Praise for The Highlander's Lost Lady:

"That is how we like our Highlanders!" **Australian Romance Readers Association**

"If you enjoy an emotional romance with derring do, a dashing, kilted hero and lots of passion, Anna Campbell's latest is for you." **Annie West, USA Today bestselling author**

"An emotional book that tugged at my heartstrings, putting tears in my eyes. I could not put this book down, but had me sobbing like a bairn! So I definitely recommend to read this book with a box of Kleenex!" **5 stars Tartan Book Reviews**

"Another enjoyable foray into Ms. Campbell's The Lairds Most Likely series." **Kathy's Review Corner**

"I have enjoyed each and every story in this series, but this one blew me away! Ms. Campbell never disappoints in delivering a well-written story, full of suspense, humor, and love. It's a fabulous story I struggled to put down. Highly recommend this book and series!" **Rose Is Reading**

"*The Highlander's Lost Lady* takes the reader on a journey through danger and betrayal, then finally, and satisfyingly, to trust, healing, passion, and ultimately – love." **Roses Are Blue**

"Anna has done it again! A braw honorable handsome Highlander and a courageous Lady. Every time I read an Anna Campbell Highland Historical Romance I am transported to the

Highlands of Scotland, the beautiful beaches, lochs, and mountains. You imagine you can smell the heather and taste the scotch whiskey. Her captivating characters are what truly make her books so wonderful. You can tell that she really loves her characters and puts all of her heart into these stories." ***The Reading Wench***

"Ms. Campbell has managed to work every known emotion into the story. The result is a mystery/thriller/romance that compels the reader to keep turning the pages to the very end." **5 stars *Amazon Review***

"So very moving, emotional and so beautifully sensual, a must read." **5 stars *Romance Book Haven***

"Luscious Highlander romance!" **5 stars *Amazon Review***

"A lovely emotional story, with a gorgeous Highlander. I loved it!" **5 stars *GoodReads Review***

"If you love some Scottish flair with your historical romance, pick up *The Highlander's Lost Lady* today." ***Bronwyn Parry***, bestselling author of ***The Clothier's Daughter***

"Another fantabulous read." **5 stars *GoodReads Review***

"I loved Diarmid and Fiona's story!! The attraction between these two was red hot!" **5 stars *Historical Romance Lover***

ALSO BY ANNA CAMPBELL

Claiming the Courtesan

Untouched

Tempt the Devil

Captive of Sin

My Reckless Surrender

Midnight's Wild Passion

The Sons of Sin Series:

Seven Nights in a Rogue's Bed

Days of Rakes and Roses

A Rake's Midnight Kiss

What a Duke Dares

A Scoundrel by Moonlight

Three Proposals and a Scandal

The Dashing Widows Series:

The Seduction of Lord Stone

Tempting Mr. Townsend

Winning Lord West

Pursuing Lord Pascal

Charming Sir Charles

Catching Captain Nash

Lord Garson's Bride

The Lairds Most Likely Series:

The Laird's Willful Lass

The Laird's Christmas Kiss

The Highlander's Lost Lady

The Highlander's Defiant Captive

The Highlander's Christmas Quest

The Highlander's English Bride

The Highlander's Forbidden Mistress

The Highlander's Christmas Countess

The Highlander's Rescued Maiden

The Highlander's Christmas Lassie

A Scandal in Mayfair Series:

One Wicked Wish

Two Secret Sins

Three Times Tempted

Christmas Stories:

The Winter Wife

Her Christmas Earl

A Pirate for Christmas

Mistletoe and the Major

A Match Made in Mistletoe

The Christmas Stranger

His Christmas Cinderella (in the anthology A Grosvenor Square Christmas)

Other Books:

These Haunted Hearts

Stranded with the Scottish Earl

The Highlander's Lost Lady

The Lairds Most Likely Book 3

ANNA CAMPBELL

To the wonderful people at the Tyrone Guthrie
Centre at Annaghmakerrig in Ireland who provided
the perfect sanctuary for a girl writing a book about
a Highlander!

CHAPTER ONE

Invertavey, Scottish Highlands, July 1819

For Diarmid Mactavish, Laird of Invertavey, a gallop along Canmara Beach was his usual way to start the day. Less usual was the discovery of two waterlogged bodies washed up on the silver sands above the high tide mark.

"What the devil," he muttered under his breath, spurring his white mare Sigurn down the dunes so fast that the sand flew up behind them.

After last night's wild storm, debris littered the beach, including, now he looked, what appeared to be the remnants of a wooden boat. Amongst the chaos, the two motionless bodies were a cruel reminder of the dangerous waters around Scotland's west coast. Stark proof of that lay in Invertavey's small, pretty graveyard which contained too many headstones dedicated to sailors known only unto God.

Diarmid drew Sigurn to a rearing halt near the first body, an old, bearded man whose gaze opened milky onto the sky. He flung himself from the saddle and kneeled at the man's side, although it was obvious the stranger was past saving. With regret for the curtailed life and what must have been a terrifying death, he reached across to close the old man's eyes.

The other body sprawled on the wet sand about ten yards away. When Diarmid realized it was a fair-haired woman, horror cramped his heart.

Most of the dead washed up on this curve of beach were sailors or fishermen. It was rare to bury a female, although in his childhood, a passenger ship had foundered on a reef near Banory Head, with the loss of twenty-eight people, including women and children. He'd been an eight-year-old boy when the *Catriona Rose* went down, and he still recalled the sad procession as the crofters carried the victims through the dunes to the village.

When he rose and crossed to the lady, his regret became even more piercing. The woman was young, not much more than a wee lassie. Even lying still and pale on the sand, Diarmid could see that she'd been pretty.

It shouldn't matter what she looked like. A life lost was a life lost. But as he stared down into her alabaster face with its straight, narrow nose and piquant pointed chin, he couldn't help grieving that he'd never see her eyes flash or that beguiling mouth curve in a smile.

He came down on his heels beside her, noting the plain, good-quality clothes, even in their sandy, soaked state. The old man was dressed like a crofter. This woman was dressed like a lady.

What had made these two people set out on unreliable waters when bad weather had been a constant the last weeks? Had anyone else drowned with them? Where had they embarked? Where were they going?

Likely he'd never find out, unless family or friends managed to track the voyage to this isolated corner of Scotland. The woman looked like she came from money, so odds were someone would seek news of her fate. Beautiful women from prosperous backgrounds were rarely permitted to disappear without a trace.

The girl's eyes were closed. In a useless gesture of sympathy, Diarmid lifted one of the slender hands that lay across her chest.

Hell...

She wore saturated gloves of lavender kid, but even through the damp material, he felt the pliability of living flesh. Now he looked more closely, her chest rose and fell with faint breath.

By God, this lady wasn't dead after all. He hauled her unresisting body up and began to pat her pallid cheeks and rub her hands. For what felt like an eon, there was no reaction. Then his heart faltered to a relieved stop as he heard her breath catch.

How the devil had the lassie survived a night outside in these temperatures? The wet sand under his knees was freezing, and the wind whipped about his ears as a reminder of last night's raging storm.

She was icy cold, and if he didn't get her back to his house, the air would finish what the sea had started. It might be midsummer, but this was the Highlands, and the water she'd come out of wasn't much above freezing.

"Miss?" He rubbed his hands over her slender body, using hard friction across her ribs and arms, and praying he wasn't worsening any injuries. "Miss, open your eyes."

He was about to gather her up and carry her over to Sigurn, when dark brown lashes flickered on her pale cheeks and a cracked groan escaped her. She twisted in his arms, and he found himself staring into pale blue eyes the color of the sea at dawn. Beautiful, unusual eyes, with a rim of deepest black around the iris.

"What? Who?" she forced out, before she raised a shaking hand to her lips. Mortification flooded her expression. "Going to be...sick."

Diarmid only just managed to turn her onto her side before she started to heave, bringing up what was mostly seawater. He kept hold of her as she jerked and shuddered, expelling what seemed to be half an ocean.

It was a lucky thing she hadn't drowned like her companion. She'd clearly come close.

By the time she'd finished, she was gasping and loose with exhaustion. Diarmid helped her sit up and settled her head on his shoulder. She lolled against him, struggling for breath.

"That will make ye feel better, lassie," Diarmid crooned, tightening his grip on her.

She smelled of the sea, and her fair hair hung in rats' tails about her bonny face. He dug in his pocket for a handkerchief and started to wipe her damp cheeks. Green still tinged the translucent white skin.

"No, I'll...I'll do it," she said unsteadily, raising an unsteady hand to take the handkerchief. He took this sign of reviving spirit as a hopeful indication that she wasn't badly hurt.

"I'm sorry," she said in a hoarse voice, caused partly, he guessed, from vomiting, but mostly from embarrassment.

"Are ye injured?" From what he could tell, he thought she'd suffered only bruises and scrapes, but he wanted to make sure.

A trembling hand touched her forehead. "I have a rotten headache."

He frowned. A head injury could be serious, although she seemed perfectly lucid. The sooner he got her to shelter, the better.

"I'm sorry to hear that. It could be dehydration."

To his surprise, her mouth quirked with unexpected humor. "I don't feel at all dehydrated. Rather the opposite, in fact."

He gave a grunt of amusement, as he registered her crisp Edinburgh accent. A Scotswoman, then. With her striking fairness, she could have washed in from Scandinavia.

Her dazed eyes looked past his shoulder at the windswept beach. "Where am I?"

"This is Invertavey, just south of Ullapool." He took back the crumpled handkerchief and stuffed it in his pocket. "My name is Diarmid Mactavish."

She stiffened against him, although he had no idea why. "Mactavish?"

"Aye. I'm laird of this estate."

"Laird…"

"I'll take ye back to my house and fetch the doctor." Her increasing distraction troubled him. He had to get her off this exposed beach fast. "Then we'll do our best to let your family know where you are."

He waited for her to introduce herself, but instead she tried not very successfully to push away from him. "Could I…could I please have some water?"

Blast him for a thoughtless fool. Of course, she wanted something to drink. He'd already guessed she must be parched after swallowing all that saltwater.

"I've got a flask tied to my saddle. Can ye manage to stay sitting up while I go and get it?"

"I think so," she said, although she was still worryingly pale, and she trembled in his arms.

With care, he slid his arm away from her midriff and edged back. Blindly she felt for the sand behind her and when she found it, she leaned back on one arm.

He surveyed her with some doubt. She looked ready to collapse again. "I could carry ye across to my horse."

"No, no, I can manage."

When he saw the effort she needed to sit upright, he commended her courage. With rough movements, he tugged his coat from his shoulders and wrapped it around her. Once he made sure she could sit without support, he rose and strode across to Sigurn, who was nosing at a clump of seaweed.

He returned to the woman and hunkered down beside her, offering her a leather flask. The hand she raised to take it was shaking so badly, he had to help her to drink.

After she'd taken a few sips, he pulled the flask away from her lips. "Och, gently now, lassie."

"That's so good," she rasped.

Diarmid could imagine. He forced a smile. She hadn't yet asked about her companion's fate, and he didn't want to tell her until he had to.

"Thank you," she said.

He gave her a little more water. "Do ye want to rinse your face and hands?"

"Yes, please."

He dribbled water on her hands and studied her with a worried frown as she wiped her cheeks. "Can ye walk?"

"I think so."

A quick survey of her pale face told him that was either optimism or bravado speaking. Her trembling had turned into full-on shivering. So much for a Scottish summer.

"If you'll let me, I'll help ye over to my horse and get you up to the house," he said. "I could go and fetch the villagers with a litter, but it would take too long and you need to warm up."

Despite her obvious exhaustion, she looked a bit better after a drink and the cat wash. "Let's try."

Diarmid rose and held his hand out to her. Her grip was weak, and he did most of the lifting as she stumbled to her feet. It turned out she was a tall woman. He was a couple of inches over six feet. When she stood, that disheveled blond head reached past his shoulder.

As her legs took her weight, she staggered, and he caught her by the waist. "Hold on to me."

She made a smothered sound and lifted her face. The wide, beautiful eyes turned glassy and to his horror, he realized she was close to falling. He wasn't even sure she could see him anymore.

With a muttered imprecation, he caught her behind the knees and swung her up. The body in his arms was rail thin. Her sodden garments accounted for most of the weight he carried.

"I'm sorry I'm so much trouble," she mumbled, closing her eyes.

Like a flower too heavy for its stem, her tousled head drooped to rest on his shoulder. She was as cold and wet as a salmon. With her cuddled up against his chest, he was soon nearly as waterlogged as she was.

Diarmid couldn't control a shiver. The wind whistling around them cut like a knife, and since giving her his coat, he was only in his shirtsleeves.

"It's no' far to the house. We'll soon have ye in dry clothes and a warm bed."

"That sounds good," she muttered without opening her eyes.

"Can ye manage to sit on my horse for a wee moment? I promise you'll be safe on Sigurn. She's well trained and as gentle as a lamb."

"I like horses," she said, then broke off on a gasp. Green tinged her complexion again.

"Do ye need to be sick?"

Her slender throat moved as she swallowed. Even as she shook her head with what he thought was an excess of foolish pride, he helped her to kneel. While she retched violently into the sand, he held her.

Poor wee lassie. After the shipwreck, her body was in such a parlous state that she couldn't even keep down a few drops of water.

Diarmid waited for her gasping to ease and watched her fumble in a pocket for her handkerchief. It was sure to be wet, but it was probably the best she could do.

"Was I alone in the wreck?" She caught Diarmid's expression before he could hide it. "I wasn't."

Hell, what was this? Didn't she know?

Diarmid frowned in confusion, but he made himself answer her. "There's a man washed up over there. He drowned. I'm sorry."

She looked sick again. "Can I see him?"

"It's probably better if—"

"Please."

Despite his better judgment, he succumbed to the appeal in those wide blue eyes. He rose and helped her up, holding tight to her elbow when her knees threatened to buckle. "He's over here."

Fortunately the dead man was only a few yards away. When they reached him, the girl straightened and managed to stand on her own two feet.

Diarmid studied her as she stared down at the body. In his opinion, she looked sad but not devastated. Probably not a family member then, which he'd already suspected given the difference in their clothing.

"Who was he?" Diarmid asked.

Avoiding Diarmid's eyes, she shook her head. "I don't know." She pressed a hand to her bloodless lips. "Poor soul."

Diarmid bit back a flood of questions, starting with a demand for the girl's name. She'd been through a horrible ordeal. He had no right to badger her. Once she was safe back at Invertavey House, they'd have time enough for introductions and explanations.

"Come." He took her elbow and angled her away from the dead man. "It's too cold for ye out here."

Their stumbling progress toward Sigurn seemed to take forever.

"You're so kind," the girl said in a choked voice, and he caught the glitter of tears in her eyes as he lifted her into the saddle. When he set her astride, her sodden skirts rode up to reveal slender calves in tattered white stockings.

"Not at all. Hold tight to the saddle while I get on."

The lass had bonny legs, shapely and with a neat ankle. He told himself that when a woman was so defenseless, he was a swine to notice such a thing. But on the other hand, the legs were very bonny indeed.

The girl was in such straits that she looked fit to slide back onto the ground. Her brief spurt of energy ebbed, leaving her even paler than before. When he found her, he'd imagined she was already as wan as a lassie could get.

He mounted behind her and curled an arm around her waist. "Lean back against me, and I'll get ye back to the house as soon as I can."

"There seems to be a lot of touching," she said uncomfortably, squirming a little.

The discomfort was probably a good sign. He managed a wry smile, although in his shirtsleeves, he was as cold as a naked Eskimo stuck in a Greenland blizzard. Despite wearing his coat, the girl must be freezing, too.

"I beg your pardon." He clicked his tongue to urge Sigurn to walk toward the dunes. "Actually, madam, I'd like to know whose pardon I'm begging. Will ye nae tell me your name?"

She wriggled weakly until she could see him. Once again, he found himself transfixed by those striking eyes. She looked pale and tense and afraid.

"Mr. Mactavish..."

His grip tightened, before he recognized that clutching her closer wasn't likely to soothe her uncertainty. He loosened his hold and lowered his voice, hoping sincerity might overcome her trepidation. "I ken I'm a stranger, and you have nae reason to trust me, but I'm only trying to help. Surely there can be nae danger in telling me who ye are. I'd like to be able to call ye something, and if I know your name, I can contact your family and arrange for them to come and fetch you. Ye have my word as a gentleman that I mean you nae harm."

She stared searchingly at him, as if trying to pierce through his skin to his soul. To his dismay, the fear he read in her eyes didn't ease. He supposed he couldn't blame her for being hesitant to confide in him—they'd known each other less than an hour after all, and she'd been through a hell of an ordeal before he found her.

After a charged silence, those thick eyelashes fluttered down and she bit her lip. "I'm sorry, Mr. Mactavish," she said in a broken rush. "I wish I could tell you my name. But for the life of me, I can't remember what it is."

CHAPTER TWO

iona Grant closed her eyes and rested her aching head against the laird's broad shoulder. His solid strength made her feel protected, even though she'd heard all her life that anyone named Mactavish was lower than a mangy gutter cur.

She sucked in a shuddering breath, wincing as her bruised ribs expanded. For a mangy gutter cur, Mr. Mactavish smelled delicious. Her clan's enemy smelled of fresh air, horses, leather, and vigorous healthy male.

Fiona had a thousand reasons to fear all men, not just those called Mactavish, but so far, this particular man had been kind to her. The care mightn't last, but in spite of the despised blood in his veins, she was inclined to believe that he might turn out to be that rarest of beasts—a man of honor.

Lying to him felt bad, when he took such trouble with her, even giving up his coat in this biting wind. She felt even worse to disclaim all knowledge of old Colin Smith, who had been a man of honor, too.

Tears too dangerous to shed gathered behind her eyes, as she struggled to hide her sorrow over the fisherman's death. How she hated that she couldn't give him his name or his due. If his spirit hovered near, she prayed that he understood and forgave her. When they'd embarked on their reckless voyage down the coast, he certainly knew what was at stake.

Now Colin was gone, she felt more alone than ever. That knowledge didn't alter her purpose, just added another layer of risk to her dangerous quest.

"Did ye hit your head when you fell out of the boat, lassie?" Mr. Mactavish asked.

"I don't know," she mumbled. She was sore all over, as though she'd endured a brutal beating. Bitter experience made that comparison more than a matter of mere imagination.

"So what do ye remember?"

Was that a note of skepticism in his voice? "I remember you finding me on the beach."

They were amidst the dunes now. Beneath her, the beautiful white horse moved easily. The man's arms were strong and sure, holding her close against his powerful chest.

She'd never imagined she'd accept a man's touch so easily, but instincts developed over the last ten years persuaded her that her rescuer meant her no harm. At least so far, when he didn't know she was a Grant.

Anyway, even if he did mean her harm, what in heaven's name could she do about it? She was weak and exhausted and sick. If she tried to run, she wouldn't make ten yards. Better to accept Mr. Mactavish's help, whatever it cost, and regain her strength as best she could before she went on.

Fiona was freezing in her wet clothes, although the man's thick coat kept out the worst of the wind. Mr. Mactavish must be suffering from the cold, wearing only his shirtsleeves, but the body behind hers was as warm as a furnace. It was a silly fancy, but those powerful arms shielded her from the wind better than his thick coat did. A thick coat that smelled most pleasantly of him, so she felt cocooned in Mr. Mactavish as the mare picked her way across the sand.

"I've heard of such things happening after a head injury," he said thoughtfully.

So had she, although only in books. But as long as she continued to deny any knowledge of her past or her identity, he could hardly call her a liar to her face.

"I wish I could tell you who I am."

"Aye, so do I," he said with a hint of grimness. They left the dunes and rode through a grove of Scots pines that provided some respite from the wind. "Perhaps once you've rested and recovered your strength, the details will come back to ye."

"Perhaps."

And perhaps not.

The horse's neat hooves thudded softly upon the carpet of pine needles, and the soughing of the branches above lulled her into a doze. The drowsiness wasn't peaceful. The moment she closed her eyes, her sensitive stomach heaved as a chaos of disconnected images from the wreck invaded her mind.

When Colin's small boat struck rocks at the mouth of the bay, the impact had flung her into raging seas. She'd fought like a demon to stay afloat, but the ocean had been like a wild animal hungry to swallow her. When she went down the last time, it was with the heartbreakingly bitter knowledge that despite all her efforts, she'd failed Christina.

Perhaps the sea heard a mother's final, despairing plea as she sank beneath the waves. The next thing Fiona knew, she opened her eyes to a dark-haired man leaning over her with a concerned expression and speaking to her in a voice as rich as good whisky.

That same voice currently murmured in her ear, promising safety and comfort. She knew better than to trust it, but she also knew that for the present she had to bide her time before she attempted escape.

"I willnae trouble ye with questions. I'm sure your head is aching. We'll get you inside and into a hot bath to get your blood flowing again. If ye think your stomach will bear it, you can have something to eat. Right now, you're safe and alive. That's the main thing."

Dear Lord above, all that sounded wonderful, even if it came from an enemy's hand.

"What about..." She stirred enough to open her eyes. They rode beside a burn that leaped over rocks down to the sea, sparkling in the light of the sunbeams that pierced the treetops.

"I'll send some lads down to the beach, once we've got ye settled."

"Thank you." She supposed this meant Colin would be buried here at—what did the man say this place was called? "Where are we? I know you told me, but..."

"Invertavey. The Tavey River reaches the sea just around the headland from where I found ye. My name is Diarmid Mactavish. I dinna blame ye for nae taking in much at first."

No, she'd had other things to worry about. Most urgently, the prospect of losing the contents of her stomach in a humiliating display before a stranger. Mr. Mactavish had been kind about that, too.

Her thoughts returned to the man who had risked everything to get her out of Bancavan. Poor

Colin, a Grant clansmen condemned to rest on Mactavish land for eternity.

As they approached the end of the wood, she swore that her faithful friend wouldn't remain anonymous. Once she was safe, she'd contact Mr. Mactavish and ask him to put the old sailor's name on the headstone. Pray God that she had a chance to do that and that a settled future awaited.

"We're nae far from Ullapool. I'll let the authorities there ken that you're here, and hopefully they can find out who ye are and where you belong. I'm sure ye must be terrified to be lost in a strange place, but there are ways we can trace your kin."

Trace her kin? For pity's sake, that was the last thing she wanted. She'd happily go the rest of her life, seeing neither hair nor hide of her clansmen.

But she could already tell that Mr. Mactavish was determined to help her in any way he saw fit. Fear, colder than the waves that had washed her up on that lonely beach, made her stiffen in the man's arms.

"There's no need to go to any trouble." She struggled to sound calm and not panicked out of her mind. Her belly clenched painfully, as she imagined what would happen to her should her rescuer locate her family. "I'm sure that with rest and warmth, my memory will return."

"It's nae trouble." He guided the horse up a rise that brought them out onto an open hillside. Even as Fiona cursed him, that remarkable, musical voice lowered to a soothing rumble. "That's all to worry about later. Right now, we need to get ye out of this weather."

She sucked in a relieved breath, although she knew her reprieve wouldn't last. After her ordeal, she wasn't up to playing mind games with anyone. She

Her last thought before she sank into oblivion was that at least she hadn't given up her fight. While she had breath in her body, she couldn't. But just now, her strength betrayed her. Whatever awaited in this stranger's custody, she had no way to defend herself against it.

Not today anyway.

Even as she surrendered to weakness, something in her recognized that the arms enfolding her were strong and sure. Mr. Mactavish's hands on her and on the horse were kind.

Long ago, she'd learned to recognize a bully. This man claimed she could trust him. Could she? Was he an exception to the rest of his sex?

God help her if he wasn't, because she was helpless in his power.

The sudden clatter of hooves on cobbles made Fiona stir. She released a muffled sound of distress and opened bleary eyes. It took her a few seconds to realize that she'd survived the wild storm and that she rested in a man's arms.

Her belly clenched on painful emptiness. She couldn't help reliving that horrifying moment when the boat crashed into the rocks with an ear-splitting crack, pitching her screaming into rough, ice-cold water.

"Whisht, lassie, you're safe," the man behind her murmured.

The man. Diarmid Mactavish.

Member of a despised clan. The laird of this place. The sole arbiter of her future, at least until she could manage more than a few steps without aid.

Fiona lacked the energy to sit up, as she struggled to make sense of where she was. A large and pleasant house rose before her, built in the fashionable gothic style. "Is this your home?"

"Aye, this is Invertavey House. I bid ye welcome, and I promise nae harm will come to you here. Ye have my word on it."

If only she could believe him. Nonetheless she dredged up a polite response. "Thank you."

He rode around the back to a neat stable block, built from the same stark gray granite as the main house. "Tam, Rabbie, are ye there?"

Two men, one young, one older, emerged from the stable's double doors, and she read astonishment on their faces.

"Och, Mactavish, what the de'il hae ye been up to? Hae ye caught yourself a wee mermaid on this morning's tide?" the older man said in a thick Highland accent. Mr. Mactavish's voice held a soft Scottish inflection, closer to the Edinburgh accents of her childhood.

"Aye, I have at that." The laird's chuckle was warm, as he brought the pretty white horse to a stop. "The lady was washed up on Canmara Beach, after a shipwreck during last night's storm."

"Och, the puir wee soul," the younger man said, his face creasing in immediate concern. "Is the lassie hurt?"

"I dinnae think so, but I'll get Dr. Higgins up to see to her, as soon as she's dry and warm and settled."

"Let me help ye with her." The older man came up and lifted Fiona down from the horse. His touch was kind, too, but he didn't smell nearly as good as Mr. Mactavish did. "Careful, lassie. You're no' looking too steady on your feet."

As Fiona found her shaky balance, she watched Mr. Mactavish dismount and take the younger man aside. He kept his voice low, but she still heard him. "There's a body on the beach, Rab. Can ye get a few of the lads down there and bring him up to the house? And send Billy into the village to fetch the doctor."

"Aye, straightaway, Mactavish."

The laird turned to where Fiona stood beside Tam, supported by one brawny hand on her arm. The ease between the master and his retainers did more to reassure her than all his promises. This clearly wasn't a man who used fear to rule. "I'll carry ye inside, lassie."

She shook her head. "I can walk."

Tam let her go, and she took a step toward the laird. She came to a stop, wavering where she stood. Her surroundings started to recede in a most alarming fashion. Pride dissolved to nothing, as she fought against crumpling onto the cobblestones beneath her feet. She felt like her very bones turned to ice, and the weight of Mr. Mactavish's coat threatened to crush her.

Blindly she reached for something solid to hold onto. Her stomach cramped, and rancid bile flooded her throat.

"I dinna think so," Mr. Mactavish said grimly.

When he swept her up into his arms, a whimper of relief escaped her. She'd learned to fear male strength, but right now that was all that saved her from falling flat on her face.

"You're a stubborn wee thing, for a lassie I could knock over with a feather," Mr. Mactavish said.

Fiona was too weak to respond, but she leaned her head on his hard chest and didn't object when he carried her across to the house. As they entered the kitchens, she was too exhausted to keep her eyes open. She heard a flurry of female voices expressing concern and curiosity, and Mr. Mactavish reeled out a list of orders for her comfort and care.

He swept along in powerful strides, carrying her as if she weighed nothing at all. Up several flights of steps. She opened her eyes to find herself in a long corridor. When she looked back over his shoulder, maids trailed after them like ducklings chasing their mother.

"I seem to be causing you a lot of bother," she said faintly, as he pushed open a door and entered a large, bright chamber overlooking a broad river and the sea.

"Och, it stops them all getting lazy, with only me to look after, lassie. Dinna fash yourself."

An older woman with gray hair glanced up at that and sent the master a narrow-eyed look that did nothing to hide the affection in her expression. "But you're a gey lot of trouble, Mactavish. Ye keep us all hopping."

"And rightly so," he said with a laugh. "Otherwise you'd be out terrorizing the parish with your wild ways, Mags."

"Aye, wild and dangerous, that's the women of Invertavey." The half dozen girls who had come in busied themselves around the room, lighting the fire and turning down the bed and setting out towels and soaps.

"I wish Mags was joking," Mr. Mactavish said, carefully setting Fiona on her feet.

She sucked in her first full breath in what felt like forever. She sensed no threat in this room. Perhaps she was safe. If just for the moment.

As long as nobody found out she was a Grant. As long as her family didn't track her down. As long as she started working on an escape plan to put into effect the second she could set one foot in front of the other without falling over.

That wouldn't be today, God help her. The legs that barely held her up felt like they were made of wet wool.

"What's the lassie's name, Mactavish?" Mags asked, as two strapping young men shouldered through the doorway, carrying a large tin bath. The prospect of soaking the salt from her skin and hair in gallons of hot water sent such a wave of longing through Fiona that she staggered.

"Careful," Mr. Mactavish said, taking her arm.

Since he found her on that windswept beach, he'd touched her a lot. Usually she hated to have masculine hands on her. But then, masculine hands in her experience bruised and hurt. There was no doubting her rescuer's strength—he hadn't even caught his breath carrying her up the stairs—but so far his hands had offered nothing but kindness and support.

"The lady cannae recall anything that happened before the shipwreck," he said to Mags.

The hubbub in the room stilled, and Fiona shifted in guilty discomfort as all eyes focused on her in avid curiosity.

"Nothing?" one of the girls said in amazement. "No' even your name?"

"Katy, mind your manners," Mags said sharply.

"I beg your pardon, Mrs. Curran." Katy dipped into a curtsy and went back to feeding the fire.

"That's better." The older woman cast a gimlet eye around the room, until everyone stopped staring at Fiona and returned to work. Mags must be the housekeeper Mr. Mactavish had mentioned on the ride up from the beach.

"Dinnae ye worry, lassie." She bustled up to Fiona and placed an arm around her waist. "After what you've been through, it's nae wonder your head is jangling. We'll soon get ye back as right as rain."

Mr. Mactavish stepped away, and ridiculously Fiona missed his nearness. "I'll leave the lady in your care, Mags."

"Aye, she needs a hot bath and dry clothes and something to eat and some sleep. Then she'll ken what's what."

Fiona suffered another pang of guilt at deceiving her rescuers. But too much was at stake for her to risk trusting them with the truth. She summoned a grateful smile. "You're all being so kind."

"Och, you've added a wee bit of excitement to our day. Most of the time, life here at Invertavey is gey quiet."

"Even with the wild and dangerous lassies we breed in these parts," Mr. Mactavish said, making Mags laugh.

"Aye, even with them."

The maids had prepared the room with quick efficiency. A fire blazed in the hearth, and the heat on her chilled skin made Fiona feel like crying in gratitude. A tray of tea and scones rested on a table, and a large bed with white sheets and feather covers awaited her. The girls trooped out, leaving her alone with Mags and Mr. Mactavish.

"I'll just go down and see what's happening with the bath water," Mags said, pouring Fiona a cup of tea. "Do ye take milk and sugar?"

"Yes, please." The kindness and the activity and the retreat of fear—although fear never altogether subsided—left Fiona feeling woozy.

"Och, sit down, lassie." Mags passed her a pretty china cup in a gold and white pattern. "Ye look likely to tumble over."

"I'm still wet." When she took a sip of sweet hot tea, tears pricked at her eyes. She was so dangerously fragile, that even simple human pleasures like a hot drink and a moment's consideration made her want to bawl like a lost calf.

"The chairs will survive. I'd put ye straight into bed, but ye don't want damp sheets. We'll have ye out of those wet clothes and in the bath in a jiffy. You'll feel better, once you're warm."

"I'll go away and leave ye in peace." Mr. Mactavish smiled at Fiona as she subsided onto a chair, although his dark eyes remained concerned as they studied her.

She blinked with astonishment as at last she took in her rescuer's appearance. In all that had happened since she'd woken up on the beach, this was the first time she'd looked at him properly. Even for a woman contemptuous of the male of the species, he was definitely worth more than one glance.

Mr. Mactavish was the most spectacular man she'd ever seen.

How on earth had she missed that? Until now, she'd been too busy deciding if he was a threat or a source of support. She hadn't registered him as an individual at all, apart from that deep, musical voice rumbling away in her ear as they rode to the house.

It turned out his voice wasn't all that was beautiful about him. With dazed eyes, she stared into that smiling face, noting the defined cheekbones and jaw, the long straight blade of a nose, the slashing black brows.

Good Lord, the Laird of Invertavey was like a prince in a fairy story.

The urge to tell him the truth rose, to throw herself on his mercy, beg his help. But she beat the impulse back.

If anyone had good cause to mistrust men, it was her. So far, he'd proven himself a good man, but she'd only known him a little over an hour. The risks of betrayal were just too great.

Fortunately he took her silence as exhaustion, not as wondering feminine admiration. So far, he'd treated her with impersonal kindness, the object of his compassion, not his desire. She didn't want him to start thinking of her as a beddable female.

"Get some sleep. Dr. Higgins will be here soon, I'm sure." He glanced across at Mags. "Look after her."

"As if I'd do anything else." Mags gave a scornful humph. "Away with ye now, Mactavish, so I can get the lassie into some dry clothes. Cannae ye see she's as cold as a wee icicle?"

His lips twitched with humor, although he didn't argue. He gave Fiona a brief bow. "Your servant, madam."

She'd been frightened since he'd discovered her, not just because he was a stranger, but because he was a man. She knew what men did to defenseless women. Yet when he left, she battled a stupid need to call him back to her side.

CHAPTER THREE

"*A* wee dram before ye go on your way, John?" Diarmid rose from behind his desk to greet Dr. Higgins, after the man descended from attending to his mysterious guest.

"Aye, I don't mind if I do."

The sun poured through the library windows to gleam off polished mahogany and the bronze celestial and terrestrial globes displayed on two ormolu tables in the center of the room. It was late afternoon, and the view across the peaceful glen belied last night's violent weather.

"Biddy Calvert's baby was safely delivered?"

"Aye, although it took all night and half the day for the wee lassie to arrive into the world."

"I'm glad they're fine. I'll call in to see the family this week and offer my congratulations. We were lucky ye were in the village when I needed you here."

John Higgins was the only doctor for miles around, and he spent much of his time riding his rawboned roan mare to isolated settlements up and down the coast and deep into the hills.

"Aye. I was lucky, too. Barring some emergency that finds me here now, I'm only a short ride from my own hearth."

Diarmid smiled. He'd always liked the spare young doctor with his wise eyes and generous heart. Passing across a glass of Bruce Mackenzie's finest whisky, he gestured Higgins toward a leather armchair. "I willnae hold ye up long. You deserve your rest."

Higgins sat and took a sip. A long sigh of pleasure escaped him, as he stretched his long legs across the Turkey carpet.

"Och, that's a bonny drop." He shot Diarmid a sharp glance, as the other man sank into the nearest chair. "I suppose you want to know about my patient upstairs."

"Aye." Diarmid sampled his own whisky. Bruce Mackenzie ran an illegal still on his friend Fergus Mackinnon's estate. Diarmid was among the lucky few away from Achnasheen who received the benefit of the crofter's illicit activities. "Is she injured?"

"No, not seriously. Plenty of scrapes and bruises after being tossed around in the wreck, but she's come through remarkably well." Higgins paused. "Apart from not remembering anything, of course."

"Aye, so she says."

Higgins's eyes remained unwavering on Diarmid's face. "You don't believe her?"

"Have ye ever seen such a thing, a woman forgetting all her past, including her name?"

"I haven't seen it." Higgins frowned thoughtfully down into his drink. "Although I've seen men lose a few days of memory after a head injury."

"This is more than that."

"I've heard of such cases."

Diarmid negated that with a gesture. "Aye, so have I. In a novel or on the stage. It always seems too convenient to be true, even in a story."

Higgins shrugged. "I can't tell if she's pretending or not. What makes you so sure she is?"

Diarmid frowned, as he struggled to put into words something that was more instinct than knowledge. "When she told me she couldnae remember anything, she wasnae frightened enough of what was happening inside her head. A past that's nothing but blankness should scare the living daylights out of her."

"Forgetting her name mightn't have her in a panic, but I get the feeling she's frightened of something. She's as nervous as a cat in a kennel."

"Ye picked that up, too?"

"It's hard to miss."

"So ye think she's a sham?"

Higgins considered his answer before he spoke. "I can't say for certain. Head injuries are mysterious beasties, Diarmid. What purpose lying to us, when surely she must want to return to her friends and family?"

Diarmid's jaw tightened. "That's the question, isn't it?"

Higgins resumed watching him. "She's a bonny wee thing."

"Aye, even when she was as wet as a herring, that was clear." Diarmid heard the betraying flatness of his tone.

Higgins's crooked smile wasn't devoid of compassion. "Not every beautiful woman is a liar, my friend."

Diarmid gave a grunt of acknowledgment. John Higgins had lived at Invertavey for five years. He was party to all the glen's secrets. Not that the late Lady

Invertavey's many infidelities and scandalous and tragic death had ever been any great secret.

"In my experience, the prettier the face, the more deceitful the tongue."

"She's not your mother."

"No," he said grimly. "But I'd still wager she's got a lying tongue."

"Who knows?" Higgins shrugged and finished his whisky, setting it on the table at his elbow. "Whoever the lady is, she's in no state to go anywhere tonight. I've given her a sleeping draft, so hopefully she'll wake tomorrow and tell us who she is. I'm a great believer in sleep's healing powers."

Diarmid made himself smile, even if the reminder of his treacherous, unfaithful mother set old anger coiling in his belly. Although of course, his mother's ghost had hovered at his side since he'd discovered the lovely waif on the beach. "Ye are due some sleep of your own."

"Aye. I'm for my bed." Higgins stifled a yawn and stood. "I'll call tomorrow and see how my patient fares."

Once Higgins had gone, Diarmid stood at the window, finishing his whisky and staring out over the estate. He didn't see the wide, sparkling river or the heather-covered hills rising away from the coast. Instead he saw a beautiful, vain woman always more interested in her latest lover than her family. He saw a good man worn down by loneliness and disgrace. He saw an only child deprived of a mother's love and gradually displaced from a father's heart, as the weight of betrayal filled up the space where paternal affection should thrive.

Aye, John Higgins was right, curse him, about Diarmid's prejudice against lovely women. But that admission didn't shift his conviction that the spectacular creature sleeping upstairs had no more lost her memory than he could sprout wings and swoop across the Minch to Lewis for a picnic.

Diarmid waited until after dinner before he went up to see his guest. Quietly he pushed the door open to find Mags dozing in an armchair beside the bed, some mending resting forgotten in her lap. A couple of candles and a roaring fire provided the only light, so the large four-poster lay in shadow.

His housekeeper started awake. "Och, Mactavish, ye surprised me." She lowered her voice to a whisper. "Come to check on the puir wee bairn?"

"Aye," he said, biting back an objection to hearing the girl in the bed described as a child. She was young, but no child. He'd guess she was a couple of years younger than his twenty-eight, and those remarkable eyes held knowledge beyond the range of any juvenile. He kept his voice to a whisper, too. "How is she?"

"Went out like a light after I gave her that potion Dr. Higgins left. She hasnae stirred since."

Diarmid hid a smile at the acid tone. Mags and Dr. Higgins had never seen eye to eye. His housekeeper was a proponent of age-old folk remedies, while Dr. Higgins subscribed to every medical journal he could lay his hands on. Even in this isolated backwater, he kept abreast of new developments in science.

"That's braw news. She was exhausted when I found her."

"Aye, sleep will do her more good than anything else."

Diarmid refrained from pointing out that Mags's nemesis had said something similar before he left. "Did she manage to eat anything?"

"Aye, she took a wee bit of supper. Skin and bones she is, and covered in bruises, too."

"The boat came to pieces on the rocks at Banory Head. She's lucky to be alive. Before she went to sleep, did she say anything that might help us find her kin?"

"No. Nothing beyond a few words of please and thank you. The lassie has bonny manners. That's no humble crofter's daughter ye found there, Mactavish. She's a lady."

Aye, she was. He'd known that the minute he'd seen those expensive, sober clothes, even torn and wet through with seawater. "Ye found her something to wear?"

"Aye, a nightgown at least, although she nearly disappears inside it. Down in the kitchen, we've done our best with what she was wearing when ye brought her inside. We may manage to rescue her frock, but I hae ma doots." Mags cast a pitying glance over the unmoving figure on the bed. "Puir wean. Imagine forgetting everything, including your name. She must be feared to death."

It was clear Mags had no suspicions that the girl lied about her memory loss. Was Diarmid too mistrustful? Somehow he didn't think so.

"You're no' sitting up with her all night?"

"Peggy's taking over at midnight."

Diarmid frowned. It was only just nine. Mags was no longer a young woman, and she'd been up at dawn to see to the day's baking. "I'll sit with the lassie until then. Go to bed."

"That's verra kind of ye, Master Diarmid."

She rarely called him that. It took him back to his childhood, when Mags had been more a mother to him than his own. "I'll see ye in the morning."

"Aye, but call me if ye have any bother." She gathered her mending and rose with a stiffness that reminded him she deserved better reward than sitting up in a chair most of the night. It wasn't precisely proper that he and the girl remained alone in a bedchamber together, but his reputation for decency should save him from too much gossip.

Once he was alone, he didn't immediately take Mags's place in the chair. Instead curiosity drew him to pick up a candle and cross to the bed. He wanted a better look at the mermaid he'd rescued from the sea.

She curled up under the covers in a pose that seemed defensive, even in sleep. Her exquisite face lay in profile on the pillow. The promise of beauty he'd seen on the beach was fulfilled a hundredfold, now she was warm and dry and at rest.

Faint pink colored her skin, and lush lips parted to reveal a glimpse of small white teeth. The wild tangle of hair had been washed and brushed into order and plaited back from her high, pale forehead. Her hair was a soft blond, with just a hint of gold to brighten the silver. The thick lashes resting on her cheek were darker, as were the delicate eyebrows.

The girl was like a lost Norse goddess, as perfect and fragile as glass. He'd thought her beautiful when he found her. Now he admitted she was the loveliest woman he'd ever seen.

Diarmid had learned early to mistrust feminine beauty. Beauty demanded too much of both its possessor and the men who vied to acquire it. His mother Ida had wielded her beauty like a weapon, laying waste to everyone in the vicinity. His mother's beauty had cursed his father's existence.

Even when he'd been too young to probe the causes, Diarmid had sensed the misery poisoning the air in this house. By the time his mother ran off to Jamaica with her last lover, to die in Kingston from some tropical fever, he knew where to place the blame. He watched how his father's frustrated yearning for his lovely wife blighted his life—and the life of his son.

He'd also seen how not even death and dishonor broke his mother's evil hold on her husband's soul. Love had weakened his father, led him to forgive every infidelity. The previous laird would have forgiven this last adventure, too, if only Ida had come back to him. Her death left George Mactavish a shell of a man. He faded from life slowly but inexorably, to die five years later, when Diarmid was twenty.

Aye, beauty was a curse to a woman and to any man unlucky enough to fall under its spell. But och, for all that, it was a powerful pleasure to behold. He raised the candle to see his mermaid more clearly. The elegant features. The skin like new cream.

Even knowing her loveliness was a cruel trick of heredity, he couldn't help staring. Nor could he stifle the rise of masculine hunger, even if he had no intention of acting on it. He was only human, after all, and the good Lord had created young men to admire a bonny face.

The girl made a sound of distress in her sleep, and the fine brows contracted in a frown as she turned away from the light. Diarmid bit back another sigh—he needed to remember that she was too pretty for him—and set the candle on the nightstand. He settled back in the armchair and fished a small volume of Robbie Burns's poetry from his pocket.

The lassie could sleep in peace. He knew better than most what it would cost him if he tried to place any claim on her.

"No..."

The soft, choked word disturbed Diarmid's restless doze. Sitting up in the chair, he muffled a groan. He was a tall man, and he'd fallen asleep at an awkward angle. His neck ached like blazes. As he raised a hand to rub the painful area, he bent forward to check the girl.

"No, not that, please."

Some nightmare gripped her. She probably relived the shipwreck. She'd been restless for a while, he could see. The quilt had slid to the floor, and the sheets were tugged loose from the base of the bed and twisted about her legs.

For a guilty, sizzling moment, he stared down at her as lust sank its claws into him. He tried to tell himself that she needed his help and that was all that brought them together. But leaning over her in this quiet room while she shifted against the crumpled sheets, he was blazingly conscious that she was a woman and he was a man.

His avid eyes devoured the slender—too slender—body stretched out before him. The white flannel nightdress billowed around her, far too big, but full of wicked tricks to trap a man's attention. Her wriggling pulled the material tight over the perfect roundness of one breast and revealed the jut of a distended nipple. The nightdress hiked up to reveal long white legs. Every drop of moisture dried from Diarmid's mouth, when he realized she wasn't wearing drawers.

Self-disgust slammed into him. He stood and turned away from temptation. Bruises and abrasions marked those sprawled legs, proof of what she'd been through. He was sick to his gut that he slavered over a helpless woman who needed his care. Worse, a woman he was convinced was a liar.

He curled one hand around the bedpost until his knuckles shone white. Behind him, the girl released another soft whimper of distress, but he hardly heard her through the blood drumming in his ears. His breath rasped on the still air.

It took far too long to leash the beast inside him, but gradually he came back to himself. By God, it was time he visited Edinburgh again. He kept his slate clean here at Invertavey, where he was laird and where his behavior set a pattern for his tenants and servants. But in the capital, he was just another rich, unattached young man seeking amusement.

How long was it since he and his last mistress had parted company? Six months? No, more.

With displeasure, he counted out the time. He and Sally had separated amicably just after Christmas, around the time his cousin Elspeth had married Brody Girvan. No wonder he was randy as an old goat. Diarmid was far from a rake—Brody was the lad who had been a devil for the ladies, until he fell under Elspeth's spell—but he was a healthy male with physical needs.

Needs that hadn't particularly bothered him until he rescued the duplicitous siren sleeping behind him. Just now, he refused to consider the implications of that fact.

He sucked in a breath and feeling more in charge of himself, he faced the bed. The girl had shifted to lie flat on her back, hands flung up on either side of her ruffled head. Her skin was so white and fine, he could see the network of blue veins running up her forearms under a mottled pattern of bruising. Another frown tightened her features, and he watched the hands on those fragile wrists close into fists.

Thoroughly ashamed of his lewd impulses, he approached the bed and tugged the nightdress down over those spectacular legs. He straightened the covers as well as he could without waking her. He pulled the quilt up, although with the fire, the room wasn't cold.

Only once she was safely tucked in did he feel able to look into her face. To find he hadn't been careful enough. Dazed blue eyes stared up at him.

Again he was struck with their beauty—and with the dread that turned them brilliant in the candlelight.

"Ye have nothing to fear, lassie," he said softly and knew himself a hypocrite when he spoke the words. Perhaps she recognized that, too, because the tension in her face didn't ease. He went on in a low soothing voice, in case she was confused to wake up in a strange place. "You're safe in Invertavey House. I'm Diarmid Mactavish, the laird here."

Her gaze clung to his face, as though she sifted his words for any hint of a threat. "I...I remember."

"Ye do?" Startled, he straightened. "What's your name?"

With obvious difficulty, she pushed herself up against the pillows. Every small movement made her wince. She might be lying about most things, but the physical toll the wreck had taken on her was no masquerade. Her suffering made him feel even more of a sick bastard for that flash of powerful lust when he'd stared at her sleeping.

"Oh, I don't remember that," she said, dismissing the idea as if it hardly mattered. She brushed tendrils of fine silver-blond hair back from her face. Her nightmare hadn't been kind to her once tidy plait. "But I remember you finding me on the beach and bringing me here. There was a woman…"

"Mags. My housekeeper. I sent her to bed a couple of hours ago. Peggy, one of the maids, is coming in at midnight to watch ye." He glanced at the ormolu clock on the mantel. "In about half an hour."

"I'm a lot of bother."

"Not at all." Her remark reminded him of his role as sickroom attendant. "How are ye feeling?"

Her lips turned down with the self-mockery that he was beginning to think might be characteristic. "Like I've been through a shipwreck."

He could imagine. "Would ye like anything? Something to eat? Something to drink? Are ye warm enough?" He stifled the memory of how she'd looked lying before him in just her nightdress.

She made an apologetic gesture. "A glass of water, please."

"On its way." He crossed to the dresser to fill a glass and carry it back to her. When she reached out to take it, the covers slipped to reveal the way her breasts pressed against the nightdress. Every cell in his body went on alert, much as he loathed the reaction.

Damn it, he should have let Mags sit with her.

"Thank you," she said, with the lovely manners he'd noticed from the first. "Please don't wait up with me. I'm sure I can sleep without supervision."

With a brooding air, Diarmid watched the girl sip the water. "Dr. Higgins says head injuries can be unpredictable. He doesnae want ye to be alone until he's sure you're out of danger." In fact, Higgins had left him with a list of questions to ask if the girl woke up. "Is your head sore? Any nausea? Any double vision?"

"Yes. No. No." A shaking hand rose to touch her temple. "I'm sure the headache is only the result of a common or garden thump on the head."

"He said to listen for slurred speech and confusion."

"I think I sound all right."

"I do, too. Apart from no' knowing who ye are."

Which he still didn't believe. Despite the unwelcome lust that had ambushed him, his powers of deduction were as sharp as they'd ever been. She took her loss of memory too easily for it to be anything but a hoax.

She grimaced. "Apart from that. I'm overwhelmed with all this kindness."

"Och, it's the Highland way to help travelers in trouble." He reached out to take the glass, which looked likely to spill in her unsteady grip. The brief brush of his fingers across hers shot a blast of heat up his arm. He'd reined in his animal awareness of her, by heaven, but he hadn't banished it. "More?"

She shook her head. "No, thank you."

He placed the glass on the nightstand. "Is your head any better?"

More humor deepened the corners of that soft, pink mouth. "I swear there's a troupe of monkeys playing cymbals and drums inside my skull."

He frowned, worried. "Dr. Higgins left a powder for ye to take if you were troubled in the night."

"Troubled. Aye, that's one word for it."

"Ye dreamed." Before he sat, he pushed his chair further away from the bed.

He was sorry he'd spoken when the hunted expression returned to her face. "Did I...did I say anything?"

He couldn't mistake her relief when he shook his head. "Nothing I could make sense of."

Which wasn't totally true.

She avoided his eyes and started to pluck at the sheets around her waist. "I must have been dreaming about the wreck."

"Aye," he said, surer than ever that she lied, however plausible it might be that she should relive her ordeal. Her lie was another reminder that even if he was prepared to disregard the rules of hospitality, he needed to keep his hands off his delectable visitor.

He stood and crossed to stoke the fire so that he didn't have to stare at her any longer. Staring at her was bad for his willpower, he discovered.

"Would you give me a moment's privacy, please?"

He turned and saw her looking uncomfortable. "Of course. Let me help ye out of bed first."

Blast it, he'd have to touch her. Whatever else he'd learned tonight, he'd learned that was a bloody bad idea.

"I'm sure I can manage."

"I'll help ye across the room, then I'll step outside."

"Mr. Mactavish, there's no need." In a clear attempt to prove her independence, she slid her feet to the floor and with some effort managed to stand.

Impressive. Less impressive when she took one tottering step toward the screen that hid the chamber pot and her knees folded beneath her.

"For God's sake..."

Before she hit the ground—before he could remind himself he shouldn't touch her—he caught her up against him.

They'd touched often. He'd touched her down on the beach, and he'd held her in his arms on Sigurn's back and when he'd carried her upstairs. But that was when he'd only thought of the girl as someone who needed his help. She'd been wet, cold and afraid, and for all her beauty, an object of pity.

In this cozy, quiet room with night crowding around them and with her wearing only a nightdress, that was no longer the case. When his arms closed around a soft, supple body, and he felt her collapse against him, heat he'd barely conquered pulsed in his blood. The fierce urge to sweep her back into that untidy bed and join her there rose like a wave.

When he'd first found her, she'd smelled like salt and seaweed. Now after a bath and sleep, she smelled like lavender soap and warm woman. With her so close, he couldn't escape the alluring scent. It permeated his every breath. That evocative perfume made his head swim, stole his ability to see clearly.

"No..." she said in a choked voice. Frantic hands scrabbled at his chest as she pushed against him.

Shame rose bitter and stabbing, made his gut cramp with self-contempt. Not least because if he despised anything in this world, it was a liar. And he'd wager his whole estate that this fragile lassie had lied from the first. Yet still he wanted her.

"Dinna worry, you're safe," he growled.

"Can you...can you help me across to the screen?"

"Aye," he said, knowing he sounded ungracious, but unable to help it. He wished to the devil that Peggy was here right now instead of him. Cursing that he had to hold the lassie at all, he adjusted his hold. "Dinna rush."

She gave a huff of grim amusement. "I don't think that's likely."

After a few unsteady steps, she found her balance. Still, the distance across the room felt like a hundred miles. By the time they reached the screen, they were both breathing hard, but she was mostly walking under her own steam. Once she made it behind the screen, she had a heavy marble-topped table to cling to.

"Shall I help ye?"

"No," she said sharply. The walk had tired her, turned her complexion ashen, but at this moment, a fugitive pink colored her cheeks. "No, I can manage. Will you please wait outside?"

Diarmid understood her pride. He wouldn't like to rely on strangers for his intimate needs either. So while he doubted the wisdom of leaving her alone, he bowed his head and stepped back. "Hold onto the washstand, if ye feel giddy."

"Thank you," she mumbled.

He turned and left the room, refusing to look back. If he did, he wasn't sure he'd keep his distance. And he desperately needed to keep his distance.

"Good God, what in holy Hades is the matter with ye, man?" he muttered, once he was safely out in the corridor and he'd shut the door behind him.

This woman was sick and hurt and in his care. Not only that, her beauty made him uneasy, not to mention that he knew he couldn't trust her an inch. She was the last person he should want in his bed.

Worse, he knew she'd sensed his masculine interest. When he'd saved her from falling, it wasn't the prospect of crumpling to the ground that had placed that terrified light in her eyes. It had been the possessive strength of his hands and the heat that flared as her body pressed against his.

Devil take her, he was a man of honor. Whatever forbidden urges might torment him, he had no intention of molesting her while she was under his protection.

Gritting his teeth and telling himself to stop acting like a bloody lunatic, he opened the door a crack. "Are ye all right, lassie?"

If she extended her stay at Invertavey and if she intended to persist with this nonsense about not knowing her name, he'd have to come up with something to call her. Another thing to worry about in the morning, when hopefully his sanity returned.

"Yes," she said in a reedy voice.

Not believing her, he stepped back into the room to find her clinging to the edge of the screen with its pretty decoration of Chinese birds and peonies. All hint of color had fled her face, and she didn't look much better than the waterlogged wraith he'd stumbled across on Canmara Beach.

"God give me strength," he bit out in impatience and strode over to pick her up in his arms.

"I can walk," she protested.

"Aye, I can see that," he said, and bit back a twinge of remorse when his sarcasm made her flinch.

Gently he settled her in an armchair near the fire, still blazing hot and high and warming the whole room. "Stay there," he said, expecting an argument.

When she didn't object, he realized she'd reached the limit of her strength. Compassion tinged his impatience, conquered it. The girl might be a liar, but she was also alone and in trouble. She deserved better than a host as grumpy as a bear because he couldn't swive her.

Under her wide-eyed stare, he restored the untidy bed to order and refilled her water glass, leaving it within reach on the nightstand. "Still nae double vision?"

"No." She looked exhausted. The fleeting spark of spirit faded away. "I'm just tired."

"And bruised and sore," he said. "Shall I carry ye?"

"I'd rather walk, thank you."

He held out his hand, expecting her to refuse it, but she accepted his assistance without hesitation. Perhaps she sensed that he was no longer any threat. He was furious with himself to think that he ever had been.

With his help, she stumbled the few steps to the bed and slumped onto the mattress with a sigh of weary relief. Diarmid arranged the covers over her.

"I'll prepare the potion Dr. Higgins left," he said.

"It made me feel so thickheaded," she said, too drained to put much force into the objection.

"Nonetheless, you'll drink it. It will ease your pain and help ye to go back to sleep."

A ghost of a smile curved her lips as she reclined upon the pillows. "Can I say again how kind you are, even if you're also a bit of a sergeant major?"

"I'd rather ye didn't," he said drily and crossed to the sideboard to mix the powder with some water.

He glanced at the clock. Blast it, Peggy should have been here ten minutes ago.

As if she'd heard him, the door crashed open to reveal the young housemaid looking flustered. "Mrs. Curran, I'm so fashed I'm late. I slept..." Her eyes widened in dismay when she saw Diarmid passing the glass of medicine to the patient. She bobbed into a curtsy so shaky, he wondered if he might have to rescue her from falling, too. "Mactavish, och, I didnae expect to see ye here."

"I sent Mags to bed," he said, keeping his voice calm. "I've seen to our guest, and she should sleep now."

"Aye. Aye, I'm sure."

"So I'll say goodnight to both of ye."

"Goodnight, Mactavish," Peggy said, eyes alight with curiosity as she stared at the girl in the bed.

"Call me if there's any change."

"Aye, Mactavish," Peggy said, managing a slightly steadier curtsy.

"Thank you," his mermaid said in a low voice. She looked to be nearly asleep.

Diarmid rescued the half-empty glass from spilling and set it on the nightstand. "Dr. Higgins will be back in the morning. Sleep now."

Her eyelids already descended over those lovely eyes. It was time he left. Good Lord, he shouldn't have come up here in the first place. He forced a smile for Peggy, as she settled on the chair beside the bed.

Out in the corridor, he came to a stop and struggled to beat back a powerful premonition of trouble looming ahead. This girl from the sea had been here a mere afternoon. Already she disrupted Invertavey's peace. Not to mention his.

What was to come? Nothing good, he feared. His heart heavy with disquiet, he made his way to bed.

CHAPTER FOUR

"*I*'m very pleased with you, lassie," Dr. Higgins said with a smile, as he mixed a draft over by the dressing table in Fiona's airy room.

Yesterday she'd been too sore and tired and frightened to appreciate her surroundings. This morning, no trace remained of the wild weather that had brought Colin's boat to grief. The windows opened on a warm summer's day, and sunlight poured into the large chamber with its pretty chintz fabrics and graceful old walnut furniture.

The day was so warm in fact that sweat prickled her skin under the tartan shawl she'd draped around her shoulders for the sake of modesty. Hard to recall how she'd shivered with cold in yesterday's howling wind.

"I'm glad," she said from where she sat up in the bed.

The doctor shot her a humorous glance from his sharp gray eyes. She liked Dr. Higgins, who was tall and spare and sinewy, and looked like a horse with his long nose and big teeth. Liked and feared—

he might practice at the back of beyond, but even yesterday, she'd recognized that he was a perceptive man. Under that observant gaze, she wasn't convinced she could maintain the pretense that she'd lost her memory.

More reason to be on her way as soon as possible.

"You don't believe me, I can see. I know this morning you're still feeling like you've been pummeled every which way, but you're bright and alert, and you managed some sleep. The bruises will fade, and your strength will return if you give it time."

She wanted to retort that time was something she didn't have, but that would blow the myth of her amnesia sky high. And while she might be desperate, she wasn't a fool.

This morning she was purple with bruises, the worst and most painful in a band across her stomach where she'd gone over the side of Colin's boat. Her muscles had seized up, too, so every movement, even something as simple as lifting a cup of tea to her lips, hurt.

If she could, she'd rise out of this soft, cozy bed and run a hundred miles. But given she needed help to reach the chamber pot—she still blushed to remember her clumsiness in front of Mr. Mactavish last night—she acknowledged she wasn't going anywhere for the moment.

"But she still cannae remember anything," Mr. Mactavish said from the window seat, reminding her, should she require it, of her most powerful reason for needing to leave this house.

He'd been kind last night, and he'd been a gentleman. Those competent hands hadn't encroached any further than was necessary to attend to her needs.

But Fiona had learned in a hard school to recognize masculine interest. Despite his gentle touch, he wanted her, and that terrified her.

She came to believe that Diarmid Mactavish was a good man, as far as that went. He'd treated her well, and she could see that the people here loved and respected him. At Bancavan, sullen resentment and constant fear infected the atmosphere, whereas at Invertavey, the ease in human relations spoke volumes for a fine and capable master.

But the laird was a man, and she couldn't trust him. When a man wanted something, he took it. She needed to be away from Invertavey before his hunger broke free of his principles.

"Och, I'm sure her memory will come back soon enough," Dr. Higgins said. "There's a reason she can't remember. Some shock. Perhaps the shipwreck itself."

"But people will be worried about her," Mr. Mactavish said. How she wished he'd leave the subject alone. "I should write to the papers in Glasgow and Edinburgh, perhaps even London, and place advertisements to see if we can locate her kin."

"No!" Fiona said sharply before she could stop herself. Shaking hands tangled in the sheets, and a towering wave of terror made her head swim. If her host traced her family, she was lost—and so was Christina. She struggled up against the pillows and with difficulty forced her tone back to its usual level. "That's too much trouble."

Those clever black eyes fastened on her with alarming interest. "Och, nae trouble at all."

"I'm sure I'll remember who I am. I'm trying." Which was an out-and-out falsehood.

Dr. Higgins frowned, as he carried the glass of medicine across to her. "That's just what you mustn't do. Turmoil and worry will only delay your recovery."

"But surely the lassie will do better with people she knows and loves, rather than remaining a nameless waif among strangers, however well intentioned," Mr. Mactavish said, that impressive jaw setting in stubborn lines.

She plucked nervously at the bedcovers gathered around her waist, then made herself stop when Mr. Mactavish focused on the betraying action. "I don't want my private troubles made public in the world. I'm a lady. A lady doesn't make a spectacle of herself."

The angle of those expressive black brows told her that he found her argument unconvincing. "At least ye remember that much, then."

Dr. Higgins cast a disapproving glance at the man who was clearly his friend. "Diarmid, don't badger her. After the wreck, she's lucky to be alive. Rest and quiet are essential for her recovery. If the lady..." He emphasized the word. "...finds the idea of a notice in the papers distressing, you need to respect that. I believe her memory will return of its own accord."

"And what if it doesnae?" Mr. Mactavish asked in a deliberately neutral voice. "Is she to become a permanent resident in my guest bedroom, like a family ghost?"

Fiona hid a wince. She couldn't blame her host for his frustration. If only she could tell him that she'd be gone the moment she was capable of travel, but that, too, would bring her lying story down around her ears.

Her quest loomed ahead, never forgotten, but suddenly overwhelming as she came to understand what a disaster the shipwreck was. She was sad Colin was dead—there were few enough good men in this wicked world. But now she faced a journey across Scotland without a man at her side. She had no illusions about the dangers a lone woman might meet on the open road. A penniless woman, at that. What little money she'd managed to scrape together over the past months had gone down with the fishing boat.

"Stop it, Diarmid." Dr. Higgins stood beside the bed and lifted Fiona's hand to count her racing pulse. "You're upsetting my patient."

Mr. Mactavish rose. Despite her dark thoughts about him, Fiona's heart skipped a beat over what a magnificent sight he made. Today he wore the kilt in the purple Mactavish plaid, and the loose white shirt did nothing to hide his broad, straight shoulders and powerful chest and arms.

She waited for him to deliver a blistering response to that rebuke from a social inferior, but to her surprise, he ran an elegant hand through his inky black hair and the taut line of his shoulders loosened. "I apologize, John. And to ye, lassie. I spoke out of turn. It's barely a day since I found ye half-drowned. It's nae wonder you're still buffle-headed."

Buffle-headed? She was speechless with shock.

Fiona tried to think of another man she'd met who might be willing to admit to a fault and say sorry for it. Even her father who had been a man of principle, unlike most of the men she'd encountered since, had been stiff-necked with pride. He'd never admitted he was wrong.

Not for the first time, she felt a twinge of guilt for all the lies she told these decent people. It didn't make her question what she did, but it was strong enough to make every word taste sour in her mouth.

Her daughter's happiness, perhaps her very life, depended on Fiona finding her. So she had to return to health in a hurry, then continue her journey. That wasn't going to be as easy as she'd hoped either. It was apparent that both these men had assumed responsibility for her safety. That spoke volumes for their generosity and kindness, but she could already see that Mr. Mactavish wouldn't send her on her way alone with a mere wave and good wishes.

She'd need to leave in secret. That would take some planning, but it wasn't impossible. She wasn't a prisoner. Although flitting off without a farewell was a shabby return for the treatment she received at Invertavey.

What alternative did she have? Explain her difficulties and throw herself on her host's mercy? Mr. Mactavish might be a superior example of his sex, but it was likely he'd take the conventional view of her rebellion and force her back into purgatory.

If he did that, Christina was lost.

No, she hated to lie, but lying was her only option while she was here. She just had to ignore her conscience's protests over how she took advantage of Mr. Mactavish's hospitality.

"I'm sorry I can't be more help," she said, meaning it more than she could tell him.

"Och, it's nothing, lassie."

"And I've disrupted your household."

"The household needed disrupting. Before all this excitement, the servants just sat around, gossiping about how dreadful the laird is."

She smiled at that. This house was well run, and the laird was firmly in charge, even if he ruled with a light hand. She'd witnessed enough bad management in her time to recognize the opposite when she saw it.

Regret stuck its claws into her. Regret and envy. How different her life would have been if she'd come to a place like this after her father's death. How different Christina's life would have been.

"At least they're not drinking your whisky when they do it," Dr. Higgins said.

"Aye. Only because I keep it under lock and key, laddie." Mr. Mactavish glanced across at her, and the brief amusement drained from his dark eyes. Which was lucky for her equilibrium. She despised the male sex, but it was hard to remember that when this handsome man treated her like they shared a joke against the world. "We still need to call the lassie something. I cannae have my guest room occupied by a lady I ken only as *la bella incognita*."

Dr. Higgins smiled at Fiona with an approval she knew very well she didn't deserve. "Indeed she is bonny."

She knew he meant only to compliment her, but fear iced her blood. Her unusual looks had always been more curse than blessing.

"Thank you," she made herself say, but she caught Mr. Mactavish's curiosity at her lackluster response.

"What about Nita?" Dr. Higgins suggested, not seeming to notice the undercurrents flowing through the room.

Her host studied her before he nodded. "I suppose it will do as well as anything else. What do ye think, lassie?"

Fiona didn't much care. She wasn't staying at Invertavey long enough to become a significant part of the household. "I'll answer to it."

"Grand to hear." Again that hint of irony. She knew her host didn't trust her, which spoke volumes for the acute brain beneath that gorgeous exterior. "Nita the lady shall be."

Dear Lord, how she wished a stupid man had come to her rescue on that beach. If Mr. Mactavish put his sharp wits to work against her, she had no chance of prevailing.

"Now it's time for Miss Nita to drink her medicine and get some sleep. All this sparkling conversation is tiring her out."

"Aye, I can see that," Mr. Mactavish said. "Perhaps with rest, she'll soon be able to tell us more."

Not likely. But Fiona obediently swallowed the draft Dr. Higgins gave her, wincing a little at its bitter, herbal taste, and rested back on the pillows. She closed her eyes, welcoming the drowsy drift of sleep as the medicine started its work.

"As Miss Nita regains her health, I hope her memory will come back," Dr. Higgins said. "In the meantime, we need to be careful not to test her stamina."

"Aye, I bow to your orders, John. I'll stop pushing the lassie to remember."

She heard the men moving away. Without opening her eyes, she spoke in a low voice. "I do appreciate all you're doing for me. I wouldn't have survived on that beach if you hadn't found me, Mr. Mactavish. And you and Dr. Higgins have looked after me splendidly since."

All of which was true. For once, it was nice not to lie.

"Don't fret, Miss Nita," Dr. Higgins said. "We'll get you well, never you fear."

"Aye, lassie, you're safe here," Mr. Mactavish said, in the black velvet baritone that always made her bones melt.

She stifled a grim laugh. Safe? If only what he said was true. But she'd long ago learned the hard lesson that she wasn't safe anywhere.

CHAPTER FIVE

"I still think you're better off staying here at the house." Diarmid stared in frustration at the woman sitting on the bed with her pale hands folded in her lap and a mulish expression on her delicate face. "Ye haven't yet recovered your strength."

His mermaid was dressed in a gown that belonged to Mags. It had been dyed black and altered to fit her. The frock was plain and practical, its high collar edged with a thin line of lace. The dress of a respectable shopkeeper's wife or an upper servant.

The dress had never looked so good on his portly housekeeper, he was grimly aware. The clothes Miss Nita had washed up in were irreparably ruined. He supposed he should be grateful they'd found anything in the place for her to wear. The house was very much a bachelor establishment these days. In those fraught, wretched weeks after word came of his mother's death beside her rakish lover, his father had burned all her clothes.

"Och, let Miss Nita go if she wants to, Mactavish," Mags said. "We'll be there to make sure she doesn't try her strength too far."

Mags stood beside the bed, and Peggy was fluttering around the bedroom, tidying something or other. After those disturbing moments during his guest's first night under his roof, Diarmid had made sure he'd never been alone with her since. It was galling to admit that he couldn't trust himself with her.

"The man traveled with me. It's my duty to attend his funeral," Miss Nita said stubbornly. "I'm much better. You know I am."

Diarmid released a huff of scornful amusement. "You'd blow over in a slight breeze, lassie."

"You'll be there to catch me."

During the last two days, he'd learned to respect this delicate creature's will. After sleeping for most of her first day, she'd spent yesterday trying to walk. First to the screen, then to the sitting room attached to this chamber. Then along the corridor.

Mags had told him about the first two excursions. He knew about the last because he'd found her close to collapse, clinging to an old oak hall chair. He'd swung her up in his arms, called for a maid, and carried her back to bed.

He could still feel the frail weight of her body and smell the subtle lavender of her soap. His sleep last night had been disturbed by feverish dreams of a slender, lavender-scented woman coming to him where he lay and kissing the soul out of his body. Dream Nita had enveloped him in flaxen tresses of silky hair, hair now pulled back in a simple knot that emphasized the stark purity of her features.

"The way I was there yesterday when ye got ten feet down the hallway before your legs gave out?"

"I'm stronger today." As if meaning to prove it, she rose to her feet.

"Be careful." He surged forward, even as he reminded himself that touching her was dangerous.

By heaven, she deserved his protection, not his lust. She was fragile and exhausted and at his mercy. He felt like a satyr every time he looked at her and imagined stripping that too-thin body bare and rolling her under him.

The girl raised a trembling hand to keep him at bay, and his gut cramped with shame as he waited for her to call him out on his shameful yearning. Instead she only offered more pride and obstinacy. "I'm fine."

His hands clenching at his sides, Diarmid battled the impulse to help her. He watched her bosom rise as she sucked in a shaky breath, then forced himself to look away out the window. In his turmoil, he hardly registered that the day was bonny, not at all funereal.

When he turned back to the room, the girl stood at the dressing table, tying the ribbons on an old-fashioned black bonnet. Another piece courtesy of Mags.

He met shining ice-blue eyes in the mirror, and a jolt of desire hit him so hard, he feared his knees wouldn't hold. Right now, he was the one who needed propping up.

The girl straightened and forced a smile to those soft pink lips. "I'm ready."

"If ye feel faint, tell me," he said.

"Och, Mactavish, stop fussing over the wee lassie. You're like an old hen," Mags said. "We'll see nae harm comes to her."

"This is against my better judgment," he said to the girl. "You havenae come near to recovering your strength."

She stiffened her spine and tilted her chin, as she pulled a pair of black gloves over her hands. "Whoever that man we're burying today may be, he was my companion. I owe him my respects."

Diarmid was convinced she knew exactly who the drowned sailor was, just as he was convinced she remembered her name and where she'd come from. Two days of sheltering a genuine invalid in the house hadn't changed his mind on that at all.

"Aye, verra well. I've ordered the carriage around, so ye just have to walk downstairs and out the front door."

"Thank you," the girl said, as collected as a queen, despite her frailty and simple clothing.

Lowering her eyes, she stepped away from the dressing table. She looked the perfect little mourner, modest and demure. Yet Diarmid would wager his next ten years that under that unassuming demeanor, she was all fire.

She made it halfway across the blue and red carpet before she showed any sign of wavering. Diarmid bit back a curse as Mags turned to him.

"Och, Mactavish, where are your manners? Give the lady your arm."

He set his jaw so hard, it ached. Damn it, he didn't want to touch the girl, largely because the devil inside him wanted nothing more. But Mags was glaring at him as if he'd gone mad—he wasn't sure he hadn't—and Peggy regarded him with a puzzled frown.

Biting back an imprecation that consigned all females to perdition, he crossed to his guest's side and extended his arm. "My lady?"

"Thank you," she said in a tight voice and curled her fingers around his elbow. The tight grip betrayed how close she was to falling down, but determination squared her shoulders. "Once I'm out in the fresh air, I'm sure I'll feel better."

"Are ye indeed?" Diarmid asked grimly, but he matched his progress to her halting steps as they left the bedroom and made their way toward the main staircase.

Fiona wasn't used to kindness or consideration, at least since she'd left her father's house. When Mr. Mactavish treated her like a fragile princess, she found it profoundly unsettling. Nice, to be sure, but a threat to her purpose. His gentleness might deceive her into thinking that the world wasn't a dangerous, cruel place.

Her perpetual war with life became even more difficult to maintain when he handed her up into an open carriage with a care that made her feel precious. He settled a fur rug over her knees.

"It's a warm day," she said, even as she pulled off a glove to bury her fingers in the silky soft pelt.

"Aye, but I dinnae want to take any chances with your recovery. Dr. Higgins expected ye to come down with pneumonia after I brought you back from the beach."

She hadn't known that. Dear heaven…

Her hand clenched in the fur throw, as she came to terms with how lucky she'd been—and how easily her story could have found a different ending. She might have drowned, or died of exposure on that wind-swept beach. She could have come down with a fever that trapped her here for weeks or, worse, killed her.

Without her intervention, Christina was doomed.

From beside the carriage, Mr. Mactavish watched her steadily. She didn't trust him—he was a man after all—but without his assistance, her quest would already have failed.

So the smile that curved her lips conveyed genuine gratitude. "You've been very good to me, sir. In fact, I owe you my life."

"Och, I didnae do anything special. It's Highland tradition to offer hospitality to strangers."

His discomfort with her thanks charmed her. And she couldn't remember the last time she'd found a male charming. The admiration glowing in his eyes made her blood flow with lazy warmth. She knew he wanted her, but at this precise moment, even that didn't seem too frightening.

Be careful, Fiona.

She stiffened in consternation, as she realized how a couple of days of kindness had weakened her resolve. It was time to go.

Today, she'd see Colin buried and name him to God, if only in her heart. Then she'd start planning her escape. While she was still woefully unsteady on her feet, two days of rest and good food had already restored some of her strength.

How strange to realize that when she ran away from Invertavey House, she'd be sorry to leave. She'd come to like blunt, good-hearted Mags and chatty, giggly Peggy and the other maids. Dr. Higgins had looked after her with stalwart dedication.

She wouldn't miss Invertavey's master, despite him being a man any woman would admire. Why wouldn't a woman admire him? He was clever, strong, good-hearted, generous, kind, and protective.

But poor Fiona could commend none of those qualities. Because if he turned that intelligence and strength against her, he'd ruin her every scheme.

Those perceptive dark eyes rested on her now, and black brows drew together over that arrogant blade of a nose. How she wished he wasn't so handsome. It was so difficult to remember that while he might look like a prince from a legend, he was just another man. And men were the enemy.

"I wish ye wouldn't do that." He started to reach for her, then curtailed the gesture and curled his long fingers over the side of the open carriage.

"Do what?" she asked, startled.

He shook his head, as if the question was asinine. "Close yourself away like that."

"I don't..."

His lips tightened in impatience. "Ye look so frightened. I loathe it."

To her dismay, he caught the hand that curled in the fur rug. He'd touched her plenty of times. When he'd found her. On that first night when she'd realized he wanted her. Since, to help her to stand, or move about when her strength failed.

But something about this deliberate clasp of his hand on hers made her shiver. For once, not with fear of a dominant, bullying masculinity. Instead more warmth stole through her veins. Not lazy this time, but urgent and beckoning and alluring.

"I wish you'd trust me, Nita. I wish you'd share what makes ye so afraid and troubled. I wish you'd let me help ye."

For a moment, she stared into his intent dark eyes and wondered if he might be someone she could rely on, someone who would hear her story and understand why she must act. Someone who would place his strength and his resources at her service, like a knight in an old story who dedicated himself to a fair damsel.

More stories again! Just the thought reminded her that outside books, perfect, chivalrous knights didn't exist.

Disentangling her hand from his required more effort than it should. "I don't understand what you mean," she said in a shaky voice.

Disappointment dulled his eyes, and his lips turned down. "As ye wish."

The problem was that nothing was as she wished. Nothing had been as she wished since she was fifteen and her father died, consigning her to a living hell. But she'd long ago learned the futility of feeling sorry for herself.

When Fiona put her glove on again, her hands were shaking, and she knew the laird noticed that she was far from composed. She stared straight ahead over the horses' backs to where the drive curved down to the road. That was the route she must follow—and soon. Before the sanctuary she'd found here in this lovely house sapped the last of her will from her.

To think, she'd spent years longing for some touch of kindness. Now she'd found it, and it turned out to be more dangerous to her purpose than years of brutality had ever been.

The carriage lurched as Mr. Mactavish stepped up and sat opposite her, his back to the horses. The coachman took his place, and the vehicle rolled away under the avenue of elms, carrying her to the funeral of her only friend in Bancavan.

CHAPTER SIX

$\mathcal{F}$iona was surprised to see how crowded the church was. After all, she was the only person here who knew Colin, and even she couldn't give him a name, not without betraying herself.

"Tears?" Mr. Mactavish asked softly, as six brawny Highlanders stepped forward to lift the plain wooden coffin and carry it from the church after the short, moving service. The congregation stood as a mark of respect. "Does that mean ye remember who he was?"

With one shaking hand, she fished a handkerchief out of her pocket. "No, of course not."

She grew to hate the way every second word out of her mouth was false, especially when the people at Invertavey had been so kind. Kind and curious. She hadn't missed the lingering glances and the whispering, when she tottered into the small stone church on the laird's arm.

She swallowed to shift the knot of sorrow that blocked her throat and silently promised Colin that one day she'd see right done by him. One day when she was safe, when Christina was safe.

But that day wasn't today, so she straightened her shoulders and set a steadying hand on the edge of the pew. Her legs felt rubbery, and exhaustion gnawed at the edges of her vision. She was appalled at how little stamina she had, when right now she needed her strength more than ever.

"Is it wrong to weep for a man lost to the sea?" she asked.

When Mr. Mactavish shook his head, a ray of color from the stained glass window above him glanced across the glossy raven-black hair. Gothic letters under a mealy-mouthed Jesus spelled out "Suffer the little children to come unto me."

Fiona didn't ask God to watch over her child. Over the last years, she'd lost any faith in the power of prayer.

God wouldn't help Christina. Only her mother could do that.

"No, especially if he's known to ye."

She dragged her attention back to Mr. Mactavish. He looked spectacular in his somber black. But then, he always looked spectacular, curse him.

"I told you, I don't remember who he is. But I must have known him once, or we wouldn't have been on that boat together." The fact that she deserved the laird's suspicions didn't make those suspicions any less annoying. "No more absurd to weep for him than for half the village to turn out to bury a stranger."

Mr. Mactavish offered his arm. She wished she could refuse it, but she didn't trust her wobbly knees to hold her up.

"People here respect the sea. If ye visit the churchyard, you'll see that many an Invertavey man has lost his life to drowning. Your friend isnae the only unknown sailor buried here either."

He unlatched the gate to the pew and helped her down the wooden step to the church's flagstoned floor. Up in the loft, the organ was playing something soft and sad. Fiona and the laird proceeded down the aisle, while the rest of the villagers filed out behind them.

By the time they reached the church door, Fiona was feeling seriously shaky. All she could hear was the blood pounding in her ears, and every step she took felt like a mile. As she struggled to remain upright, her fingers formed claws against the fine black wool of Mr. Mactavish's coat.

The world tilted and reeled as she found herself swept up in Mr. Mactavish's powerful arms. "Ye really shouldnae have come," he said.

She drew a breath to clear the fuzziness from her head and sent him a disgusted look, even as her arm curved around his neck. "If you say I told you so, I'll bite you."

He stifled a laugh inappropriate to the solemn occasion. Fascinating creases deepened around his eyes as he smiled.

Spectacular she'd called him? The word didn't do him justice.

"Och, I might like that."

Before she could muster a reply to that taunting remark, Dr. Higgins had come up to them. She'd smiled at him in the church, but he'd been too far back from the Mactavish family pew at the front for her to speak to him. "Is Miss Nita all right?"

"She wasnae ready to come out in public." Mr. Mactavish's grip on her was firm yet gentle. "Will ye take her back up to the house, John? I should go to the graveside."

"With pleasure."

"I can speak for myself." She winced at how childish she sounded.

Mr. Mactavish stopped and directed a mocking lift of a dark eyebrow at her. "Would ye like to go back to the house, lassie? I could carry ye into the churchyard, but we're causing enough talk as it is."

She looked around and saw that everyone was staring at her in the laird's arms. Uncomfortable heat prickled her cheeks.

"No, I'll...I'll go back to the house." She mustered a stronger tone. "You know, you don't need to haul me about like a bag of flour all the time."

He gave a sardonic grunt. "I do, when you turn as white as that flour. I cannae have strange women fainting at my feet and littering the church. People might trip over ye and do themselves a mischief."

Fiona didn't want to laugh, but she couldn't help it. She was annoyed with him. And she was genuinely sad that they buried old Colin Smith today. If he hadn't agreed to help her, he'd be tucked up safely beside his fireside in Bancavan.

Mr. Mactavish's efficient care belied his sardonic manner. She soon found herself in the open carriage with the luxurious rug wrapped around her once again.

As Dr. Higgins took the seat opposite, Mr. Mactavish tipped his hat to her, then turned to his friend. "Stay on for a wee dram, if you're no' in a hurry to be elsewhere."

"Aye, I will. Thank you."

As the driver clicked his tongue to the horses and the carriage rolled away, Fiona couldn't help turning her head to watch Mr. Mactavish stride after the coffin.

I'm sorry, Colin. I'm sorry I got you into this. I'm sorry you died. And I'm sorry I'm too feeble to see you safely placed in your grave.

"The service didn't spark any memories for you?" Dr. Higgins asked.

She'd forgotten he was there, she was so busy staring after the laird, who towered above everyone around him. There was no reason to blush. She didn't harbor wicked intentions toward Mr. Mactavish, however handsome he was. But blush she did, even as she brushed a tear from her eye and said a silent farewell to Colin.

"No." She avoided his gaze and stared down to where she ripped at her damp handkerchief. "I'd tell you if it did."

"I'm starting to agree with Diarmid. We need to do something to locate your family. This is the third day after the wreck. They must be frantic for news of you."

"No…" She raised horrified eyes to meet the doctor's kind but perceptive gaze. She gulped in some air and struggled to steady her voice, although she feared he'd recognized her panic. "I'm sure in time my memory will come back. I don't want to put you or Mr. Mactavish to any inconvenience."

As if he spoke the words, she saw the thought run through the doctor's mind that she could hardly disrupt Mr. Mactavish's household more than she did right now. But he was too polite to point that out, even if they both knew it was true.

Staring out at the small village, she swallowed to shift the bitter taste of all her lies. Invertavey was neat and prosperous and well managed. The laird was a good master. Compared to rough, rundown Bancavan, Invertavey was Eden.

She hadn't paid attention to the scenery on the way to the church. When Mr. Mactavish was with her, she never noticed much else. Dr. Higgins was more restful company, or at least he had been until he mentioned taking measures to discover her identity.

As they trundled along the cobbled street, people turned to watch her. She supposed her dramatic arrival set tongues wagging, especially as she'd taken up residence in the manor with a bachelor. Another reason for going sooner rather than later. Mr. Mactavish didn't deserve to be the target of gossip as repayment for his generosity. A woman in dire straits could spend a couple of days under his roof without raising too many eyebrows. But if that turned into an extended convalescence, questions would be asked.

Nor would her presence remain a secret outside Invertavey if she lingered. News had a way of spreading like rings of water in a pond after someone threw in a stone. She couldn't take the risk of word reaching the Grants that an unknown woman had washed up miles down the coast from Bancavan.

"Miss Nita?"

How she hated that stupid name, too. Every time she heard it, it reminded her that she was a foul liar.

"Yes, Dr. Higgins?" She didn't look away from the road. They'd turned onto the long drive leading up to the house.

"Diarmid Mactavish is the finest man I know. There's no better friend in adversity. If you're in trouble, tell him. You can trust him."

Dr. Higgins's quiet, sincere words had tears pricking at her eyes, tears too revealing to shed. How she wished she could ask for her host's help, but she couldn't take the risk that he might decide to tell the Grants where she was.

Fiona wasn't lost to the irony of her situation. All her life, she'd been taught to loathe the Mactavish name, yet now the only man she came close to trusting was a Mactavish.

Blinking away her tears, she braced to tell more lies. She sucked in an unsteady breath and faced the doctor, seeing his concern and his integrity, and knowing she could rely on neither. She even managed to muster a brief smile.

"Once my memory comes back, I'll be able to answer all your questions. Right now, that's my only trouble—and regaining my strength. Mr. Mactavish has been so good to me, and so have you, Doctor. Whatever happens, I'll always cherish the welcome I received at Invertavey. No lady in distress could have found a better sanctuary."

That at least was true, although it didn't ease the doctor's frown as he studied her. Mr. Mactavish had never believed that she'd lost her memory. She had a sinking feeling that Dr. Higgins became more skeptical by the hour.

It was time she went, before these kind people realized that they'd sheltered a deceiver. One more night at Invertavey to gather her strength, one more day. Tomorrow night, once the household was abed, she'd brave the open hills and make her way to her daughter.

CHAPTER SEVEN

*S*hielding her candle with one hand, Fiona crept down the imposing oak staircase to Invertavey House's ground floor. Her other hand clung to the carved banister, with its fanciful dolphins and mermaids and tritons, more reminders that the house was beside the sea, if the view out the window wasn't enough to convince a visitor.

She'd returned from Colin's funeral exhausted and heartsick, not just with grief for the loss of a good man. Her quest had forced her to make some hard decisions, and none harder than this. What she intended to do now broke every law of hospitality and was a betrayal of all the generosity she'd received here.

After the funeral, she'd slept for hours and managed a good dinner. This was the first time since the shipwreck that she started to feel more like herself. For days, she'd felt like she was made of wet string, scarcely able to stand on her own two feet. Now her legs hardly trembled as she inched her way downstairs.

This morning on the way out, she'd caught a quick glimpse of the rooms leading off the hall. She made for the one that seemed to be a study or library. What she wanted might be there. If not, she'd search for an office, or down in the kitchens.

At the doorway, she paused, loathing what necessity made of her. Then as so often before, she set aside her qualms and stepped into the dark room, quietly closing the door behind her.

Nothing mattered beyond Christina's safety.

In grim, loveless Bancavan, everything was locked away, including the women. So when she put her candle on the large leather-topped desk before a tall window, Fiona expected what she wanted to be out of immediate reach.

Picking simple locks was a skill she'd learned over the last wretched years. But when she tried the top drawer, it opened at her first touch. A sigh of relief escaped her. Here in happy, well-managed Invertavey, the laird didn't secure his valuables. He trusted the people around him. Shame tasted rusty in her mouth as she realized she was about to prove him wrong.

Flickering candlelight revealed a jumble of bits and pieces. A silver compass. A gold watch on a chain. Pens. Pencils. Notebooks. Bent nails. Bird feathers. Seashells. And a scatter of what she sought—cold, hard cash.

Instead of reaching for the money, Fiona paused to fight a wave of poignant tenderness. She couldn't afford to give in to weakness, but the mess in the drawer was so unexpected. She'd imagined Diarmid Mactavish would be orderly in his habits. He always seemed so in command of himself.

This untidy drawer revealed a boyish tendency to collect odds and ends and pile them together in a chaotic heap. Her powerful response to this surprising side to her host's character took her unawares. Somewhere in the last days, she'd developed a genuine respect and liking for the master here.

Fiona stared down at the tangle. More than likely he didn't know how much money was here. She could take a little, without him noticing the robbery the moment he opened the drawer.

Her conscience stabbed her. Theft shouldn't be so easy.

Without hesitation, she picked out some notes and a handful of coins and wrapped them in a handkerchief. Her hands were shaking so hard that it took several attempts to tie everything up in a tight bundle.

"Two gentlemen to see ye, Mactavish," Mags said from the library door.

Diarmid looked up from the plans to drain a low-lying field where he wanted to graze cattle. "Two gentlemen?"

Obviously whoever his visitors were, they weren't from the estate. Mags knew everyone on Invertavey as well as he did. "Did they give their names?"

"Aye, they did." Her tone was uncharacteristically cool. "Allan and Thomas Grant of Bancavan."

Diarmid stifled a sigh. Over past centuries, the Grants and the Mactavishes had been mortal enemies. Rivers of blood had been spilled on both sides, and clan lore was rife with tales of raids and battles and kidnappings. But in this modern era, with the Highlands at peace, he had no patience with feuds extending back into the mists of history.

"Did they say what they want?"

"No, they didnae." Mags's sternness didn't ease. "Probably the clan silver."

Standing, Diarmid cast her a disapproving glance. "You'd better show them in."

"I hope you've got your pistol handy, in case they try something."

"Mags, those days are past."

"No, they're not." She didn't wait for him to put her in her place. "I'll gae and get them, but I'll be listening at the door. If ye want help, you just need to shout."

Considering she was all of five feet tall, that made him smile. "Verra reassuring," he said drily.

Mags stumped away while he put on his coat. By the time his two visitors stepped into the library, he looked every inch the Laird of Invertavey.

"Diarmid Mactavish?" the older of the two men said with a hint of suspicion. "I'm Allan Grant of Bancavan, up by Durness, and this is my brother Thomas. Good of ye to see us."

Diarmid stepped forward and shook the older man's hand. The younger man avoided any friendly overtures and regarded him with barely concealed hostility. Clearly Mags wasn't the only one recalling old troubles.

"Aye, I'm Diarmid Mactavish. What can I help ye with?"

The man's handshake was brief and dry and made Diarmid feel vaguely unclean. Perhaps he wasn't quite as removed from clan prejudice as he'd hoped.

There was no mistaking that the two men were brothers, tall, stringy, red-haired—although with a good bit of gray—and with the characteristic long, pinched Grant features. Both were respectably dressed in black frock coats. As Diarmid took in their flinty expressions and cold gray eyes, he couldn't help thinking that they looked like a pair of particularly unsympathetic undertakers.

"We believe you're harboring Fiona Grant, my brother's runaway wife, in this house. We're here to fetch her back to her kin and her bairn."

Runaway wife? Bairn?

Diarmid only just saved himself from staggering as the unacceptable words battered at his uncomprehending brain. For God's sake, was the bonny lass upstairs like his faithless mother?

Surely not.

Except…

Except he'd always known his mermaid lied about her loss of memory, and now he had an inkling why. She might be gloriously beautiful, but he knew better than most that beauty was no guarantee of honesty.

His late mother had been famously beautiful—she'd taken London by storm when she made her debut and had made a brilliant marriage to a rich man, despite her relatively humble birth. A brilliant marriage that soon deteriorated into a nightmare of infidelity and recrimination. His mother had loved nobody but herself. Not even her child had counted for her.

His father had loved his wife, forgiven her over and over for her escapades. But years of playing the cuckold had turned his soul to stone.

Despite his mother's many sins, her death had devastated what remained of his father's life. The previous laird never ceased to grieve for the woman who had brought him endless heartbreak and humiliation.

And Miss Nita—no, that wasn't right. What did they say the girl's name was? Fiona?—was just such another as his selfish, wanton mother? A woman prepared to abandon a child in her reckless pursuit of pleasure?

Anger knotted his gut, while a betrayal he had no real right to feel left a rotten taste in his mouth. The girl didn't owe him her loyalty. As if such a woman knew the meaning of the word.

Still he felt duped and used. Despite his mistrust, over these last days, he'd developed a reluctant liking for her. He'd imagined he saw qualities that he admired, qualities like courage and consideration for others.

Dear heaven, he was as big a fool as his father. Instead of bringing her to his home, he should have tossed her back into the sea.

Shame turned rage to bitter aloes. To think, he'd wanted her, despite knowing all the time that she lied. After what his mother had done, he should be immune to a woman's wiles. But it seemed wretched experience made him no more proof against beauty than any other man.

Even as fury darkened his vision and nausea churned in his gut, some element of rational thought stirred. He was reluctant to call it hope.

"Are ye sure this is the lassie you're looking for?"

Although how many stray females wandered along the Scottish coast?

"We've been working our way south from Bancavan, asking after my wife," the other man said.

The other man? Curse him, he was more than that. This unimpressive, hatchet-faced bastard was Fiona's husband, if what they said was true.

"When we arrived at Invertavey and made inquiries, we heard of a shipwreck in the last few days," Thomas continued. "A beautiful lady and a dead man washed up after a storm. It could only be my wife. The dead man is Colin Smith, a fisherman on the estate. We asked if anyone had seen the woman, and it turns out that she was in church only yesterday. The description made us even more certain. She's tall and skinny. Pale blond with blue eyes."

A prosaic accounting of the girl's remarkable looks, but unmistakably accurate. Diarmid cursed himself for being a thick-headed fool, still hoping against hope that the Grants were mistaken.

"That sounds like her. I'm sorry that we werenae in touch with ye. The lassie who arrived in such poor shape has lost her memory, so we were unable to discover her identity and contact her kin."

He could see that the memory loss struck these men as convenient, just as it had always struck him. "Perhaps seeing her husband again will restore her mind," the older Grant—Allan—said flatly.

It struck Diarmid that these men might wonder if he was part of a conspiracy to keep the girl for himself. "I'd like to make it clear that the lady..." He used the term with emphasis. "...has been treated with the utmost care, respect and honor. After the shipwreck, she was dangerously weak, and she remains far from recovered. If ye have any doubts about her health, I advise you to talk to the village doctor, John Higgins."

He saw that both men understood his meaning, although he was uncomfortably aware that his guest's fragility hadn't stopped him wanting to possess her.

"We appreciate your kindness to our wayward kinswoman, Mr. Mactavish," Allan Grant said, with just enough irony to grate on Diarmid's nerves. "We're sure ye did everything in your power to aid her recovery."

Perhaps it was the lingering ghost of the old feud, but a prickling at the back of his neck told him that he neither liked nor trusted these two men. On the surface all was politeness, even smarminess, but he sensed rage from both, and an iron determination to have his will from the older Grant. The other man, Fiona's husband, showed no pleasure in tracking down his errant wife. Diarmid struggled against imagining that dried up old husk using the girl's slender body, but it was impossible not to.

Again he reminded himself that none of this was his concern. He was in no position to judge. Who knew what a dance the wee besom had led her family?

He opened the door, expecting to see Mags hovering outside, but she wasn't there. Instead, Peter, a shy new footman, was polishing the windows in the hall.

"Peter, will you please go upstairs and ask Miss Nita..." Blast it, he wouldn't call her Mrs. Grant until he was absolutely sure of her identity. He knew he clutched at straws, even as his mind told him he was a naïve idiot to give her the benefit of the doubt. "...if she'll come downstairs to the library for a moment?"

"Aye, Mactavish," the young man said.

Diarmid returned to the Grants. "If the lady is your missing kinswoman, I'm more than happy for her to stay until she regains her strength. I'd be pleased to offer ye both the hospitality of Invertavey House as well."

"That's grand of ye, Mr. Mactavish," Allan Grant said, and Diarmid would wager his estate that the man meant precisely the opposite. "But we dinna need to put ye out. We'll take my sister-in-law back to where she belongs, to her kin. She's had her wee adventure. It's time for her to come home and resume her duties."

Was Diarmid oversensitive to find it both odd and suspicious that neither man seemed noticeably relieved that the girl was safe? Again, none of his concern. But he had a grim feeling that her kin felt little affection for their lost lady.

"She shouldnae be long. While we're waiting, may I offer ye a wee dram?"

"No, thank ye, Mr. Mactavish. We'll just be collecting Fiona and taking our leave. She's been gone from Bancavan long enough already."

An awkward silence fell. The Grants wouldn't sit down, which left them all standing about in an uncomfortable circle. With every moment, Diarmid found it more and more incongruous that the beautiful girl upstairs was married to the nonentity before him. The fellow must be more than thirty years older than she was. Perhaps her reasons for running away weren't so hard to fathom after all.

With a soft knock, the door opened to reveal his mysterious guest. As she paused in the doorway to take in the scene, her eyes widened in unmistakable horror and the color leached from her face.

"Fiona!" Thomas said, surging toward her.

"No!" She whirled around as if she intended to run, but Allan, despite his age, was too quick for her. He grabbed her wrist in what Diarmid saw was a bruising grip. Before he remembered he had no rights here, he'd stepped forward to protest.

"Time to come home, lassie." Allan hauled her into the library and kicked the door shut with a crash.

The girl was visibly shaking, as Allan wrenched her closer. Thomas took up a place in front of the exit, blocking her escape route.

Despite his lifelong contempt for faithless women, Diarmid couldn't let this go on. "Mr. Grant, there's nae need for violence. May I remind ye the lady has been unwell? Pray release her immediately, and let's see what she has to say."

"I don't know these men, Mr. Mactavish." Huge blue eyes, glassy with terror, focused on him. In spite of all he knew of her, Diarmid fought the urge to rip her away from her captor. "They're strangers."

Diarmid wished to blazes he believed her. But even without that panicked denial when she came in, he saw recognition in her eyes, and the kind of fear that was always missing when she claimed to have lost her memory. He couldn't doubt that she knew the Grants, and his faint ridiculous hope that there was some confusion about her identity faded to nothing.

"Mr. Grant?" he repeated.

He prickled as he saw the reluctance with which the older man lifted his hand.

The girl immediately made for the open window behind the desk. It was a purely animal reaction. There was nowhere for her to go.

Recalling that she was still frail after the shipwreck, Diarmid went after her. Thomas shoved him out of the way and caught her arm in a grip hardly less brutal than Allan's. "You'll no' run this time, Fiona. Your place is at Bancavan with me."

"No..."

But her denial this time conveyed despair rather than defiance. She looked pale and ill and more like the drenched waif Diarmid had discovered on Canmara Beach than she had since she'd arrived.

When she raised her beautiful eyes to his face, they were dull with misery. "Please don't let them take me, Mr. Mactavish."

"Mrs. Grant, if these people are your family..." He struggled against the ludicrous instinct that he gave her up too easily.

What could he do? He had no claim over her, and it seemed these men did.

Thomas gave her a savage shake. "That's enough of that, lassie."

Before Diarmid could protest, a knotted handkerchief slipped from her pocket and landed with an unmistakable clink on the Turkey carpet at her feet.

A bristling silence crashed down. Mortified on the girl's part, curious on the Grants', while Diarmid's stomach cramped with a caustic disappointment he shouldn't feel. After all, he'd always known her as a liar, and today's revelations proved her to be a faithless wife. But somehow this seemed the worst treachery of all.

As if he touched something poisonous, he bent to pick up the heavy little bundle.

"Don't..." she said in a constricted voice that once might have touched his heart.

"You stole from me?" Through the thin lawn handkerchief, he felt the hard metal roundness of coins and the crackle of pound notes.

"I had to." Shame flooded those lustrous eyes and a remorse he almost believed was genuine. "I wish to heaven I could make you understand."

"After all the kindness you've received in this house, this is the best return ye can make?"

She flinched under the biting question, and her eyes fluttered down in a silent admission of wrongdoing. "I hope you'll forgive me," she mumbled. "You've all been so good to me."

He bit back a host of melodramatic responses. He could call her a snake and a liar and a doxy. But what was the point of berating her? She was leaving today with these austere, unpleasant men, and he'd never see her again.

Right now, that seemed a blessing.

"I'm just glad to see ye restored to your kin," he said, and knew himself for a hypocrite, because the chaos of wild emotions swirling in his belly included nothing so benign as gratitude.

"There's nae more to be achieved here, Mactavish," Allan Grant snapped out, and Diarmid heard the subtle contempt he injected into the last word. It was clear that the Grants remained set on pursuing the feud between their families. "It's a good few days traveling back to Bancavan, and there's work to be done in the fields. The estate cannae afford to be without us at this time of year."

Poor bloody Fiona. Despite everything, Diarmid couldn't quash a pang of sympathy for his duplicitous guest. Her kin would blame her for the trouble she'd caused, he could see, including making her husband and brother-in-law chase halfway down the coast.

"Ye must see she's been ill. Surely you're able to stay a night or two until she's well enough to travel," he said, before he reminded himself that the besom had broken every rule of hospitality. Not to mention that the virulent dislike he rapidly developed for her clansmen made the idea of extended contact unappealing.

"Thank ye, Mactavish, but we'll be on our way," Allan said. "She'll manage the trip, and she's better with her own flesh and blood than among strangers."

The discovery of the stolen money had whipped the fight out of the girl. Or perhaps two attempts at escape had sapped what small strength she had.

She looked ready to crumple to the floor. How the devil was she going to cross the mountains and glens between Invertavey and her home?

Diarmid reminded himself that, too, was none of his business. She'd get there one way or another. She might be a liar and a thief, but her courage had been real. "Verra well. I'll have my housekeeper pack her a bag."

"Did ye manage to salvage her belongings from the wreck?" Allan asked sharply. "The villagers gave me to understand nothing survived the sinking."

"Nothing did, except the lady," Diarmid replied in a dry tone. "But we've lent her clothing and…"

"Dinna fash yourself, Mactavish. A Grant doesnae need your charity," Thomas said. "The lassie will get along fine as she is until she's home."

Diarmid wanted to protest at sending the girl off without so much as a hairbrush or a change of linen, but she wasn't his responsibility. His bow was chilly. "As ye wish."

Thomas's rough jerk had Fiona stumbling after him as he headed for the door.

"Thank ye for housing our kinswoman and restoring her to her family, Mactavish," Allan said. "The lassie caused ye a gey lot of trouble, and we commend your generosity."

That must have nearly choked him, Diarmid thought. "It was the least we could do."

"We'll be saying our goodbyes, then."

Both men were at the door, the girl between them, hedged in like a horse in harness. It was clear they'd allow her no more chances to run.

Diarmid had taken a step to drag her away from them, before he recalled that she wasn't his to defend. Even if he wanted to help her, given what he now knew about her.

He wanted, devil take her. That was beauty's power over a frail male will.

Hadn't he seen that destructive influence working on his father, when he accepted his wife back time and time again, no matter what she'd done? Until the last time when she and her lover came to grief. Then absence proved even more excruciating than awkward forgiveness.

So Diarmid made himself remain where he was. Neither Grant had offered him a hand in farewell.

Even with everything that had happened, he couldn't let her go like this. He swallowed the acrid denial in his mouth and spoke as if nothing of significance had occurred. "Goodbye, Mrs. Grant. I wish ye well."

She somehow found the strength to resist the arms pushing her out the door and turned back long enough for him to catch fear and desolation in her lovely eyes. "You're too good, Mr. Mactavish. I wish things had been different."

"Come, Fiona, enough of that," Allan chided her. "It's time to go."

Her shoulders slumped in visible defeat, and she trudged out of the room without looking behind her. When the door closed on a thud, Diarmid realized with a sense of unreality that his dealings with his mystery woman were at an end.

He shifted to the window and watched as Thomas lifted her onto a large roan, then climbed into the saddle behind her. Husband or not, it was clear that his touch was unwelcome. She strained away, as he slid an arm around her waist and turned his horse for the gate. Allan followed on a powerful bay.

Diarmid stood at the window until the riders were out of sight. And well after that.

While all the time, a voice in his head screamed that, whatever the law might say, he'd just made the greatest mistake of his life.

CHAPTER EIGHT

"Icalled in to see my patient, but Mags tells me the lassie has gone."

At the sound of John's voice, Diarmid turned his head from where he stood, staring sightlessly over the empty drive. The clock on the mantel chimed the quarter hour, and he realized with a shock he'd been brooding out the window for nearly two hours.

"Good evening, John." He struggled to sound as if nothing important had happened. "Aye. It turned out she was on the run from her husband and bairn."

John's response was thoughtful, rather than surprised. "So you know her name now."

"Fiona." He made himself go on, although giving his mermaid her marital name tasted like vinegar on his tongue. "Fiona Grant. Her husband and his brother took her away."

Now John looked troubled. "And you let them?"

"What the hell else could I do?" Diarmid made an angry gesture, although he couldn't have said whether his resentment was directed toward the Grants, his deceitful former guest, or his friend. He had a sick feeling that most of all, he was angry with himself.

How had he been so easy to dupe, when he had such good reason to mistrust beautiful women? How could he still be regretting that she'd gone?

"There was nae question she was the lass they were looking for. They gave me a description when they turned up. Anyway, the moment she saw them, it was clear that she knew who they were."

John came further into the room. "So she went willingly?"

His gut knotted with guilt that he shouldn't feel, as he recalled Mrs. Grant's violent resistance to departing with her kin. "I wouldnae say that."

John didn't remark on the girl's eagerness to escape, but Diarmid could see his friend adding that fact to the picture he built in his cool, scientific mind. "So she regained her memory?"

His lips twisting in bitter humor, Diarmid dropped into a chair. "I'd wager half of Invertavey that she never lost it."

"She put up such an elaborate masquerade. There must have been a good reason."

Diarmid paused to note that John didn't argue about the false amnesia. "Aye, doubtless a lover somewhere. There usually is."

John's expression didn't ease, as he stepped toward the sideboard. "If you want a medical opinion, you look like you need a wee dram."

"No' so wee," Diarmid admitted with a heavy sigh.

The silence that fell wasn't entirely easy. John poured the whiskies and settled in the chair opposite.

Not even the liquor's warmth melted the cold, sick feeling in Diarmid's belly. For God's sake, what was his problem? He'd done exactly what the law demanded. The girl deserved neither his good opinion nor his help.

"The lassie wasn't wearing a wedding ring," John said.

"Wedding rings can be removed, or she might have lost it in the wreck." Diarmid scowled at his friend. "I have nae doubt she's who the Grants say she is."

"Oh, I'm sure she is. But we still don't know why she ran away."

"Dinna look at me like that. We ken she's a liar. Worse, she stole from me. I caught her with a bundle of money just before she went, and she certainly didnae have that on her when she arrived."

He still flinched to recall that appalling moment when the handkerchief full of money had tumbled from her pocket. The strangely pathetic bundle still sat disregarded on the corner of the desk. He hadn't had the stomach to open it up and see just how much she'd taken.

"She must have been desperate," John said in what Diarmid recognized as a carefully neutral voice.

"Desperate to escape her responsibilities."

To his relief, John didn't remark on the similarity with his mother. John didn't have to. It was brutally obvious.

This silence was as uncomfortable as the last one.

Eventually Diarmid broke it. "She was their kinswoman, the younger Grant's wife. I had nae right to keep her here."

"Except the right of care." John's gray gaze was stark. "She was in trouble. Whatever else you think of her, you must see that much was true."

"Trouble of her own making," Diarmid growled, even as renewed guilt added a sour flavor to the words.

Although he doubted she'd spoken one true word since she'd arrived at Invertavey, he couldn't forget the expression in her eyes when she'd thanked him for taking her in. The dread and despair—aye, and grim courage, much as right now he didn't want to credit her with any finer qualities—in those azure depths still haunted him.

"Did she offer any explanations for her behavior?"

"No, although when she tried to run, that told me her feelings about going back to her family."

"And what breed of men were the Grants? Mags wasn't too impressed."

"You've lived in this glen long enough to ken nobody called Grant will ever be welcome among my clansmen."

"Aye."

John and his blasted silences. Eventually Diarmid answered, although by God, he didn't want to. "They didnae strike me as...kind."

"Diarmid..."

He stood and prowled across to slam his crystal glass down on the sideboard with a loud crack. "Hell, she's gone. Let that be an end to it."

"It's not, though, is it?" John said slowly from behind him. "You're not happy you let her go."

"She belongs to them."

"I don't believe in ownership of people, whether man or woman." He paused. "And neither do you."

"What the devil can I do, plague take ye?" His hands fisted on the polished mahogany. "It's over."

John shifted to stand beside him. "At this time of year, there's plenty of light. And there's only one road out of Invertavey and one inn where a traveler can pass the night if he's headed north."

"Are ye suggesting I go in with all guns blazing and rip the woman away from her lawful husband? And what in heaven's name do I do with the lassie then?" He squashed completely unacceptable fancies of luring her to his bed and burying himself and his turbulent reactions in her pale body.

John shrugged, unimpressed by Diarmid's heated tone. "What you do with her depends on what you find when you catch up with the Grants."

"I might find her relieved to be on her way home."

He didn't believe that for a moment. The flare of primitive panic in her face when she saw her kin had been unmistakable.

Diarmid hated a faithless woman more than he hated anything else on earth. He should be saying good riddance to the lying baggage. But that fear had been too stark to forget. Its memory had tortured him since she'd left.

"She was a gallant creature." It was as though John peered into Diarmid's mind.

"She was a liar and a thief."

"But brave for all that. She was in a dreadful state when you brought her in, yet I heard not one word of complaint from her."

That was true, damn it. Diarmid couldn't help recalling how stoically she'd borne her pain that first night, when he'd been alone with her.

"Aye, she was brave." Despite everything, his voice softened.

"If she was as scared of the Grants as you say, that indicates she had cause."

"She's the man's bloody wife," Diarmid bit out, knowing he fought a losing battle, but not quite ready to admit it.

"That doesn't give her husband the right to mistreat her."

Diarmid at last turned to face his tormentor—and close friend. "It does under the law, ye know."

John's lips tightened. "Then the law is an ass."

And so, Diarmid feared, was he. It was all very well for John to urge him to pursue Mrs. Grant, but he was dangerous to her, too. His honor offered frail defense against lust.

He wondered what his friend would say, if Diarmid confessed his wicked yearning. John wouldn't be so quick to advise him to ride after her like a knight on a quest, then, by Jove.

But as he met that calm, understanding gaze, he had a nasty suspicion that his yen for the bonny deceiver was no secret. Shame spiced the uncomfortable mixture of emotions roiling in his gut.

"Ye forget there's a bairn."

"I knew she'd given birth."

"Ye never told me."

"She was my patient. She has the right to her privacy. There was also a mark on her finger that hinted she once wore a wedding ring."

Diarmid scowled. "And ye never told me that either?"

"There were bruises, too."

"Of course there were blasted bruises. She'd just been through a shipwreck."

John shook his head. "These were older, from what I could tell."

Queasiness set up home in his stomach. The thought of anyone lifting a hand to that graceful girl made him want to vomit. "Oh, hell."

"So you're going after them?"

Impatience tightened Diarmid's lips. He was taking on a world of trouble, and God knew where it would all end up. In a mess the size of bloody Scotland, he could already predict with grim certainty.

He sighed and ran his hand through his hair. Bleak resolution weighted his voice as he responded. "Aye, I'm going after them."

CHAPTER NINE

*D*iarmid crept along the shadowy upstairs corridor at the Thistle Inn. The hostelry was three hours north of Invertavey, and he'd spent the whole ride wondering if he was about to make a huge fool of himself.

He still wasn't convinced he should be here, but once John told him—too blasted late—about Mrs. Grant being beaten, all choice was gone. The idea of someone striking that girl made him blind with rage. And he was accounted the most even-tempered of men. If he'd known about the violence before the Grants turned up on his doorstep, they'd have received a very different reception.

So far, his luck had held. The evening had stayed bonny, and Sigurn had made braw speed along the narrow road. Rose Hulme, the landlord's wife, had been born a Mactavish, so she'd asked no awkward questions when he expressed an interest in a party of two older gentlemen and a younger lady stopping overnight on their way north.

His luck had held there, too. The Grants were famously parsimonious with their blunt, but on this occasion they'd decided to pay for a room. Even if only one for all three of them.

Diarmid had arrived at the Thistle about an hour after his quarry did. Why should they rush? They had no reason to fear pursuit, or to imagine that the man who had so easily handed the lassie over now intended to take her back.

Back to where, God alone knew.

He'd waited in the kitchens, praying that the Grants would be hungry enough to pay for a meal and that they'd leave Mrs. Grant upstairs alone. He relied on them wanting to deprive her of any opportunity to appeal for help in the taproom. It was a frail enough hope, and not the end of the world if it didn't come to pass. If he didn't catch the girl alone here, he'd track her further north. Somewhere on the road, he'd see his chance to steal her away. When Rose told him the two Grant brothers had come downstairs to eat, Diarmid had asked her to delay them as long as possible.

The Grants' room was at the end of the building, only a few steps from the servants' stairs. When he tried the door, it was locked. Fortunately Rose had given him a key.

He hoped to hell Mrs. Grant didn't scream when he barged in on her.

He hoped to hell she was alone.

He hoped to hell she hadn't changed her mind about wanting to break away from her family.

When he opened the door, the room was shadowy with late summer light. So far north at this time of year, it never got completely dark.

At first, Diarmid wondered if the room was empty. Then he heard a muffled whimper from the corner.

When he located the girl tethered to the bed like an animal, the anger that had sustained him this far spiked. The Grants were lucky they were downstairs, because at that instant, he was ready to do murder.

Hands shaking with rage, he strode forward and ripped the gag away from her mouth. "Mrs. Grant, are ye all right?"

Blue eyes huge with astonishment stared up at him. "Mr. Mactavish, what on earth are you doing here?"

Her voice was dry and scratchy, he imagined from having her mouth covered with what he now saw was a rough linen neck cloth.

"I'm taking ye away." He started to tug at the knots on the ropes lashing her to the bed.

"But you gave me up to them."

"Bugger." He gave up on knots that would do justice to a sailor and slid his dagger from his belt. "I shouldnae have."

"But you must hate me. I lied to you. I *stole* from you."

"Aye, ye did," he said grimly. "That's something we're going to talk about. But no' here and no' now." With a couple of ruthless movements, he cut the bonds attaching her hands to the posts on the headboard.

"They'll kill me if I run away again." Her flat tone robbed the statement of all melodrama.

Diarmid set his jaw against a resurgence of choking rage and slid the hem of her plain gray gown up just far enough to allow him to cut the ropes around her feet.

"Ye dinnae want to come with me?"

When she tried to sit up, he realized she must have been tied up for a couple of hours. The awkward position had left her stiff and clumsy. Despite Diarmid's urgency, his touch was gentle as he helped her onto the edge of the bed.

"Don't be a fool." Her familiar wry smile contrasted with the dried tearstains on her wan cheeks. "Of course I do."

Despite all the evil he knew of her, he couldn't help smiling back. John was right. She was brave. Her courage touched his heart in a way he knew was dangerous.

Any delay was risky, but he filled a glass with some water and passed it to her.

"Thank you," she murmured in a croaky voice.

As she drank, he inspected her for signs of injury. "Have they harmed ye?"

"Not yet." Her lips turned down with more of that grim humor, as she returned the empty glass. "They're storing up my punishment until we're back at Bancavan and there's no chance of interference."

Fury prevented him from speaking. He set the glass on the chest of drawers with a crack.

How could anyone hit this beautiful woman? The idea made him nauseous.

With difficulty, he swallowed the lump of outrage blocking his throat and held out his hand. "Can ye walk?"

"Believe me, if it means getting away from the Grants, I can fly."

More courage. It made her so blasted irresistible. Her courage, and her spellbinding beauty. He'd wondered if knowing of her faithlessness might weaken her power over his senses. It turned out there was no chance of that.

She accepted his hand and lurched to her feet with reckless speed. He barely had time to register the tingling warmth of her touch, before she stumbled.

Without thinking, Diarmid caught her up against him. In a flash, he was back in the Chinese

Room at Invertavey with a sweetly scented woman clasped in his arms.

A storm of impressions flooded his mind. She still smelled like the soap she used at Invertavey—and horses and a trace of sweat. Those Grant bastards hadn't even given her a chance to wash before they tied her up. Even more than that, she smelled like Miss Nita.

That alluring scent had woven itself through his dreams ever since he'd met her. Dreams where honor held no sway, and she arched up in welcome as he thrust hard inside her. Dreams where that pale blond hair floated around him like a veil of silk and he knew nothing except how much he wanted her.

She gasped and stiffened in his hold, although God forgive him, he took a few seconds to register her resistance. Azure eyes shadowed with exhaustion darted up to his face.

He saw more than weariness. He saw alarm.

What a savage he was. Self-disgust loosened his grip on her.

"Nae need to be frightened, Mrs. Grant." He shifted away and spoke in the soothing tone he'd use to a nervous horse. "I'm only here to help ye."

He hoped to Hades it wasn't a lie.

For days, he'd battled his craving for this woman. After today, she was even more out of bounds. Now he knew she was another man's wife, and she'd given him even fewer reasons to trust her than he'd had before the Grants took her away.

But every time he was with her, he learned the bitter lesson that principles and propriety offered no defense against desire.

"I still don't know why you should," she said, and he cursed the husky edge to her voice. It put him in mind of her murmuring seductive promises in bed.

"Save your questions for when we're safe." With her so unsteady on her feet, he kept hold of her slender waist. "I've got the landlord's wife doing her best to keep your kin downstairs, but I fear they're no' men to linger over their dinner and leave their captive unsupervised."

Her lips tightened. "No."

"Are ye able to stand without help?"

He hoped to blazes she was. Touching her like this tested every ounce of his willpower.

"Aye."

He let her go.

She staggered.

He caught her arm. "Damn it."

"I'm sorry."

"Nae need. You're still no' recovered from the wreck."

"I can make it. I can make it to wherever you take me. Please..." The delicate throat moved as she swallowed. Desperation glittered in her eyes. "Please don't leave me here."

Despite everything, a smile tugged at his lips. "Whisht, ye daft lassie. I've gone to all this trouble to find you. I'm nae going to abandon ye because you're a wee bit rocky on your feet."

"You're a fine man, Diarmid Mactavish." Her expression remained grave. "Better than I deserve."

Shame twisted in his gut. If she guessed how she made him hunger, and her another man's wife, she wouldn't say that, by God.

"Save your breath to cool your porridge." He glanced around the room. "Do ye need anything?"

"Only my freedom," she said. "Let's go."

He took her hand before he carefully opened the door. To his relief, the corridor remained empty. Rose had told him the inn was full, but at this hour, most of the guests would be downstairs at dinner.

He drew Mrs. Grant—how he loathed calling her by that name—outside. Her grip on his hand tightened, silent confirmation of her trepidation. After shutting the door, he turned back to her. She looked pale but determined.

"We just need to make it down the stairs and into the stables."

"I'm ready."

They'd reached the end of the hall when he heard someone coming up the main staircase.

"If we dinna stop on the way, we'll be home tomorrow night," Allan was saying.

"Do ye think the besom will last another hard day's travel?" Thomas asked.

"She'll have to. If she's uncomfortable, it's her own damned fault. Once we get her home, I'll show her what uncomfortable is, the insolent witch."

Diarmid heard Mrs. Grant muffle a gasp as he hauled her into a dash for the backstairs. She managed a few steps before she stumbled.

"Oh, hell," he muttered.

Knowing that he invited trouble but unable to do anything else, he swung her up in his arms and whipped around into the narrow stairwell. Adjusting his grip on her, he rushed down the steps, praying that the Grants wouldn't hear the thud of his boots on the wooden treads. Or if they did, they'd just assume it was a servant on his way back to the kitchens.

The girl curled up against him, as if making herself smaller would aid their escape. Her erratic breath was warm on the side of his neck.

"Hold on," he whispered, as he started down the last flight of stairs. When they rushed through the hot, crowded kitchen, he caught a host of curious glances, then he was crossing the yard at a run.

Rose was already leading a saddled Sigurn out of the stables. "I'm gey sorry, Mactavish. I tried my best to keep them downstairs. But they're awfu' sparse conversationalists."

"Thanks, Rose." He tossed Mrs. Grant into the saddle and mounted behind her. As his arms closed around the girl's trembling body, he cursed the fact that more physical closeness was inevitable. "Ye did your best."

"I've told my people that if any of them says a word about what's happened, they're out of a job. I willnae have your name or the lady's disparaged in my hearing. And I've packed some food in your saddlebags."

"You're an angel."

She smiled at him. "Aye, that's me."

Angry shouting rose from inside the inn. Diarmid had a suspicion that the staff were doing their best to impede the Grants' pursuit. Rose wasn't the only Mactavish working at the Thistle.

He caught up the reins. "God bless ye, Rose."

"And God go with ye, Mactavish."

He clattered out of the yard while behind him, the Grants rushed into the open, yelling blue murder. When he heard the sharp crack of a gunshot behind him, his principal reaction was rage rather than fear.

What the devil did those madmen think they were doing? To Hades with them.

The stakes, already high, rocketed up into the sky, now that this rescue turned into a killing matter. With a muttered curse, Diarmid dug his heels into Sigurn's sides and urged her away from the inn.

CHAPTER TEN

After the terrifying gunshot, Fiona heard Allan shout after them to stop. She suppressed a whimper and shrank against Diarmid Mactavish. She didn't like men touching her, but at this moment, that strong chest behind her seemed the closest thing to safety she'd known since her father died.

Mr. Mactavish's grip tightened, and he urged the horse to greater speed, as they raced along the pale ribbon of road toward the hills. "They willnae catch us. Dinna be afraid."

Stupid that those words of reassurance in his deep, musical voice should soothe her rising panic. But they did. He'd balanced her across his saddle bow, and one powerful arm lashed around her. She wasn't afraid of falling. He wouldn't let her go. "We're still too close to the inn."

"They've got to saddle their horses before they come after us, and Rose will make sure that's no' easy. Even then, they dinna ken these hills like I do."

"But the road..." They were riding between two hills with a river running along beside them. When she looked back, she could no longer see the inn.

"We're no' staying on the road. Trust me."

Despite everything she knew about the male sex, she'd almost started to trust Diarmid Mactavish. Until he handed her over to her tormenters, and she had to accept that despite Colin's death and all her frantic efforts, she'd failed Christina.

Fiona had spent the ride from Invertavey to the Thistle lost in a thick fog of despair. Even Allan's spite hadn't had the power to hurt her.

Now she took her first full breath since Mr. Mactavish had appeared in her room at the inn. The Grants' arrival at Invertavey had crushed all hope. It revived now, frail and uncertain. But definitely there.

"Hold on." He angled the horse down the steep riverbank, and the sudden lurching had her clutching at his waist.

"They'll find a way to follow us," she said, partly to hear him deny the fact.

As they splashed across a ford, he cooperated, bless him. Every time he spoke, she felt stronger, as if she might have a chance of winning after all. "We're well ahead of them."

She wanted to argue that it wasn't enough, but what was the point? For the moment, she was free. When Allan Grant tethered her to that hard little bed at the Thistle, she'd feared she'd never be free again.

The horse labored up the opposite bank. The hem of Fiona's dress was heavy with water. The eerie half-light of a summer night in the northern Highlands revealed more hills and a narrow track winding ahead. Mr. Mactavish ignored the track and guided the horse along the lush, green bank. Brambles caught at her wet skirts as they progressed.

She lifted her head until she could see his expression. He looked stern and distant, even as his arm clasped her close. "Why did you come for me?"

"Whisht, lassie. No' now. We'll talk when we stop for the night. Right now, I need to concentrate on getting us to safety."

Safety. What a glorious word.

Although when they stopped, he'd expect her to tell him everything, and she was so used to keeping secrets. But the jut of that impressive jaw hinted that she'd wheedle nothing more out of him until he was ready. So she rested her head on his chest and let weariness wash over her.

After following the bank for about half a mile, they turned off onto a trail so faint Fiona wouldn't have known it was there. A sheep track, she supposed. Since leaving the inn, they hadn't met any people or passed any houses. This was like fleeing into an endless wilderness.

As the ground firmed, Sigurn settled into a smooth canter. Fiona soon lost any idea of which direction they went. The trail twisted and turned, but as they wended through the treeless hills, Mr. Mactavish seemed to know his way with unerring exactitude. From the first, she'd noted and admired his air of easy competence. She started to believe him when he said they'd evade pursuit. At least for tonight.

They were pressed so close together that his rich scent invaded her nostrils. Strangely pleasant. She was used to the musty smell of old men. Sitting much as she did now, she'd ridden north on Thomas Grant's horse, trapped in the miasma of his dry, unpleasant stench. She'd come close to gagging, dreading the fact that soon he'd be even closer, if he got his way.

But Diarmid Mactavish didn't smell anything like Thomas Grant. He smelled of open air and health. She sucked in a great gulp of air, relishing that fresh scent. The shirt beneath her cheek was clean, with a hint of lavender and fresh sweat. The combination was surprisingly heady. As they rode into the night, she drifted into a pleasant doze, where the scent of Diarmid Mactavish's skin became the scent of paradise.

When the horse stopped, she stirred. "What is it?"

Groggy, Fiona struggled to sit up straight. She cuddled up to Mr. Mactavish, as though they were eloping lovers instead of reluctant allies. If they were even that.

His grip tightened. "Dinna be afraid."

She bit back a snort of disbelieving laughter. Of course she was afraid. She was always afraid. Fear was the air she'd breathed for ten lonely years. As if the Grants might rise out of the ground like the dead at the Last Judgment, she cast a wary glance around the small glen with its stand of spindly scotch pines and narrow burn.

All was calm and peaceful. The sky was lighter, as the early summer dawn approached. Birds chirped from the trees, and she saw a fox slink up the brae on his way home from a night's hunting.

Fiona felt a pang of compassion for his prey. She knew what it was like to be hunted.

"Are they coming for us?"

"I'm sure they'll try, but they'll never follow us this far into the hills."

"Then why have we stopped?" She realized her arms were still looped around Mr. Mactavish's waist. With a blush, she pulled free.

"Sigurn needs a spell. I thought ye might, too."

He dismounted and reached for Fiona. He'd been holding her close for hours, so she shouldn't tremble when he touched her. But she was shaking as he set her on the ground.

"Are ye cold?" He helped her across to the hillock. Sitting on the horse for so long left her stiff and clumsy.

"No." With a sigh of relief, she sat. Her legs felt like rubber.

The laird slid off his coat and dropped it around her shoulders. "Wait there, and I'll get us something to eat."

She wrapped the coat around her. More of that delicious smell. She'd never imagined she'd enjoy a man's scent, but Diarmid Mactavish's was a tonic. So was the fresh summer air. The light wasn't bright as day, but she could see well enough. "Where are we going?"

He crossed to where Sigurn nosed at the grass and untied a saddlebag. Sweat streaked the horse's glossy sides, proof of the long ride with a double burden.

With an easy kindness that made Fiona want to weep, he patted the horse's neck. "Good girl, Sigurn. You're a bonny wee lassie."

Until she'd met the Grants, kindness had seemed such a humble virtue. After ten years of brutality, she'd come to view kindness as the greatest gift one human could give another.

She'd found kindness at Invertavey House, and repaid it with lies and theft. Shame coiled in her empty belly. When she and Mr. Mactavish finally talked, it promised to be a humiliating experience.

"There's an abandoned crofter's cottage a few glens away." The laird left his horse and walked toward Fiona. "Hopefully we'll reach it before the rain starts."

Surprised she looked around, noting the cloudless sky and Venus winking at her over the horizon. "Rain?"

"Aye. Only a couple of hours away, I'd say. That's to our advantage. It will give the Grants even more trouble tracking us."

It also meant she'd be stuck inside a small cottage, alone with Mr. Mactavish. Would he demand the obvious reward for helping her? Nobody did anything for another person without recompense, and she knew he wanted her. Perhaps that was why he'd saved her, to turn her into his whore.

The thought wasn't as bitter as it might have been. She'd already decided that in return for his aid, she'd do whatever he wanted. Pride and morality might object, but she'd long moved past the point where either of those things mattered. If Mr. Mactavish wanted to use her body, she could endure it. After all, it would only be another loveless coupling, and she was used to that.

He dug in the bag and passed her a crusty roll full of pink ham and hard yellow cheese. "Are ye hungry?"

When her stomach gave an audible growl, he laughed. Despite everything, so did she. "I haven't eaten since I left Invertavey."

His smile died. "Those bastards didnae feed ye?"

Fiona took a bite of the roll. The delicious taste of the simple fare almost made her weep. She only just resisted the urge to devour the whole roll in a couple of bites.

"It was part of my punishment for running away," she said through a mouthful. "I'm used to going hungry."

He sat beside her, keeping a decorous distance. Wearing only his shirtsleeves, he looked magnificent. Broad-shouldered and strong.

As the slight breeze ruffled his thick dark hair, a muscle jerked in his cheek. "Dinna start telling me everything now. We'll talk when we get to the bothy. I have a feeling ye have a lot to say, and I want to make sure the weather willnae interrupt us."

To her surprise, she realized she'd wolfed down the whole roll, while he hadn't touched his. "I'm sorry I stole from you," she mumbled.

Mr. Mactavish turned to face her. "Ye must have had good reason."

His black eyes glittered, and that muscle still danced in his lean cheek. He was furiously angry, but not with her. Relief tinged the breath she drew. "I did."

He took a bite of his roll before he set it on the grass. "Later."

Another rummage in the bag, and he passed her a second roll and a flask. "It's ale. Or I can fetch ye some water from the burn, if you prefer."

"Ale is fine, thank you." She took a long drink before she returned the flask.

His strong throat worked as he swallowed. Watching him drink from the same vessel felt like an act of breathtaking intimacy.

Realizing that she was staring, she looked away. Heat prickled her cheeks, as a wicked thought rose in her mind. Perhaps if she gave herself to Diarmid Mactavish, it might end up being more than mere self-sacrifice. The act itself might disgust her, but the prospect of that vigorous body joining with hers made her shiver. And not with revulsion. The messy, uncomfortable invasion might be worth it, in return for those brawny arms holding her close.

A strangely peaceful silence fell, as she ate her second roll more delicately than the first. Sigurn's bit clinked as she grazed closer to the burn.

"Mrs. Grant?"

She looked up to realize he held the flask out to her. "Thank you."

His fingers brushed hers and despite everything, a tingle of warmth rippled up her arm. As she drank, forcing the liquid down a tight throat, he produced some dried apple from the bag.

She accepted a few pieces of fruit. As the intense sweetness hit her tongue, she closed her eyes. It took her back to childhood, to the days before she'd learned to fear the world.

"Would you like some more ale?" she asked through a foolish urge to cry. What she'd give to be that innocent girl again.

Then she realized that if she were that innocent girl, she wouldn't have Christina. Nothing was worth missing out on that.

"You're tired." Mr. Mactavish took the flask and stoppered it. "I'm sorry."

"No, I'm fine."

"You're no' fine. But can ye go a wee bit further?"

He was a considerate man. She'd been in his house long enough to recognize that his people served him because they loved him, not because he bullied them into obedience. He'd always been considerate of her, too, even when he'd handed her back to the Grants.

"Yes," she said.

"Then we should go. I dinna fancy being trapped out on the braes, when the storm comes through." He rose and extended a hand. "Mrs. Grant?"

She didn't immediately take his hand. "Please don't call me that."

He frowned. "That isnae your name?"

To her everlasting regret, it was. "It is. But it reminds me..."

She didn't know what Mr. Mactavish saw in her face, but compassion softened the dark eyes. "Would ye prefer Miss Nita?"

"No." Reaching for his hand, she stood.

She felt better after the meal. A couple of hours away from the Grants made her feel even better.

"We dinna have far to go."

She withdrew her hand. "If it means escaping Allan and Thomas, I can ride forever."

"Hell, I cannae believe I handed ye over to those bastards." Mr. Mactavish looked sick, and his hands fisted at his sides. "I should never have..."

For so many years, nobody but Christina had been angry on her behalf. How gratifying to know that at last she had someone on her side. She managed a smile.

"You came to get me. There's no need for remorse." Especially when she'd dealt him such poor gratitude in return. "You may call me Fiona, if you like."

She watched him struggle to overcome his disgust with himself for letting the Grants take her away. "It's a bonny name."

"Thank you." He crossed to catch Sigurn, and buckled on the saddlebag. With obvious affection, the horse butted her master. Aye, he was a kind man. Sigurn knew that, and so did Fiona.

He brought the horse back to where Fiona waited. "Ye should call me Diarmid. Mr. Mactavish is too much of a mouthful, when we're going to be alone together for the next wee while."

If anyone but Diarmid Mactavish had said that, she'd be terrified. But somewhere between the two rescues, she'd accepted him into the very exclusive category of people she trusted. As far as she trusted anyone. Of course, he was yet to hear her confession, but something told her that he'd listen with his usual intelligent tolerance.

She found herself smiling with genuine pleasure. "Then Diarmid it shall be."

"Excellent."

He came close and for a mad moment, she wondered if he meant to kiss her. Even madder, she wondered if she might kiss him back. But he merely caught her waist in his strong hands and tossed her into the saddle. Sigurn whickered and sidled under Fiona's weight, but stilled at a soft word from Mr. Mactavish.

Diarmid.

He mounted behind her and when he settled her against him, she had to fight more foolish tears. Already his embrace seemed safe and familiar. It was so long since she'd felt safe.

"Let's go." He clicked his tongue to Sigurn, and they set off at a smart canter.

CHAPTER ELEVEN

As the short summer night brightened toward dawn, they rode up to a turf-roofed cottage. Fiona felt close to exhaustion, and Sigurn wasn't in much better state. Even the indomitable Diarmid showed signs of tiredness.

When he lifted Fiona from the saddle and set her down on the grass, her legs folded under her. Only his swift action saved her from hitting the ground. She was sick to the devil of not being able to stand on her own two feet, but there was little she could do about it. It was only a few days since she'd nearly drowned in the shipwreck that had killed Colin.

With grim stoicism, she submitted as he carried her inside and set her on a rough cot against the wall. The interior of the cottage was dim, but she caught an impression of a few simple pieces of furniture and a cold hearth. At this point, she hardly cared, as long as there was a bed and the roof was intact.

She was too tired to talk much, but one thing she had to say. "Thank you."

"Och, it's nothing, lassie," he said gently, kneeling to remove her half-boots. "Sleep now."

"Aye," she whispered before she fell asleep, worn out with fear and the long ride, and the day's turbulent emotions.

Sometime during the day, Fiona stirred to hear heavy rain pounding on the thatch. The laird had been right about the weather. She hardly cared. She was warm and safe—when the weather turned dreich, there were worse places to be than a snug Highland bothy. A fire blazed merrily in the grate, and Diarmid had covered her with his coat. His spicy scent filled her senses once more, helping to calm her fears.

On the far side of the cottage, the laird slept on the packed dirt floor. He used his saddle as a pillow. The sight of him gave her the same reassurance as his scent. She settled back into immediate slumber.

Now Fiona emerged from the deep sleep of exhaustion. She opened blurry eyes on lamplight and a tall, dark-haired man watching her from where he sat among the shadows.

Mr. Mactavish. Diarmid.

She felt no disorientation. She knew exactly where she was.

"Better?" he asked softly.

Gingerly, stiff from the long ride, she slid away his heavy coat and shifted to perch on the side of the bed. She felt like she'd been beaten—and she knew that feeling well enough. Aggravating how weak she still was. She needed to regain her strength soon, or she'd be no use to Christina.

"Aye, thank you."

"I'm glad. I'm sorry I pushed ye so hard last night."

Her lips turned down in a smile that was close to a grimace. "I'm not, if it means we outrun the Grants."

"I wouldnae worry about them for the moment." He shrugged. "I'll be verra surprised if they track us so far."

So would she. She ran a hand over her untidy mess of hair. What an absolute fright she must look. Diarmid would wonder if he shared the house with a witch.

Her mind slammed to an appalled standstill. Good Lord, when had she started to worry whether a man approved of her appearance? At Bancavan, she'd tried as hard as she could to avoid masculine notice altogether. "What time is it?"

"About four."

"In the afternoon?" If it was, she'd slept most of the day away.

"Aye."

He rose from his spindly chair and crossed to offer his hand. "There's a bucket of water in the corner, if you'd like to wash."

"Thank you," she said, taking his hand. She stumbled as she stood but gestured him away when he made a move to pick her up again.

"No, don't carry me. I need to stand up for myself."

His lips twitched. "As long as ye are managing to stand."

She tottered toward a chair and watched as he tugged his coat over his shoulders. "Are you going out in the rain?"

"I willnae melt, lassie, and the lean-to is only across the way. I'll go and check on Sigurn to give ye some privacy. Take your time. When I get back, I'll fix us something to eat. The laird here keeps the bothy stocked, in case travelers are stranded. As you've seen, the weather in these braes can turn on a sixpence."

"Thank you." She started to feel like a parrot, saying the same thing over and over again.

Only after he'd disappeared out the door did she notice that the water he'd left her was steaming with heat and he'd set a folded handkerchief near the bucket. He'd also put out a small cake of soap and a comb.

More silly tears stung her eyes. Such simple concessions to bring her to the brink of losing control, but for years she'd survived without an ounce of kindness or consideration from people who owed her their care. Diarmid's thoughtfulness made her feel like sinking down to the ground and howling like a lost bairn.

By the time he returned, she felt much better. Taking a cat bath in hot water had felt almost luxurious. Tidying the birds' nest of her hair made her feel less like something that same cat had dragged in.

Without a mirror, she didn't try to do anything elaborate with the style. Once she'd combed out the knots, she braided it into one long plait and tied it with the pale blue ribbon threaded through the neck of her chemise.

How she wished she had some fresh clothes to put on. After yesterday's travel, her plain gray frock was stained and creased, and she'd love a change of linen.

Diarmid appeared in the doorway and flung off his coat. Fiona was used to seeing him dressed *comme il faut*. The man before her was no longer the elegant Laird of Invertavey. His thick dark hair was wet and windswept, and after the long ride and sleeping rough, his shirt was in worse state than her dress. Dark stubble shadowed that determined jaw and lent him a disreputable air. Even a frightened mouse of a woman like her found this rough-hewn version of her rescuer intriguing.

"Sigurn is all tucked up and enjoying her oats." That sharp black gaze ran over Fiona with more concern than covetousness. Still, an instinct of self-protection had her folding her arms in front of her breasts.

"I'm sure," she said, and heard a trace of nervousness in her voice. "I hope you gave her an extra pat for me."

"Aye, I did."

"Thank you...Diarmid," she said. Shaping his name with her lips felt like a forbidden thrill. "I feel considerably more human after my wash."

Another expression of gratitude, although at least this time she managed to stand firm on her feet while she made it. She was sick and tired of drooping around like a cut rose left too long in a dry vase.

His smile of approval shouldn't make her feel like he'd just given her a wonderful present. But the flash of straight white teeth against the darkness of his beard set her heart leaping about in a most disconcerting manner.

"Sit down while I make us a meal." He pulled one of the chairs out from the table. "There's some of Rose's food left, enough for a bit of supper, anyway."

"Let me help."

He made a dismissive gesture. "Och, you'll just get in the way, lassie. Take the chance to rest while ye can."

"What about you?"

"Dinna worry your head about me. I'm as tough as old boots, no' a delicate wee bluebell like ye."

A delicate bluebell? Nobody named Grant would call her that. More of those silly tears pricked at her eyes as she watched the laird bustling about. He treated her like a lady. He always had, but something about his courtesy now, when they were alone together in this hidden glen, sliced at her heart.

"What if it keeps raining?" she asked as he sat opposite her.

On the table, he'd set out two wooden plates with a couple of wizened apples from last year, some hard yellow cheese, and half a small loaf of bread. Wooden cups held more ale.

"There's a stock of basic food in the cottage. We willnae go hungry if we're trapped here. In any case, the rain will only last a few more hours."

This time, she didn't waste time questioning his prediction. Instead, she turned her attention to their makeshift meal. It was a long time since they'd stopped and eaten. She was starving. Only with difficulty did she stop herself falling on the food like a hungry dog on a bone. The bread from the Thistle was a day old, but she didn't care. The cheese was deliciously sharp, and the apples had a rich sweetness.

"Where are we heading?" She knew enough of Diarmid to guess that he wasn't wandering around the wilds with no idea where he wanted to go. More of that appealing competence.

"My friend Fergus Mackinnon is Laird of Achnasheen. He'll offer us a safe place to stay, while we decide what happens next. I cannae take ye back to Invertavey. That's the first place the Grants will look."

"Is it far?"

"We'll stay here tonight, until the weather clears. If we leave early tomorrow, we should make Achnasheen by nightfall."

She was surprised to look down and find her plate empty. When she glanced up again, she caught

Diarmid watching her with a steady gaze. His expression was grave, almost austere.

"Now, Fiona, it's time ye told me exactly what's going on," he said in a voice that invited no argument. "And nae more lies."

She'd felt better after some food. Now her dinner coagulated into a cold, bitter lump in her stomach. Her hand shaking, she set her cup on the table. After all he'd done for her, she owed this man the truth. But telling him everything exposed her as a liar and a thief.

And an ingrate. Even before he risked his life to save her, she'd given him poor return for his hospitality.

"Diarmid…" she said, still not used to saying his name, even less used to hearing him call her Fiona. It shouldn't sound like an endearment, especially when his tone was so stern. But it did. God help her, it did.

He slammed one palm flat on the table. The sudden display of anger startled her and made her regard him with wary eyes.

"Enough," he snapped. "Nae more evasions. Nae more prevarications. By God, you've put me on the wrong side of the law, Fiona. The least ye owe me in return is to tell me why."

CHAPTER TWELVE

*D*iarmid battled his unaccustomed surge of temper. He didn't want to frighten Fiona, when he could tell she'd been frightened too often already, but he'd been seething since he'd discovered her tethered to that bed in the Thistle.

"The law?" Her eyes widened, and a puzzled crease appeared between her fine eyebrows. "What do you mean?"

"For pity's sake, stop lying to me," he said in frustration, running one hand through his still-damp hair. The crossing from the lean-to to the bothy had been dreich in the extreme. "Ye cannae trust me even now?"

After nearly a week of her deceit, he should be proof against the palpable innocence in her expression. But despite knowing that every second word out of that rose-pink mouth had been false, he still wanted to believe her.

As he'd grown up, a reluctant hint of contempt had tinged his sympathy for his father. When it came to forgiving his faithless wife, the man's gullibility had begun to seem like willful stupidity. After a few days with Fiona Grant, Diarmid understood his father much better.

"I'm not lying." She must have read the way his expression closed against her, and she went on more urgently. "Not now. I know I've lied to you in the past, and I'm sorry. I had no choice in what I did. I hope you'll see that when I explain. But I truly don't understand what you mean when you talk about breaking the law. I...stole from you, but that's me, not you. And while it's no excuse for taking your money, I can't tell you how much I loathed doing it."

That he believed. When the purloined coins had hit the floor, she'd looked sick with shame.

"That's no' what I mean," he said, although he'd been appalled to discover that she was a thief as well as a liar, and probably an adulteress as well. Why else did a woman leave her marriage, if not to run to a lover? His mother had never had any other reason. "The Grants could bring a case against me for kidnapping."

"Kidnapping?" she echoed, as if the word made no sense.

He got up. He was rarely angry. In the week since meeting Fiona Grant, he'd been angry more often than he'd been in all the previous ten years. Now he was too furious to sit still. He stalked across to the fire and stoked it until its heat rivaled the blaze inside him. Although he kept his back turned, Diarmid felt her watching as the poker stabbed at the burning peat.

Impatience sharpened his voice. "You're a man's wife, and I've stolen ye away."

When he turned to face her, shock had made those already wide eyes impossibly wider. "Mr. Mactavish—Diarmid—I'm nobody's wife."

A flush marked her slanted cheekbones, but her eyes didn't waver. She was so beautiful. Why did she have to be so bloody beautiful? If anyone should be proof against a pretty face that concealed a false heart, it should be him. But each time he looked at Fiona, every muscle clenched with helpless longing.

"Your finger shows the mark where ye wore a wedding ring." Stinging bitterness edged his answer. He still didn't like a liar, even if it seemed he'd thrown in his lot with one. "John says you've borne a child. Ye answer to Mrs. Grant. Allan Grant says you're Thomas's wife."

The cynicism hardening her expression sat oddly with her elegant prettiness. "And you believed him without question?"

"I had nae reason no' to."

"No, I suppose you didn't," she said grimly.

Diarmid made an irritated sound in his throat. How the devil did she manage to make him feel like he was in the wrong?

"I always knew ye were lying. Right from the first. When the Grants turned up looking for their lost kinswoman, at least I knew why. You're a wife on the run from a husband she doesnae overmuch like."

She stood to face him. "No, that's one thing I'm not. I was married for nine years to Allan and Thomas's brother. Ian Grant died a year ago, and I'm his widow."

A widow...

Although she'd spoken softly, the words resounded in his ears like the toll of a huge bell. Diarmid stared at her in shock and sagged as his self-righteousness flowed away, taking all his breath with it.

It was the obvious answer. Why didn't he think of it before? More proof that this girl turned his usually reliable brain to porridge. "I...see."

That clear blue gaze sliced at his heart like a razor. "If you believed I was an adulteress on top of all my other sins, why on earth did you come to get me?"

"Devil if I ken," he snapped, suffering a shame of his own. He wanted her, he always had. While he had no intention of doing anything about it, he was still uncomfortably aware that he wasn't as white as snow when it came to mixed motives. "I didnae trust the Grants."

A crooked smile twisted that lush mouth. "That speaks well of your instincts."

"And Allan and Thomas werenae kind."

Her slender throat moved as she swallowed. "No, they're not."

"And on top of all that, I'm a blasted fool."

She shook her head. "No, a good man, but one who perhaps suffers from an excess of chivalry." She paused. "I'd think after what your mother did, you'd have no sympathy for a woman who abandoned her family."

Shock clouted him on the head, hard as a lump of wood. "You ken about that?" Before she could answer, he went on, his voice heavy with weariness. "Why would ye no'? My mother's adventures were the most exciting things to happen at Invertavey until...well, until you arrived, frankly. I assume Mags told ye."

"Not Mags. She was the soul of discretion. But the younger lassies were a wee bit more forthcoming when I asked about you."

"I suppose ye wanted to know what manner of man had taken you in," he said with a hint of grimness. Diarmid wasn't used to people questioning his character.

"I knew what manner of man you were," she said in a level voice. "Or at least I soon did."

"Then why did ye no' trust me enough to tell me the truth?"

Her lips turned down. "I'd learned the hard way that I was better off relying only on myself."

He hid a wince at "the hard way." He'd seen and heard enough since he'd met the Grants to guess what that meant. Hell, what he'd give for a chance to smash Allan Grant's smug smile back behind his yellow teeth. "If you'd told me ye were in trouble, I'd have offered to help, instead of handed ye over to those bastards."

"By the time I'd worked that out, I was too deeply mired in deception to fight my way out." Her gaze settled on his face. "I owe you my gratitude and an apology."

He made a dismissive gesture. "I dinna want either. What I want is the full story."

Diarmid crossed to pull her chair out for her. What he really wanted to do was take her hand and offer some physical comfort. He knew better than to risk the contact. Not with only the two of them in this cottage and a bed waiting against the wall behind him.

The last thing she needed was his desire. Now he looked more closely, he saw the marks of a hunted animal in her demeanor. Vulnerability flashed in those winter blue eyes and as she faced him down, she looked both alone and lonely.

"Thank you," she whispered, sitting with the instinctive grace that always made his heart lurch. "After all my lies, I can't blame you for being suspicious of me."

"Och, the time for keeping secrets is well and truly past. Tell me everything, Fiona." Wanting to reassure her, he dredged up a smile as he took his seat. "I cannae help ye, until I ken just what we're up against."

We ...

Fiona stared at this remarkable man who proclaimed himself so unconditionally her defender. Since her father's death ten years ago, nobody had championed her. Hearing someone declare they were on her side was overwhelming. After being alone and powerless for so long, the change was too much to take in.

As she surveyed that dark, intense face, something told her that she was safe to trust Diarmid Mactavish. Her gaze dwelled on the strong bones of his face. The wide forehead. The marked black brows, currently drawn together in a frown of concern—for her. The high Celtic cheekbones. The lordly nose. The determined jaw.

He'd taken her in and asked nothing in return for his kindness. Even after she'd repaid his hospitality with lies and theft, he'd defied the Grants to save her. And believed he was risking arrest by doing so.

Over and over, he'd proven himself worthy. She owed him the truth, even if the habit of hiding away from questions had become so ingrained, it was part of her.

"My father was a Grant," she said, steadying her voice and laying her hands flat on the rough pine tabletop.

Fiona waited for Diarmid to question the odd beginning to the tale. But he leaned back in his chair with every sign that he was happy for her to proceed as she wished. That was something else she liked about the Laird of Invertavey. His patience.

Her constant fear fluttered down to rest, as she sucked in a deep breath. She'd spent the last weeks feeling like an iron vise tightened around her ribs. Now she felt free as she hadn't felt free since she'd lived in Edinburgh as a child.

"He was Allan Grant's cousin and given all sorts of privileges because he was his mother's favorite and the child of his father's old age." She glanced down at the table again. Something about Diarmid's unwavering attention made her feel strange, unlike herself. It set up a strange wobble inside her, like butterflies beating their wings against the walls of her stomach. "Because of this, he was the only Grant ever allowed to leave Bancavan to get an education. Not just that, he was clever. He ended up teaching at Edinburgh University, which was where he met my mother and married her. She was the daughter of one of the masters."

As ever when she spoke of her parents, grief gnawed at her. Both had been good people. Both had passed away far too early.

"What did he teach?" Diarmid asked gently.

Her eyes swept up to his face, and she saw he'd heard both the love and sorrow in her voice. Yet again, she noted what a perceptive man he was.

At Diarmid's house, that perception had scared the life out of her. It still did, but not because she feared he might see through her lies. Now she feared that he might see the dangerous confusion she felt when she looked at him. She'd never found a man attractive. Ten years of abuse had killed any yen she might feel for a handsome face. Or at least so she'd believed, until she met the Laird of Invertavey.

"Mathematics." Despite everything, a fond smile curved her lips. "If that implies a certain unworldliness, you're right. You'd have liked him. Most people did." All urge to smile faded away.

"When I was nine, my mother died giving birth to a baby boy."

"You have a brother?"

"No. He never took a breath."

"I'm sorry. About the bairn, and about your mother."

"So am I." She braced to continue. Already this was hard, and she hadn't reached the worst part. "Papa struggled on for another six years, but he was never the same after Mamma died."

"So ye were left alone at fifteen? That's a vulnerable age for a lassie."

Wasn't it just? Grim humor flattened her lips. "I'd have done better alone, I think. Here's where Papa's unworldliness becomes crucial. He didn't make a will. If something happened to him, I'd always assumed I'd live with Mamma's parents in Edinburgh. But Allan Grant descended on the funeral and claimed rights over me as chief of my father's clan. He took me back to Bancavan and within a fortnight, married me to his younger brother Ian. Not that Ian was that young. He was only two years younger than Allan." Her hands clenched against the tabletop as she forced herself to look back on those appalling weeks of sorrow and dread and bullying.

"Fiona—"

"I should have resisted. I tried." She rushed on before Diarmid could tell her how sorry he was. At this moment, his pity would destroy her. "But they locked me up in the cellar and beat and starved me until I agreed."

"I should have shot the bastards before they had a chance to cross my threshold," he said flatly. "Ye were a child. A grief-stricken orphan. Ripped away from everything you'd ever known. What they did was unconscionable. I assume there was a dowry involved."

"Aye. Papa wasn't rich, but there was a house in Edinburgh, and Mamma had a small inheritance. The Grants like to amass property. Once they've got it, they don't like to let it go."

"And their idea of property includes their womenfolk."

She swallowed to shift the boulder of hatred blocking her throat. "It does."

He leaned forward. "Puir wee lassie, ye must have felt like you'd been stolen away to hell."

"Life in Edinburgh was calm and happy and civilized. The Grants live like animals."

"With Allan the king of the beasts."

"None of the others have the backbone to stand up to him."

"I loathe that this happened to ye." Bristling with tension, Diarmid rose and crossed to stand in front of the fire. His voice vibrated with emotion. "Given over for an old man to rape."

She flinched at the stark description. "I was Ian's wife. He owned me." Bitterness sharpened her tone. "There's no rape in marriage."

Diarmid's shoulders moved with a sigh. When he turned to face her, she saw that he was struggling to contain his outrage. "Were ye willing?"

"Once he had my vow, I owed him the use of my body."

"Were ye willing?" His tone was implacable.

"I was obedient."

Her belly knotted in a queasy tangle, as she recalled Ian grunting and sweating over her. The first time he'd taken her, he'd hurt her so badly that she'd vomited. That had earned her a beating from Allan, after Ian complained of his bride's lack of enthusiasm. After that, she learned to lie still until the foul act was over.

She straightened on her hard wooden chair and steeled herself to go on. It wasn't just that she hated to recall those nights when Ian's scrawny old body had heaved about on top of her. Something about discussing such a private topic with Diarmid Mactavish set those crowds of butterflies in her stomach madly fluttering once more.

"Ian died nearly a year ago. He hadn't been well for a long time before the end. For most of our married life, I was more nurse than wife."

God forgive her, she'd been grateful when her husband's debilitating illness left him incapable of his husbandly duties. She'd been hard put to summon any pity for his sufferings either.

One of the most disturbing parts of the last ten years was the creeping fear that constant misery gradually turned her as evil as Allan Grant. The nightmare of her existence at Bancavan poisoned any sweetness and softness she'd ever possessed.

"Couldnae ye leave, once you were a widow?"

"I had no money and nowhere to go." Looking back, she realized that unending brutality had cowed her into sullen compliance. "And I had a year ahead with no man in my bed. Allan wanted to wait to see if there was another child."

"There wasnae?"

"No. Ian had hardly touched me in two years, but I wasn't going to tell Allan that." Odd how they kept circling back to this topic of marital relations. "But I couldn't keep the ruse up forever. Allan pushed the marriage with Thomas, despite the fact that a union with my brother-in-law isn't strictly legal."

"Another old man."

"Old men get the pick of the women in Bancavan."

"Is that why ye ran away?"

She shook her head. "No. I ran away to save my daughter."

Something tightened in his expression. "Allan said ye had a bairn," he said slowly. "Is the lassie still at Bancavan?"

"No. They fostered my daughter out to a clansman near Inverness." She swallowed against a surge of bile. Thinking about Allan's plans for Christina always made her feel sick. "She's nine years old. When she's thirteen, they'll marry her off to one of her cousins."

A muscle flickered in Diarmid's cheek and even across the room, she read his anger. "So she's fated to go through the same horror ye did."

He did understand. "Aye."

"And ye cannae bear that."

"No. I won't have it. I won't." Her voice shook, as it hadn't when she described her own trials. The idea of her beloved child becoming nothing but a drudge to the Grants, with no hope of joy or love, made her want to scream.

"So ye ran away to find her."

"Colin Smith was one of the few men on the estate who maintained a shred of humanity. He deserves better than to lie in an unknown grave at Invertavey."

"I'll see he gets a fitting memorial. But what were your plans? Ye must have known the dangers you faced. Did ye have any money?"

"Only a few shillings. But I had a wedding ring to sell, and I'm strong and willing to work. I planned to snatch my daughter away, then disappear somewhere. Glasgow. London. America, if I must."

Diarmid looked troubled. "It's a flimsy plan, and one sure to lead to trouble. You're unprotected and defenseless. The world can be cruel to a woman on her own."

"The world can be cruel to any woman," she said bleakly.

"At least at Bancavan, ye had a roof over your head. If you'd gone ahead, it's likely you'd end up selling yourself on the streets to keep body and soul together."

Disappointment soured her anger. She'd expected his support, not his criticism. "You're saying I should accept my lot?"

"No, no' for a minute, but I am saying you should use your brain before ye set out into an uncaring world."

"I didn't have any choice. Christina's whole life was on the line."

"Christina? Is that your daughter's name?"

"Aye. It was my mother's name. Ian didn't care what I called our child. When she turned out to be a useless girl, and not the lad he wanted, he took no interest in her."

"How old were ye when you had your baby?"

"Just past sixteen."

His lips tightened. "By God, it's like ye were banished back to the Middle Ages."

"I doubt life has changed much at Bancavan since then. Not in essentials. The Grants never forgot the feud with the Mactavishes, for example."

"Och, even if they had, this will reawaken it."

"I'm sorry I dragged you into this," she mumbled, staring down at the worn table. "When the Grants turned up, I was on the verge of leaving Invertavey."

"And I let them take ye," he said bitterly.

"Why wouldn't you? I'd done nothing but lie to you." Fiona returned to a memory that still seared like acid. "And I stole your money."

"Och, ye were desperate." He made a sweeping gesture, as if wiping her theft from the record. "I cannae blame ye anymore, although if you'd trusted me with your story, it would have saved us some time."

"You don't owe me your help."

"Aye, I do. Out of common decency, if nothing else."

As she looked at him, brave and determined and most of all, on her side, she wished she'd confided in him earlier. Because Diarmid was a good man, she said what she must. "You've taken on a mountain of trouble with this fight. Allan is stubborn and spiteful. Even if I go on without you, he'll seek to pay you back for helping me to escape."

"I can handle Allan." That formidable jaw hardened. Diarmid's strength was quiet, but she couldn't doubt its power. "And what's this about going on alone? Your first plan was insane, surely ye see that. A beautiful woman with nae money and nae friends faces only one fate."

She twined her hands together on the table. "For my child, I'd sell myself."

Although the thought of strangers using her body made her skin crawl. It had been bad enough doing...that within the lawful bonds of marriage.

"And who will look after Christina when ye do?"

Diarmid's harsh assessment of her scheme made her flinch. "I'm not a fool, although I know I must seem like one to you. What choice do I have? I have to get Christina away from the Grants. While they have her, they have power over me and they know it. Once I've got her, I can decide what to do and where to go."

In the firelight, his face was austere. "I have a better idea."

Her heart sank. She already felt guilty about how she'd disrupted his life. "You're going to be heroic, aren't you?"

Bleak humor lengthened his lips. "I dinna ken about that, but I'm certainly going to help ye. We'll go to Achnasheen tomorrow and talk to Fergus. He's a clever laddie. He'll have some ideas about what we can do. Ye can rest there for a couple of days to regain your strength, knowing we're safe from the Grants. Then we'll go and get Christina, openly or by stealth."

"That sounds too good to be true." Hope, frail, painful, but invincible began to unfurl in her heart. "It *is* too good to be true. Allan will never let me go. He'll never leave me in peace. Especially if I turn to a Mactavish for help."

"But your circumstances have changed." A purposeful light glittered in Diarmid's black eyes. She almost believed that if anyone could defeat the Grants, it was this stalwart man. "Ye have powerful friends now. Allan might bully an adolescent girl. He'll have less success against the combined might of the Lairds of Invertavey and Achnasheen."

"It's too much," she said faintly, wanting to cry, wanting to tell him that she could succeed without putting him at risk, yet knowing that she couldn't. "I have nothing to give you in return."

Diarmid made a dismissive gesture. "No gentleman could abandon ye to your distress."

"You'll never see the end of this."

When Diarmid shrugged as if it hardly mattered, she wanted to tell him that he underestimated the Grants. But shameful self-interest kept her quiet.

"We'll come through. Dinna be afraid anymore, Fiona."

She bit back a sharp retort. Of course she was afraid. Now not just for herself and her daughter, but for gallant Diarmid Mactavish, too.

"Thank you." The words were inadequate recompense for what he'd done and even more, what he was about to do.

She was right to fear for the health of her soul. If she was a good woman the way Diarmid was a good man, she'd refuse to drag him any further into her difficulties.

CHAPTER THIRTEEN

At the first soft touch of Fiona's hand on his shoulder, Diarmid woke immediately from where he slept wrapped in his coat and with his head resting against the rough sod wall. The room was dim and shadowy, lit only by the banked peat fire. In the gloom, she was a dark shape kneeling at his side. He couldn't see her expression, but he read the tension in her body. Behind her, the bed showed traces of her restless sleep. The blanket sagged toward the floor.

"Fiona?" he asked groggily. "What is it, lassie? Is everything all right?"

An unwelcome thought struck him, and he reached out to catch her hand where it hovered above his shoulder. "Is it the Grants? Have they found us?"

Curse his blasted complacency. How could he have gone to sleep instead of sitting up to watch? But he'd been sure Allan and Thomas would never find this isolated bothy. And after all those long hours of riding, he'd been stupid with exhaustion. Not even the hard dirt floor and his raging desire could keep him awake.

He strained to hear some hint from outside that they'd been discovered, but there was only the crackle of the fire and the faint rasp of Fiona's breath. Even the rain seemed to have stopped.

He struggled to sit up. Hell's bells, he ached. It was a long time since he'd spent so long in the saddle.

"No," she said on a whisper of sound. "No, it's not the Grants."

Her answer emerged in jerky gasps, and while he was relieved to learn their pursuers hadn't caught up with them, he wasn't reassured. "What's wrong? Are ye ill?"

"No. No, not ill." The hand he held trembled, but she didn't try to draw away.

"Then what the devil is it?" Even as he battled the mists of sleep clouding his mind, he started to get seriously worried.

"It's...this."

He was still so dazed and bewildered that even when she leaned in over him, he didn't understand what was going on.

Then her lips crashed into his, and all rational thought disintegrated to ash.

Her lips were soft, and her scent, warm and womanly, flooded his head, made him drunk on Fiona. Riding across the hills, he'd spent hours cuddling her close. That scent had become a familiar torment. It was a lying promise of what could never come to pass.

Now, unbelievably, she'd come to him. He'd never imagined she would.

Masculine triumph gripped him, and arousal so powerful, it verged on painful.

Without thinking—when she kissed him, she incinerated his brain—he lashed his arms around her and dragged her across his body. She fell against him in an ungainly tumble, and her hands clawed at his arms.

Fiona made a faint sound. By all that was holy, he wanted to interpret it as a sigh of pleasure. But it sounded more like a whimper of distress.

No. No. No. No. No.

She was here. She was in his arms. She'd made the first move, for pity's sake.

But his shocked pleasure at her invitation already receded, even as the weight in his balls became more excruciating than ever. Much as he battled against accepting the return of reality, his mind started to function.

Diarmid knew what a willing woman felt like. Fiona didn't feel like a willing woman.

Her slender body was stiff and awkward. Her lips were tight and closed, as if she had no idea how to kiss a man.

He reached to frame her face, to tell her she didn't have to do this. What he found made him feel like taking an ax to the whole world.

He ripped his lips free of hers. "Stop, Fiona, stop."

More roughly than he should, he shoved her away. He was half-mad with wanting her and with dredging up the willpower to deny her.

To his dismay, she resisted his attempt to put some space between them. Instead she tried to plaster herself against him again. "You want me," she muttered. "I know you want me."

He wished to blazes he didn't. But draped across his lap as she was, she couldn't miss his readiness, damn it.

"For the love of God, let me go," he grated out.

"No," she said in a broken voice.

She was shaking the way she had when he'd saved her from the shipwreck. And not, blast her, with desire, although he'd give up ten years of his life for one minute where he could genuinely believe she found him appealing.

"Aye," he snapped, struggling to get a firmer grip on her so he could push her off.

In the struggle, his hand curled around one soft breast. A lightning strike of heat sizzled through him.

As she cried out in surprise, he bit back a savage curse. This time, he caught her arms and wrenched her to the side. He staggered to his feet and backed away until he hit the wall behind him.

"Dinna touch me," he said, holding his hands out to keep her away, as if she had some dreadful disease. "In the name of heaven, dinna touch me again."

Closing his eyes, he said a silent, despairing prayer for strength. Then he stumbled across to the hearth and stoked up the fire until the blaze turned the room bright. He ground his teeth as he fought the urge to take her anyway. After all, she was no man's wife. She was free to give herself to him. Hell, the fire raging in his loins proved he was more than ready to accept what she was offering.

But as his vision started to work again and the hot tumult of his blood ebbed, he looked at her and knew he couldn't give in to his base impulses.

She remained where he'd left her, huddled against the ground. In the stronger light, he saw her clearly at last. And wished to Hades he'd left the room in darkness.

Fiona looked afraid and defeated. Her face was pale, and her huge blue eyes were bruised and desolate as she stared at him in complete bewilderment. Worse, the flickering light picked up what he'd felt when he touched her cheeks. Tracks of tears. Tears she still shed. It was eerie, how silently she cried.

The lips she'd pressed so hard against his were red and swollen. He refused to call that desperate contact a kiss.

When he made a sweeping gesture in her direction, she flinched.

The anger and frustration churning in his gut turned to sick horror. Surely she couldn't imagine he meant violence. Of course she did. What else did she know of men but brutality? His loathing for the Grants rose another notch.

"Don't be frightened," he said, his voice bitter. "You're safe."

Because they both knew she'd come close to not being safe at all. There had been an instant in that excruciating embrace where he'd nearly hauled her under him and thrust inside her.

He watched her straighten and slide back. She pressed against the wall, as if she tried to burrow her way out of the cottage. He finally realized what she was wearing, and dangerous male hunger stirred to life once again, making a travesty of his belief that he'd regained his self-control.

Her flimsy shift did little to hide her body. The long, graceful legs. The alluring line of hip and waist. The luscious roundness of her breasts with their beaded tips. He wasn't fool enough to imagine that those hard nipples meant she was sexually excited.

The first night after he found her, he'd seen her close to undressed. The memory had tortured his every moment since. Now, God damn it, fate delivered another image of Fiona Grant's half-naked body to drive him insane.

Diarmid stood still, breathing deeply and battling for restraint. It was a long time before he felt sufficiently in charge of his impulses to approach her. When she flinched away again, guilt knotted his belly.

Stopping a couple of feet away, he fished his handkerchief out of his pocket. As he held it out to her, he struggled not to stare at the delicate architecture of her collarbones under the sagging shift. "Wipe your eyes."

She swallowed. He felt her hesitation like a blow to his solar plexus, before an unsteady hand reached to take the handkerchief.

Fiona didn't immediately wipe her cheeks. Instead she kept staring at him with that wounded, questioning gaze, while she twisted the square of white lawn between shaking hands.

On unsteady legs, Diarmid backed away, hoping a greater distance between them might reassure her. The wild race of his heart slowed. She looked so frail and defenseless, he felt like the worst kind of degenerate for what he wanted to do to her.

Wanted to do even now, as the fraught silence built between them.

She bit her lip and raised her chin. These signs of returning self-possession eased his tension, until she spoke.

"Why?" she asked, her usually sweet voice a croak.

He didn't pretend to misunderstand. "Ye dinna want this."

"You do." The self-hatred that flooded her face made his guilt rear up like a striking cobra. "Or did I get that wrong?"

God give him strength. He wasn't sure he was ready to talk about his unwelcome desire for her. But her aching vulnerability meant he had to.

"No, ye didnae get that wrong," he muttered.

She made a helpless gesture. "Then..."

His mouth tightened. "I've never taken an unwilling woman in my life. I'm no' going to start now."

"I came to you."

"Ye dinna owe me anything."

To his surprise, grim amusement tugged at that lush mouth. "Of course I do, Diarmid. And this is all I have to give in return."

She was so proud, it threatened to tear his heart to shreds. What chance did he have against her? He'd wanted her like the devil, even when he believed her a thief and a liar. Now he knew the full extent of her courage and her sacrifice, she was utterly irresistible.

But resist her he must.

She'd already ceded too much to selfish male power. He wasn't going to add himself to the list of men who took advantage of her.

For the sake of his sanity, he needed to cover her up. He returned to where he'd slept and picked up his coat. "Here. You'll get cold."

She was cold now, if the pointed nipples were any indication. He struggled to ignore the way her breasts filled out that infernally transparent linen.

Her breasts were larger than they'd been when she arrived at Invertavey. A couple of days of good food had added a beguiling roundness to the skeletal figure he'd carried from the beach.

Another unwelcome jolt of desire shook him, as he recalled holding her breast. Soft. Round. The perfect size for his palm.

God help him, that wasn't something he needed to think about when another day's riding lay ahead. A day when he had to hold her in his arms and devote every agonizing second to reminding himself that she didn't want him.

Diarmid wished he'd thought to bring a second horse and a cohort of his clansmen on this rescue mission. All this privacy with Fiona tested his honor to breaking point.

"Thank you," she stammered, and he saw a flush rise in her cheeks.

"Ye dinna have to trade your body for my help." As he watched her tug the coat around her with shaking hands, he felt utterly disgusted with himself. "If you'd gone ahead with what ye tried to do, it would have turned our alliance into a squalid transaction. I pledge myself to your service, Fiona. You're a victim of huge injustice. My word is enough to bind me. Ye dinna have to confirm my allegiance in any other way."

Humiliation flooded her face, and he realized that he was right to think that what had just happened stemmed more from calculation than gratitude. The elegant jaw hardened. "I won't let my daughter suffer my fate."

Diarmid remembered back to that awkward moment when she'd slammed her mouth into his, more an act of violence than of desire. Her lips had been closed as firmly as a bank safe. A man might almost imagine the girl had no idea how to kiss, which was ridiculous, given she'd been married and borne a child.

He bloody well had to keep his hands to himself. Fiona needed his help, not his seduction. Chivalry forbade him from asking for anything in return.

But as he stared at her across the room, chivalry's voice was a feeble whisper against the drumroll of craving.

I can keep my hands off her. I can.

Diarmid wasn't sure he believed it. Because even when she'd trembled with fear, his hands had adored her slender shape, his senses had filled with the warm, floral scent of her skin, and those taut, closed lips had tasted like heaven.

He clenched his fists at his sides and prowled across to the door. "I'm going out to check on Sigurn."

"You don't have to go." Fiona scrambled to her feet, giving him a glimpse of long, coltish legs and bare, narrow feet. "I won't...I won't do that again."

Her slender hands twined in front of her. The heavy folds of his coat covered her like a nun's habit. He should feel less on edge, now he'd restored her modesty.

He felt like he teetered on the brink of a precipice. Because he'd seen more than enough of her tonight. Enough to know he'd never forget the sight of her clad in only a drift of white linen. Plague take her, she could stand before him wearing sackcloth and ashes and he'd want her.

And tonight he'd touched her. His hands could never unlearn the satiny softness of her skin.

"Aye, I do," he said grimly, opening the door. Out of the corner of his eye, he saw her take a step in his direction.

"You'll be cold out there."

"No, I bloody willnae," he muttered. "And if you've got an ounce of sense, lassie, ye willnae follow me."

Blindly Diarmid blundered out of the bothy and stood shaking with reaction in the soft summer gloaming. He gasped for breath as if he'd run up Ben Nevis.

By heaven, the sooner he got his charge safely to Achnasheen, the better. He hoped to hell that seeing Fergus and Marina would remind him that he was a man who had a few principles.

It took far too much effort to force himself to make the short journey to the stables, where he intended to stay until they rode out in the morning. Two nights with Fiona Grant, and already he felt wrong when she wasn't sleeping within reach.

CHAPTER FOURTEEN

It was the evening of the next day when they came over a ridge and Fiona found herself looking at a scene from a fairy tale. From where she sat, warm and safe in Diarmid's arms, she drank in the spectacular landscape. The green slope swept down to a turreted castle standing guard over a glittering loch, with the sea a shining silver mirror behind it. Across the water, a line of jagged hills rose against the clear violet sky.

She must have made some sound, because Diarmid pulled a tired Sigurn to a halt on the brow of the hill. "Bonny, isn't it?"

Through this long day on horseback, he hadn't talked much. She supposed he was still angry with her for last night's failed seduction. Nor had she tried to coax him into conversation. She'd been too busy cringing at the memory of her clumsiness. The constraint between them had made a hard journey more exhausting than it needed to be.

"Aye," she said softly, wanting to apologize for making herself cheap, for everything, really. She'd brought him nothing but trouble.

But what was her apology worth, when for Christina's sake, she'd do it all again?

Humiliation still churned inside her, made today's skimpy rations lie like stones in her belly. He'd known straightaway that her kisses last night were a self-serving attempt to bind him to her. She owed him her gratitude, but gratitude wasn't the reason behind that disastrous encounter.

If she became Diarmid Mactavish's mistress, he wouldn't abandon her before they rescued Christina. She'd steeled herself to endure a man's possession. Only to have her shabby bargain rejected as unworthy of her. And of him.

When he said no, he exposed the rot in her soul. He'd recognized her seduction as the counterfeit it was and sent her back to her bed, alone and ashamed.

And even more astonishing, a little miffed. Not to mention...disappointed.

That unacceptable disappointment was the hardest memory of all to bear. She'd gone to Diarmid feeling like a brave martyr for a good cause, and he'd left her with the knowledge that she was nothing more than a wee hypocrite.

"That's Achnasheen." The way he spoke the name rippled through her like music.

After years of nothing but harsh voices, the sound of Diarmid Mactavish's deep baritone always made her want to weep. It reminded her of a time when every word wasn't angry or critical or peremptory.

"That's where we're going?"

While she made herself appear cheerful, she shrank from meeting Diarmid's friends. She must look a fright, not to mention she arrived in their home, after spending days in the company of a man to whom she wasn't married.

The world would condemn her as a slut. And if Diarmid told his friends the full story, they'd know she was not only a slut, but a liar and a thief. If it meant saving Christina, she'd suffer any derision, but still her pride smarted.

"Aye." He clicked his tongue to Sigurn, and the horse set off at a gentle canter. The mare, too, must want food and warmth and rest. "We'll stay here while we decide what we do next and while ye recover your health. You'll like Fergus and Marina."

"Right now I'd like anyone who offered me a bed and a hot meal."

"I can promise ye that much."

She supposed she should welcome the presence of other people. It might ease the tension simmering between her and Diarmid.

But even after last night, the thought that they'd no longer be alone together stirred a forbidden regret. Since her father's death, she hadn't enjoyed any amiable or interesting company. While their circumstances over the last few days had been uncivilized, Diarmid hadn't been. He'd remained courteous throughout, treating her like a lady, when surely she'd relinquished any claim to the description.

Over the last ten years, she'd fought for her very survival. Life's more sophisticated pleasures hadn't got a look in. But since meeting Diarmid Mactavish, she'd remembered that every minute didn't need to be a brutish scramble. She hadn't realized how she'd missed that gloss of grace and manners. If she failed, if her daughter stayed out of reach, if she had to return to Bancavan, life there would be unendurable now she'd glimpsed something sweeter.

As they neared the castle, she realized it was bigger than she'd thought. The fairy-tale magic hardened into a fearsome defensive structure.

She liked that. The days of sieges might be over, but even if the Grants found her here, she'd be safe behind thick stone walls.

Today, the portcullis was raised, and Diarmid rode in without a challenge. They trotted through a dark tunnel where the weight of centuries-old stone pressed over her head. Then they emerged back into the evening light.

"Good evening, Jock," Diarmid said, as a burly Highlander rushed out into the large courtyard to take Sigurn's reins. "I hope Fergus and Marina are at home."

"Good evening to ye, Mactavish. Aye, the Mackinnon and his lady are here."

The doors at the top of the impressive stone staircase opened, and a tall and spectacularly handsome man with auburn hair ran down to greet them. "Diarmid, this is an unexpected pleasure. Ye sent nae word you were coming."

"Aye, well, it was a spur of the moment thing. Can ye offer a friend and his companion shelter?"

"Shelter, is it? That sounds dire." An expressive russet eyebrow tilted in inquiry. "Last I heard, Invertavey House was still standing."

"Aye, it's standing. But it's no' safe for us right now. I have a tale to tell, but no' in the middle of the yard. Is it all right if we stay for a wee while?"

The tall man made an expansive gesture. "Och, my doors are always open wide to a friend in need. Although you've caught us at a difficult moment."

"Marina?"

"Aye. The baby's due in the next few weeks."

Fiona made a sound of protest. "We can't inconvenience you, sir."

Steely gray eyes had already subjected her to a swift, but thorough inspection. "There's plenty of room, Miss..."

Diarmid's arms tightened around her waist. "This is Mrs. Grant."

She assumed Mr. Mackinnon must know about the history of violence and hatred between her family and the Mactavishes, but he didn't mention it. Nor did he comment on her married name. "May I help ye down, Mrs. Grant?"

She was strangely loath to leave Diarmid's arms, and she wondered if he felt the same. He seemed reluctant to release her. "Thank you. You must be wondering why…"

Mr. Mackinnon took her by the waist and lifted her to the cobblestones where she staggered. After a day in the saddle, she was stiff and awkward. He kept hold of her arm and saved her from a tumble.

"Steady there, lassie. There's nae need for explanations on the doorstep. Come away inside and have a hot bath and something to eat. We can save getting acquainted until you've settled in. Any friend of Diarmid's is a friend of mine."

She wasn't sure if she was Diarmid's friend. She didn't know how she'd describe what drew her and the Laird of Invertavey together. Nothing as benevolent and uncomplicated as friendship, that was for sure. But after the last few days, she was exhausted and heartsick. A chance to catch her breath before she shared her story with yet another person was a blessing.

Behind her, she was aware of Diarmid dismounting. She was always aware of where he was and what he did. He loomed up behind her and as if at a silent signal, Mr. Mackinnon released her arm. She was firmer on her feet now, but even so, she appreciated the warm strength of Diarmid's hand at her back.

"We're grateful, Fergus."

"Och, it's nothing. It's no' as if we dinna have the space, laddie. And Marina might like another lady in the place at such a time."

Fiona took a deep relieved breath. So far, thank heaven, their host didn't seem ready to treat her like a scarlet woman. The silvery eyes that settled on her were bright with curiosity, not condemnation.

"Jock, will ye take Sigurn?" Diarmid asked. "She's had a rough few days and come through like a champion. A bit of your famous touch with horses willnae go astray."

"Och, she is a bonny champion. All of Banshee's get have hearts as big as the Highlands. But I can see she's due to be treated like the queen she is. Leave her to me, Mactavish."

"Come away in," Mr. Mackinnon said, gesturing toward the stairs. "We're due to have dinner in an hour or so. We'll put it back half an hour, so ye can slough off the travel dust. Diarmid, you'll join us?"

"With pleasure."

"Mrs. Grant? If you'd rather have a tray in your room, we can arrange that. I can see this dunderhead has put ye through the wars."

A night to herself? It sounded like paradise, but she couldn't rest easy until she'd explained herself to this man who seemed so ready to accept her at face value.

"No, I'll join you for dinner. Thank you."

Mr. Mackinnon offered his arm. "Then welcome to Achnasheen."

Fiona curled a trembling hand around his elbow. What on earth was she getting into? If Diarmid hadn't been just behind her, she might have taken to her heels and run.

CHAPTER FIFTEEN

ithin half an hour of his arrival, Diarmid was downstairs. Weariness thickened his head and made his muscles ache, tugged at him with every step. Weariness, and his uncertainty about the best way to help Fiona. But a good wash and some clean clothes, courtesy of Fergus, left him feeling more like his unflappable self.

He'd visited Achnasheen since he was a boy, so he needed no guide to find the library where Fergus usually enjoyed a wee dram before dinner. Before Fiona joined them, he wanted a quiet word with his friend.

"Fergus, may I come in?" he asked from the doorway.

"*Buonasera*, Diarmid." Fergus's striking half-Italian wife looked up from her seat near the window. "This is a treat to have you here."

Diarmid had last seen Marina in Edinburgh in April, at the triumphant opening of her exhibition of Scottish landscapes. She was a famous artist whose work was in demand across Europe. Fergus had told him then that he and his wife expected their first baby in August. Over the last few months, she'd grown large with child.

Now she sat in a leather armchair with her feet up on a stool. As usual, a sketchbook lay open on the table next to her elbow.

He smiled at Marina with the genuine fondness he'd always felt for her and crossed to kiss her olive-skinned cheek. "Och, I hope you'll still say that, once I've explained myself. I ken it's an inconvenient time. But we had nowhere else to go."

"That sounds desperate, laddie." Fergus crossed the room to push a glass of whisky into his hand.

"I'm afraid it is," Diarmid said somberly. He accepted Fergus's offer of a chair and took a sip of his whisky, relishing the smoky flavor. "But first, how are ye, Marina? You're looking blooming."

Marina made an unmistakably Continental sound of contempt. "I'm looking like I'm about to explode. This baby must be the size of a horse. *Porca miseria*, I'm beginning to wish I'd married a skinny man who was five feet tall, instead of this brawny Highlander."

"Ye dinna mean that, *mo chridhe*," Fergus said gently.

With obvious difficulty, she shifted. She was a tall, naturally slender woman—or at least she had been. "Don't I?"

But the glance she shot her husband from her bright black eyes was loving.

Diarmid felt a sharp pang of envy for his friend's happiness, although this outspoken, independent woman was the precise opposite of the docile, biddable wife Fergus always said he wanted.

It was difficult to imagine that such a happy union awaited him. After his mother's antics, he was too reluctant to trust, and it was clear that mutual trust formed the basis for the love between Fergus and Marina.

Och, stop feeling so blasted sorry for yourself, man. You've got more important things to worry about than your uninspiring love life.

"I want to explain what I'm doing here, and why I need your help. Then if ye wish, you can send me to the devil."

Fergus crossed to stand behind his wife and rested one hand on her shoulder. "Diarmid, we've been friends most of our lives. If I can help ye, I will. Ye know that."

"That's what I hoped you'd say. Although ye might end up being sorry you did."

"Diarmid, you've never brought a woman here with you before." Marina raised her hand to lay it upon Fergus's. "Who is she?"

"She's no' my mistress," he said quickly.

Marina shrugged. "*Per pietà*, I don't care if she is. You vouch for her. That's enough for me. She's a married woman? Fergus called her Mrs. Grant."

His hostess took a refreshingly broadminded attitude to life, he'd long ago discovered. Years on the road as a working artist in her father's company, not to mention associating with people from all levels of society, had shown her more of the world than most gently bred Scottish girls ever saw.

"A widow." He took another mouthful of the fiery spirit and launched into the tale of Fiona's arrival at Invertavey, the Grants' appearance, the chaotic rescue, and the wild chase across the hills. To give Marina and Fergus credit, they were bonny listeners, only interrupting when he told them what he'd recently discovered, the reasons behind Fiona's reckless quest.

"Oh, *la poverina*," Marina said. "What cruelty she's endured."

Diarmid hadn't spoken at length of what he'd learned or guessed about life at Bancavan. That was Fiona's business. But he'd clearly said enough for Marina and Fergus to reach their own conclusions about her sufferings.

Fergus now sat on the opposite side of the fire. His expression was austere. "She'll be safe here."

"The problem is that the Grants must ken Fiona plans to rescue her daughter. They dinna need to go to the trouble of tracking us all over Scotland. They just need to hold onto the girl and wait for us to turn up."

"Like spiders in a web," Marina said in a grim tone.

"Aye."

A sound at the door made Diarmid look up. Fiona hovered at the entrance, and Fiona as he'd never seen her. She wore a pale blue evening gown that made her eyes look like the sky, and she'd arranged her moonlight hair in an elaborate style that made her seem an aristocratic stranger.

By God, she was bonny. He felt like someone hit him with a hammer. He'd always been painfully conscious of how exquisite she was. But when he saw her dressed in silks, her beauty thumped him in the belly like a punch. Before he even thought to stand, he found himself on his feet.

He moved to take her hand, then remembered he had no real right to touch her, even if she'd rested in his arms all day as they rode across the hills. Damn it, he felt awkward, as he rarely had until he met her. He turned the gesture into a sweep of his hand toward Fergus and Marina.

"Fiona, come away in and meet our hosts."

After a hesitation, she stepped into the room, as graceful as a doe picking her way into a forest clearing. He couldn't mistake the caution in her expression. Like him, she'd learned that trust must be earned. "I hope I'm not intruding."

Marina came up to Diarmid's side, her hands extended. Fiona in her borrowed finery had so dazzled him, that he hadn't even noticed his hostess rising to her feet. "Of course not. *Benvenuta a* Achnasheen, *Signora* Grant. I'm Marina Mackinnon, and this is my husband, Fergus. We're so pleased you came to us in your time of trouble."

The warm, spontaneous welcome took Fiona aback, Diarmid saw. There was an uncomfortable silence, then Fiona's rare, radiant smile lit her features and she curtsied. "You're too kind."

"Not at all, *signora*." Marina took her hands. "I see Sandra has worked her magic."

"She's amazing." Fiona self-consciously touched the becoming curls framing her face.

"*Certo*, she is. I bless the day she decided to come to Scotland with me, instead of staying in Firenze. When I heard you'd arrived without any luggage, I knew if you had something *bellissimo* to wear, you'd start to feel at home."

Fiona glanced down at the pretty dress with an expression of wonder. "It's a beautiful gown."

"*Certo*, but that blue never did very much for me, whereas it's perfect for you."

"Thank you."

"*Prego.* Come and join me, *bella*." Marina brought Fiona across to a sofa and sat beside her.

As Diarmid turned back to his chair, he caught Fergus's interested gaze from where he stood near the unlit hearth. Embarrassment prickled his skin. He had an unpleasant inkling that his reaction to Fiona's arrival had revealed too much to his sharp-eyed friend.

"Would ye like a glass of wine, Mrs. Grant?" Fergus asked. "I imagine you're hungry. Dinner willnae be long."

Fiona's gesture was apologetic. "You must curse me for arriving uninvited at such a time."

"We'd do anything for Diarmid," Marina said. "And he's just told us a little about your difficulties."

As she accepted a glass of hock from Fergus, the inquiring glance that Fiona sent Diarmid wasn't altogether friendly. "Did he?"

"Aye, I did," Diarmid said. "Ye can trust Marina and Fergus, and I'm hoping they'll help us against the Grants."

"Indeed we will," Marina said, squeezing Fiona's hand. "I think you've been so brave, *poverina*."

"Desperate, more like." Fiona's lips turned down. "I know the shipwreck was a disaster, not least because a good man lost his life to the sea, but I was lucky to wash up on Diarmid's beach. Without him, I dread to imagine where I'd be now. The more I think about it, the more I realize I had no chance of succeeding on my own when I ran away from Bancavan."

Fergus emptied his glass and gave her an encouraging smile. "With Diarmid's help and now with ours, the odds have changed in your favor, Mrs. Grant. It was indeed a lucky thing that ye made land at Invertavey."

Fiona didn't smile back. As Diarmid recovered from the shock of seeing her dressed like a lady of fashion, he realized that she looked tired and uneasy. The last days had been long and hard, and telling him her story had been draining. Not to mention that since she'd kissed him, hostile awareness had buzzed between them like a low, irritating hum. It had worn at his nerves all day. He suspected she must find it just as grating.

"I don't know why you'd pledge yourselves to my cause," Fiona said gravely. "You know nothing about me."

Marina's eyes were dark and serious. "*Signora,* we told you—we'd do anything for Diarmid. It's enough that he's on your side. Even before he told us your circumstances. Your daughter is in trouble. So are you. Accept what help we can give you. Don't let your pride get in the way of your good sense."

Fiona tugged her hand free, and her expression didn't lighten. "But one of the problems is that I'm not sure why Diarmid is on my side."

"That's easy to answer." Fergus's laugh held a hint of fond mockery. "At heart, my stalwart friend is a white knight. Your plight is a chance for him to devote all that chivalry to a lady in distress. You're doing the laddie a favor. Life at Invertavey is so peaceful, he was getting too lazy and complacent for his own good."

Diarmid ignored his friend's good-natured jibes. "I saved your life, Fiona. It puts me eternally at your service."

"Shouldn't that work the other way?" Fiona retorted.

"I told you when I saved ye that you'd never break the bond between us."

He wanted to sound jocular, to ease the heavy atmosphere building in the room. But the words emerged like a vow.

Fiona looked troubled and didn't reply. He waited for Fergus to scoff at him or for Marina to break the weighty silence that descended. But neither spoke.

Instead two pairs of astute eyes leveled on him. The intense scrutiny made him rise from his chair and turn toward the window to avoid the discomfiting knowledge he read in his friends' faces.

When Kirsty chose that moment to come in and announce dinner was ready, Diarmid sagged with relief. For a moment there, he felt like he stood on that precipice again. And this time, he'd been on the brink of jumping.

CHAPTER SIXTEEN

Fiona was so used to sleeping with one ear alert for danger, that she woke the minute she heard distant sounds in the castle. She opened her eyes to firelit darkness. After a warm, fine day, the weather had closed in. By the time she came upstairs, she'd been grateful for the blaze in her hearth.

She had no idea what time it was. Not late, she suspected. The exhaustion weighing her body hinted she hadn't slept for long.

Before she thought what she did, she was up with a shawl wrapped around her borrowed nightdress. When she opened her door, the long corridor outside was empty. Had she imagined the sounds of doors opening and closing?

She retreated into her room to light a candle from her fire. As she stepped out once more, the house lay quiet around her, but instincts honed over years with the Grants told her something was afoot. Further down the hall, another door opened, and Diarmid emerged wearing breeches and his loose shirt untucked around his narrow hips.

"What is it, Fiona? Are ye all right?"

He, too, carried a candle. The frail light turned his chiseled features into a symphony of shadows. His hair was wildly disheveled, falling in charming disarray over that noble brow.

"Did I wake you?" she asked, telling herself it was idiotic to blush. "I'm sorry."

He padded toward her on bare feet. His shirt was open over his chest, revealing a scattering of black curls. For the last two nights, they'd shared sleeping quarters. This midnight encounter shouldn't feel so forbidden. But it did. Perhaps because Diarmid hadn't undressed when they'd been traveling, and now it was clear that he'd woken and tugged on whatever clothing lay near to hand.

"I heard your door." It seemed he, too, remained attuned to danger.

"Is it the Grants?" She clutched at her shawl, as if the soft wool provided some protection.

"I hope to God it's not." He strode past her toward the staircase.

"I thought I heard people moving about."

"I only heard ye." By now, voices rose from the great hall downstairs, too muffled for her to catch any actual words. "Stay there, and I'll see what I can find out."

For a moment, Fiona remained where she was, her eyes feeding on the sight of Diarmid retreating down the corridor. Heaven help her, the view from the back was almost as good as the view from the front.

The sheer shirt and tight breeches revealed every line of that powerful back and those taut buttocks. She licked her lips again, as something warm and liquid swelled inside her. Then she reminded herself that she had more important things to worry about than her white knight's shapely backside.

She wrapped her shawl more securely around her shoulders and followed him. If it was the Grants, she wanted to know sooner rather than later. At Invertavey, their arrival had taken her by surprise. This time she'd be prepared.

Diarmid stood on the landing at the top of the imposing stone staircase that led down to the great hall with its medieval tapestries and displays of arms. She blinked at the brightness. Every light in the house seemed to be burning.

One of the maids who had served them at dinner scurried across the flagstones below and disappeared down a hallway. She carried a large china ewer. Mr. Mackinnon appeared from the opposite doorway.

"What's happening, Fergus?" Diarmid called out. "Have the Grants followed us here?"

When Mr. Mackinnon looked up, the light was stark on his strained features. With a shock, Fiona realized he looked afraid. When she'd met him, he'd seemed as impervious to fear as a rock.

"No, it's the baby. Damn it, Diarmid, it's early. We thought we had until the end of August."

"How is Lady Achnasheen?" Fiona asked, descending a few steps.

She recalled that her hostess hadn't eaten much at dinner, and she'd been pale and quiet and in obvious discomfort by the time everyone went upstairs. Nobody had lingered over the meal. Fergus had helped his wife to climb the steps, and Fiona and Diarmid had both been exhausted and grateful to retire to their chambers.

"She's…" He made a despairing gesture, and his rugged features tightened.

Fiona had already noted that the Mackinnons shared a rare bond. Now Mr. Mackinnon's love and terror for his wife lay unconcealed in his face.

"Have ye sent for the doctor?" Diarmid asked.

"Aye. But ye know he's miles away. Jenny's up there with her. There's nothing she doesnae ken about bringing new life into the world. I'd trust her over the sawbones any day."

The words lacked conviction. Fiona descended until she was close enough to touch the man's arm. They were strangers, but she couldn't resist offering a moment's comfort.

"Can I help? For the last ten years, I've helped with births at Bancavan, and your wife might appreciate another pair of skilled hands at her lying in."

When both men regarded her dumbfounded, she bit back an impatient retort. She knew she looked likely to blow away on a stiff breeze, but she was strong. To survive under Allan Grant's rule, she'd had to be.

"Would ye?" Gratitude eased the tension in Mr. Mackinnon's features. "Marina is healthy, but..."

Fiona stepped aside to allow another maid to scuttle past with an armful of fresh towels. "I'm sure everything will be fine."

She wasn't surprised that he didn't believe her. Hiding a shudder, she remembered the times when she'd attended births that hadn't been fine at all.

The Grants didn't believe in paying for a doctor's services. Instead they relied on the clan's womenfolk to assist in delivering any babies. Not that Fiona had anything against wise women. Christina's birth had been long and difficult. Only the midwife's skill had saved both mother and child.

"Thank you." Mr. Mackinnon's smile was an obvious effort, and she commended his courage. "I'll take ye up to her."

"I'm glad I can repay some of your kindness, sir." If only she could repay Diarmid, who had done even more for her. But he'd rejected the one thing she had to give, and she didn't know what else to offer him.

Except as she studied the two men, she realized that helping Lady Achnasheen would go a long way toward compensating Diarmid. She'd recognized immediately not just that the Mackinnons loved one another, but that powerful ties of friendship united them both to Diarmid.

When her hosts said they'd do anything for Diarmid, the words were no idle promise. At dinner, Diarmid had told her how the connection began. Mr. Mackinnon had rescued Diarmid and his cousin after the younger boys became lost in the hills behind Achnasheen. It was clear that this friendship established twenty years ago was deep and enduring.

"I told you, ye owe me nothing. In fact, if you help to bring my wife safely through tonight, I'll be eternally in your debt." He turned to Diarmid. "It's the middle of the night, and you've been in the saddle all day. Why no' go back to bed?"

Diarmid gave a contemptuous snort. "And leave ye all alone to fret yourself daft? Not likely, my friend. I'll see ye down in the library, where a dram or two of Bruce Mackenzie's finest awaits."

Mr. Mackinnon didn't even try to hide his relief. "I willnae be long. Dinna drink it all before I get there."

Diarmid laughed, as he was meant to. But Fiona had come to know him over the last week, especially in these last days when they'd hardly been apart. She read the concern in his dark eyes, as he studied his friend. Concern they all had a right to feel when a first baby arrived early.

"Come away with me, Mrs. Grant." Mr. Mackinnon gestured for Fiona to precede him up the stairs, as Diarmid descended to the hall.

She would have preferred to change out of her nightgown, but the only other dress she had was that elaborate silk gown. When she was in the bath, the maids had whisked away her plain gray dress. Once she'd checked what was happening with Lady Achnasheen, she would set about finding something suitable to wear.

Wrapping her shawl around her shoulders, she wished she'd waited to put on the slippers Marina had sent along with this pretty white lawn nightdress. Despite it being summer, the stone stairs were cold under her feet.

They climbed higher and higher, and she realized they must be entering one of the castle's towers. When they reached the landing outside a closed door, she heard a long, broken groan from within.

"Marina!" Mr. Mackinnon cried out and pushed past Fiona. He shoved the door open so hard that it crashed against the wall.

As he rushed forward, Fiona took in a candlelit room. Lady Achnasheen was bent over the back of a wooden chair, gripping the top railing with white-knuckled hands. She wore a white nightdress, and her black hair snaked around her shoulders in a wild tangle. She was pale as milk, and her great dark eyes looked like bruises in her face as she panted for air.

"Marina, *mo chridhe*." Mr. Mackinnon slung an arm around his wife's swollen body. A flood of urgent Gaelic escaped him as he supported her through her pain.

While her parents had only ever spoken English, Fiona had picked up some basic Gaelic at Bancavan. She heard him call his wife his heart and his darling. But she only made out a few words of his desperate pleas, which seemed to combine prayers to the Almighty with encouragement to his wife.

"Fergus…" Lady Achnasheen rasped out, straightening gingerly from the chair and sagging against him. Tearstains marked her cheeks, and Fiona didn't need to recall her agonies with Christina to know what the woman endured. "*Madonna*, you shouldn't be in here."

The room contained four women, other than her hostess. Three maids and an older woman who must be Jenny, the local healer. This woman turned away from the sideboard where she was setting out an array of vials and bottles and marched up to the laird.

"Aye, my lady is right, Mackinnon. It's nae proper for ye to be here. Bringing bairns into the world is women's work."

Fiona's eyes rounded at the peremptory tone. If anyone spoke to Allan Grant that way, they'd be lucky to escape with a clout around the ears. She'd seen her husband's brother kill a servant boy who wasn't quick enough bringing him his wine at dinner.

"It's my bloody house, ye old besom." Mr. Mackinnon tightened his grip on his wife. "Can ye no' see she's in pain?"

"Och, aye, she is." Even more surprising, the woman didn't quail at the angry response. "And she'll be in more pain before she's done. It's nature's way. If the Good Lord wills, the mistress will come through like the braw lassie she is. She's strong, and she's got a lot to live for."

"The bairn is early."

"Aye. He's an impatient wee laddie, just like his daddy was. Dinna fash yourself, Mackinnon. It will all work out in the end."

"He?" Marina asked in a breathless voice.

Jenny shrugged. "Just a wee feeling I have. Ye carried the bairn just like the Mackinnon's mother carried him. High and forward."

"*Per dio,* so I'm to welcome another stubborn male into my life?" Fiona was glad to hear Lady Achnasheen sounding more like herself, although she still leaned heavily on her husband.

"Aye, that goes without saying, my lady. Now, away with ye, Mackinnon, and leave us to get on with things without ye fidgeting around us like a cat on top of a hot stove."

"She needs me," he said with the stubbornness his wife had mentioned.

"No, my bonny laddie, she doesnae."

Lady Achnasheen turned her dark head to stare up into her husband's face. His features were strained with worry and love. "Jenny's right, *caro.* Trust that everything goes as we hope."

He leaned in and kissed her, clearly not reassured at all. "I hate to think of ye suffering, *mo leannan.*"

"*Per pietà,* it can't be helped, *tesoro.* Although I wish it were otherwise." She looked past her husband to see Fiona. Fiona realized that until now Lady Achnasheen had been so focused on what was happening in her body, she hadn't realized her guest had come upstairs to join her. "*Signora,* what are you doing here?"

"I've assisted at every birth at Bancavan since I arrived there." She stepped forward. "I'm here to help."

"That's very kind of you."

Jenny surveyed her with sharp blue eyes. "I'm no' sure a fine lady is what we need, lassie."

Fiona bit back a contemptuous snort. "Believe me, I know what's required. If you find I'm more trouble than I'm worth, I'll go away again. But if I were you, I'd welcome an extra pair of experienced hands."

Jenny still inspected her, as if waiting for her to swoon at the first sight of blood. Fiona raised her chin and returned the old woman's steady gaze.

"I'd like Mrs. Grant to stay, Jenny," Lady Achnasheen said. "She sounds like she's used to bringing *bambini* into the world."

"As long as she's willing to take orders," Jenny said doubtfully.

"You're in charge," Fiona said.

Lady Achnasheen gasped and bent against Fergus's arm. The faint color that had returned to her face drained away.

"Marina!"

"Mr. Mackinnon, really you should go." Fiona came around to support her hostess from the other side, rubbing her back in firm circles. "She's more worried about frightening you than she is about the work she has to do."

"There's..." Lady Achnasheen stopped to draw a shuddering breath. "There's a reason they call it labor, you know."

The small joke didn't make her husband smile, although Fiona had noticed that her hosts communicated with a fond teasing that did nothing to hide the love flowing beneath the humor. "I want to stay."

With a tenderness that made Fiona's heart clench in envy, Lady Achnasheen touched his stricken face. Nobody had ever loved her like this. She'd borne Christina among people who had no affection for her at all, and her husband had cared only if she delivered a boy. His disappointment at the arrival of a girl had been unconcealed. A disappointment the whole clan had shared.

"*Per favore, amore mio*, go downstairs. I'll send for you if I need you."

His gray eyes troubled, Mr. Mackinnon stared into his wife's face. Then with a reluctance Fiona could see, he gave a brief nod. "I love you, Marina. I hope ye know how much."

The tension leached from Lady Achnasheen's body, and Fiona braced as the weight shifted from Mr. Mackinnon onto her. "*Sì, lo so. Ti amo anche io, caro. Va tutto bene.* All will be well."

Fiona saw that he wanted to argue, to insist on his place at her side. She didn't mistake that it was an act of enormous devotion when he slid his arm from her waist and stepped back. "God keep ye, *mo chridhe*."

"And you, my beloved husband."

"Do you want to walk?" Fiona set her arms more firmly around Lady Achnasheen. "It might ease the pain."

"Aye, that's it, my lady. We willnae see anything to carry on about for another couple of hours yet." Jenny sent Fiona an approving glance. "Ye have done this before, it seems."

"Yes," she said. "And borne a child of my own. You won't be sorry you let me help."

"You should call me Marina." Her hostess's smile was tight-lipped with strain. "*Oddio*, I have a feeling we're soon going to be on very close terms indeed."

So did Fiona. She smiled back at the tall, dark-haired woman. "I'd be honored. And please call me Fiona."

CHAPTER SEVENTEEN

*D*iarmid glanced up as Fergus trudged into the library, and his greeting died unspoken. His friend always bestrode the world as if he owned it, especially here at Achnasheen where he was master. But tonight trouble weighed him down and cast a pall over his powerful personality.

Reminder, should Diarmid need it, of the price love extracted from its victims. Look at his father, destroyed by his enduring love for a woman who didn't know the meaning of the word.

But when he looked at Fergus, he couldn't maintain his habitual sourness on the subject of love. The circumstances here were different. The love Fergus and Marina shared had enriched both of them, brought out a generosity of spirit in her and a humility in him that had made them better people. On their own, both had been strong, but together they were stronger.

He found himself saying yet another silent prayer that the birth went well. Fergus had been married a little less than two years. He and his beloved wife deserved many happy years together, and God willing, a tribe of healthy children to bring up to find happiness of their own.

"Here." He stepped forward to offer his friend the dram he'd poured earlier. "Ye look like you need this."

As he accepted the glass, Fergus's hand was shaking. Diarmid had never seen his friend afraid, had never imagined he could be. "Thanks."

The raw anguish in Fergus's expression as he raised his eyes shocked Diarmid. He turned away to stoke the fire, to give him a moment's privacy. After a decent interval, he set down the poker and picked up his whisky.

Fergus had already drained his glass and now poured another. He lifted the decanter in a silent invitation, but Diarmid shook his head as he sank into his chair. "How are things upstairs?"

"How the hell would I know?" With a helpless gesture, Fergus slumped into the chair opposite Diarmid's. "It looks like life and death to me, but Jenny appears to be taking it all in her stride. Mrs. Grant seems verra capable."

"She's stronger than she looks. Nobody knows that better than I do. Through all that rough travel, she never uttered one word of complaint." Diarmid stared into his half-empty glass. "Between Fiona and Jenny, I'm sure Marina will be all right. She's got everything to live for, after all."

Fergus hadn't yet started his second whisky. Instead he dangled the hands holding the glass between his spread legs and stared blindly into the fire. "Diarmid, I dinna ken what the hell I'll do if Marina doesnae make it." His voice cracked with emotion. "I never thought I could love anyone the way I love that lassie. She's my soul, the reason behind my every breath."

Diarmid had never heard Fergus talk like this. In other circumstances, he might have been uncomfortable. But he could see fear for Marina drove Fergus to the brink of his control.

By God, he envied his friend. Whatever happened tonight, Fergus had experienced a great love. Diarmid wondered whether he was so clever after all to steer clear of emotional entanglements.

"Did Jenny mention how long she thought it would take?"

Fergus looked up from where he brooded into the flames. "Hours, she said."

If the child was slow arriving, Fergus would go mad with only his fears to entertain him. With sudden purpose, Diarmid stood and crossed to an inlaid wooden box on the desk. "Let's play piquet. A penny a point."

Fergus looked up with a dazed expression. "What did ye say? I wasnae attending."

"Cards." Diarmid held up the pack. "It will pass the time until we have news."

Fergus looked terrible, haggard and miserable, and the skin clung tight to the powerful bones of his face. "Ye arenae tired?"

Diarmid began shuffling the deck. "Not too tired to beat ye into penury, laddie."

With a sigh, Fergus rose. "It's the one time in history ye might have a chance of coming out ahead."

Relief flooded Diarmid. While he knew that nothing except news of a healthy mother and baby would ease Fergus's panic, a few hands of cards would help fill the wait. He opened up a mahogany games table and placed two chairs on either side. He sat on one and set the cards in the center of the green baize top.

"Ye keep telling yourself that, my friend. It might ease the pain of your drubbing."

Actually he and Fergus were very different players, but well matched for all that. Fergus played with dash and brilliance, whereas Diarmid was cool-headed and strategic. Despite his taunting, he wasn't expecting an easy win.

With another sigh, Fergus sat opposite him and the hand that cut the cards was almost steady.

Summer sun flooded into the tower bedroom through the tall windows. Marina slumped exhausted against the pillows, her face so pale that the dark circles under her eyes stood out in stark relief. Beneath the sheet, her stomach rose hard and swollen.

Fiona stood by the dressing table and prayed they would soon have an end to this. Marina was strong, but the night's travails sapped even her impressive stamina.

Someone who showed no signs of flagging was Jenny. Now she bustled across to give her mistress some herbal concoction that seemed to soothe her.

In the corner, Marina's maid Sandra fiddled with the elaborately decorated crib. Fiona hoped to heaven there would be a child to fill it before too long. They'd already been here over eight hours.

As she straightened her back, she bit back a groan. The days on horseback, ending in this difficult night, wearied her, too, although her aches and pains were nothing compared to Marina's.

For the moment, the contractions had stopped. Even Jenny seemed worried, although she did a good job of hiding it.

Berating herself for borrowing trouble, Fiona picked up Marina's brush and comb. She hoped that the smile she plastered to her face looked more convincing than it felt. "Can you sit up?"

Marina managed a smile in return. In her drawn face, her lips were bloodless. "I'm sure I can."

In such a dire situation, you learned a lot about a person in a short time. Fiona couldn't believe she'd met this woman mere hours ago. She felt like they'd been through a lifetime together.

Fiona couldn't imagine a better companion. Marina Mackinnon was brave and strong and considerate of others, even in her extremity.

"If I plait your hair away from your face, you'll be more comfortable."

"Thank you," Marina said in a whisper, struggling to shift against the pillows.

Fiona slid onto the bed behind Marina and helped her lean forward. She began to run the brush through the skeins of sweat-soaked hair clinging to face and neck.

"It shouldn't be long now," Jenny said, approaching the bed with a bowl of warm water and a flannel. With gentle efficiency, she wiped Marina's face before shifting to her arms and hands under the nightdress's loose sleeves. "You're a braw champion, my lady."

"*Per dio*, I don't feel like a champion. *Ahi, madonna...*"

Marina stifled a whimper, as another contraction shuddered through her. Fiona abandoned the half-finished plait and slid her shoulder behind the woman. When she caught Marina's hand, she hid a wince at the painfully tight grip.

"Aye, you're doing grand, my lady. That's it the noo. Breathe deep and ride out the pain."

Fiona's eyes met Jenny's, as the older woman folded up the hem of the nightdress. It was time for the baby to arrive. The contractions now came so close together, they seemed as one. Marina sank her teeth into her lip deep enough to draw blood and groaned as she pressed back into Fiona's hold.

"Scream, Marina," Fiona said, squeezing her hand. "We're almost there."

The shriek was so distant, it could be a bird flying over the loch. But it disturbed Diarmid who had drifted off in his chair near the fire. In the opposite chair, Fergus immediately stirred from his wakeful doze and leaped to his feet.

"What...what is it?" Diarmid asked groggily, rubbing his face and feeling his beard scratch under his palm. With the next cry, he recognized the sound as a woman in agony.

"That was Marina." Fergus glanced at the ormolu clock on the mantelpiece. It was after nine. "I cannae bear it. I'm going up there."

Before Diarmid struggled to his feet, Fergus had slammed out of the library. Diarmid cast a quick look around the untidy room, with its dirty glasses and playing cards scattered across the gaming table. They'd played until dawn, when even his attempts to make sure Fergus won weren't enough to distract his friend from what happened upstairs. He knuckled the sleep from his eyes, stretched, and set off in pursuit of Fergus.

The screams grew louder and longer and more guttural, the closer he got to the tower. When he reached the top of the stairs, he also heard Fergus arguing with someone. He turned onto the landing and saw skinny, diminutive Sandra ranged in front of the closed bedroom door like Cerberus guarding the gates of the underworld.

"*Non può entrare, signore. Non è appropriato.*"

Fergus's fists bunched at his sides. "Blast ye, get out of my way, Sandra."

"*La signora* Marina, she in good hands," Sandra said in a fractured mixture of Italian and English. "*Va tutto bene.*"

Another broken cry from inside made Diarmid question that reassuring statement. Anxiety knotted his gut. Until tonight, when there was a chance they might lose her, he hadn't realized how much he'd come to love Marina. And dear God above, he doubted Fergus would survive if the worst happened.

"Fergus, dinna shout at Sandra," he said in a calming voice, stepping up and taking his friend's arm to stop him barging into the room. "You ken that men have nae place in the birthing chamber."

"Ye dinna understand." Fergus turned a despairing face on him, and Diarmid's stomach clenched with agonizing pity when he saw tears glittering in his friend's eyes. "I have to be with her."

Another scream from inside, then a silence descended. Diarmid's grip on Fergus's arm tightened.

That silence couldn't mean Marina had lost the fight. It just couldn't be true. By all that was holy, it couldn't.

"Fergus..."

The silence went on and on. Diarmid's blood turned to ice.

Finally and unmistakably through the closed door came the sound of a baby crying.

"What the devil..." Fergus choked out and broke free of Diarmid. Pushing Sandra out of the way, he shoved the door open and stood on the threshold. Behind him, Diarmid peered into the room.

Marina leaned against the pillows and reached out to take a remarkably red and noisy scrap of humanity from Fiona's arms. Marina's face was drawn and pale, and glowing with an elation that made mockery of all the pain that had gone before.

Jenny stood beside the bed, looking every one of her seventy-odd years, but he couldn't doubt her joy either. Fiona glanced up as she passed the baby to Marina, and the smile she gave Diarmid sliced a hole in his brimming heart.

"Marina?" Fergus asked, his voice thick with emotion. He took an unsteady step into the room. "*Mo leannan?*"

"*Caro...*" she began, as her arms closed around the baby.

Jenny stalked across to him, speaking over whatever Marina meant to say. "Ye shouldnae be here, Mackinnon. Let me get your lady all clean and tidied up, and the wee bairn as well. Then ye can greet both of them properly."

"To hell with that." Fergus strode forward past Jenny. "Are ye all right, *mo chridhe?*"

"Mackinnon..." Diarmid could hear that the laird's presence offended every scrap of Jenny's sense of decorum.

Marina's tired smile for her husband was so laden with love that Diarmid looked away, uncomfortable to intrude on this private moment. "Come and meet our daughter, then you'd better go before this dragon turns you to ash, *tesoro.*"

Astonishment and gratification filled Fergus's face as he approached the bed, hesitant as Diarmid had never seen him hesitant. "Och, our daughter?"

"*Sì, nostra figlia, amore mio.*"

Diarmid watched Fergus reach out to touch the baby's cheek, then he turned and left the room. Fergus didn't need him anymore, and at this time, he had no place in his friend's communion with his family.

He shut the door behind him and stopped on the landing to catch his breath. A wide smile curved his lips. Hurrah for Fergus. Hurrah for Marina. He couldn't be happier for them. And hurrah for the bonny wee lassie, too, whatever her name was going to be. She'd had a big night of it as well.

Behind him, the door opened, and he turned to see Fiona carrying a pile of dirty towels. "Diarmid..."

She looked tired. She looked relieved. She looked heartbreakingly beautiful.

He frowned. "What the devil are ye wearing, lassie?"

She glanced down at her loose linen blouse and red and black plaid skirt, caught at the waist with a black leather girdle laced in front. Her lovely hair was plaited away from her face in a simple style. "I couldn't stay in my nightdress when I had to run up and down stairs all night. Kirsty, one of the maids, is about my size, so she lent me this."

A tired laugh escaped him. The world had been a cold and empty place before he'd heard that baby's cry. Now it seemed full of warmth and promise. "Ye look like a shepherdess in a folk tale."

With a weary gesture, she brushed stray tendrils of hair back from her forehead. "If I do, I'm a shepherdess in need of a good wash."

He frowned at the laundry in her arms. "Ye dinna have to rush around like a servant."

She shrugged. "The lassies have been up all night, too. Jenny told them to go to bed a couple of hours ago, but they're sitting down in the kitchen to hear the news. I'm off to tell them, so I may as well take something with me when I go."

Jenny appeared in the doorway behind her. "Fiona, come back as soon as you've told them downstairs that all is bonny. We havenae finished here yet."

"Jenny, she's been up all night…" Diarmid said.

As an eleven-year-old boy, he'd met Jenny the same day he'd met Fergus. After he'd spent the night stranded on a mountain with his cousin Hamish, the old woman had checked him for any ill effects. Since that day, she'd never treated him with particular deference. Now she sent him a reproving glance. "Och, Mr. Diarmid, dinnae ye take away the best pair of hands I've had to help me in years. When the job's done, we can all sleep."

He'd noticed before that Fiona had a talent for making people like her. It had happened at Invertavey with John and Mags and the rest of his household. He shouldn't be surprised that it happened here, too.

"I'd like to help, Diarmid," Fiona said.

"Aye, your lady's been a marvel. It was lucky ye brought the lassie here. There were a few moments when I couldnae have managed without her."

His lady? If only Fiona were.

Idle thoughts. His mermaid was only interested in his ability to rescue her daughter. The surprise was that he looked at her now and realized that he'd give his right arm to change that.

Because God help him, when he'd seen his best friend smiling down at his wife and child, the woman who had filled his mind wasn't Marina, but Fiona.

CHAPTER EIGHTEEN

"By God, Bruce Mackenzie makes the finest whisky in Scotland," Diarmid said on a sigh of pleasure, as he leaned back in his usual chair in Fergus's well-stocked library.

Fergus smiled at him from the other side of the hearth. "Aye. The laddie has a touch for it."

A comfortable silence fell, broken only by the crackle of flames in the grate. It was late. Fiona and Marina were upstairs with Fergus's three-day-old daughter, Eilidh. The household slowly began to settle into a new routine after her dramatic arrival.

The doctor had turned up the same afternoon Eilidh was born and had pronounced mother and child to be in perfect health. But while Eilidh might be in perfect health, she was far from a perfect sleeper. Both Fergus and Marina were looking frayed, as they adjusted to life as new parents. Frayed but happy. Diarmid surveyed his friend now and could almost see a golden glow of contentment surrounding him.

Another thing that pleased him was that so far, there had been no sign of the Grants. Achnasheen proved to be the perfect sanctuary. He doubted they'd ever guess where he and Fiona had taken refuge.

The problem, as he'd told Fergus and Marina the night he arrived, was that as long as Fiona's kinsmen kept Christina, they knew she must eventually come out of hiding. If this turned into a waiting game, the Grants had all the advantages.

The thought darkened his easy mood. While he and his mermaid lingered in comfort at Achnasheen, a wee girl remained in the clutches of her brutish relatives.

"Recent events have distracted us from your problem," Fergus said, proving his thoughts moved along similar lines.

"A worthwhile distraction."

"Aye." Fergus smiled. His friend had smiled a lot since Eilidh and Marina had emerged unscathed from their ordeal. "I willnae argue with that. But it's time we decided what to do about the Grants."

Diarmid sat up and set his glass on the table at his elbow with a determined gesture. "Fiona and I have to go and get Christina."

Fiona had suggested several times that they leave, but he'd argued her into waiting until she regained her strength. Her agreement had been reluctant. He sympathized with her impatience, but only today had he believed that at last she was up to traveling across Scotland.

"Aye. But it willnae be easy. The Grants will expect ye to turn up, and they'll do their best to hold onto the bairn."

"And to get Fiona back, too. Allan is set on marrying her to his brother, and they've already taken a deal of trouble to track her down to

Invertavey. They willnae surrender her without a fight."

Fergus frowned down into his half-full glass. "I've been thinking about your dilemma."

"Aye?"

"Aye." Fergus looked up. "While ye go and try to get Christina, I'll head for Edinburgh and see what legal routes are available to restore Fiona's daughter to her. For a start, under law, she must have some claim to a widow's portion from Ian's estate. Ye also mentioned there was a house she inherited."

"That's a bonny idea." Diarmid wanted to kick himself. He'd been so focused on prizing Christina out of the Grants' clutches, he hadn't considered bringing the weight of the law against them. Yet he was accounted to be a thoughtful man who considered every angle before he acted. Fiona Grant had him in a spin, for sure.

"Och, I do have the occasional spurt of inspiration," Fergus said drily. He paused and shot Diarmid a look he didn't altogether understand. "If it comes to a court case, which it verra well may, telling the court that Fiona has means of her own puts her in a better position to gain custody of Christina."

"Fiona's nae longer a penniless runaway. She has powerful supporters. Ye and Marina. Me. Hamish, once I get him involved."

"Aye, that's true."

When Fergus paused again, Diarmid frowned. His friend built up to saying something important. He knew the signs.

Fergus drank some more whisky before he went on. "Although her position would be even stronger, if she was married to one of those powerful supporters."

A silence as hard and sharp as a slap crashed down and sucked all the air from the room.

"Married..." Diarmid said stupidly, feeling like that one word from Fergus punched the breath out of him.

"Aye. It would solve a gey lot of problems."

His hands clenched on the arms of his chair, and every muscle tightened in rejection. "It's..."

Fergus's eyes were compassionate as they rested on him. "It's a big step. And really ye dinna owe it to her. After all, it's only chance that got ye involved in this mess in the first place."

Chance or destiny?

From the moment he found Fiona on that beach, he'd felt fated to become her defender. These last days of fleeing the Grants and finding shelter at Achnasheen had only strengthened that conviction.

"I can see the idea doesnae appeal." Fergus rose to pick up the decanter and refill their glasses, as if he hadn't just shattered all Diarmid's ideas about his future. "Forget I said anything."

Married to Fiona? The suggestion was absurd.

Except it wasn't.

It was no real effort to picture her as mistress of Invertavey. God forgive him, he could picture more than that. Fiona in his bed every night. Fiona presenting him with a child and wearing that same proud, exhausted smile he'd seen on Marina's face three days ago. Fiona at his side as they made plans and established a life and grew old together.

No. No, it was impossible.

"She doesnae want me." His tone was grim. He couldn't help recalling that farrago of an attempt at seduction in the bothy.

Fergus considered that statement with a frown. "But ye want her."

It wasn't a question. Why would it be? Diarmid might struggle to hide his powerful yen for the woman he'd brought to Achnasheen, but Fergus knew him like a brother.

He made a helpless gesture. "Och, how could I fail to want the lassie? She's brave and stalwart and in trouble."

"And bonny." Fergus set the decanter back on the sideboard and sat down, his attention unwavering on Diarmid. "Ye always swore you'd never marry a beautiful woman."

An unamused smile flattened Diarmid's lips. "After what happened between my parents, can ye blame me?"

Fergus shook his head. "Fiona's no' like your mother. Your mother followed her passions, with nae thought for her responsibilities. Fiona has put herself at considerable risk to save her daughter, including trusting herself to strangers for help. I'd say she has a loyal and gallant heart."

"Nobody ever said that about my mother," Diarmid said bitterly.

"No." Fergus lifted his glass to take a sip. After a thorny silence, he went on. "It's a huge change, a lifelong commitment. You'd forsake any chance of finding a woman ye loved and marrying her."

Diarmid tried to imagine such a lady, but it was impossible when Fiona's face filled his mind. "After what Fiona's been through, I doubt she wants another husband."

"No, I ken that. She's like a mistreated filly, shying at the sight of the bridle."

Dash it, Diarmid should reject this outlandish scheme out of hand. Marriage to Fiona was a crazy idea. After all, a fortnight ago, he'd had no idea she even existed.

If he went ahead with this, it was possible he'd never have a wife in his bed or legitimate children to succeed him. Fiona's painful, arousing, distressing attempt at seduction had shown him that any man who wanted her needed to be kind and patient and ready to forsake his expectations of passion. At least in the short term.

But he was kind. And he was patient. And if a marriage protected her from the Grants, he had time to help her face her fears.

Heat flooded him as he imagined luring Fiona into pleasure's realm. Too quickly, the heat threatened to turn into a conflagration. He struggled to clear his head and made himself think of what else Fergus had said. "Do ye think a legal challenge is feasible?"

Fergus shrugged. "I'm no' an expert, but I imagine Fiona has grounds to claim her daughter back. Whether a court would go so far as to agree with me, I dinna ken. But it's worth asking the question."

"A legal solution offers a permanent defense against the Grants."

"It means she wouldnae have to hide for the rest of her life—or flee to America."

Diarmid frowned. "She believed those were her only alternatives. Abandoning the child to her kinsmen is unthinkable. The girl will be forced into marriage when she's little more than a bairn. Fiona already knows what hell that promises. She's lived through it."

"I agree." Fergus paused. "If we take this matter to court, the mother's moral character will come into question. I've never met the Grants, but ye give me nae reason to expect a clean fight."

Temper had Diarmid surging to his feet. "Are ye casting slurs on the lady's reputation?"

Fergus didn't shift from his chair, although his russet eyebrows rose with eloquent mockery. "Hell, laddie, you've got it bad. It's perfectly clear that you've never laid a finger on the lassie, if only because frustration's got ye wound tighter than a watch spring."

A painful flush burned Diarmid's cheeks. With a defeated sigh, he slumped back into his chair. "I dinna ken what the devil's the matter with me."

"You're in a tizz over a lass." Fergus raised his whisky in his direction. "It happens to the best of us."

Diarmid ground his teeth. "She's everything I dinnae want."

"And everything ye do."

"Aye, that she is," he admitted glumly and lifted his own glass to drink. But not even Bruce Mackenzie's finest could shift the desolation settling in his heart. "But she's been hurt. Hurt deeply. I'd rather cut off my hands than hurt her again."

Impatience flattened Fergus's lips. "Then don't." He took a mouthful of whisky. "But getting back to what I was saying—"

"Before I tried to knock your block off?" Diarmid said in self-derision.

"Aye, then. Ye know that she's as chaste as the driven snow. So do I. But she was alone with this drowned fisherman."

"He was an old man."

"Old men have urges, as your lady could tell ye better than most." Fergus didn't wait for Diarmid to argue. "Then she was alone with ye at Invertavey."

"Hardly alone. The place is crawling with servants."

"Your servants."

"And she was half-dead when I carried her up from the beach. Only a barbarian would have—"

"I'm looking at things the way the Grants will, as they'll try and get a judge to see it. If there's even a whisper that Fiona has taken a lover, the court case will have nae chance of succeeding."

"I can produce witnesses to swear that my behavior was all that was proper."

He stifled the memory of that first night in Fiona's bedroom. On that occasion, if she'd been another woman in other circumstances, events would have turned out very differently.

But then if she'd been another woman, he wouldn't have wanted her so desperately.

"I'm sure. But what about your two nights alone in the hills? And there's an inn full of patrons to swear ye rode off with the lassie with nae chaperone in sight."

"Oh, hell," Diarmid said, his self-righteousness crumbling to nothing. "I swear I didnae touch her."

That wasn't true either. If he'd accepted what she'd offered, however reluctantly, they'd have become lovers in that isolated bothy.

"I believe ye. But it's the appearance of sin that's the issue, no' whether ye sinned."

Fate had indeed stalked Diarmid ever since he'd met Fiona. The conclusion became inescapable. "I'll have to marry her," he said slowly.

Fergus's gray eyes were alight with sympathy and understanding. Too much understanding, if you asked Diarmid. "I believe ye do."

"She may no' have me." He wasn't sure whether he spoke the words in despair or hope.

Fergus set his glass down on a side table. "If it means strengthening her hand with Christina, she'd marry ye tomorrow."

"Aye, I know." He felt trapped. Even worse, Fiona would feel trapped. "I dinna want to marry a woman who only takes me as a means to an end."

A woman who might never accept his touch as a man. Especially when he had a horrible suspicion that his desire for her was a lifelong affliction.

Fergus looked somber. "I'd always hoped you'd find the same happiness in marriage that Marina and I enjoy."

Diarmid grimaced as cruel reality overwhelmed him. This ending had been ordained since he'd ridden up to the Thistle. Good God, before that. From when he'd brought his mermaid back to the house after the shipwreck.

"I should have realized it would come to this."

"Aye." Fergus's expression remained austere. "Of course, there are those who would argue the lassie is nothing to ye. Not kith or kin. A stranger. You've already done plenty for her. Making this final sacrifice asks too much of ye."

Diarmid met his friend's steady regard. "I've offered her my help. I've pledged my allegiance. As far as she trusts any man, she trusts me. I cannae leave her flat. And what becomes of her if I do? Ye and I both know the likely outcome if she runs off with Christina, without a shilling to her name and with nobody to protect her. She'll find herself on the streets. And her daughter, too."

"Aye. And that's if she manages to winkle Christina out of the Grants' clutches."

"If she doesnae, she'll end up either having to sell herself, or give up and marry Thomas. If they dinna kill her first. She hasnae said much, but it's clear they've abused her. They'll have a burden of anger to work off, now she's put them to all this trouble. Damn it, but right from the start, I dinna see what else I could have done."

"I dinna either. You and your infernal chivalry. It's really got ye into trouble this time, laddie. You've always been a white knight."

"Now I'm paying for it," he said. "Worse, Fiona will pay for it."

Fergus rose and clapped him on the shoulder. "Chin up, laddie. This tangle is still a mess of knots and snarls. There's a gey lot of untangling yet to do. We'll find our way in the end."

Diarmid raised his head and made himself smile, although in his chest, his heart was leaden with foreboding. "Wish me happy, Fergus. I have a feeling I'm getting married this week."

CHAPTER NINETEEN

The next morning, Diarmid knocked on the tower room's door. He'd hoped to catch Fiona at breakfast, but she'd come down early then gone upstairs to help Marina with Eilidh. Kirsty opened the door and bobbed in his direction, before she headed downstairs on some errand. A new baby at Achnasheen meant people were always running up and down stairs.

"Diarmid, *buongiorno*," Marina said with a smile, one hand tugging up the bodice of her dress while the other cuddled dark-haired Eilidh close. "Come in."

He'd interrupted the baby's feeding. Embarrassed, he hovered on the threshold, feeling he had no right to enter this purely feminine domain. "Marina, I dinna want to intrude."

Fiona wore her borrowed blouse and plaid skirt and sat on the window seat. Her glorious hair was confined in a plait. The bright sun flooding through the windows lit her in gold and made her look like a princess, despite her humble wardrobe.

Diarmid bit back a groan. Right now, he didn't need any more reminders of how bonny she was.

She was sewing something small and white for the baby. The smile she greeted him with was an uncomfortable reminder that he'd promised to do everything in his power to help her. Last night's discomfiting discussion with Fergus had revealed just how far that promise extended.

"Good morning, Diarmid," she said.

"Good morning, Fiona. It's ye I've come looking for, actually. Would you care to join me for a walk in the rose garden?"

Marina shot him a sharp look, full of inquiry. He wondered if Fergus had told his wife about their conversation. He suspected his friend had. "First come and say hello to your goddaughter."

Shock banished his conflicted feelings about what he was about to do. "Goddaughter?"

"Didn't Fergus ask you last night?" She sighed with fond irritation. "*Cavolo*, we arranged that he was going to. Men!"

He and Fergus had had other business to cover in the library. But even that grim thought couldn't altogether stifle his pleasure. "Are ye sure?"

"I can't think of anyone I'd rather have as my daughter's spiritual guardian. Fergus and I already think of you as part of the family. This makes it official. I hope you'll say yes."

"I'd be honored." He meant that to his marrow. Fergus and Marina were the finest people he knew. Swallowing a lump in his throat, he crossed to kiss Marina's cheek. "Thank ye."

"Would you like to hold her?"

"Aye, I would indeed."

With confident hands, he reached for Eilidh. He was well used to weans. As Laird of Invertavey, he met all his tenants' babies, and several of his cousins had children.

Eilidh grizzled at the unwarranted jiggling. When she settled, she opened cloudy blue eyes and stared up at his face. He knew it was too early for her to make any sense of what she saw, but he couldn't help feeling that this moment established a lifelong link.

"She's beautiful," he said softly.

Tiny, rosy, and with perfect wee toes and fingers. With a pang, he wondered if he'd ever hold a child of his own like this. Should Fiona agree to his proposal, there was a good chance he wouldn't.

He'd never much thought about children. He'd never much thought about marriage, except as a duty awaiting him in the distant future. How very sad that only now, cuddling Eilidh, did he realize how much he'd like children. Just at the point when it was likely that he signed away any chance to have them.

"Good morning, wee Eilidh. I'm your godfather, don't ye know?"

The baby wriggled and made a fearsome face. He laughed and passed her back to her mother. "I think this bonny lassie needs some attention, Marina."

"*Porca miseria*, she always needs attention," Marina said, clearly not minding at all. She rested Eilidh on her shoulder and started to pat her gently on the back.

Diarmid was impressed at her adept handling of the baby. Up until now, those slender olive-skinned hands had been more used to wielding a paint brush than cradling an infant.

When he looked up, he caught Fiona watching him with an arrested expression on her face. He arched a questioning eyebrow at her, and to his surprise, she blushed and fixed her attention on her sewing.

"Fiona, are ye free to speak to me?" If they were to do this mad thing, better they did it quickly, before Fiona's reputation suffered any more damage.

"I'll just finish this," she mumbled, still avoiding his eyes.

"Very well. I'll meet ye downstairs when you're ready."

The hand holding the scissors she used to cut the thread was shaking. He supposed that seeing Marina with Eilidh must remind her of Christina. He said his farewells and headed out the door.

Fiona took longer to arrive than he'd expected. He had time to look around the sunny enclosed garden and wonder if perhaps this wasn't the most appropriate place for his proposal. The rich scent of roses made his head swim, and while the ancient walls had a practical purpose, built to keep out the persistent winds, they also created an air of privacy that suggested a lovers' tryst. A small statue of Cupid held court over the scene, and brightly colored butterflies fluttered from flower to flower.

As Diarmid took in the grassy hollow with its neat beds of lushly blossoming rosebushes and fragrant climbing roses nodding against the soft red brick, he couldn't help noting the romantic picture it made. Definitely not the atmosphere he wanted. What he was about to do held no trace of romance at all, damn it.

Something told him he was no longer alone. He glanced up to see Fiona framed like a painting in one of the lichened stone arches.

"You've changed," he said stupidly, as though it mattered. This drugged air played havoc with his common sense.

She glanced down at the russet muslin gown. Her hair was pinned up in a mass of curls, just untidy enough to summon images of her rising from her bed.

Diarmid looked at her and felt sick with longing. And knew it did him not one ounce of good.

He tried not to think of how bonny she'd looked when she smiled at wee Eilidh.

"Yes, it's hard to keep neat and tidy around a baby." With a self-conscious gesture, she smoothed the richly colored skirt. "And Sandra got a maggot in her head, and wouldn't let me go without doing some titivating."

"To good effect," he said with a delayed attempt at gallantry, and made himself smile. "Ye look lovely."

"Thank you," she said uncertainly. Around her neck, she wore a small cameo pinned to a black velvet ribbon. One white hand rose to touch it, as if for reassurance.

"Please sit down." He gestured to one of the stone benches set in alcoves around the garden.

She moved to perch on the seat. As she settled, the soft material drifted around her slender body. Diarmid found himself wishing that this was a real proposal leading to a real marriage, one promising mutual affection and desire.

That dream shifted out of your reach the minute ye decided to help Fiona, laddie. Even if you knew then what it was going to cost you, could ye have left her to die? No' bloody likely. Every step you've taken since that morning at Canmara Beach has brought you to this point.

"Is it the Grants?" she asked in a small voice.

"Aye." When she stiffened, he made a placatory gesture. "No, they havenae caught up with us. As far as I ken, they still have nae idea where we are. But Fergus has been looking at the best way to proceed against them. And he feels—we feel—that regularizing our association is essential."

She looked both puzzled and wary as she studied his face. "Regularizing?"

"We need to get married, Fiona."

CHAPTER TWENTY

"No. Never." The denial escaped before Fiona even had a chance to think about it.

Although her knees felt like jelly and ready to fold under her, she surged to her feet. She stiffened against the weakness. By heaven, she refused to fall down. Over the last week, she'd spent far too much time crumpling into a helpless heap. No longer.

Diarmid whitened, and a tiny muscle in his cheek began to jerk and dance as if he ground his teeth. "I know ye dinna want to marry me."

Despite her rudeness, his voice remained calm. She'd never been so grateful for his self-control. It was one of the things she most admired about him. At Bancavan, the men used their fists first and thought about why later. If at all.

Not that Diarmid was likely to hit her. She'd come to trust him that much.

"I don't want to marry anyone," she said, barely hiding a shudder. Her retreat came to an abrupt halt when she bumped into the bench behind her.

He managed to dredge up a reassuring smile. Somehow that just made everything worse. The understanding in his expression made her cringe. "Will ye let me explain?"

His face was serious and earnest, with no hint of covetousness. Her mind moved past the instinctive urge to run and hide and began to consider what happened here. This wasn't a man inviting a woman he wanted to swive to become his wife. This was something to do with strategy. Her answer must remain no, but at least she felt calm enough to hear him out.

"Very well," she said through stiff lips. "I'll listen, but I can already tell that it's going to be some mad scheme that will do nobody any good."

"I hope you'll change your mind about that by the time I've finished," he said calmly.

Without shifting her gaze from him, she subsided back onto the bench. "Tell me."

He'd asked for her attention, but now seemed at a loss as to how to continue. He ran a hand through his thick black hair, leaving it disheveled. Even someone as impervious to masculine attractions as Fiona couldn't help thinking how charming confusion looked on Diarmid Mactavish.

"Last night in the library, Fergus and I had a long discussion about your situation," he said eventually.

"Did you indeed?" Her shock at the idea of marriage had receded far enough to leave room for a moment's irritation. "It didn't occur to you to include me in your deliberations?"

The surprise in his eyes revealed that it hadn't. And reminded her that for all his fine qualities, he was still a man with all the effortless assumption of privilege that implied. "We started talking, and things went from there."

She linked her hands in her lap and kept her voice steady. "I've hardly been at my best since we met, and I've relied on you far too much. But believe me, I'm more than capable of choosing my own future."

"I know ye are." A smile eased the stern line of his lips. "I wouldnae dream of trying to bully ye."

More charm. Because she found herself weakening, she sounded more annoyed than she was. "Yet that's what you're doing. I won't marry you, just because you propose and say it's the best thing to do. So far, you've made all the decisions without consulting me. I won't have it anymore."

"I owe you an apology." He ran his hand through his hair again. It was a characteristic gesture when he was at a loss, she'd noticed. "I'm used to being in charge."

"Aye, you are." His apology went a small way toward mollifying her ruffled feelings. "And you must know I'm grateful for everything you've done. But that doesn't give you the right—"

"To take over? No, it doesnae, but I hope you'll see the reasoning once I set it all out."

"Please sit down." She shifted along the bench and gestured to the space beside her. "I feel like I've been hauled into the headmaster's office because I'm in big trouble."

Fiona was struggling to maintain her emotional distance, but it was difficult when he gave her another smile, sheepish this time. "Duly chastised, I take my place. I humbly beseech my lady to hear my plea."

"No need to go overboard."

As he sat beside her, she couldn't stop her lips twitching at his exaggerated manner. She noted that he kept a couple of inches clear between them.

No, this proposal was nothing to do with ardor.

An unexpected pang of disappointment stung her, although ardor was the last thing she wanted from her champion.

He didn't start where she thought he would, with talk of marriage. "Fergus thinks that ye may have some legal recourse against the Grants."

Surprise made her sit up straight. "In the courts?"

"Aye. You're of age. You're the child's mother, a closer relative than any of the Grants. It would be different if Christina's father was still alive, but he's not. If you want to sue for custody of your daughter, ye have a strong case. Especially if you make it clear it's in the child's interest. It's still legal for twelve-year-old girls to marry in Scotland, but the practice is considered barbarous and old-fashioned."

Good Lord, she was so unworldly. It hadn't even occurred to her that she had any choice but to steal Christina away and disappear to somewhere the Grants would never find her. "But that means—"

"A permanent solution where ye can keep your identity and so can Christina. God willing, you might even have some hope of squeezing an allowance out of Allan Grant. Ye brought assets to your marriage with Ian. And you're Allan's brother's widow. Under the law, ye have rights."

She stamped on the seedling of hope that sprouted in her heart. "Allan will never let me go, and he's chary to put out a penny, once it's found its way into the family coffers."

"If there's a judgment in your favor, he'll have nae choice."

"It sounds grand." She made a helpless gesture. "I have no money for lawyers. I may be naive. But I know these things cost good coin. I don't even own the clothes I stand up in."

"We'll talk about money after it's all done."

Meaning he intended to pay for any legal action. The weight of what she owed Diarmid Mactavish was already crushing. She couldn't bear to fall further into his debt.

But that was an argument for later. "And the courts will take forever, while all the time, my daughter suffers in captivity."

"As it's urgent, we may be able to request an emergency session. Fergus is going to Edinburgh to see what his solicitors have to say about your circumstances."

Someone else to whom she'd owe a crippling debt. "But he's just become a father. This is so much trouble for him. Why on earth…" Then she stopped. "I see. It's because of you, not me. He and Marina said they'd do anything for you."

He looked a little uncomfortable. "They like ye, too."

"They've known me all of four days. I'm a stranger."

"Who's suffered a great injustice."

"Which is enough to make someone extend the hand of sympathy, not to send a man dashing off to Edinburgh when his child is scarcely a week old. And what do we do in the meantime? Stay here and twiddle our thumbs?"

"No. We go back to your original plan. We find Christina and steal her away. The minute the Grants hear of any legal case, they'll whisk the girl off to where we'll never find her."

She straightened. This sounded more like what she had in mind. The legal angle was promising, but what she wanted most of all was her child in her care and safe from the Grants. "Really?"

Diarmid smiled at her. "Really."

"Then let's go." She rose to her feet.

He studied her from where he sat on the bench. "No' yet. That's where the other part of the plan comes in."

The prospect of setting out to retrieve her daughter had almost made her forget where this conversation had started. Her excitement disintegrated, and dread tasted bitter on her tongue.

"You want to talk about getting married," she said flatly.

"Aye, I do." His expression was implacable.

"I don't want to marry again." She was already shaking her head. "If you knew the nightmare I've been through, you'd have enough pity not to ask me."

As he stood and caught her hand, his eyes softened. "Fiona, I ken—or I can guess—what you've endured. I wouldnae ask this, if it wasnae the only way."

For a moment, Fiona let her hand rest in his. It was mad, but his strength flowed into her, bolstering her against quaking terror.

But his strength only weakened her resolve against doing what he wanted. She wrenched away and began to wring her hands in distress.

"It can't be the only way. I won't believe that. How can we marry? I've only known you for a couple of weeks."

She was grateful that he didn't try to touch her again. "That's long enough for ye to learn I've got your best interests at heart."

Hot tears of rage and frustration pricked her eyes. She had the odious sensation that he backed her into a corner.

"And what about your best interests, Diarmid?" she asked in a broken voice. "Don't they matter?"

"I said I placed myself at your service. I meant it."

"And you get nothing in return?"

"I get the satisfaction of doing down the Grants. Since Allan Grant tried to shoot me, no' to mention discovering what they did to ye at Bancavan, trust me, that's a major inducement to help."

She shook her head again, not that it seemed to make any mark on his determination. "It's not enough."

"It's something." His voice hardened. "A legal solution is the only way ye and your daughter can have security, Fiona. The courts willnae give a child to a single woman without means. They will give her to Lady Invertavey, who has the full backing of her powerful husband, a laird and a magistrate. No' to mention a man with a network of aristocratic connections throughout Scotland."

"I can't do this to you," she said dully, looking across the garden and seeing only darkness instead of the spectacular roses. The awful truth was that she was mightily tempted. She wasn't blind to the good sense of what he said, but her conscience balked at tying him to her for life. "I just can't. Don't ask me."

Diarmid went on as if he hadn't heard her. "The courts willnae give Christina to a woman living openly with a man to whom she isnae married, nor to a woman who has been alone in that man's company as they traveled halfway across the Highlands."

Shock made her face him. "But we didn't..."

"I know," he said gently. "But as Fergus said, the appearance of sin is what counts, no' the sin itself."

This time her tears welled up beyond her control and trickled down her cheeks. "Diarmid, I'm sorry. I'm so very, very sorry."

His mouth curved down in a bleak smile, as he passed her his handkerchief. She always seemed to rely on him for a handkerchief. She relied on him for more than that.

God help her, if they went through with this lunatic plan, she'd be relying on him as long as she lived.

The thought stiffened her backbone. She couldn't believe he offered to do this for her. His generosity and self-sacrifice beggared imagination. But despite that, she couldn't allow him to proceed.

"If we marry, it's forever," she said in a thick voice.

"I know." Almost hesitantly, he took her arm and steered her back to the bench. He sat beside her, keeping that decorous distance between them.

"What happens if you find a lady you want to marry, and you can't because you've done this mad, gallant thing?"

He didn't answer immediately but stared down at where his elegant hands rested on his knees. "Ye heard all about my mother when you were at Invertavey."

She frowned. The statement seemed a million miles from his attempts to coax her into accepting his proposal. "She ran away with a lover and died in the Indies, they said."

"They were right." That muscle in his cheek returned to its erratic dance. She could see he loathed talking about this. "They probably didnae tell ye that my father fell in love with her at first sight at a ball in London. She was one of the Macgrath sisters, two famously beautiful girls from a humble background. Both of the lassies made stellar marriages, at least in a worldly sense."

"No love?"

"Och, there was love, all right," he said bitterly. "My father worshipped my mother until the day he died. He died with her name on his lips, though by that time, she'd been buried five years in a fever pit in Jamaica, with her twenty-year-old paramour dead beside her."

"Your father had a steadfast heart," Fiona said, still unsure what Diarmid was trying to tell her.

"A heart that stayed steadfast through years of infidelity and humiliation."

She frowned. "Are you afraid I'll lead you a similar dance?"

"No, you're nothing like my mother." He turned his head to give her a brief glance. "But because of what she did to my father—and to me—I always swore I wouldnae marry a beautiful woman. And you're the most beautiful woman I've ever seen, Fiona."

It was absurd, but even at this harrowing moment, she felt a trickle of pleasure to know he thought her beautiful. Particularly absurd when until now her looks had brought her nothing but trouble. "I'll never take a man into my bed."

"I believe ye," he said. "I wonder if perhaps ye and I can find a wee measure of happiness with a bond closer to friendship than the mania my father had for my mother."

"Don't you want what Marina and Fergus have? They're happy, and it's clear they love one another."

"Aye, they do. They're lucky."

"You could be lucky, Diarmid."

"Ye don't understand." He shifted on the seat until he looked into her face. "I'm saying this isnae a love match, what we're talking about. But that doesnae mean it cannae work. You and I could establish a good life together with Christina. Ye like Invertavey."

"How could I not? That was where I experienced real kindness for the first time since my father died."

His tone turned hesitant. "And I think...I hope ye like me."

"Of course I do." She spread her hands in a helpless gesture. "You're a good man."

"Then let's try this. After we've seen off the Grants, if ye discover you cannae endure living with me, I promise to give you an allowance and set you and Christina up wherever ye choose. I swear you willnae be worse off for knowing me, Fiona."

"But you will be." Damn it, she was starting to cry again. One shaking hand raised his handkerchief to wipe her eyes, as she went on in a raw voice. "Because marriage is more than chats by the fireside and jolly outings and running an estate. A marriage is a man and woman in bed together, and I told you, I'll never willingly do that again. Even with a husband. Even with someone to whom I owe so much."

Fiona could see that he didn't like the way she harped on obligation, but surely he must know that what he offered placed an intolerable burden of gratitude upon her.

"If I can bear a chaste marriage, I'm sure ye can," he said with the first hint of resentment he'd shown.

"But you shouldn't have to." She blinked back more tears. "And don't you want children? What about an heir for Invertavey?"

She couldn't help remembering how right he'd looked holding Eilidh. This was a man who was born to be a father. The sight of big, powerful Diarmid Mactavish cradling the wee baby had stirred a strange longing inside her.

"The estate isnae entailed. I can leave it where I wish." That muscle still danced in his cheek, proof that he wasn't as composed as he seemed. "I can leave it to ye or to Christina. Or my cousin Hamish and any bairns he might have."

She stood up and stared at him, appalled at what he was giving up for her sake. "That can't be enough for you."

Diarmid met her eyes, and she read both resignation and stalwart strength in his eyes. Neither reassured her. "It will have to be."

"I can't accept this sacrifice. Not from a stranger." She made a sweeping gesture of denial. "Not when it costs you so much and costs me nothing."

His lips flattened, and he looked old as she'd never seen him before. "Your pride objects to what I'm offering."

"My pride. My principles. My heart. My soul. You've already done so much for me, more than any other man would ever have done. And you've asked nothing in return." She swallowed to loosen a throat so tight that it hurt to speak. "I honor you for it. I'd reached a point where I believed true goodness was unknown in this wicked world. You've shown me I was wrong." Her voice lowered to an urgent rasp as she went on. "It would be heinous to repay that goodness with an act that deprives you of the hope of love, an heir, grandchildren, the life that you have every right to lead. I won't do it, and you can't make me."

Fiona folded her arms and stood square facing him, for once firm on her feet. Nothing he could say would shift her. She'd decided her fate, and she meant to abide by that decision. There would be some other way to defeat the Grants. There must be.

Diarmid didn't immediately respond to that defiant little speech. Instead, he bent forward and linked his hands between his spread knees. His dark head lowered in thought.

Fiona's stomach clenched with foreboding. She'd hoped she'd won the battle, but she knew him well enough to guess he only summoned more arguments against her.

It didn't matter. Nothing he could say would change her mind. Nothing.

Because lying unspoken on the air was yet another argument against this marriage. The fact that he wanted her. She and desire were only the most distant of acquaintances. But she knew enough to recognize that if he promised never to touch her, this union would become the vilest torture for him.

Eventually he raised his head, eyes as black and lightless as coal. "What about Christina?"

She frowned, feeling like she'd prepared for a head-on attack, only to find herself assailed with a sudden flanking movement.

"Christina?" she said, faltering back. Because she could guess what was coming.

If she was right, she'd surrender. She'd have no choice, and that knowledge tasted bitter as aloes in her mouth. She'd do this tremendous wrong to a man who didn't deserve it, who had already done too much for her.

The unfamiliar ruthlessness in Diarmid's face disturbed her. Usually he was the kindest of men.

"Aye, Christina," he said in a hard tone. "Marrying me is your best chance of getting your daughter back, certainly the best chance of establishing anything like a happy, comfortable and safe life with her. Will your pride hold out against your daughter's future?"

"There are other alternatives." She sounded shaky. She was shaky.

"You're nae fool, Fiona." His lips flattened with impatience. "Ye ken how risky any other plan is, how fragile, how vulnerable you'll be. How vulnerable you'll both be."

She did, God help her. "Why are you doing this?" she asked in a ghost of a voice, twisting the damp linen handkerchief between her nervous hands.

Diarmid sat up, still staring at her. He hadn't touched her. He hadn't moved closer, but with every second, she felt more trapped.

"Because I've pledged to help ye."

"There's help, and there's ridiculous self-sacrifice. You'll regret this."

"However this works out, I'll find my reward in knowing ye and your child are safe." His voice turned implacable "Will ye marry me, Fiona?"

Despair flooded her and a guilt so sharp, it made her feel like vomiting. But he had too many weapons against her. She had nowhere else to go, no other choice to make.

Because the bitter truth was that when she was backed against the wall, she'd sacrifice anyone and anything for her child's sake. Even Diarmid Mactavish.

She bowed her head and blinked back more tears. Crying struck her as the height of hypocrisy when she achieved just what she wanted, a genuine chance to get her daughter back.

But at what cost to her? What cost to Diarmid?

After a long delay, her voice emerged low but certain. "Aye, Diarmid. I'll marry you."

CHAPTER TWENTY-ONE

On a perfect Scottish summer morning, Diarmid waited for his bride in Achnasheen's library. He remained unsure whether Fiona would balk at the last minute, so when she and Marina appeared in the doorway, his first reaction was surprised relief.

The four of them had spent yesterday making plans to defeat the Grants. Fergus, who stood up with him now, would travel to Edinburgh next week to seek legal advice about Fiona's circumstances. Fiona and Diarmid would leave today and journey across to Inverness, from where they'd assess the situation with Christina's foster family. With Fiona married to a rich, influential man, it was possible they could just collect the child and return to Invertavey.

Possible, but not likely.

The final resort was to snatch the girl from her guardians and spirit her away somewhere secret until the legal issues were resolved.

It wasn't going to be much of a honeymoon for the bride and groom. But then he was grimly aware that it wasn't going to be much of a marriage.

Diarmid hadn't touched Fiona since she'd agreed to marry him, not even so much as a hand on her arm as they went into dinner. She probably thought he was being considerate of her feelings. When he'd proposed, he was shocked to realize that she'd developed an unrealistically rosy view of his character.

The humiliating truth was that if she gave him an inch of encouragement, he didn't trust himself to keep his promise about a chaste marriage.

As he turned to watch her walk in, he bit back an agonized groan. This marriage would send him mad, if he wasn't careful. Marina must know this was no love match, but it seemed she couldn't resist turning Fiona into an unforgettable bride.

The cream gown was made of heavy silk and swept down into a graceful train. The tight bodice clung to Fiona's bosom in a way that set his blood churning. The rich buttery color only enhanced the satiny whiteness of her skin. A collar of pearls circled her slender throat, and her moonlight hair was caught up with more pearls.

Her blue eyes sought him out, and a nervous smile hovered around those lush pink lips. Lush pink lips he'd never kiss in passion.

He'd get used to the idea of never possessing his beautiful bride. Devil take him, he had to.

Marina bustled in behind Fiona and smiled at Diarmid in an obvious attempt to bolster his spirits. "Doesn't Fiona make a *bellissima* bride? Sandra was in alt when I told her we needed to make a wedding gown. *Certo*, she didn't even complain about having to do it in a day."

"It wasn't necessary to go to all this trouble," Fiona said, accepting a bouquet from Marina. When Diarmid noticed it was made up of roses, he felt like someone punched him in the stomach. The most romantic of flowers seemed to be haunting him. "I didn't wear anything special for my first wedding."

When she'd been a frightened fifteen-year-old girl forced into an old man's bed. Diarmid caught Marina's eye, and knew she shared the same thought.

"Even more reason to make an occasion of your second wedding," Marina said.

Fiona sent her a reluctant smile. Even from across the room, Diarmid could see that she was as taut as a violin string.

Why wouldn't she be? A second husband was the last thing she wanted, and she wasn't reconciled to what she saw as taking advantage of him. He'd tried to explain that he claimed responsibility for her welfare. But how could he explain what he didn't understand himself? All he knew was that he felt a fierce need to see her safe and happy.

A fierce need that this wedding answered, despite all the problems surrounding it.

Right now, when he looked at his glorious bride, he knew that in giving her his name, he provided her with a security she'd never had before. He suddenly felt at peace with his decision in a way he'd never expected.

Perhaps he and his father had more in common than he knew. His father had dedicated himself to one woman, despite knowing she'd never give him what he wanted. Fiona was a different creature from his reckless, faithless mother, but the end result was the same. Diarmid, like his father, would spend his life hungering after what he couldn't have.

Perhaps it was time to stop blaming his mother for not loving his father and seeking her happiness wherever she could find it. One thing Diarmid had learned lately was that few emerged unscarred from the perilous jungle of the human heart.

For the first time since he was old enough to understand the tension between his parents, he drew a breath untainted with bitterness over his mother's betrayal. To his surprise, the air tasted sweet. He'd carried his resentment around for so long, he only now realized how the burden had weighed him down.

Rest in peace, Mamma.

As he crossed to take Fiona's arm, his smile was genuine. Who knew how this marriage would play out? He already owed his reluctant bride a debt for helping him to see his unhappy parents with adult eyes, not the eyes of an abandoned child. "Ye look bonny, lassie."

When his hand curled around her silk sleeve, she gave a start. But her voice was steady as she replied. "Thank you. So do you."

Ridiculously, like the schoolboy he hadn't been in years, he found himself blushing under her admiring gaze. "Och, Fergus came to the rescue."

Luckily he and Fergus were of a height and of a similar build. The superfine black coat might hang a wee bit loose on his lean frame, but at least he looked a proper bridegroom for his wedding.

He smiled at Fergus and Marina. "We both owe ye more than we can say."

"Any time, laddie." Fergus turned to face the minister who waited in front of the unlit hearth with a prayer book in his hands. "Shall we proceed, Reverend Angus?"

"Aye, if Mr. Mactavish and Mrs. Grant are ready."

"Are ye ready?" Diarmid murmured to Fiona.

"Are you?" Wide blue eyes full of doubt focused on him. "There's still time to change your mind about this outlandish scheme."

"This is the only way to save Christina, Fiona." He paused. "I have a feeling we were heading for this moment since we met."

Her lips turned down with the familiar self-mockery he liked so much. "You should have left me on that beach."

"No, lassie, that I couldnae do. Ye made the place look untidy."

As he brought her forward to the minister, he heard her stifle a huff of laughter. Not a bad way to start a marriage, he thought.

The ceremony didn't take long. To his surprise, Fiona spoke her vows in a confident voice. Her demeanor gave no hint that she harbored doubts about this union. She held her head high, and her spine was as straight as a ruler.

Because she was a widow, he supposed a new bride's blushing hesitation was inappropriate. Hell, what reason did she have to blush anyway? She'd slept undisturbed since he met her, and she'd sleep undisturbed tonight, too.

Damn it.

Even that thought couldn't cast a pall over what they did, although he wasn't foolish enough to imagine he'd remain quite so reconciled to his cold marriage as time went on. Just now, he wasn't ready to borrow trouble. Something felt right about this simple ceremony in this room he'd always loved, with his dearest friends by his side. There were worse ways to pledge your life to a woman.

As he'd known it would, the most uncomfortable moment came at the end of the ceremony, after he'd slid the gold ring Fergus had found for him onto Fiona's slender finger.

"Now ye may kiss the bride," Reverend Angus said, closing his prayer book and regarding Fiona and Diarmid with misty-eyed approval.

With a hesitant smile, Fiona turned to face him. Diarmid couldn't help remembering her awkward kisses in the crofter's hut. When it had taken him far too long to realize that she was as unresponsive as a stone in his arms.

Still, he had an image to keep up. If the Grants decided to question the validity of this union—and it might well come to that in the end—he wanted the parson to say that all was done in accordance with law and tradition.

Not wanting to frighten his bride, Diarmid leaned in to brush his lips against her cheek. But at the last second, Fiona shifted and her lips met his. This close, he couldn't miss her swift intake of breath.

For an instant that seemed to extend into eternity, her lips remained motionless under his, before he felt a faint flutter as, unbelievably, she kissed him back. He hardly had time to register that tremulous response, before she'd pulled away.

For a blazing instant, he stared into blue eyes shadowed with uncertainty and astonishment. He struggled to mask the titanic effect that kiss had on him.

It was over so quickly, now he wasn't even sure he had felt her kiss him. Dazed, he turned to Marina who embraced him with an enthusiasm he'd never encounter in his bride.

And yet...

"Diarmid, I'm so pleased for you. Congratulations, *caro*. I know you and Fiona will be very happy together."

By God, he didn't. But he owed Marina so much, not least for her generosity when he brought a stranger to claim her help and hospitality. He made himself smile. "Thank ye, Marina."

"Congratulations, old man." Fergus came up to shake his hand. "She's a wonderful lassie."

"Thank ye." He glanced at Fiona, and acknowledged that Fergus was right. Fiona was wonderful. Beautiful and brave and steadfast.

The undeniable truth that her steadfastness wasn't focused on her new husband didn't take away from how exceptional she was.

"Congratulations, Mr. Mactavish and Lady Invertavey," Reverend Angus said. "I've got some papers for ye to sign, then I believe you're both acting as godparents at the christening I'm to perform the noo?"

"Aye," Diarmid said, noticing Jenny had slipped into the room carrying a sleeping Eilidh. That peace wouldn't last, heaven help them.

Fiona had already left his side to go across to take the baby in her arms. He'd been touched when Marina and Fergus had asked his bride to join him as a godparent to their first child. Fiona had looked completely overwhelmed at the offer, reminding him yet again how lonely her life had been over the last years.

Aye, however it turned out in the end, he did a good thing this morning.

"After this, we've put together a *piccolo* wedding breakfast," Marina said, tugging him away from his solemn thoughts.

Diarmid frowned. "That's kind of ye, but we must start on our journey. We have a long way to go today."

Marina took his arm with a naturalness he wished his wife would emulate. "Diarmid, *per dio*, don't be such a spoilsport. You both need to eat, and it's a day when we should take time to celebrate. It's not every day our best friend decides to take a wife."

"What do ye think, Fiona?" he asked, conscious that from now on, he had to consider someone else's wishes with everything he did. The short ceremony changed his life in ways that he'd hardly started to imagine.

She looked up from staring down at Eilidh and summoned a smile. Nobody would call her a radiant bride, but she'd handled the difficult day with her usual stoic courage.

"A chance to say goodbye to Fergus and Marina would be nice. Another hour or two won't make much difference, when the light lingers so late and the weather promises fair."

"Excellent," Fergus said.

It was only as Diarmid turned to thank the reverend for conducting the ceremony that he wondered whether perhaps Fiona seized the chance to delay being alone with her unwanted bridegroom.

CHAPTER TWENTY-TWO

After the wedding breakfast, Fiona and Marina went upstairs to the lovely bedroom overlooking the loch. A room that she was sorry to leave, where she'd slept in a security she couldn't remember enjoying since her childhood.

Heaven knew where she'd sleep tonight. Heaven knew if she'd be alone. Diarmid had promised he wouldn't demand a wife's duty from her. But however honorable he was, was that a promise too far?

A strange shiver rippled through her, and to her surprise while it contained fear, it held no trace of revulsion. She couldn't help remembering how that kiss at the ceremony had made her blood rush.

"That went well." Marina smiled at Sandra, who turned from laying a pretty dark blue traveling gown across the bed. "You're a lucky *ragazza*, Fiona. I know of no better man than Diarmid, and if he pledges himself to you, he'll never falter."

The praise had Fiona hiding a wince. She didn't want to hear about what a fine man she'd wed. Not when she wanted to run for the hills and ignore the fact that she'd remarried, despite swearing she never would. She owed her new husband so much, yet she gave him so little in return. No wonder she'd approached her wedding with mixed feelings.

She bit back a snort. Mixed feelings? She'd been a jangled mess of nerves and self-disgust and guilt. Marina was right—Diarmid was too good for her. He deserved better than a damaged woman, who married him purely out of self-interest.

He deserved...love. The kind of love she'd stopped believing in, once she realized fairy tales were cruel lies.

After coming to Achnasheen, she could no longer pretend she didn't believe in love. With every moment she spent with Marina and Fergus, she witnessed its power.

"I wish you 'appy, *Signora* Mactavish," Sandra said in her broken English. "*Il Signor Diarmid è un uomo eccezionale. E molto bello.* You are blessed."

Aye, her husband was *molto bello* and *molto buono,* and *molto* cursed to be tied up with her and her troubles. "Thank you, Sandra," she mumbled.

In liquid Italian too fast for Fiona to follow, Marina spoke to the woman. The maid curtsied and left the room.

"*Andiamo, bella.* Let me help you change," Marina said. "I'll miss you. It's been nice having another woman of my age to talk to."

Fiona smiled at her. Unlike her gratitude to her new husband, no shadows tinged her gratitude to this remarkable woman. "You must have wished us to perdition when we turned up at such an awkward moment."

Marina shook her head emphatically. "No, not at all. *Per pietà, cara,* I only survived Eilidh's arrival with your help."

"I was glad to be there. It was the kind of day that stops people being strangers."

"*Sì, certo.*" Marina's smile was wry. "It was also the kind of day that reveals a person's true colors. You came out pure gold, Fiona. Diarmid's a lucky man, too."

She couldn't agree. She suspected he wouldn't either, although she'd lay good money, if she had any, that her white knight would never admit that, even under torture.

"You're so kind." She touched the beautiful collar of pearls around her neck. "Thank you for my wedding gift and my lovely gown. I felt much more like a bride than I did at my first wedding."

She bit her lip to force back rising tears. It had been an emotional day. She'd started it with a good cry. Because she was about to marry a wonderful man, and all she could offer him in return was heartache. This should be a joyous morning, and she'd spent it feeling like she went to the guillotine in a tumbril.

As Marina crossed to stand behind Fiona and unhook the cream gown, her expression softened. "You married a much better man this time round."

That was true—and Fiona repaid him with poison coin. They'd settle into things, she supposed, if the unbelievable happened and they retrieved Christina and set up home together. In time, she assumed he'd take a mistress. Men had needs, and Diarmid would reach a point where he could no longer bear their unnatural chastity.

"*Oddio*, what's the matter, Fiona?"

Fiona realized she'd gone as stiff as a board. She struggled to relax, but it was harder than it should be. How addled she was to choose to avoid Diarmid's bed, yet to loathe the idea of someone else taking the place she denied herself.

"Nothing," she muttered and drew a shuddering breath. "Sorry."

Her self-contempt deepened another few notches. Every cell in her body revolted at the thought of her tall, handsome husband kissing another woman, or putting those elegant hands on another woman, or sharing his strong, vigorous body with another woman. The mere idea made her feel sick.

After a pause, Marina went back to unfastening the dress. "At least I don't need to talk to you about what happens tonight."

"We haven't…" she began, as Marina lifted the rustling silk over her head. She emerged from all that shiny material to catch sight of Marina smiling in the cheval mirror in front of her.

"*Credimi*, I know. I haven't seen so many longing looks since last year when Fergus took me to see 'Romeo and Juliet' at the Theatre Royal in London."

"We don't…" Devil take her, why couldn't she finish a sentence?

Marina laid the extravagant frock over a chair and crossed to the bed to lift up the hardly less extravagant traveling dress. "You do."

"Diarmid is…" Another sentence that frayed at the ends before she completed it, but she balked at telling anyone, even Marina, that this was to be a chaste marriage. Even she could hardly believe that Diarmid had given her his name and his protection, with no plans at all to enjoy the use of her body.

"In a complete spin over you. Which is nice when you're in a complete spin over him, too."

Fiona met worried blue eyes in the mirror. A shaking hand rose to her throat, where her pulse fluttered like a moth trapped in a bottle. Of course she was in a spin, but not at the prospect of her husband's passion. She was in a spin because they would soon confront the Grants, and because even with only a good night's sleep waiting ahead of her, there was something unsettling about a wedding.

She stepped closer to the mirror, because even she didn't believe that. What on earth was the matter with her? That couldn't be yearning in her eyes. The marital act had always repulsed her.

"He's a good man." While that was true, it went nowhere near to expressing her turbulent feelings about Diarmid.

Marina made a disgusted face, obviously agreeing with that assessment of her lukewarm comment. "And handsome and virile and mad for you."

She bit her lip and ventured to speak as much of the truth as she dared. "My first husband wasn't kind."

"*Cavolo,* I'm such a blundering fool." Marina dropped the beautiful dress back on the bed and rushed across to hug her. "*Mi dispiace. Mi dispiace.* I'm so sorry, Fiona. I should have realized. You're nervous about sleeping with Diarmid, even though you can hardly wait. No wonder the two of you have been dancing around one another. Don't worry. Your husband's a clever man, and he cares for you. He'll give you pleasure."

"I've never felt...pleasure."

Marina drew back and subjected her to a searching inspection. "Trust me, you will tonight. All that desire raging between you is going to lead to lots of lovely explosions."

"Explosions?" Fiona went rigid. "That doesn't sound very nice."

A note in Marina's laugh made her shift in discomfort. Her friend's black eyes were bright with certainty—and secret knowledge.

"They're better than nice. They're…" A smile little short of gloating curved her lips. "You'll see. Trust me. And trust Diarmid."

Fiona's cheeks burned with embarrassment—and chagrin. Because what Marina didn't know was that this wedding night would be as lonely and barren as all the nights preceding it.

"It seems you did need to talk to me after all." Marina's expression sobered, and she hugged Fiona again.

After a moment, Fiona sagged and hugged her back. Because while she'd done her best to hide it, she was afraid and confused and far from certain that she should have married Diarmid.

Marina drew away, and Fiona was shocked to see tears glittering in her eyes. "*Per pietà*, it's a happy day. I shouldn't be upset. But when I think of all the things you've missed, everything stolen from you, it just makes me so angry."

"My daughter."

Marina wiped her eyes with an unsteady hand. "*Sì, certo, la tua figlia.* But other things like the pleasures of the marriage bed." She must have caught a hint of Fiona's skepticism, because she gave her a misty smile. "You'll see. Giving yourself to the man you love is a joy. The greatest joy. I hope you discover that tonight with Diarmid. You both deserve to be happy, and I'm just so glad that fate decided to bring you two together."

"Oh, Marina…" Fiona said in dismay.

Because none of what her friend predicted with such well-meaning optimism was going to come to pass. Suddenly that seemed a tragic waste.

"Now let's get you ready to face the world." Emotion thickened Marina's voice, as she turned to pick up the traveling dress once more.

"You've already given me so much, how can I ever repay you?" Fiona asked.

Marina's smile turned tremulous. "If you make Diarmid happy, you'll repay me a thousand times over."

Acrid self-loathing cramped Fiona's heart. Today's marriage promised her new husband nothing but danger, toil, misery and frustration. God forgive her for what she did. She should never have agreed to marry him, whatever Christina's straits. Now it was too late to do anything about it.

CHAPTER TWENTY-THREE

hen the door connecting Diarmid's room to his wife's clicked open, immediate concern had him sitting up against the pillows. Fiona hovered in the doorway about ten feet away, twining her hands at her waist in what he'd learned was a sign of nervousness—or fear. She was dressed for bed, in a white nightgown, and she'd draped a pretty paisley shawl around her shoulders.

"Fiona, is something wrong?"

The lamps in the cavernous chamber were lit, although it was late and the day had been long and fraught, with the wedding and miles of travel to follow. Fiona had used Fergus's luxurious coach, and Diarmid had ridden ahead on Sigurn. His friend had cast him a curious glance when he didn't join his bride in the carriage. But even for the sake of appearances, he couldn't face sharing that confined space with his wife. The woman he could never touch, despite what the law might say about her being his.

They'd arrived at this bustling inn on the main north road in time for a very late dinner. The Northern Lights offered more luxurious accommodation than anything else on the way to Inverness. He'd taken a suite of rooms. While their private arrangement might be unconventional, he wanted to honor his bride with worthy lodgings on their first night as a married couple.

"Fiona?" he asked with a hint of sharpness, when she didn't immediately answer. He was renowned for his patience, but the day's tensions had tested him to the limit.

"No," she answered on a breath of sound. Her gaze dipped to his bare chest, then rose again. Pink tinged her cheeks as she took a step closer. "Nothing's wrong."

Diarmid immediately regretted his irritation. After all, this cold wedding night was what he'd expected. He made himself smile in what he hoped was a reassuring manner and set aside the volume of Hazlitt's essays he'd taken from Fergus's library. When he'd opened it tonight, he'd wondered how many other bridegrooms went to bed with an improving book on their wedding night.

By God, not many, he'd wager. No, those lucky sods had something much more entertaining to look forward to than finding pleasure in an elegant turn of phrase.

"Dinna be afraid." He kept his tone soothing. "The Grants dinna ken we're here. Even if they did, you're my wife now. They have nae more legal claim on ye."

"I know," she said, her voice still so low, it was almost a whisper. Those busy hands twisted over and around one another in an agitated dance.

"Then what are ye doing here?" The question emerged much more baldly than he'd intended.

Curse him, he wished he'd turned down the lamps. The light was more than bright enough to reveal every detail of her appearance. He tried to tell himself he'd seen her in her nightdress before, but Mags's acres of billowing flannel didn't give the same impression as this fine—and much more closely fitted—sheath of white clinging to his wife's slender body.

The sheer material revealed that a couple of weeks of decent meals had filled out Fiona's curves in a way he cursed right now. The girl he'd rescued had been gaunt. The woman he'd married was a miracle of graceful dips and hollows and soft female roundness. His hands curled into fists in the crisp linen sheets, as he struggled to remember that he'd sworn not to touch her.

Damn it, he should have told Marina to pack sensible nightwear, not this instrument of torture in silk and lace. Damn it, he should have locked the connecting door between the rooms, even if having his wife sleep nearby was the main reason he'd chosen this inn.

He closed his eyes briefly, but that didn't help. Fiona's alluring image was burned on his retinas. Nor did it help that under the covers, he was naked. His body reacted in a predictable manner to a beautiful woman's arrival in his bedchamber in the middle of the night.

Still her hands twisted. "I..."

She'd never exactly been a chatterbox, but this was pushing taciturnity to its limits. Not wanting to frighten her, he raised his knees to hide his arousal. "Then what is it?"

When his edgy tone made her bite her lip, he felt lower than a worm. With the courage he'd come to recognize as an essential part of her, she raised her chin. Standing before him, she looked both vulnerable and invincible. Like a schoolgirl with her hair tied back in a simple plait. Like a woman who knew all the secrets of Eve.

He bit back a groan and told himself that Fiona had already married one selfish swine. He didn't want her finding out that her second husband was no better. He'd get used to treating his wife like a sister. In about a thousand years.

Maybe.

Another step closer. Another flickering inspection of his bare chest. Her shy interest in his body sent forbidden heat swirling through his blood.

"You're not asleep."

Obviously.

He stifled the sarcastic response. She didn't deserve it.

"I couldnae settle. It's been a big day. You're no' tired?"

"No. I slept in the coach."

Lucky lassie. "It's more comfortable than traveling two to a horse, I'm sure."

Familiar humor quirked her lips. "Riding on Sigurn was enjoyable in its way."

What in blazes was this? Diarmid frowned in bewilderment. If she were another woman, he'd think she was saying that she liked being in his arms. But this was his untouchable bride, so she must mean something else.

He sighed, recognizing that he was in line for more torture. She showed no sign of wanting to go back to her room. "Would ye like some company?"

She eyed him as though she expected him to bite her, then nodded. "Aye. My room feels lonely."

Lonely? Everything he knew about her should make a solitary wedding night her idea of heaven. For pity's sake, she'd send him deranged. Worse, he'd signed up for a lifetime of having Fiona within reach, yet off limits.

When he proposed marriage, he'd vowed that his willpower would outstay his hunger. Cracks already riddled that vow. If his wife made a habit of midnight visits to his bedchamber, his honor would soon crumble to dust.

On the other hand, he couldn't bear to think of Fiona afraid and alone and fretting over the possibility that despite all their efforts, they still might fail.

"Are ye already regretting marrying me?" He wasn't sure he wanted to know the answer.

"No."

Well, she sounded sure about that at least. "That's good."

Another comprehensive, if swift survey of his chest. She really should stop doing that. It tested his self-control. He wished his shirt wasn't hanging from a hook on the other side of the room.

When she edged closer, he read the troubled expression in those clear blue eyes. "Are you?"

"No." At this precise moment, he wasn't sure he meant it.

"I'm glad."

A thorny silence descended until unable to bear the crackling tension, he said, "Let me pour ye a wee dram. It might help ye sleep."

"Will you join me?"

He'd rather someone hurled a caber at his head, but his turmoil wasn't her fault and he wanted to start his marriage with some vestige of civilization. "Aye, but first, you'll need to pass me my robe, then turn your back."

The rounded eyes that focused on his lap did nothing to quell the storm in his blood. She made a move toward where the red velvet dressing gown Fergus had lent him lay tossed across a chair near the fire. "You sleep naked?"

St. Peter and all the little fishes... Did his bride think he was bloody well made of stone?

Although one part of him did its best to imitate good Scottish granite.

"Aye," he bit out with a snap of his teeth.

When that uncertain blue gaze rose to his face, his discomfort increased. "I've never seen a naked man."

If she hung around much longer, that would change. He ground his teeth and told himself to settle down. Then he realized just what she'd said.

What the hell? That couldn't be right. Perhaps the thunderous pounding in his ears meant that he'd misheard.

"But your husband..."

Her lips turned down. "When we...did that, it was always in the dark. Ian would lift up his nightshirt, and then..."

Almighty God above. He couldn't sit here and listen to her talk about the sexual act. Not without jumping out of this bed and giving her a good eyeful of what a naked man looked like. A rampantly aroused naked man, at that. "He took ye."

She looked thoughtful, as she considered his response. Her hands remained linked at her waist, but at last they were still. "Yes, it was taking."

"Did he hurt ye?" he couldn't help asking, although the wisest move was to exile her to her room with orders to stay there.

"At first. I had no idea what to expect, and I fought him."

Sick pity clenched Diarmid's belly. How could he resent her reluctance to sleep with him, after she'd been through such suffering?

If only she'd never met the Grants. Deep within her, she contained the promise of passion, but that promise would never find fulfillment.

What a crying waste. The idea of awakening an innocent Fiona to the potential of pleasure stirred not just his raging senses but his aching heart.

And it was all too blasted late.

Damn the Grants. All of them. Allan. Ian. Thomas. And the rest of the pestilential breed. They deserved to fry in the lowest circle of hell.

"Fiona..."

She went on before he could express his horror at the way those brutes turned something magnificent into violence, degradation, and misery.

"At least it never lasted long, and once Ian's health started to fail, he lost the capacity to..." Her gesture encompassed both her husband's impotence and her relief at no longer having to endure his attentions.

"You're safe now."

She looked nervous again, although he couldn't imagine why the hell she should. He'd given her his word he wouldn't insist on his husbandly rights. What man with an ounce of conscience would force his attentions on this woman?

"Yes, I am safe. Thanks to you."

"Ye dinna have to spend the rest of your life making recompense. That will drive us both mad."

A hesitant smile curved her lips, and she took another step forward. Plague take her, he wished she'd go away. He meant well by her. Of course he did. But it was torture to have her hovering at his bedside in the middle of the night. And not just any night, but his wedding night.

"I do have to make recompense."

"No, ye don't. Knowing that you and Christina are safe and happy will be reward enough."

"You're such a good man, Diarmid." The smile broadened. "Such a good man—and such a liar."

Shocked, he sat up straight, sending the sheet slipping dangerously low. "What in Hades…"

She made a gesture of repudiation. "That's not going to be enough for you, and you know it."

Diarmid was slow to anger. He always had been, although once he decided against someone, he was steadfast in his dislike. But now powerful rage began to coil in his gut, fueled with frustration and barely controlled desire.

"Fiona, what the devil do you want?" he snapped out. "We've been through this. When I proposed, I swore I wouldnae touch ye. But we both know I want you. Plaguing me like this is cruel and unfair, beneath ye. I'm no' made of wood. Stop teasing me, and go back to bed. We're never talking about this again. Leave me some pride, blast ye."

To his surprise, she didn't retreat. "I have my own pride."

Under the paisley shawl, her breasts rose as she sucked in a deep breath. His hands made claws in the sheets as he battled the itch to grab her. She was mere feet away, and he could quiet any scruples by telling himself that she'd asked for trouble by coming to his room and ignoring the danger signs.

"More than is good for ye," he grated out. "But if you're playing some sort of game here, I'll never forgive ye."

She looked horrified as she shook her head. "No game, Diarmid, I swear."

"Then what is this about?"

She twined her hands together once more. The shawl shifted to reveal the outline of one pert breast beneath the clinging silk. He went back to grinding his teeth and staring above her head at the lamplit shadows dancing on the wall.

"It's about my pride."

"What?" he snarled, not brave enough to look at her.

"Ever since we met, you've given to me. It makes for an uncomfortably lopsided bargain. I'm always grateful, and you're always in charge."

Resentment made him look at her and—almost—overcame his craving to feel her body under his hands. "Now we're married, it will take time to work out how we're going to proceed. You'll find your way. I know I still feel like a stranger..."

"You don't feel like a stranger."

He didn't want to explore that. Not when only a sheet and a thin layer of silk separated them from being naked together.

"You'll feel more like a partner in this match, once we've sorted the Grants out and you've taken over as lady of Invertavey and you're raising Christina without your kin's interference."

Her hands dropped to her sides, and she leveled an unwavering blue gaze upon him. "I'll feel more like a partner when I am one."

He knew she was sending him a message, but for the life of him he had no idea what it was. "Aye, once we've found Christina and—"

"No. Now."

Another silence descended, this time as sharp and heavy as a honed ax. Diarmid's heart gave a mighty thud and crashed against his ribs. He gulped for a breath in a futile attempt to steady his reeling mind.

"What?"

"I'm offering to be your wife in every sense, Diarmid."

He started to reach for her then drew back. "I ken ye hated lying with your husband."

She tilted her chin in such a Fiona-like move that his yearning heart performed another somersault. "Perhaps I wouldn't hate it with you."

"And perhaps ye will."

"Marina says it can be good. With the right man."

"It can." He wondered why he tried to argue her out of doing what he wanted more than he wanted his next breath. Except he knew why. He only had to recall the strain that tightened her delicate features when she spoke about Ian Grant. "But after what you've been through, it's likely there's damage."

"You're saying I'm incapable of a woman's responses?"

"I'm saying that violence and pain leave scars, even if invisible ones. In time…"

One hand sliced the air in denial. "No, not in time. I can't bear to be your charity case any longer. I want to be your wife, your equal. I want a true marriage."

"So do I," he said quietly. "But it's insulting to come here without wanting me and expect me to jump to your command."

He could have wept when he saw her incomprehension. "But you want me."

"Aye." No point denying it. "It's no' enough."

"Perhaps you can make me want you." She verged nearer. "I know you won't hurt me, and trust will surely help us."

"It will."

She was close enough now to reach for him. "Diarmid, I'm tired of being broken and alone." Her voice throbbed with conviction. "I want you to show me what I'm missing."

He didn't take the proffered hand. "Fiona, ye dinna have to do this."

"Yes, I do," she said stubbornly.

He sighed. Somehow they'd moved from something that was impossible to something that might just happen. "You ask a lot of me. What if I let ye down?"

"You won't." She swallowed. "Let's start with something small. Will you teach me how to kiss?"

"Kiss?"

She'd kissed him at the bothy. That night, too, she'd offered herself. The similarities to tonight hadn't escaped him.

He'd dismissed her clumsiness then as a result of fear and desperation and unwillingness. But maybe...

"You've never been kissed?"

"You kissed me today at our wedding."

"Aye." The experience had threatened to send him up in smoke. "What about before that?"

"My late husband didn't waste time on anything but the essentials." She lowered her hand and shifted from one foot to the other. "I kissed you at the crofter's cottage. Perhaps you've forgotten."

A derisive huff of laughter escaped him. "Dinna be a fool, lassie. Of course I remember. Ye don't know how close I came to losing control that night. I was in agony."

He expected his admission to daunt her, but to his surprise, she looked gratified instead. "Are you in agony now?"

"Aye." The answer was a groan.

"You want me so much?"

"Fiona, dinna be a wee cat. Ye ken what you do to me."

With a radiant smile that set his poor overburdened heart cartwheeling again, she drew herself up and sent him a direct look. "Then it's time, my husband, that you kissed your bride."

CHAPTER TWENTY-FOUR

Fiona sounded braver than she felt. When Ian Grant went to his final rest, she'd sworn that she'd never again submit to a man's demands. But these days in Diarmid's company had made her wonder if the male touch must always be harsh and greedy and frightening.

She'd never felt desire, but she couldn't deny that sometimes when she looked at the man she'd just married, wanton curiosity stirred in her blood.

Ian Grant had made her skin crawl. Diarmid Mactavish's touch made her feel safe and cherished, even before he took the astonishing step of marrying her to keep her safe. If gratitude and liking meant anything, she could endure what was to come. At least he didn't smell like an old man, and his breath was sweet.

Men enjoyed the vile act. She couldn't imagine women ever did.

Except all day, Marina's words had played in her mind. As Fiona stood beside Diarmid's bed, she couldn't help wondering if perhaps there might be...more.

This time when she offered her hand, he took it. As those strong fingers closed around hers, heat surged up her arm and settled around her stuttering heart.

"Ye do me such honor, Fiona." His dark eyes were steady. "I promise I willnae hurt you."

"I know you won't." She believed that at least he'd try.

"If you're frightened, tell me and we'll stop." He frowned. "Your hand is trembling."

"I'm nervous. That's natural." She made herself meet that perceptive gaze. It was difficult not to keep staring at the muscled expanse of his bare chest. She'd never imagined she'd find a male torso quite such a compelling sight. "But today I promised you my body. Don't make me dishonor my word."

"Verra well," he said softly.

"What should I do?"

Tenderness softened that searching black stare. "Venturing a wee step closer might help."

She blushed. For heaven's sake, she'd been married nine years and borne a child. Stupid to feel as uncertain as a maiden with her first lover. "Are you staying in the bed?"

Self-mockery twisted his expressive mouth. "I fear if I throw the sheets aside, you'll run screaming from the room."

Her eyes settled on the way the loosely draped sheet tented below his waist. All the moisture dried from her mouth, and her pulse fluttered erratically. That was the part of him he'd shove into her. She struggled not to remember how it had felt when Ian strained and grunted.

"I'm made of sterner stuff than that." She prayed she spoke the truth.

The smile deepened, and so did the tenderness. "Let's no' put it to the test just yet."

Something in his expression set up a thrumming pulse in the base of her belly. She bit her lip and cast a nervous glance around the room. "Before we go any further, shouldn't I extinguish the lamps?"

"No."

"No?" The question emerged as a squeak.

He shook his head. "I want to engage all your senses, including sight." The comprehensive survey he gave her body made that throbbing between her legs more insistent. "I've dreamed of seeing ye."

She licked dry lips and noticed with another jolt of awareness how his eyes flared when they focused on the betraying movement. "You have?"

"Aye." The fervor in the simple answer made her tremble. "Take off your shawl and come and sit beside me, Fiona."

She'd always loved how he said her name. Right now, with night surrounding them and the prospect of his possession looming, her name turned into music on his lips.

Fiona couldn't force a word through her tight throat, but with her free hand, she slid the pretty shawl Marina had given her from her shoulders and let it fall to the floor. Her nipples beaded against her silk nightdress, as Diarmid subjected her to another of those leisurely inspections.

"Now come nearer." His voice sounded gruff, and his fingers tightened around hers.

Again, speech was beyond her. Feeling like her legs were sure to collapse, she took one faltering step, then another until she stood right above him. She fought the urge to cover her breasts.

This close, awareness of his vigorous male beauty shuddered through her like an earthquake. The lamplight turned his skin to gold, lapped across the broad shoulders and powerful chest with its scattered covering of black curls. When he turned his head, light cascaded over his shining hair, black as a crow's wing.

She shifted on her bare feet, as the throbbing inside her approached the pitch of discomfort. Heaven help her, she could look at him forever.

There was more to come than just looking. Feeling bold, she perched on the edge of the bed, her feet still on the floor. It took all her courage to twist her body until she met that fathomless dark gaze.

He kept hold of her hand. Odd how the simple connection felt strong enough to defy the world.

Without shifting his gaze from hers, he raised her hand and kissed the back of it. The courtly gesture made her breath catch in an audible gasp. She felt tremulous and uncertain, eaten up with fascination.

"You're taking your time." Her voice was husky with nerves and what she couldn't help recognizing as sensual interest.

His smile was sweet, with no hint of the usual irony. "Why would I no'?"

"Ian was always in a hurry. He'd have me under him by now." By heaven, he'd have finished and rolled away to snore the night away.

"Och, lassie, ye shock me." One sleek black brow rose in teasing inquiry. "Are ye telling me to get a move on?"

Color burned her cheeks. "I won't back out."

He placed her hand flat on his chest, where she felt the solid thud of his heart. His skin was warm, and when she instinctively rubbed the firm muscle, his hair created a pleasant friction under her palm. That restless feeling tightened her stomach and made her feel like she'd swallowed a hundred grasshoppers.

"You can if ye want to. You've been bullied enough."

She stared at him, trying to make sense of what he offered. "But you want...me."

His hand flexed over hers. "Aye, I do. From the first." His lips quirked. "Well, perhaps no' when I picked ye up from the beach. You were as waterlogged and sandy as a lump of seaweed then, but definitely after we'd dried you off and put you in Mags's nightie."

To her surprise, the memory made her smile. At the time, his desire had terrified her. "It was a tent."

"It was." His eyes flickered down to encompass the silk that barely covered her. "I like this one much better."

She bit her lip again. "What should I do now?"

"Kiss me, Fiona," he said softly.

"Very well." She sucked in a nervous breath. "But it's at your own risk."

He laughed softly. "I'll survive. Stop putting off the evil moment, lass."

It took her a few seconds to gather the nerve to lean in and touch her lips to his. Immediately a barrage of familiar impressions engulfed her. Warmth. The firmness of his mouth. His tangy scent, edged with something she recognized with an alarmed thrill as arousal.

He made a purring sound of pleasure, and she pressed harder. Her fingers clenched against where his heart accelerated.

Oh, Lord, she started to feel like she was drowning. Fiona wrenched her head up. It took her a few seconds to clear her vision.

"Was that right?" she asked shakily. She could taste him on her lips.

The tenderness was back. "It's a start." He reached for her shoulder. "Lie back against the pillows, and we'll try again."

"Under the sheets?" More of that wanton curiosity had her wondering just what he hid beneath the bedclothes.

His lips twitched. "No' yet."

He brought her down beside him and shifted to lean on his elbow. She hated the way she stiffened in wariness, but lying next to a man like this reminded her too vividly of her first husband. "Diarmid…"

"Whisht, lassie," he murmured, trailing his fingers along her hairline and across her ears and down her cheeks. "You're awfully bonny. Later, I'd like to take down your hair. I've had a thousand fantasies involving your hair."

"My hair?" she asked, unable to hide her astonishment.

He laughed softly and kept up those teasing, unthreatening touches. "Aye, your hair. It's beautiful."

"I assumed you'd only think about…"

A smile hovered around his mouth, as those drifting fingers trailed heat wherever they touched.

"Och, I've thought about that, too, never ye fear, sweetheart." He caught her chin and angled it up. "But that's all for later—or perhaps never. Now I'm going to teach ye how to kiss a man."

She should be frightened, but fear had moved further out of reach than she'd ever imagined it could. "A man?"

"Well, me. I'm hoping you'll find the lesson so satisfactory that ye won't want to broaden your range of kissees."

"Kissees?" she queried on a gurgle of laughter. "Is that a technical term?"

"Och, aye. Ye need to learn the correct words for what we do together."

"How...educational."

"I aim to please."

He bent in so close that his breath made the sensitive skin of her lips tingle with what she was shocked to recognize was longing. Another shock shivered through her as she realized she'd laughed. In bed. With a man. Who was going to push inside her before the night was done.

Lying with Ian had always been an act of grim endurance. When she'd come to Diarmid tonight, she'd been keyed up for an onerous experience. She hadn't expected this enchanting lightness.

He brushed his lips across hers. Automatically, she closed her mouth and her eyes.

When nothing else happened, Fiona opened her eyes to find him watching her with a fond amusement that had her silly heart performing wild acrobatics.

"Why do ye shut your mouth so tightly?"

"Aren't I meant to?"

"If you're kissing your grandfather, perhaps." When his fingers caressed her jaw, her lips loosened of their own volition. "Relax a wee bit, and follow my lead."

He bent his head again, and this time her nervousness receded to a point where she moved her lips against his. The tingling sensation increased and spread until she felt the contact across every inch of her body. When the pressure on her lips shifted and changed, she tried to imitate it.

After a few seconds, he raised his head. "Better." His breathing was unsteady. "Shall we try again?"

"Yes," she said on a whisper.

This time the pressure was more purposeful, and she felt the flicker of his tongue. When she whimpered in protest, he stopped.

"Ye dinna like it?"

She gasped for air, and her heart banged in her ears like a madman's drum. "I'm...I'm not sure."

"Perhaps I'm going too fast."

He returned to playful kisses that teased her into yearning up toward him. Little glancing touches that surprised and tantalized. His hand cupped her jaw and held her still, as he kissed her lips then shifted to quick kisses across her cheeks and eyelids and chin and nose.

A choked giggle escaped her. "It tickles."

"In a nice way?" He punctuated each word with a brief kiss somewhere on her face.

"Yes, very nice."

Diarmid returned to her lips, and this time the glide of his tongue had her following instinct and parting to take in more of his taste. He made a low sound of approval and slipped his tongue into her mouth with fleeting importunity. Her heart slammed hard against her ribs, as a wave of sensation crashed over her.

He tasted like the peppermint powder he'd used to clean his teeth. He tasted of heat and hungry male.

She'd learned to fear masculine arousal, but now she opened her mouth wider. Another rumbling growl of encouragement, and the kiss changed. Flared into desperation and craving.

Through quaking astonishment, Fiona summoned the courage to greet him with a flutter of her tongue. Then everything melded into a tumultuous symphony of question and response, as he sucked her tongue into his mouth and she returned the favor.

By the time he lifted his head, she was shaking, her toes curled, and her hands were clawing at the bedsheet beneath her. Her lips felt full and damp and eager for more.

Fiona forced heavy eyelids upward. Diarmid looked ruffled and intent, and his black eyes were glowing. "Would ye like to touch me?"

"T...touch?" After those dazzling kisses, speech was difficult.

"Aye. Put your hands around my neck."

"Would you like that?"

"Aye."

Tentatively she curled a hand around his nape, feeling the way his soft dark hair tickled her fingers. Her other hand curved around the ball of one brawny shoulder.

He'd been warm when they started kissing. Now he radiated heat like a great furnace. His scent had changed, too, become richer and muskier. She gulped in a mouthful of that delicious fragrance.

"More?" he asked.

Fiona stared up into a face drawn tight with reined-in hunger. She'd never felt like this before, hot and eager and daring. The restlessness inside her might even be passion stirring to uncertain life. "Yes, please."

So far, he'd touched her face, holding her still for those breathtaking kisses. Now he slid his hand around her back and angled her toward him.

This time, she had an idea what to expect from his kisses. So when his mouth opened over hers, she parted her lips and kissed him with no trace of her earlier hesitation. His hold firmed, and he rolled over so she felt the hard outline of his body through the sheet. Even that didn't make her want to stop.

As long as he kept kissing her, he could do whatever he liked with her. With a sigh, she yielded to the wild seduction of her husband's lips.

CHAPTER TWENTY-FIVE

*P*leasure pounded through Diarmid. Pleasure and rising hunger. But when he recalled that he'd had to teach his wife how to kiss, he leashed his impatience.

The more he discovered about Fiona's previous marriage, the more he understood her skittishness. He refused to let her put him in the same category as that clumsy swine who had frightened this treasure of a woman away from sensual fulfillment. The fact that she was here in this bed at all told him that she trusted him as she trusted no other man.

That was a heavy responsibility. Even if it killed him, he wouldn't betray her by pursuing his own delight ahead of hers.

How strange to hold this bonny woman in his arms, a woman who had married and given birth to a child, and recognize that he must treat her like a virgin. Because in every sense but the most prosaic, she was a virgin.

Hell, she hadn't even kissed anyone properly until tonight.

The memory of coaxing her lips to open for him and the rapture that followed drew him back from the brink of passion. Every time he touched her, he was torn between overwhelming desire and a tenderness so poignant, he felt like someone stuck a harpoon into his aching heart.

Her burgeoning response made his blood rush and his head swim. She tasted so sweet, like honey and flowers and warm female. Her scent, more flowers, more warm female, was intoxicating.

God bless her, her hands started their own exploration. They raked through his hair, traced the shape of his shoulders and arms, stroked his naked back. With a soft sigh, she arched toward him.

Still he kissed her, teaching her the dance of tongues and teeth and lips. A teasing foray, a strategic retreat, a nip here, a more thorough invasion there. Until on a growl of frustration, she set out to pursue him with all the skills he'd lavished on her.

With a breathless laugh, Diarmid pulled away to lean on one elbow. "You're getting too good at this."

Hazy blue eyes stared up at him, as she gasped for air. Her breasts rose and fell under the frail silk covering.

When she caught his hand and brought it to her lips, more tenderness threatened to choke him. Even if they stopped now, she'd turned a wedding night that he'd dreaded into an occasion of extraordinary joy.

She brought his hand down to her breast. "Touch me," she whispered, pressing his palm against that luscious roundness.

"Fiona..." he forced out through a throat jammed with pleas and questions and, damn it, piercing emotion. He bit back a groan, as he shaped his hand to her. When his thumb brushed a hard nipple, she gave a huff of surprise.

"If I do, I'll…" He couldn't finish. She knew what he wanted.

"I want to give you pleasure." She seemed to have no trouble putting a sentence together, whereas words scattered in front of him like seagulls running across the beach at Canmara. "Let me give you this."

"I…" He wanted to tell her he could wait, but his hand tightened on her breast.

She released his hand and fumbled with the hem of her nightdress. During their voracious kisses, it had ridden high over her slender thighs. Now she bunched it in her hands and tugged it up to reveal a tangle of ash blond curls at the base of her flat stomach. Lamplight glistened on damp, feathery hair, proof of her arousal.

Diarmid swallowed the jagged boulder that blocked his throat and made himself say what he must. "Ye dinna have to do this."

"Aye, I do." To his surprise, she smiled with an openness he'd never seen before. "Not just because you're my husband and I owe you my duty. Diarmid, I want to give myself to you."

In his wildest dreams, he'd never imagined Fiona saying those words. Her admission filled him with gratitude and astonished joy and scrambled every coherent thought in his head.

He kissed her to try to tell her what he couldn't say. When he raised his head, she trembled, but he was—almost—certain that this was desire, not fear of a man's possession.

Releasing her breast, he slid his hand down to the soft plain of her belly. He paused to explore the pale, satiny skin, then ventured a few inches lower to cup her mound. She gave a start and bit the lips he'd kissed over and over tonight.

"Should I stop?" he asked.

She flattened her hand over his chest, where his heart labored as if he pushed a loaded wagon up a hill. "No."

"You dinna sound too sure."

"I'm sure."

Diarmid didn't quite believe her, but while she might be nervous, she was aroused, too. Need darkened her eyes, turned them heavy. Her nipples pressed tight and hard against her silk nightdress.

He kissed her again. At first, she was awkward in his arms, but soon she kissed him back with gratifying enthusiasm. Only then, while his lips still teased at hers, did he launch a gentle invasion of her body's secret hollows.

"I love to touch ye," he whispered, nibbling a line down her neck and feeling her shiver as he scraped his teeth across the nerve where her neck curved into her shoulder.

Fiona tangled her fingers in his and after a pause that seemed to last an eon, she relaxed under him. Her legs parted to allow his caresses where, God willing, he'd soon join his body to hers.

She was sleek and hot. As his seeking fingers met the proof of her response, relief washed through him. She hadn't lied about wanting him. Slowly he explored the satiny folds.

Her hand clenched in his hair. "What are you doing?" she asked unsteadily.

"Ye dinna like it?"

"I'm not..."

As he caressed the sensitive pearl of flesh, another huff of surprise escaped her. "Oh."

Once again, he thought how virginal she was. She knew nothing of her body's potential for pleasure. How could she, married off as little more than a child to a brute who made no attempt to teach her about enjoyment?

Diarmid leaned in and took one beaded nipple between his lips. The silk was a tantalizing barrier. He burned to rip away this rag of a nightdress. But some corner of his brain retained enough grip on strategy to recognize that once she was naked, her fears might resurface. Right now, she was drunk on new sensations, not thinking beyond the next delightful shock.

As he drew on her nipple, his touch between her legs became more purposeful. One finger circled the entrance to her body, then slid inside. He tensed his jaw as she closed around his finger. Even aroused, she was tight.

Carefully he withdrew, relishing how she clung to his finger. The promise of being inside her thundered through him like an earthquake. He reached a point where the sheet could no longer ensure restraint.

Diarmid shoved the hampering linen out of the way and settled between her slender thighs. The trust and barely hidden uncertainty in her eyes hit him harder than his discovery of her desire.

"Shall we proceed, lassie?" The question emerged as a growl.

She studied his face as if seeking the answer to some eternal question. He gritted his teeth and told himself that despite bollocks as heavy as cannon balls, he could stop.

He'd limp for a month, but he could stop.

Her courage once again stole his breath—if he had any to steal. Whatever she saw in his face must have reassured her, because she gave a small nod and stretched out her legs. A slight smile fluttered around her lips.

"Yes."

A long groan of relief escaped him. "Hold onto my shoulders. And bend your knees. It will be easier for you."

He wished he sounded more like a lover and less like the sergeant major she'd once called him, but stringing any words together was almost beyond him. Urgent hands caught her hips and angled her upward.

He could hardly believe this moment had arrived. Fiona in his bed, willing and ready for his possession.

With a smoothness that set his heart crashing against his ribs, he pushed forward. At first, he met tension, then her body adjusted to take him and with a broken sigh, she accepted his entire length.

His breath escaped in a great whoosh. He buried his head in her shoulder and kissed the damp skin in an ecstasy of thankfulness.

He'd wanted her so long. He'd dreamed about her. But not even his most feverish fantasies came near to the joy of uniting his body with hers. He shifted to settle more deeply.

Through the elation, some shred of care lingered. He raised his head and stared down into her face. Her cheeks were flushed, and her lips were red and swollen with kisses. "Are ye all right?"

Another brave little smile. "Of course." She softened the prosaic answer with a gentle caress along his jaw. "Are you?"

Despite his urgency, a grunt of laughter emerged. "Och, never better."

"Good." She wriggled, a subtle twist of her hips that threatened to take him over the edge.

He groaned and closed his eyes as he fought to master his animal impulses. "If ye do that, lassie, this is going to be a verra short encounter."

"Oh." Fiona went still, and her eyes opened very wide.

Her hands tightened on his shoulders, as he began to move in and out. Fiona surrounded him. She was the whole world. Gradually every need faded under the pounding drive for release. Through the hot fog in his mind, Diarmid felt her rise to meet him. Her moans of blossoming pleasure were sweet music.

Every time he thrust, she clenched around him. He wanted her to find her peak before he finished, but he was only flesh and blood and he'd wanted her for so long. Too soon, his deliberate movements turned choppy. His seed rose on an irresistible tide.

Shaking, he kissed her hard on the lips, glorying in her swift response. Then darkness crashed down over him like a thunderclap. He thrust once, twice, then surrendered to a vast swell of sensation as he yielded to her.

The wild rush threatened to shatter him. It was fierce and magnificent and savage. Fiona cried out as he heaved over her, filling her with every drop of his passion.

Finally it was over. He was so exhausted that it was an effort to move to roll over and lie next to her.

He flung one arm across his eyes to close out the world. Self-loathing festered in his gut, souring the lingering pleasure. Because while physically he'd never felt better, his soul was black and sick.

Fiona didn't speak, although as his heartbeat steadied, he could hear her erratic breathing.

"I'm sorry, lassie," he muttered, without looking at her.

"Sorry?" she whispered.

"Aye, to the depths of my heart," he said grimly.

Because he'd broken the promises he'd made to himself when he started. Tonight Diarmid might have discovered an ecstasy to shake the heavens, but Fiona hadn't joined him on the journey to the stars.

CHAPTER TWENTY-SIX

"I don't understand," Fiona said dully, staring up at the shadowy ceiling and trying not to cry.

She felt wet and brimming with Diarmid's seed. She also felt alone and inadequate and confused. The worst of it was that for a good while before the act's ending, she'd believed that she pleased him.

His vigorous possession had left her aching. She felt stretched and pummeled, and the slightest move set off twinges she hadn't experienced in years. Not that he'd been rough. Even when he'd pumped into her, he hadn't hurt her. But it was a long time since a man had used her body, and Diarmid was much more impressively endowed than her late husband.

Fiona would dearly love to leave the bed, go back to her own room, and wash. She felt sticky and uncomfortable. That, too, was familiar.

But Diarmid was clearly in a funk about something, and she had a nasty suspicion that abandoning him at this moment might set up a permanent rift between them.

"I didnae wait for ye," he said in that same desolate tone.

He still spoke in riddles, although she knew even without seeing his face that whatever troubled him was no minor matter.

She braced for him to turn on her and blame her for her failure. She'd tried. She'd tried so hard. When he'd lost himself in that groaning, ferocious release, she'd felt proud of herself for giving him such pleasure.

She'd got that wrong. Her ineptitude made her feel like she'd swallowed hot lead. She couldn't summon the courage to look at him. She steeled herself to ask the humiliating question. "What more did you want from me?"

The bed shifted as he turned on his side and rose on one elbow to study her. "What on earth did ye say?"

"Don't worry about it," she mumbled, cringing away from talking about what had happened between them. It was all too embarrassing.

"No, what did ye mean?" He frowned. "Tell me."

Ian Grant hadn't been much of a talker, especially when it came to marital matters. Faced with more than six feet of naked male on the hunt for answers, Fiona wondered if perhaps that might be one thing she commended in her first husband.

Her eyes flickered from Diarmid's stern expression down over that splendid chest to where his rod lay upon one powerful thigh. Even flaccid, it emerged large from a nest of black curls.

She knew she shouldn't stare, but she couldn't help it. She'd never seen that part of a man before. Ian's fumblings had all been under cover of darkness, and she'd been so lost in her astonishing reactions to Diarmid's touch, she hadn't looked before he pushed inside her. Fighting the urge to touch it, she whipped her gaze back up to the ceiling and clenched her hands in the sheets.

"Fiona?" The wry humor in his voice told her he hadn't missed that lightning inspection of his body.

Diarmid was a clever man. He never missed much.

"You put your rod inside me and gave me your seed," she said in a choked voice. Could her cheeks burn any hotter? "Surely that means I pleased you."

"Of course ye pleased me," he said with a hint of impatience.

It nearly killed her to turn her head and meet his glittering eyes.

For a dazed moment, she lost herself in admiring his handsomeness. With those pure Celtic features, he really was a gorgeous man. "Then why in heaven's name are you grumbling?"

He looked startled. "Ye should be the one grumbling. You didnae find your pleasure."

Her brows drew together. "Yes, I did."

Thick black eyebrows lowered over brilliant eyes. "Dinna lie to me."

She flinched. After all the lies between them, the accusation left a sting.

"I'm not. You must know I liked kissing you." Her eyes fluttered down. She'd never had a conversation like this in her life. "And what you did when you touched me down there...was wonderful."

His expression didn't ease. "But you felt nae more when I was inside ye?"

Good Lord above. "More?"

She watched understanding light his expression, and wished to the devil that she understood.

"Diarmid," she said slowly, "I don't know what you're talking about. If you enjoyed what we did, isn't that enough?"

He shook his head. "My dear, ye married a fool."

Fiona placed a hand on his shoulder, before she wondered if she had the right to touch him, now the act was done. She'd never wanted to touch Ian, but the turmoil in her mind made her need the solid reassurance of contact with Diarmid.

Before she could withdraw, he turned his head and placed a quick kiss on her fingers. Relief filled her. Clearly he didn't mind her touching him.

"I think I must be the fool," she said huskily. "Please explain what you mean, and keep it simple."

His smile was rueful, and so charming that her heart did another of those disorienting flips. "A woman can enjoy congress as much as a man."

Her eyes rounded, even as disbelief added a skeptical note to her reply. "I doubt it."

"I'd like to prove it to ye."

"You want to do that again," she said in a flat voice.

"Aye, I do."

A quick glance toward his thighs confirmed that he wasn't exaggerating. "Is a man capable of doing that more than once a night?"

"He is indeed. Can ye bear it?"

Fiona found the courage to tell him the truth. "If you kiss me and touch me again, I'll be delighted."

He kissed her with a sweetness that thickened her blood to syrup. "I dinna think ye know what delighted means, my darling."

Her heart squeezed hard at the endearment. "You're still speaking in riddles."

Diarmid studied her as if she belonged to some strange new species. "You didnae feel there was something missing at the end? Ye were definitely on the way."

"After the kissing, I didn't mind what you did."

"High praise," he said with a hint of sarcasm.

"I don't know what you want me to say. You made me feel things I never had before, and I loved that I gave you ease."

"Aye, I've been in a state about ye since we met."

She thought back over the evening's astonishing events. Diarmid's kisses had swept her into a sublime world she'd never known existed. His caresses had roused strange but enjoyable quakes. Were they the explosions Marina spoke about?

When he moved inside her, those shivery little explosions had risen again. She'd loved hearing his groan of completion as he filled her. What else could there be?

Apparently more.

At least she hadn't been wrong about pleasing him. When she feared she hadn't, she'd wanted to shrivel up and die. "What should I do?"

A slow smile curved his lips. Suddenly steadfast, upright Diarmid Mactavish looked dauntingly devilish. "Och, just lie back, lassie, and let me do all the work."

"That doesn't seem fair."

"You'll get your turn."

She was still blushing. "Do you mind if I have a wash first?"

"No' at all."

"Thank you."

Fiona slid out of bed, tugging down her nightdress with a modesty she knew was absurd now he'd touched every inch of her. As she walked across to the connecting door, a cascade of aches reminded her of what they'd just done to one another. And what Diarmid meant to do again.

The heat that stirred in her loins wasn't nearly so unfamiliar as it would have been an hour ago. His desire no longer felt like a threat. It felt like a gift.

She prayed that whatever this mysterious other was, she could give it to him. The thought of satisfying her husband made her feel very wifely indeed.

When Fiona returned to Diarmid's room, she was relieved to see that he wore his robe. She was curious about his body in a way that she'd never been curious about Ian. But she wasn't yet ready to cope with a naked man prancing about the chamber.

He'd built the fire and straightened the disordered bed. He turned from the sideboard to offer her a glass of whisky, then stopped with a spellbound expression. "Your hair."

Self-consciously she touched the tumble of hair floating about her shoulders. "You said you wanted to see it loose."

"It's beautiful." As he came closer, she read awe in his eyes. "You're beautiful."

"Thank you." Pleasure at his appreciation rippled through her.

His hand ran down the fall of blond hair. The caress conveyed a reverence that made her shiver with awareness. That odd restlessness inside her became more urgent.

He passed her the glass. "Drink up, Fiona."

Diarmid stepped away and picked up his whisky to down it in a single mouthful. She sipped at her drink and felt the warmth seep into her bones.

"You must be hungry." He offered her a plate of oatcakes and cheese. "I rang for some food."

"But it's the middle of the night."

"They managed."

She reached out for an oatcake. He was right. She was hungry. She'd hardly touched the extravagant dinner he'd ordered. Nor had she eaten much at the wedding breakfast. She'd been so jittery, she hadn't been able to swallow a thing.

She sank into a chair near the fire. "This reminds me of our meal on the road."

This reprieve was welcome. She'd expected Diarmid to leap on her the minute she came back into the room. She should have known better. He was taking the time to ease her into whatever happened next.

If it involved more kissing, she approved of his plans. She'd loved his kisses.

"We've been through a lot, ye and I," he said, offering her another oatcake. "Here."

He sat down in the chair across from her and subjected her to an intent stare. "How are ye feeling?"

"Better." She was surprised that it was the truth. "But, Diarmid, I'm still not sure I can give you what you want."

"I don't believe that. I want to make ye mine."

Puzzled, she let the hand holding the oatcake drop to her lap. "You've got me."

"No' fully."

They veered back toward that confusing conversation, where he seemed to think she had more to bring to him than she already had. "That might be all there is."

It was possible she was unnatural. Or Ian had damaged her. Diarmid had said something about her bearing scars from her marriage.

"I dinna believe that."

Her appetite deserted her. She set the half-eaten oatcake on the side table. "I've given you more than I've given any other man. You had my willingness. You even had my enjoyment."

He listened with a concentration nobody else had ever devoted to her. It was daunting and flattering in equal measure. "Tell me how ye felt."

A shiver rippled through her, as she recalled the passionate heat of his lips. "Shaky, and...needy, and weak in the knees, and dizzy."

A grunt of amusement escaped him. "That doesnae sound too good."

"Actually it was lovely." She couldn't help smiling. "The loveliest thing that's ever happened to me."

She had a sudden memory of Marina's expression as she'd talked about making love to her husband. Her friend had meant more than kisses. The look in her eyes had made Fiona envy her, even if she didn't know precisely what she was envying.

"I'm glad." Diarmid looked relieved. "I was so afraid of hurting ye. You've been hurt too often."

She regarded him in horror. "Of course you didn't hurt me. I liked it."

Her cheeks were hot again. She'd blushed more in these last hours than she ever had in her life. Something about the purposeful light in her husband's eyes told her that before the night was done, more blushes were forecast.

"Even the last bit?"

"Even the last bit." When she saw he remained dubious, she struggled for words to explain something beyond words' power. Her voice lowered, and she twined her hands in her lap. "I liked that you gave me everything you had."

"I certainly did that," he said drily.

"I made that happen, Diarmid." Her cheeks had heated to the point where they threatened to turn to flame. "For once, I wasn't the mere recipient of your charity."

He flinched as if she'd hit him. "That's no' fair."

"You know, it really is. It's humiliating to take, take, take, with no choice but to accept your generosity, and no way to repay you."

He looked troubled. "I'm no' keeping a ledger, Fiona."

"I am."

"That's nae way for us to go on." He looked displeased and unhappy. "Will ye keep this up for the next fifty years? Every time I give you a new dress or a new bonnet, will ye feel obliged to martyr yourself to me?"

"No, of course not. I imagine as time goes on, we'll settle into a more equitable relationship." Her voice shook with the force of her feelings. "But I can't spend the rest of my life feeling like I owe you a debt I can never repay."

"I'm no' asking ye to," he said with barely concealed frustration. "Anything I do for ye, I do willingly."

"And what I do for you, I do willingly," she said with a trace of heat. He needed to understand this, or they had no chance of finding their way together. "Over the last ten years, I've had every ounce of power stolen from me. I couldn't say who I married. I couldn't decide where I lived. I couldn't even control what happened to my child. Allow me the privilege of choosing what I share with you."

Diarmid sighed and ran a hand through his ruffled dark hair. He looked breathtaking, sprawled in the oak chair and wrapped in his rich red dressing gown. "It would be churlish to object."

"It would." His acceptance stuck a pin in the bubble of her self-righteousness. "Even if what we do together never goes beyond what just happened, you made me feel more fulfilled than I ever have before." Her lips turned down. "So I suppose I'm still grateful to you."

"I dinna want ye feeling like you owe me anything, Fiona. That will only poison our life together." His expression turned somber. "You speak as if I think of ye as feeble and weak, a clinging vine. That couldnae be further from the truth."

She gave a gasp of surprise. "Don't you?"

"Hell, no. I cannae think of anyone I respect more. Ye broke away from the Grants, you faced every peril to save your daughter. You stuck to your purpose, even though it meant lying and stealing and taking any chance ye could."

"That wasn't courage. I was desperate."

"It was courage."

Her guilt at the way she'd repaid his kindness at Invertavey remained. "Are you saying you forgive me?"

"Of course I do." He looked shocked. "I forgave ye as soon as I learned the truth."

"Even though I stole from you?" She still cringed to recall that ghastly moment when the coins dropped from her pocket and he realized she'd broken into his desk.

"Fiona, what's mine is yours. Everything I am and everything I have is at your service."

The words struck her like blows. She couldn't doubt he meant them. Fiona made herself smile, although poignant emotion turned her voice husky. "That sounds like a vow."

"Aye, it is." He didn't smile. "A vow as binding as the ones I spoke today in front of the minister."

More binding, she suspected. He'd promised to love her then, too. She had no illusions that he cared for her that way. "I don't deserve you, Diarmid."

One hand slashed the air. "Any debt between us became null the moment ye married me."

Fiona could hardly credit his generosity. A few hours ago, she'd never have imagined finding the nerve to do this, but she stood and crossed to stand before him. She caught his face between her hands and met his intense black stare.

"I honor you, Diarmid Mactavish, my husband. And while I know you don't want my gratitude, you have it. I promise I'll do my best to be a good wife and to make sure you never regret taking me as your bride."

"Fiona..." he said in a raw voice.

Before he could deflect her thanks, she bent to press her lips to his mouth.

The kiss was unprecedented in her experience, a step beyond even those heady kisses they'd shared before he used her body. He'd been very much in charge of those, for all her enjoyment and enthusiastic response. Now she made the choices. His lips were soft beneath hers, and he let her take the lead, so the contact conveyed more tenderness than passion. Although passion hovered close, a whisper from taking over.

Slowly she drew away. He rose to his feet and settled his hands at her waist. The light in his eyes made her stomach clench on more of that piercing emotion she still couldn't identify.

"I'm glad I married you." Something else she'd never imagined saying before tonight.

"And I'm glad I married ye." The sincerity in that deep voice settled inside her like a warm ember at the heart of a fire. "We've made a bonny start, I think."

"I think so, too." She lowered her hands to those broad shoulders. She loved his strength. Another first. Male power had only ever been a threat until she met Diarmid. "Shall we take the next step?"

"Aye." He kissed her again, and she realized with a shock, that for the first time in her life, she came to a man's bed with joyous anticipation.

CHAPTER TWENTY-SEVEN

Fiona expected Diarmid to pull her nightdress over her head that very moment. She knew he wanted to see her naked. But he seemed content to stand here and keep kissing her, until her knees threatened to fold beneath her.

Hard to believe at the start of the night, she hadn't known how to kiss a man. Now she knew about playful kisses and teasing kisses and wet, open-mouthed kisses that were all tongue, and that set her blood thundering. She knew about long, lazy kisses that lured the soul from her body. Hard, thorough kisses that ignited flashes of excitement, hot and bright as lightning. Sweet, quick kisses that sparked pleasure wherever they landed. An eyelid. Her nose. The tip of her chin. The whisky they'd shared added a honey flavor, but the richest flavor of all was Diarmid himself.

It was impossible to ignore the hard flesh rising between his thighs. She'd learned to fear that part of a man, but tonight his excitement presaged the joining to come. Not cruel and inescapable, but a promise that she'd bring him joy.

The voluptuous dance of their lips made her audacious. How odd to find herself seeking contact, when before tonight, she'd always shrunk from it. It seemed Diarmid gave her yet one more gift, a nascent sensual courage.

She bent to nip and lick at the bare chest revealed under the open vee of his robe. He tasted delicious, and the heady scent of his skin intoxicated her. When she scraped her teeth down the center of his chest, he shuddered. The frail seedling of her bravery shriveled, and she raised her head to meet blazing black eyes.

"I didnae teach ye that," he said in a hoarse voice.

"I...I wanted to taste you," she said uncertainly.

He closed his eyes, and that telltale muscle flickered in his cheek.

"I'm sorry." She started to shift away. "I thought you'd like it."

His hands tightened on her waist. "By God, I do."

She regarded him doubtfully, although she stopped retreating. "You don't sound as if you do."

"Ye took me by surprise. You've been so afraid..."

As he stood before her, she saw a legion of reactions in his face. Care. Consideration. Desire. Nothing even close to disgust. "I'm becoming less afraid by the minute."

"Well, that's encouraging." A ghost of a smile deepened the corners of his mouth, fuller than usual after all those urgent kisses. "Would ye like to try again?"

"Only if you would."

"My body is at your command, lassie." He kissed her quickly, then stepped back. "Make braw use of it."

A couple of hours ago, that invitation would have had her quaking with nerves. What had she cared then for a man's body? The thought alone promised only pain and degradation.

But this was Diarmid, and she'd wanted to touch him for a long time. Despite her fear, his male beauty had always drawn her.

Now he was hers to explore.

"What should I do?" she asked again, as her hands itched to discover the hard planes of his torso.

He spread his arms out and smiled at her with a delight that chased away the shadows in her heart. "Whatever ye want."

"But will you like it?"

"I'm sure I will. I'll like it even more if ye like it, too."

She bit her lips and wondered where to start. Her touch tentative, she placed her hands flat on that triangle of skin where she'd kissed him.

"You're so warm," she said almost to herself.

His muscles bunched under her caresses. This time, she didn't read the response as rejection, but as stirring need.

"I burn for ye," he said softly. "You must ken that by now, Fiona."

She did. It was lovely knowledge. With growing confidence, she spread her hands wider, pushing the heavy red velvet aside to reveal flat brown nipples.

He'd liked it when she'd been bold. Perhaps she should be bold again. The breath caught in her throat as she leaned in to kiss each nipple in turn.

She heard Diarmid stifle a groan of pleasure. When he'd suckled her breasts, wild, shivery sensations had rocketed through her. Could she do that to him? She placed her mouth over one nipple and drew hard until the point hardened. She swirled her tongue over the nub until he was shaking.

"Dinna...stop," he said in a cracked voice she'd never heard before.

She caressed his ribs as she nibbled her way across his chest. Avid hands pushed at the dressing gown, edging it down until it hung loose around his waist.

In a fever of carnal curiosity, she fumbled to untie the belt. But her fingers couldn't make sense of the knot.

He caught her hands. "No' yet."

"I want to see you." Enough of the former frightened Fiona remained for her to marvel at the demand.

"Last time, I rushed ye."

Her hands stilled, and she stared up at him, puzzled. "No, you didn't."

"Aye, I did." That crooked smile she'd come to love turned his lips down. "If ye undress me, I'm likely to rush you this time as well. That would be a pity when there are things I want to do to ye first."

A luscious ripple stirred her blood. "That sounds—"

"Terrifying?"

Once, perhaps. No longer.

The answer she settled for didn't come near to expressing the turbulent storm raging inside her. "Interesting."

"I hope you'll think so. Will ye follow where I lead?"

She smiled. "That's what I promised in front of the minister."

He caught her hand and placed a quick kiss on her fluttering fingers, before he drew her across to the bed. "Thank ye."

He'd explored her most intimate flesh, moved inside her. In comparison, these little gestures of affection shouldn't contain such power. But the sweetness of his lips on her knuckles transformed her blood to melted sugar.

In a daze, she let him push her down to sit on the edge of the bed. When she shifted, the slide of her nightgown beneath her bare buttocks felt like yet another sensual tease.

Diarmid kneeled before her. "Part your legs for me."

"But you'll see…"

Familiar amusement creased his cheeks. "Aye, I will indeed."

Fiona set her hands flat on the mattress either side of her and slowly spread her thighs. The loose nightgown dipped to preserve her modesty, but she wasn't naïve enough to imagine it would stay that way.

Diarmid moved in until her legs framed him. Instead of doing anything shocking, he put his arms around her and tilted her down for more kisses. He was so tall, she didn't need to lean far.

By the time he drew away, her heart was racing and she couldn't muster a sensible thought. Her hands were buried in the black silk of his hair, and the neck of her nightgown gaped to allow him an unimpeded view of her breasts.

His eyes flared, and he licked his lips with unabashed appreciation. Instead of hitching up the nightgown to cover herself, she leaned forward and ran one hand down the side of his face. When she felt the faint prickle of whiskers, she recalled the short beard he'd grown in the hills and how dashing it had made him look.

Then he'd looked like a pirate. Now kneeling before her, he looked like a knight of legend beholding the Holy Grail.

Except she couldn't imagine Sir Galahad's eyes ever gleaming with quite that sensual fire.

"Touch me, Diarmid," she whispered.

He caught her breasts through the silk. Her nipples tightened into yearning points. He played with her breasts, squeezing, cupping, pressing them together, rubbing the silk across the sensitive peaks until she whimpered with longing. By the time she caught his busy hands and tugged them down to her lap, she was shaking so hard she could barely sit up.

"Wait," she said breathlessly. "Shift back a wee bit."

Fiona stood to pull the nightdress over her head. She felt she offered him her nakedness like a gift. When his eyes worshipped her, she received a reward of her own. She'd expected to see salacious hunger, but he looked transfigured. His fists closed at his sides as if he hardly dared to touch her.

Dear heaven, how she wanted him to touch her. Liquid heat welled between her legs, and her breasts swelled in flagrant need.

"Fiona..." he said in a choked voice. "I'm no' worthy."

Tenderness crushed her heart into an aching mass. She slid her fingers through his hair. "Of course you are."

Diarmid's movements always expressed manly grace and power. But as he reached for her and buried his face in her belly, eagerness made him clumsy. His hands shook as he caught her buttocks.

This time, the tenderness sliced so deep, it carved a rift across her heart. Her hand curled around his head and pressed him closer. She bent over until her hair drifted about him like a veil.

She didn't know how long they remained in that desperate embrace, but eventually he raised his head and stared up at her from where he kneeled at her feet. The fond amusement was back, but beneath the smile, deep emotion lingered, like the last traces of sunset in a night sky. "You're glorious."

"I'm glad you think so," she said in a thick voice, still playing with his hair. "I want to please you."

"By all that's holy, ye do." He caught her hips and pushed her back until she was sitting again. "Let me please ye in return."

When her legs spread and his eager eyes fell on her...there, she blushed with a mixture of embarrassment and excitement.

"Bonny," he said with a trace of his earlier awe. Gently he caught her thighs and slid her forward to the edge of the mattress. "Lean back on your elbows."

Fiona sucked in a breath laden with the spice of arousal and obeyed without hesitation. When Diarmid stroked her legs, starting at her ankles and venturing higher with each pass, she gasped. She craved his hands where she was wet and needy. With a shiver of voluptuous nostalgia, she recalled how he'd touched her there.

By the time he reached the top of her thighs, she was panting. Then her breath stopped altogether, when he caressed her feminine folds until they felt full and hot and swollen. Each brush of his fingers teased a place that left her shuddering with reaction.

A strange, powerful sensation rose. A little like what she'd felt when he'd joined his body with hers. But compared to the mighty waves crashing over her now, that had been a mere wisp of response.

She gave a whimper and shifted to urge him on. Impatience made her restless.

Diarmid leaned closer and placed his mouth where his hands had created such havoc. Shock made her stiffen and cry out as wet heat settled over her.

He raised his head and sinful surprise gripped her to see his lips glistening with her female juices. Until tonight, she'd never been wet with need. Until tonight she'd never known that a woman could need.

"Diarmid..."

"You'll like this. Trust me."

"I do, but..."

Devilish knowledge lit his face. "I've wanted to taste ye since that first night."

"This seems so wicked," she said weakly.

A huff of laughter escaped. "Och, I certainly hope so."

Before she could digest that answer, he lowered his head to kiss her private places. Astonishment held her quiescent under his mouth, before a blast of sensation so pure and piercing struck that she cried out again. In helpless surrender, her thighs opened wider to invite him to feast on her.

He did.

Fiona felt the scrape of his teeth and the soothing flicker of his tongue. Except the touch wasn't soothing at all, but teasing and taunting and tormenting.

Another shudder jolted through her. And another. Until the quakes came so fast, she could no longer count them. Boneless with bliss, she flopped back onto the sheets and gave herself up to his brazen incursions.

At first, she was only aware of the unprecedented sensations rushing through her body, turning her blood to flame. Gradually her response focused on one particular place that his mouth returned to over and over.

Something new and overwhelming began to coil in the base of her belly. Like an ever-tightening spiral of brightest gold. She gasped as the feeling grew sharper. Her hands tangled in Diarmid's hair, while she fumbled for purchase in this whirling new world.

Sounds of sensual enjoyment escaped him, something between a purr and a growl. His hands stroked up and down her legs, the caresses creating a counterpoint to the movement of his greedy lips.

Fiona should be shocked. She'd never imagined anyone doing such a thing to her—or wanting to. But she'd moved into a universe completely alien from what she'd known before. She lay beneath his attentions and let the pleasure build layer by layer.

Because even in her innocence, she couldn't call what flooded through her anything but pleasure. Even if it was pleasure with an edge of striving, of insistence for an end.

Instinctively she pressed up toward his mouth. Then—heaven save her—the pressure changed. She could hardly believe that he'd pushed that clever tongue inside her. With a broken moan, she tugged sharply at his hair.

Still he went on. Still that wild longing rose and rose, until she was entangled in suspense close to pain. Her breath emerged in ragged gasps, and tears pricked at her eyes.

"Diarmid..." she moaned, at the point of begging him to stop, to end this torture that hovered so close to ecstasy.

He didn't answer her. Or not in words.

Instead he returned to that place that throbbed with need. Fiona sank into a dark velvet world charged with lightning, as he circled that place with his tongue, then drew hard.

A towering surge of heat flooded her. She felt his teeth on that sensitive spot, and everything dissolved into white-hot, perfect rapture that buffeted her across some invisible barrier. She tumbled into a dizzying free fall, where she swooped through endless skies of brilliant light.

Through the clamor, she released a high, broken sound of ecstasy. Every muscle clenched as she writhed in delight. She closed her eyes and vanished into the wild colors rioting through her head, the incendiary waves battering her body.

How long did she remain pinned to that starlit rack? Who knew? Her body seemed to shudder for an eternity. When she slumped back against the sheets, she felt as loose as a bolt of silk draped across the bed.

She gulped to fill lungs that ached after the violent, astonishing, transfiguring paroxysms. Slowly she opened eyes that until now had been blind to so much. Hazy sight took in the black beams on the whitewashed ceiling.

That couldn't be right. Surely she should see the vaults of heaven instead.

Fiona was still lost in the mists of what had happened. What on earth had happened?

She was only vaguely aware of Diarmid shifting. Her legs sprawled around his shoulders. Some last shred of modesty made her wonder what he could see. But she couldn't summon the energy to sit up and close her thighs.

After tonight, her body held no more secrets for him. He'd fed on her, and she'd gloried in every moment.

She felt so luxurious and lazy, she might never move again. Diarmid would have to build a special litter for his sloth of a wife, who lay around all day waiting for him to transport her to paradise.

"Something funny?" Even through her satisfaction, she heard the purr in his voice.

Fiona kept staring at the ceiling. "I want to stay like this forever. I've never known…"

Words fluttered away from her like butterflies over a field of wildflowers. Although even at her sharpest, she'd never be able to describe that extraordinary event.

He placed a kiss on the base of her stomach, just above the curls hiding her sex. Slowly she wafted back to the workaday world. But it was a workaday world now tinged with magic, thanks to Diarmid.

The bed sagged beneath her, and Diarmid's face appeared between her and the ceiling. "Ye were created for pleasure," he murmured and bent his disheveled dark head to kiss her.

His lips tasted salty. She took a few seconds to realize she tasted the flavor of her intimate flesh. The thought made her shiver with arousal.

With Ian, the marital act had been an unforgivable invasion. With Diarmid, she welcomed every profligate incursion.

So after a surprised hesitation, she caught Diarmid's shoulders and kissed him back with succulent enjoyment. He began to rain kisses across her neck and breasts.

There were a few beguiling, awkward moments while they shifted from lying across the bed to lying along it. Her feet no longer dangled onto the floor, and he stretched out beside her, still kissing her as if he hardly knew which part of her he wanted to taste next.

This playful, passionate seduction had her blood rising like the tide. As he teased her, she moaned with burgeoning desire. Then cried out when at last he lowered his lips to her breasts. She bowed up to encourage him, as a deep, pounding demand set up in her secret places.

Now she had some idea what that thick pulse promised.

"I want you, Diarmid."

After a conversation formed of sighs and moans and gasps of appreciation, words seemed a shocking intrusion. He went still under her stroking hand and raised his head. A glittering black gaze pinned her in place.

"Say that again."

Fiona tangled her fingers in the soft curls at the base of his skull. This ease with touching him was new, too. She even summoned a smile. "I want you."

Before he could answer, she went on, needing him to know how he'd changed her. "I've never said that to a man in my life. Before tonight, I wouldn't have known what it meant. Thank you, Diarmid. Thank you...my husband."

He looked overwhelmed. "Fiona..."

"Kiss me again." She gave his hair a gentle tug. "And perhaps it's time, my dear, for you to take off that dressing gown."

CHAPTER TWENTY-EIGHT

*D*iarmid's heart squeezed tight, as he rose on one elbow to stare down into Fiona's breathtaking face. He couldn't help recalling her desperate bravery when she came to him hours ago and offered to make this a real marriage.

She was still brave, and she was still desperate. But now, praise heaven, she was desperate for him.

He could hardly believe it, although that long, quaking response to his intimate kisses had made him hope that he might lure her into enjoying the union of their bodies. At least he'd assuaged her fears that she was unnatural, incapable of a woman's full pleasure.

He'd loved the rich, salty flavor of her sex. He'd loved the little gasps and murmurs of surprised joy that greeted every daring incursion of his lips. Most of all, he'd loved feeling her spasm and writhe under his mouth, as she reached her first climax. Her startled cry would echo in his mind forever.

When she'd succumbed with such enchanting, unfettered astonishment, he'd struggled not to take her. He'd been ready for so long, but the bitter recollection of finding his release and leaving her behind proved a great spur to restraint. Perhaps now patience found its reward.

He sat up on the mattress and with a few fumbling movements untied the cord holding his robe in place. He was so het up, even the slide of the velvet against his skin threatened his control. He kneeled before her in all his hard male insistence and waited for her to retreat in terror from his nakedness.

No male organ had given her pleasure. Not even, to his shame, Diarmid's.

Her curious gaze settled on the flesh swelling between his thighs. "Good Lord above."

"I want ye, too."

When she licked her lips, he bit back a pained groan. In most respects, she was still an innocent. He shouldn't be imagining those satiny red lips closing around his dick.

"I...see."

She continued to stare at his cock. Lack of blood started to make his head swim. "Are ye...are ye afraid?"

For her sake, he could hold back. Or at least he'd do his damnedest.

Fiona licked her lips again. Hell, he wished she'd stop doing that.

The delay before she replied threatened to blast him into tiny, steaming pieces. "You know, I don't think I am. May I touch you?"

He was so stupid with wanting her, he wasn't sure he'd heard her aright. "Aye."

She pushed up against the pillows and stretched out one unsteady hand. Diarmid felt like he was strangling. His hands curled in the sheets beneath him, and he braced for her touch as if awaiting a blow.

Although the contact was over in an instant, it rushed through him like a tidal wave. He shut his eyes and groaned, as he battled for control.

"Oh!" she said on a soft exclamation of surprise that made him grit his teeth. "You're...hot."

By the devil, he was. Hot enough to burn to ash.

"May I do that again?"

"Aye." The word was a harsh rumble.

"Are you sure?"

He opened his eyes to see her regarding him uncertainly, but not, thank God, with any fear.

"Of course I'm sure." The prospect of her hand on him made his blood rush with wild anticipation. "I'm an inch away from grabbing ye. You must know by now that I want ye to the point of madness."

A frown drew her fine brows together as she digested his words. "How..."

Perhaps his need troubled her or, even worse, disgusted her. Breath jammed like hot coals in his throat, as he waited for her to finish the sentence.

"...delightful."

Dazed, bewildered, he stared at her. He was so used to seeing Fiona frightened, it took him a few moments to recognize that her expression conveyed curiosity and something that might almost be need.

"What?"

She shrugged, and her soft red lips curved in a smile tinged with gloating. "After what we just did—what you just did to me—I'm glad I can return the pleasure."

"A hundredfold," he said on a groan. He caught her hand. "Shall I show ye another way of giving me pleasure?"

The smile deepened, and sensual interest sparked in the blue eyes. "Yes, please."

When he placed her hand on him, the heat threatened to incinerate him. He ground his teeth, as he hardened, when he'd already been as hard as an iron bar for what felt like hours.

He waited in a lather of suspense for Fiona to pull free. Instead, she shaped her hand to fit him, stroking his length, then curling her fingers around him. The night turned into exquisite torture.

"You like this?"

The husky question penetrated the uproar of blood in his head. "More than I can say."

"I'm glad."

"Move your hand up and down." Although he wasn't sure how long he'd last if she did.

After a vibrant pause, she obeyed. Fire engulfed his body, and his balls tightened to agony, but he couldn't summon the words to stop her.

"Tighter," he growled, his hands fisting in the bedclothes.

Diarmid watched Fiona learn how to touch a man. Her face was stern with concentration, but the hectic color in her cheeks betrayed how what she did stirred her.

He cupped one lovely breast. She shivered under his touch, and the rhythmic squeezing faltered before she resumed his torment.

His thumb teased her nipple until it pearled. He wanted to take her into his mouth, but if he did, she might stop touching his dick.

She leaned in and kissed him. Her lips moved over his with a luscious sweetness that threatened to tip him over the edge.

"Fiona…" he groaned when she lifted away, her name both plea and demand. He raised his hand to catch her shoulder. "I cannae…"

"Show me, Diarmid."

He caught her hand and lifted it away from him. "Lie back."

As she complied, he couldn't mistake her eagerness. He prayed that this time she'd reach her climax. With him so close to the edge, he wouldn't wager on it.

When he shifted over her, she opened her legs to welcome him. He bent to kiss her, silently asking for permission to continue. She returned his kiss, running her hands up and down his back, then to his shock, catching his buttocks and squeezing them.

With a shaking hand, he stroked her cleft. She was slick and ready. He wanted to bring her to orgasm again, but he'd reached the limit of his control. His urgency to be inside her made him blind to everything but the woman beneath him.

"Don't make me wait," she said breathlessly, hands clenching on his arse. "I've never felt like this before."

A reminder, should he need one, of what was at stake. Diarmid clasped her hips in tender hands. With a gentleness that belied his fierce need, he tilted her toward him. Instead of plunging into her as hunger demanded, he slid forward carefully. When hot wetness clasped the head of his cock, he tensed every muscle against spilling himself. With steady power, he forged ahead, until he was seated fully inside her.

Diarmid rose on his elbows to see her face. Fiona was flushed, and her mouth was red and parted as she gasped for air. With a sigh, she closed her eyes, and angled up in wordless encouragement.

He needed no better incitement.

Fiona felt cherished and complete, in a way she never had before. When she shifted, Diarmid settled more deeply. He stretched her, touching places Ian had never come near to discovering.

Also new was the emotional connection, even stronger than a physical connection that left her floundering. The mercifully rare encounters with her first husband had never impinged upon her essential self. Now her essential self was naked and vulnerable. The strangest element was that she wasn't afraid, when fear was the air she'd breathed every day for the last ten years.

Diarmid's thrusts shook her body and pressed her into the mattress. After that extraordinary explosion of delight when he kissed her between the legs, she recognized the swirling rise of arousal. But this was better because he was with her. Every time he slid deep, he became part of her in some way she didn't understand, but couldn't deny. The union extended beyond two bodies in a bed to verge on the holy.

When she lifted her hips to meet him, an immediate thrill rewarded her. Muttering something unintelligible, he caught her waist. Firm hands took her with him as he rolled onto his back. Now she was kneeling over Diarmid, with his body hard and insistent inside her.

"What on earth..."

Before she could shift away, he seized her hips in adamant hands. "Ride me, Fiona."

"I can't..." she said, even as this position pressed his length against new and needy parts of her.

A smile eased his tension. "Aye, ye can." As the smile faded, dark eyes met hers with a piercing alertness that she felt to her bones. "This act has never been yours. Now it is. Use me for your pleasure."

This agony of gratitude she suffered felt like so much more. He understood her better than she understood herself. If she wasn't so avid for his possession, the idea would terrify her.

"Diarmid..." she said in a broken voice.

Words failed her, and she leaned forward to kiss him with a luxurious languor that thickened her blood to honey. Her breasts pressed into his chest, creating a beguiling friction against the crisp curls of dark hair.

She lingered over the kiss, before she rose with fresh confidence. Holding that impressive column of flesh beneath her, she angled over him. It was easier than she'd imagined to take him inside her, although the action seemed outlandish, almost unnatural.

"What should I do?" she asked uncertainly.

"Whatever ye like." Humor creased his eyes, as he caught her hips in a light hold. "But I fear if you delay too long, I mightnae stay the distance."

"You're a hero, Diarmid. You'll manage."

She meant it, although his grunt of amusement told her he thought she was teasing.

Teasing...

Slowly, knowing it would both tantalize and please him, she rose. Every nerve in her body sparked to life. Her startled gaze met his. He watched her with a powerful mixture of tenderness and hunger.

Fiona tightened and squirmed, until he groaned. Stoking the heat inside her to a blaze, she settled into an undulating pattern. When he cupped her breasts, a spike in pleasure made her circle her hips.

He groaned again and pinched her nipples, propelling her spiraling need ever upward. Her movements became more uneven, as each wave hit harder. He tugged at her nipples and jutted his hips higher into her.

The subtle change in position swept her across into rapture. She convulsed over him, as rivers of fire flashed through her. Vaguely through the glory, she felt his hands tighten on her hips. He rolled her under him again. As he shifted over her, she felt the mattress give beneath her back.

Diarmid groaned and thrust hard. In a heated gush, his seed flooded her womb.

In perfect, unprecedented peace, Diarmid sprawled over Fiona. His galloping heart slowed from its headlong rush. This time he felt neither guilt nor dissatisfaction. She'd found her peak, just before he'd delivered himself over to a fulfillment deeper and more powerful than anything he'd ever known.

For a few seconds, he lingered dazzled in that heaven, his cock still inside Fiona, her arms holding him close, the broken whisper of her breath in his ears. Then he stirred and raised his head.

"I must be crushing ye."

She always looked beautiful, but the ease in her expression as she stared up at him made her so bonny that he caught his breath. Her eyes glowed, and the ever-present strain was gone. "I like it."

"You're a strange wee lassie," he murmured and kissed her quickly. Her lips moved under his with tenderness, but no passion.

Despite her beauty, she looked weary. It had been a long and eventful night.

Gently he wrapped his arms about her and moved onto his side, taking her with him. They remained joined. He had an uncanny feeling that after this miraculous night they'd shared, in some indefinable sense, they'd remain linked forever.

He'd liked and enjoyed the women he'd taken to his bed before his marriage. But the act of love had never touched his soul the way it did with Fiona. She'd pleasured his body—he felt so pleasured, he feared he'd never walk again—but she'd also filled some hollow in his heart he hadn't even known was there.

Perhaps it was because they were husband and wife. He and this woman would create a family, live together as long as the good Lord granted.

Fiona studied him, as if profound thoughts troubled her, too. "I feel...married."

Suddenly and illogically happy, he smiled. He bumped his hips forward and felt her tighten around him as if she, like he, couldn't bear to break the connection. "By God, so do I."

"I'm glad I came to you tonight."

"I never imagined ye would."

The joy in her smile made his heart turn a clumsy somersault. "To think, we can do it all again and again."

"Aren't we lucky?"

"And..." A yawn interrupted her. "Actually I might need some sleep before we get too adventurous."

"You've been worrying yourself sick for days, haven't ye?"

She'd looked gorgeous at the wedding, but frail and on edge. He hadn't missed the violet shadows under her azure eyes.

He'd been fair bedeviled himself. The prospect of Fiona becoming his bride but never his wife had robbed him of sleep.

"About Christina."

"Aye."

"And about you. You made such a dreadful bargain when you decided to help me."

He kissed her softly on the mouth. "Right now, it doesnae feel too dreadful."

"No, it doesn't," she said. "Thank you, Diarmid. You've banished my fear."

"I'm glad." He wanted to say more, something significant, but the right words hovered out of reach. "Sleep now."

"Aye." Her eyes searched his face as if she sought answers to questions she hadn't yet asked. "May I stay?"

This kiss lasted longer and to his astonishment, his body stirred. He raised his head. "I'd like that. I hated asking for that second room."

"At the next inn, you should save your silver and take one bedroom." Charming humor lit her tired eyes. "I'm speaking as a thrifty housewife."

His brief laugh was appreciative. "What a wee treasure I've found."

Diarmid tried to speak lightly, but the words emerged weighty with meaning. Because he did think she was a treasure. She wasn't anything like the woman he'd ever imagined marrying, but he wasn't blind to her quality. Now she was his wife, he intended to guard her well and do his best to make her happy.

"I've brought you a lot of trouble." Her smile faded. "I hope you still think I'm a treasure, after we've defeated all our dragons."

"I will," he said, although he could see she remained unconvinced.

He sighed. Time was the only thing that would prove him true. "Stop worrying, Fiona. You're safe, and we'll get Christina back. Everything else can wait."

"You're right," she said softly, and leaned in to kiss him. Every time she seized the initiative, she took him by surprise. "I don't want to spoil our glorious night."

"Glorious?" he said, his heart brimming with happiness.

With a tenderness that had the same giddy effect as her kiss, she touched his cheek. "Aye, glorious. Although I suspect our glorious night has turned into glorious morning."

So did he. As if to confirm what she said, a blackbird began to sing outside the curtained window.

"Try and sleep. I want us on the road early." He paused. "I'm sorry it's no' much of a honeymoon."

Not that he'd expected anything like a traditional honeymoon. He'd assumed that he'd spend his wedding night alone and yearning. Fiona might be astonished by what had happened between them, but then so was he.

"I wish things were different," she said with a trace of wistfulness.

"I hate what you've been through. I hate that your child has been stolen away. But I cannae hate the circumstances that brought us together."

By the light of the guttering candles, she studied him. "Do you mean that?"

"Aye, with all my heart."

"You're a good man, Diarmid," she said softly and kissed him again.

He wished to heaven she'd stop saying that. He wished to heaven she felt more for him than gratitude.

But that was an argument for another time, if ever. Diarmid didn't mistake the damage ten years with the Grants had wrought on his bonny wife. He wasn't fool enough to think that one night of passion could heal those wounds and leave her whole and ready to face the future at his side.

But she was brave, his Fiona. And she was stalwart. Tonight had made up for a lot of what she'd suffered.

It was a start. In fact, it was a damn good start.

They had another long day of travel ahead, and he was lethargic with the remnants of pleasure. Right now, he could wait to find solutions to their problems. He'd worry about the future when the future arrived.

So he didn't say anything but good night when his wife settled with her back against his chest. He cuddled her close and buried his nose in the tangled silvery hair that smelled so evocatively of Fiona. When he crashed into a dreamless sleep, a contented smile curved his lips.

CHAPTER TWENTY-NINE

"Have a look," Diarmid said, passing Fiona the pocket spyglass.

They were hidden in a grove of trees on a rise overlooking a rundown house that showed failed ambitions of becoming a castle. The tower over the gatehouse was crumbling, matching the unmistakable signs of neglect he'd noted across the rest of the estate. The boundary walls were also in disrepair. It had been a simple matter to sneak onto the grounds of Trahair House unobserved.

That had worried him, still did. Even five minutes in Allan Grant's company had persuaded him that the man might be a stone-hearted bastard, but he was a clever, stone-hearted bastard. He wouldn't make it easy for Fiona to get onto the property where he held Christina and spy out the situation. In fact, he'd be lying in wait to seize Fiona back under his control.

But so far, Diarmid hadn't seen Allan or Thomas—or a wee lassie of Christina's age. He hadn't seen much of anything, if truth be told. At this time of year, the estate should be bustling with preparations for the harvest, but the fields lay fallow, and the few people who appeared didn't seem too bothered with anything like work. Trahair was a poor place.

"You don't think she's here, do you?" Fiona said flatly, lowering the spyglass.

"There's nae sign of her. There's nae sign they're preparing to fend off a rescue attempt. There's nae sign of Allan or Thomas." He caught bitter disappointment on her face. "I'm sorry, lassie."

He reached for her hand and squeezed it. After three days of hard travel, she looked exhausted. Diarmid wasn't feeling too sprightly himself. It was difficult to sleep when his wife lay chastely in his arms and he was hard and aching for her.

They'd arrived at each inn late, eaten a quick dinner, then tumbled into bed for a couple of hours before they hit the road again at sunrise. It was a punishing schedule, and he hadn't had the heart to press his wife to make love to him when her tension increased with every mile they covered toward Inverness.

Now with a trust that made his heart skip a beat, she curled her fingers about his. "Perhaps it looks easy to break in because it's a trap."

"Perhaps."

She looked across at him. "You still think we should approach them directly?"

"Aye. Your circumstances have changed. You're now Lady Intertavey. The Grants nae longer have any claim on you. Nor are ye destitute and alone anymore."

Her lips twisted with the ironic humor that he now recognized as her defense against the onslaught of crippling pain. "What an unflattering description."

He squeezed her fingers again. "Shall we say you're still brave and determined?"

"Determined anyway." She frowned. "If we turn up at the front door, we'll show our hand."

"It's the only way to discover the lay of the land. If there was a village where we could ask for information, the way the Grants did at Invertavey, it would be different, but nobody here seems to set foot more than a stone's throw from the house. Certainly nobody does a lick of work."

Diarmid didn't try to hide his disgust. He hated to see a property left to fall into ruin.

Fiona pulled free of his hold and squared her shoulders. "In that case, let's proceed," she said, passing back the spyglass.

As Fergus's traveling coach rolled across the weedy gravel in front of Trahair House, no grooms ran out to hold the horses. No footmen opened the house's main door and stood to attention to welcome visitors. Up close, the neglect was even more apparent than it had been when Fiona had looked through the small telescope.

Her heart shrank as she contemplated what lay ahead. She still wasn't convinced confronting the Grants was wise. At Bancavan, she'd learned that subterfuge was the only way to outsmart her kinsmen. She reminded herself that she now had Diarmid on her side. His description of her former self as poor and friendless might chafe, but she couldn't argue with its accuracy.

Beneath her misgivings lurked burgeoning anticipation at the prospect of seeing her daughter at last. She assumed Allan received regular news of

Christina from his cousins, but he'd never shared a word of it with her.

He'd always enjoyed tormenting Fiona. They both knew that he'd never cowed her rebellious spirit, however docile she might pretend to be.

From where he sat opposite her, Diarmid took her hand. "Courage, lassie."

She'd come to rely on her husband's quiet, steady support. Since their wedding night, he hadn't claimed her body. She wasn't sure if she was relieved or disappointed. Circumstances hadn't encouraged further pleasurable interludes. The inns had been rough, and their halts had been short. Eating and sleeping were the focus.

Each time they stopped, Diarmid was all business, more like the benevolent autocrat of Invertavey than her passionate lover. And she'd been so tired, not to mention taut as a violin string. Her mind was all on getting her child out of the Grants' clutches.

Now she turned to him. "Diarmid, kiss me."

In the dim interior of the carriage, she caught the startled flash of his eyes. She couldn't blame him for his surprise. Over the last frantic days, an inevitable physical distance had grown up between them.

Leaning in, he pressed his lips to hers. It was over almost before it had begun. Then he reached across to open the door. "Let's see what we can discover."

He stepped out and extended his hand to help her down. Disappointment at the curtailed kiss stirred in her belly, even as she reminded herself today was all about Christina. She'd hoped for one of those deep, passionate kisses that had punctuated their lovemaking after their wedding. A kiss like that would distract her from her fears. Instead, all he'd done was remind her that once Christina was safe, she still needed to negotiate the terms of their marriage.

As she emerged from the coach, her eyes searched the façade of the house. Was Christina at a window, wondering who arrived? Did her daughter sense that her mother had come to take her away?

Not that Fiona imagined it would be so simple. She knew Allan Grant better than that.

At least she looked ready to take on her clansman as an equal. The collar of pearls circled her neck, and her beautiful dark blue gown was the height of fashion, thanks to Sandra. One of the maids at the inn in Inverness had arranged her hair in an elaborate style. When she'd looked in the mirror, she'd hardly recognized Ian Grant's downtrodden widow, or the ragged waif who had washed up on Diarmid's beach.

"The moment they see ye, they'll ken things have changed," Diarmid said with an encouraging smile. He was thinking along the same lines she was. That happened with surprising frequency, she'd noticed. "Ye look bonny. More to the point, ye look like a rich man's wife."

Fiona made herself smile back, although Diarmid's rueful gaze told her she wasn't nearly as skilled as he was at masking her trepidation. She took in how elegant he looked in his borrowed clothes. "The rich man looks rather impressive himself."

"Thank ye." He drew her toward the crumbling stone stairs that led up to a closed oak door. "Good luck."

She straightened and plastered a haughty expression on her face. Diarmid might know she was on edge, but to her enemies, she meant to present an appearance of confidence and power.

They climbed the steps while behind them, Fergus's coachman kept the horses quiet. Diarmid lifted the large iron knocker. The hollow crash echoed the terrified bang of her heart. She tightened her hold on Diarmid's hand and braced for what was to happen.

At first, nothing did happen. The door seemed to take an inordinately long time to creak ajar.

"Aye?" The person hiding in the shadows was a woman, but that was all Fiona could tell about her.

"Is the master at home?" Diarmid asked in an imperious tone Fiona had never heard him use before.

"Aye." The door remained open a mere crack.

"Kindly inform Mr. Grant that Diarmid Mactavish of Invertavey and Lady Invertavey wish to see him."

"He's awfu' busy."

"Nonetheless, pass on the message."

"Aye."

When the woman moved neither to open nor shut the door, Diarmid reached out and pushed it wider. "Is this Highland hospitality, to leave guests standing on the front step?"

Fiona found yet another reason to be grateful to her husband. His cool, commanding manner had them over the threshold and standing in a dusty hall without a stick of furniture to relieve the bleak emptiness. The elderly woman who let them in regarded them with a sullen wariness that made Fiona's stomach knot in familiar dismay. The servants at Bancavan had worn that exact expression. Although unlike this shabby house, Bancavan was run with sparse but military efficiency.

"Ye show nae courtesy to your kinswoman," Diarmid said.

"Kinswoman?" The woman's eyes rounded as they settled on Fiona. "Ye said Mactavish."

With everything else going on, Fiona had forgotten the feud. No wonder they received such a meager welcome.

"Aye," Diarmid said sternly. "But my wife is a Grant. Or she was until we married. Ye have her daughter Christina here. We'd like to see the lassie."

The woman's expression closed against them. "You'd better talk to the laird."

"Is Christina in the house?" Fiona asked, unable to help herself. "Is she well?"

The flash of pity in the woman's glance sent a ripple of foreboding down Fiona's spine. "Please wait here."

"Diarmid…" Fiona whispered, her fingers turning into claws on his arm as the servant shuffled away.

"Whisht, lass. We've got further than I thought we would. Dinna give up hope yet."

Settle down, Fiona.

He was right. She was on the verge of panicking, and that would do no good at all. She stiffened her backbone and sucked in a deep breath to soothe rioting nerves.

The woman was only absent a few minutes. When she returned, her expression was unreadable. "This way, if ye please."

They left the hall and followed a corridor to a closed door. The maid opened it. "Fiona Grant and her man, sir."

The fellow behind the desk was old and decrepit, and as he limped forward, Fiona smelled whisky and stale sweat. William, Laird of Trahair, was pudgy and gray-faced, but beneath the fat, she could make out the familiar Grant features.

"Allan said you'd turn up, and I was to watch for ye, Fiona." He didn't offer his hand, and he spoke with blatant contempt. "Och, I never thought to hear a Grant had sunk to marrying a Mactavish. That is if ye are married. Thomas seemed to think ye are betrothed to him."

Fiona didn't falter, although she'd been nervous about this encounter with her daughter's jailer. Last time she'd seen this man, she'd been hysterical, fighting to prevent Christina falling into his clutches. Now she realized he was yet another satellite of Allan Grant's, impotent away from his cousin's reach.

"Good afternoon, William," she said coldly. "I'd thank you to keep a civil tongue in your head."

"Would ye indeed, ye wee besom? And ye whoring yersel' around the Highlands. Worse than harlotry. You're sleeping in a Mactavish's bed."

Diarmid stepped up to the man until he towered over him. "Ye will apologize to my wife, sir."

"I willnae." Bleary eyes stared up at him. "I heard about the trollop carrying on with ye."

"I hesitate to strike a man in his own house, but I will if ye dinna withdraw that remark."

"Aye, aye, nae need for that. I meant nothing by it." Fiona watched William cringe away from the threat. "I beg your pardon, Fiona."

She'd met him several times at family weddings and christenings. She'd never liked him. "Is Allan here?"

He looked shifty. "No."

"But he has been here?" Diarmid asked.

"Aye, why no'? He's my cousin."

"I want to see Christina," Fiona said.

William retreated behind his desk, clearly relieved to put a barrier between himself and

Diarmid who still conveyed a belligerent air. "Och, ye cannae."

"My wife is the girl's mother," Diarmid snapped. "She has a right to see her bairn."

For the first time, a smug smile creased William's pasty face. Fiona knew what he was going to say before he said it.

"That's all braw and bonny, but the brat's gone back to Bancavan. Allan was here a few days ago and took her." He shot Diarmid an assessing glance. "And he left ye a message, Mactavish. He said if ye want the lassie, come to Bancavan and see how well ye fare. He also said if Fiona sees sense and returns to where she belongs, he's willing to let bygones be bygones."

"Did he indeed?" Diarmid said in a grim voice. "I'm assuming this forgiveness involves appropriate punishment, followed by a quick wedding to Thomas."

William shrugged. "If it's true that she married ye, she cannae marry Thomas. Unless of course something happens to ye." He didn't bother to hide his satisfaction at that prospect. "If you'll take my advice, laddie, you'll steer clear of Bancavan. Swine by the name of Mactavish dinnae receive much of a welcome in the Grant family keep."

"Och, I'll keep that in mind," Diarmid said sarcastically.

Disappointment at the news of Christina's absence left Fiona staggering. She'd been keyed up to see her daughter, whatever the outcome of today's negotiations.

"How was Christina when she left?" she asked, abandoning pride.

William's glance was hostile, but he answered readily enough. "When Allan promised that she'd see her mam, she went willing. Glad to see the back of her, if truth be told. The brat's been nothing but trouble. Tried to run away. Blockheaded idea. Where the devil would she go? As pudding-brained as her mother. I hope Allan intends to teach her better manners, before she weds my lad in a couple of years."

"She'll never..." Fiona caught Diarmid's eye and swallowed the rest of her denial. There was little point fighting with William. At best, he was Allan's cat's paw. He had no influence over the result of this particular game.

"In that case, we'll take our leave," Diarmid said.

"Aye, get out of my house, you stinking Mactavish, and take your stinking wife with ye. I'm glad to be shot of ye."

With drunken violence, he rang the bell. The woman who had let them in appeared so swiftly, it was clear she'd been listening at the door.

Diarmid took Fiona's hand, but she hardly noticed. The poison in the air here took her back to the years at Bancavan. She felt like she couldn't breathe. The idea of her daughter in this spiteful drunkard's custody made her stomach heave. Blindly she let Diarmid lead her back to the hall, then through the open door.

As the maid turned to go, Fiona struggled to speak. "Christina was well and unharmed last you saw her?"

The woman kept going. For a moment, Fiona thought she wasn't going to answer. Only as she reached the corridor did she mutter without turning around. "Aye, she was."

"Thank God," Fiona said, knees sagging with relief.

"But Allan was in a gey evil mood when he was here." As the woman looked over her shoulder, her eyes were sharp. "I wouldnae like a bairn of mine in his care."

A choked sound of distress escaped Fiona, and she stumbled. "Do you mean…"

But the woman had gone.

Fiona felt like vomiting. From bitter experience, she knew what Allan was like when he was displeased. Poor, poor Christina.

"Sweetheart, dinna give up hope." The deep voice seemed to come from a different universe. "We'll get her back, I swear."

"We've come so far for nothing," she whispered, as Diarmid pressed her close to his side. Her mind told her he was warm and strong, but her despairing heart felt only an icy cold. "I can't believe it."

Carefully he helped her down to their coach. He said something to the driver before he handed her inside the cabin. Fiona hardly noticed or cared. Blackness enveloped her. Christina was lost to them.

"We'll never get her out of Bancavan," she forced through a throat as tight as a knot. "It's a fortress. Anyone called Mactavish will get a dirk in his ribs the minute he sets foot in the glen." She slumped on the seat and stared sightlessly ahead. "It's hopeless."

"We're no' beaten yet." Diarmid sat next to her and put his arm around her. "Chin up, Fiona. This is only the first step."

"I told you." As the coach lurched into movement, Fiona turned to the man she'd married. She was too stricken to cry. "You'll never break into Bancavan. If you try, it means a death sentence."

She'd come back to herself enough to notice that he looked determined, not defeated. That impressive jaw was square and stubborn. "The solution is easy to see. We have to get Allan and Christina away from Bancavan."

"He's not a fool. He'll never release her."

"Whisht, lassie." She didn't resist as Diarmid drew her head down to rest on his broad shoulder. "We'll find a way."

If only she could believe him. But as they drove away from Trahair House, a premonition of inevitable failure crushed her heart.

CHAPTER THIRTY

Trahair House lay in an isolated glen twenty miles from Inverness, so it was late by the time Fiona and Diarmid returned to their inn. Not finding Christina at Trahair had been a blow, but Fiona couldn't give up. Her daughter's safety and happiness were worth any sacrifice. By the time the carriage rolled into the inn yard, she felt capable of sitting up and facing what came now. She smoothed her hair and straightened her skirts.

In the dim light, Diarmid studied her with a searching gaze. "Better?"

"I haven't seen Christina in so long." She made an apologetic gesture. "When Allan wasn't there lying in wait for us, I'd hoped…"

"That we might get her back. I know."

"Or that at least I'd get to see her."

"I'm sorry, lassie."

Something in his tone made her eyes sharpen on him. "You're not surprised we didn't succeed."

An ostler opened the coach door and let down the steps. Diarmid descended and turned to help her out. In the soft gloaming, his expression was serious. "Nothing you've said indicates that Allan will give

Christina up without a fight. Or the dowry he stole from ye. Or, in fact, you yourself. Allan strikes me as a canny laddie, who keeps a tight grip on what he decides belongs to him. That means all the clan's assets, material and human."

"That's true." Fresh despair washed over Fiona, leaving her feeling as heavy as lead. "You must know that William will write to him about our visit. My marriage to a Mactavish will have Allan seething."

"Och, I count on it." Diarmid tucked her hand into the crook of his elbow and drew her toward the open doors.

Surprise made her misstep. "You do?"

"Aye. I want him thinking with his spleen, no' his head. He'll be easier to defeat."

"Allan will want you dead so that he can marry me to Thomas."

"Dinna fash yourself, lassie." To her surprise, Diarmid's voice was warm with affection and humor. "I've got nae intention of letting Allan kill me, and he's no' going to get ye back."

"That's all very well, but as long as Allan has Christina, I'll never be free of him," she said bleakly.

The innkeeper bustled up, asking about dinner and their plans for staying on. Through the turmoil in her mind, she heard Diarmid order a meal to be served in their sitting room.

Fiona wanted to tell him she wasn't hungry. Fear, worry and disappointment made her queasy. But by the time she summoned the words, the landlord had gone.

"Come away upstairs, lassie." Diarmid's smile was gentle, even tender, as he took her arm. "I've ordered baths for both of us. We'll have something to eat and decide our next step."

"Is there a next step?"

"Och, there's always something to be done. Dinna give up hope."

They climbed the stairs to their spacious rooms overlooking the shallow sweep of the Ness River. "But after today…"

"We've had a setback. It doesnae mean we've lost the war."

"I know you mean to be kind, but there's no need to treat me like a child," she responded with a hint of a snap.

He laughed, as he opened the door. "Braw to hear ye sounding less like a wet hen."

"A wet hen?" she spluttered, turning on him. "You know what this means to me."

To her surprise, he caught her up against him for a quick kiss. Despite her pique, she sank into him. During their rushed trip across Scotland, she hadn't slept much, but when she had, she'd dreamed of kisses and the touch of those strong, competent hands.

She staggered as Diarmid stepped away. Then she blushed to realize a servant had come in. Her husband took everything in his stride, directing the man to set up the tray of wine on the sideboard and standing back as more servants arrived to prepare the bath.

The thought of soaking away the day's troubles in hot water was ridiculously appealing. After years of straitened living at Bancavan, a bath still seemed a great extravagance.

By the time Fiona was settled behind a screen and lying back in steaming, scented water, she realized she didn't feel nearly so crushed as she had when they'd left Trahair. Diarmid's conviction that they would prevail lifted her spirits.

She ran the fine rose-scented soap over her breasts and couldn't help remembering the way

Diarmid's hands had followed the same path. The memory tightened her nipples to hard, sensitive points.

Her voice was husky as she called out, "So what happens now?"

There was no answer.

"Diarmid?"

Fiona rose from the bath and wrapped a generous towel around her wet body. She stepped away from the screen. The large, opulent bedroom was empty.

Diarmid rested his head on the end of the bath and closed his eyes in weariness. Today had been discouraging, although unlike his wife, he'd never imagined that the visit to Trahair House would end their troubles. At the very least, he'd expected a confrontation with Allan. But the bastard had been clever enough to make himself scarce and remove Christina to a secure location. With the girl at Bancavan, the quest became more complicated, certainly, but not hopeless.

Nothing more could be done tonight. He was so bloody tired that he might even sleep, despite the distraction of holding Fiona in his arms. She was exhausted, too, and struggling to cope with the continuing separation from Christina. When they left Trahair, his wife had looked devastated. She'd reminded him of the waif he'd rescued from the shipwreck.

The sound of the dressing room door opening made him raise his head. It was too soon for Allan Grant to send an assassin—Diarmid didn't make light of Fiona's warnings about his enemy's murderous intentions. He'd already asked the landlord to tell him about any strangers asking after the Laird of Invertavey and his lady.

He expected a servant, perhaps to top up the hot water. But the person hovering on the threshold to this small room with its cot bed and shelves for clothing and luggage was no servant.

"Fiona?" He reached for a towel. "Is something wrong?"

"No." She gestured for him to lie back. "I just wondered where you were."

"Having a bonny soak. I thought you'd take longer over your bath."

She shrugged, still without stepping into the dressing room. He sank deeper into the water. Since their wedding night, he'd hungered for her. But she'd been so lost and despairing after they left Trahair. He couldn't imagine she was interested in bed sport tonight.

His understanding was no defense against his natural reaction to being naked in front of her. Especially as she was dressed the way he dreamed of seeing her—when he dreamed of her dressed at all.

She wore the cream silk nightdress from their wedding night, although the loose peignoir she'd flung around herself almost made it respectable. Her magnificent hair cascaded around her shoulders. His hands clenched on the sides of the tin bath as he fought the urge to make a rope of those silky tresses and use it to drag her down for his kiss.

"I worried when you didn't answer me."

"I told ye I'd ordered baths for both of us."

"I assumed you'd bathe in the bedroom after I finished."

"Och, I'm all about efficiency, me," he said drily, as he tried to ignore the excitement kicking his heart into a gallop.

"So I see."

When she turned away, he wasn't sure whether he was sorry or relieved. She looked beautiful, all rosy and damp. The way that sheer material clung to the graceful curve of hip and breast tested his self-control.

Diarmid slumped back into the water, only to sit upright once more when she returned with two glasses of claret. She passed him one, before with a whisper of cream satin, she settled on the stool beside the bath.

He gritted his teeth. He'd hoped a bath would relax him. Having his wife within reach left him anything but relaxed.

"Fiona, I dinna think it's wise if ye stay."

She frowned. "I want to talk to you."

God give him strength. "Better when I'm dressed, sweetheart."

"Oh." Her gaze dropped to where his cock rose hard and insistent. "I see."

"Ye do indeed." He tried to speak lightly, but the words emerged as a strangled growl. He took a gulp from his glass, but mere wine couldn't douse the heat blazing inside him.

Fiona hadn't seen him naked since their first night together. He'd taken to sleeping in his dressing gown.

"You know, I'm your wife." That conversational tone shouldn't make him burn.

"I know." Another strangled yelp.

Her gaze lingered on his erection, then she raised her blue eyes to his. "You have every right to use me as you wish."

She leaned forward until the loose nightdress dipped to reveal the top of her breasts. He swallowed to moisten a mouth as dry as dust. His hand clutched the glass so hard, surely it must break.

"You're tired after traveling."

"So are you."

A grunt of bitter laughter escaped him. "I'm never too tired for that."

She sighed and sat back just in time to save his ragged composure. "Then what's stopping you?"

He felt his jaw drop. "Are ye saying you want…"

"Why not?" It was her turn to look uncomfortable. Color rose under her gardenia-petal skin, but she held his gaze. "You know I liked what we did. I thought you did, too."

"I did indeed." Although "liked" was a lily-livered word for the sea of irresistible pleasure that had swept him to paradise in her arms.

Her lips tightened with disapproval. "Must I ask you whenever I want to do…that?"

"It would help to know I'm no' bullying ye."

Something glowed in her eyes, before her lashes fluttered down to hide her expression. "It might be nice to be invited. So far, I've asked you twice, and you haven't asked me at all."

"For the love of God, Fiona," he bit out, setting his wine on the floor and starting to climb out of the bath, only to stop when she gave him a small wave of discouragement.

"Perhaps not right now," she mumbled, although the gaze that ran over his wet body sent another message entirely.

Confused, feeling like she played with him, obscurely hurt, he subsided with a splash. "But ye said…"

She made a helpless gesture toward the door. "Dinner will be here in half an hour. I'd rather…"

He groaned in self-disgust. Of course it would. These last few days, he'd teetered on a knife edge. Now the idea that she might welcome his attentions chased every other thought out of his brain.

"I'm sorry. I didnae think."

She still watched him. He was calm enough now to recognize the keen interest in her expression. "We don't have to linger over our meal."

"No, we damned well don't." His voice deepened into seriousness. "Are ye feeling better?"

"You said you had a few ideas about Christina." She took a sip of her wine. "Will you tell me?"

"Let me get out first."

The flush in her cheeks deepened. "I'm happy to let you finish your bath, as long as you don't mind me being here."

He settled back. "If you'll pour in some hot water, I'm happy to stay until our dinner arrives."

"Perhaps I could wash your back."

Heat stirred anew, but lazy this time and laden with sweet anticipation. He was even able to laugh softly. "Och, that would be grand."

The sultry look she directed toward him was a surprise. She bent to pick up his wine and pass it across. "It would make me feel very wifely."

"Then kiss me, and I'll tell you what's in my mind."

Another comprehensive inspection of his body, before she leaned in and gave him a claret-tinged kiss. "I know what's in your mind, husband."

A wolfish smile curved his lips. "In that case, wife, let me tell you what else is in my mind."

CHAPTER THIRTY-ONE

Fiona settled on her stool beside the bath and tried not to stare at Diarmid the way a rustic stared at the glories of Edinburgh. But it was nearly impossible when he reclined naked before her, his broad chest glistening with moisture and his thick, dark hair clinging in unruly curls to his head. Not to mention the sight of the part of him that she'd once felt grow hard and insistent under her hesitant caresses. When it came to her second husband, she'd chosen a magnificent specimen.

"Fiona, if ye keep looking at me like that, I'm afraid I'll let dinner go to hell. No' to mention we'll shock the servants."

She blushed and brought her wineglass to her lips to hide her embarrassment. "Do you mind me looking at you?"

He gave a grunt of amusement. "What do ye think, sweetheart?"

She swallowed her wine and told herself to settle down. He often used endearments. They didn't mean anything in particular.

"I think you need to tell me what you're planning. If it's a full-on assault, you're wasting your time. Bancavan has never been taken, despite the best efforts of generations of Mactavishes."

"I ken the old stories, too." The humor she loved twisted his lips. "Anyway the days of private armies are over."

"You can use the law against Allan, but it will be slow, and it gives him too many chances to spirit Christina away. Once she hits twelve, he'll marry her to William's son. Whatever the legalities, the courts are inclined to let consummated marriages stand."

"I ken time is of the essence. Tomorrow, I'll write to Fergus and tell him what happened at Trahair."

"Good."

As he sipped his wine, Diarmid's expression turned thoughtful. "In all those hundreds of years of feuding, the Grants didnae have everything their own way."

"No, the Mactavishes were always sneaky."

"Canny."

"Underhanded."

"Cunning as foxes."

Fiona straightened on her low stool and placed her hand on the side of the bath. She leaned forward eagerly. "You have got a plan."

When she saw Diarmid's smile, she found it in her to feel a brief twinge of pity for her vile brother-in-law. Allan had made an implacable enemy in the powerful Laird of Invertavey.

"Aye, I do."

"Well, don't keep me in suspense, Diarmid, blast you."

He laughed and leaned forward to kiss her with more intent. "It was something ye said."

She frowned, as she attempted to focus a mind whirling after that kiss. "Was it?"

She'd said a lot about the Grants. None of it seemed remotely likely to result in Christina's rescue.

"Ye said Allan never met a penny he didnae like. In that case, the prospect of a pound should drum up a fever of excitement."

She sat back. "Aye, he likes to hoard his gold, does my revered brother-in-law."

"I'll offer him a thousand pounds for Christina."

"Diarmid!" she said in astonishment. Another act of lunatic generosity from her husband. She gulped back an automatic protest about the extravagance of the payment.

"It's the perfect solution."

She felt torn. For ten pounds, Allan would walk barefoot to John o'Groats. For a thousand, he might even give up Christina. "I'm sure Allan has never seen that much money in one lump."

"It will be irresistible. And by far the best solution to our dilemma. Nobody gets hurt. A nice, clean transaction. Cash for the girl. And Allan Grant signing away any rights he imagines he has over either ye or your daughter."

"It's too much money, Diarmid. A fortune, in fact." Only minutes ago, she'd been giddy with hope and looking forward to a night of passion. Reality's abrupt and unwelcome return left her reeling. "I shouldn't let you do it."

He set down his wine and regarded her with a somber expression. "Do ye recall our vows?"

The question disoriented her. She'd expected an argument. "Of course."

"So do I. I pledged all my worldly goods to ye."

She, too, put down her wine. Drinking it now would make her heave. "But we don't have a real marriage."

One sleek black eyebrow tilted. "No?"

Did they?

The silence reverberated with a thousand questions, none of which she felt capable of asking.

"It feels rather marital to be sitting in my bath, while you're watching over me in your nightie."

It did feel marital. So had the hours they'd spent traveling together across Scotland. In nine years with Ian, nothing had felt as intimate as the most casual word she spoke to Diarmid.

"I suppose it does," she said slowly.

"Are my causes yours?"

"I don't know what your causes are," she retorted.

"At the moment, my causes are to disentangle my wife from her villainous relatives and bring her daughter to live with us."

Her lips turned down, although her heart was so jammed with poignant emotion, she felt close to crying. "How you must curse the day you found me on that beach."

His smile held no shadows. "Never."

However sincere he sounded, she couldn't believe him. "Let me top up your hot water while we talk about this outlandish idea."

Two large cans waited near the door. As she emptied them into the bath, she realized that Diarmid was right. Somewhere in the last few days, she'd turned into a wife, not a bride. She couldn't put her finger on the precise difference, but there was one.

"Thank ye," he said softly.

She subsided onto her stool and took another mouthful of her wine. It didn't taste half as good as Diarmid's kisses. "I still hate to think of you giving all that money to a toad like Allan."

"No' even to save Christina?"

Her gesture expressed irritation. "You used that argument to convince me to marry you."

"It still packs a punch."

It did, damn him. "Gratitude can smother, you know."

He didn't look happy. He understood what she was saying. "Fergus is looking into getting your property back from the Grants. You'll feel more in control of your destiny, once you've brought a dowry to the match, I know."

"Good luck to him. He'll need pliers to winkle so much as a penny out of Allan Grant. That man loves money almost as much as he loves the clan's unquestioning obedience."

"I'm banking on that." Diarmid paused. "Are you truly so stiff-necked with pride that ye willnae accept my help, even though when we married, I placed my entire fortune at your disposal?"

Her grip on the glass tightened, and her tone turned bitter. "You're always accusing me of pride, when you must know that the Grants humiliated me over and over."

The mocking fondness in his expression made her feel like he caught her heart in one powerful hand and squeezed it. "Darling lassie, without that pride, the Grants would have beaten every scrap of spirit out of ye. I'm devilish grateful for your pride. Without it, we'd never have met, because you'd never have found the nerve to defy Allan and run away." He went on before she could remind him yet again of all the trouble she'd caused him. "But sometimes ye must set pride aside to achieve the larger goal. Getting Christina back is our purpose. Nothing can come between us and success."

She shifted uncomfortably on her stool. He made her feel petty and ungracious—and like a bad mother. "If you go to Bancavan with a thousand pounds in your pocket, we'll see neither you nor the money again. Allan will shoot you, steal the gold, and bury you where nobody will ever find the body."

"I'm sure you're right." A ruthless light entered Diarmid's eyes. "Which is why I propose to meet him on neutral ground."

"He'll still try and bring you down."

"Has he committed murder before?"

She tightened her grip on her glass. "I saw him kill a servant boy in a rage. Beyond that, I can't say for sure, but I wouldn't put it past him."

Fiona recalled a fractious nephew who was there one day, then never seen again. And a kitchen maid who fell pregnant to Thomas and made a great fuss about expecting him to marry her. She'd disappeared, too.

"I wouldnae either." Diarmid's tone was grim. "We'll do the exchange on my cousin Hamish's land. Or near it, anyway. Glen Lyon isnae far from Oban. A good distance from both Invertavey and Bancavan."

"Allan will never agree."

"He will, if he wants his thousand pounds."

"He'll try and squeeze more money out of you. He's a repulsive human being, but he's as wily as a weasel. He'll scheme to get the money, keep Christina, and destroy you. He knows how much I want Christina. He knows as long as he has her, he's got the winning card."

"That arrogance will bring him down, Fiona. He's too used to getting his own way. We can beat him. He'll make a false step."

"Not if he puts a bullet in you the second he sees you," she retorted.

For so long, Christina had been her only reason for living. Now she discovered that the thought of becoming a widow for the second time was utterly unacceptable. "I'll take it very ill if you get yourself killed, Diarmid Mactavish."

He looked startled. "Would ye indeed?"

"I would."

"I wouldnae like it much myself," he said drily. "Trust me, I willnae face Allan alone."

"Will you take Fergus?"

"No. He's got his work cut out with the lawyers. My cousin Hamish looks like a marauding Viking. He'll make even the doughtiest Grant tremble in his boots. He's just the laddie to join our fight."

"You're lucky to have people you trust to stand beside you." She watched him steadily. "I never did."

That ruthless light hadn't faded from his eyes. "That's changed, Fiona. I told ye when you agreed to marry me that ye were no longer alone and defenseless. Allan Grant might bluster and bully his way around Bancavan. But you're away from there and ye now have the Mactavishes, the Mackinnons, and the Douglases on your side. I'd dare the king's entire army to try and best us. Will ye let me go ahead with this?"

What choice did she have? She owed her daughter not just her love but her protection. So far, she'd been a miserable failure when it came to keeping Christina safe.

She still wondered at the sick terror she felt at the idea of Diarmid coming to grief. He was brave and strong and palpably capable of looking after himself. But on the other hand, he didn't know Allan like she did. Diarmid was a lion, and the Grants were a pack of hyenas.

But a pack of hyenas could bring down a lion.

"Do I have any say?"

"Certainly ye do. We're in this together."

She frowned, unhappy at the idea of him risking his life in a direct confrontation with Allan, but feeling trapped into accepting. "You know I'll agree."

"I hope ye will. This seems the simplest way to get Christina."

After a moment, she nodded. "Then all I can say once more is thank you."

His jaw set in a stubborn line. "I wish ye wouldnae."

She could see that he was in no mood to hear an argument. Sighing, she slid to her knees and pushed up the sleeves of the extravagant robe Marina had given her. "Pass me the soap and lean forward."

He cooperated with her request. "So that's a yes?"

She stared at his long, powerful back. Yes, it was strong. But she feared the obligations she laid upon that impressive back might end up breaking him.

"It is." With another sigh, she began to wash the smooth white skin. "Although with misgivings."

"I'll take it." His voice was a rumble of pleasure.

For a long while, the gentle splash of bathwater was the only sound in the room. Fiona's disquiet eased as she started to enjoy having her husband at her mercy. By the time she rinsed the soap away, sensual anticipation weighted her stomach.

When he spoke, he startled her. She'd fallen into something of a trance. "Ye ken, it's no' all bad news."

"It's not?" She stood and reached for a dry towel.

"We'll have to stay in Inverness while we arrange for the money and wait for answers from Hamish and Fergus and Allan."

He rose from the water. The sight of over six feet of virile male, sleek and wet after his bath, filled

Fiona's vision. The languorous interest swirling in her blood sharpened to desire.

"Do you think that will take long?" she made herself ask, when what she really wanted to do was run her hands over every inch of that powerful form.

"Long enough for us to stay in one place and have a real honeymoon."

"Oh."

Diarmid's smile made her heart jump like a bannock on a hot griddle. "Ye dinna like the idea?"

"I...do," she forced out.

With a soft laugh, he plucked the towel from her hands. Seeing him in his potent glory had made her forget to pass it over. "I can see ye do."

She licked her lips, as she noticed he liked the idea, too. Potent glory indeed.

"Let's...let's have dinner," she said in a shaky voice.

"Aye," he said on a deep rumble that vibrated in her bones. "I'm suddenly verra hungry."

CHAPTER THIRTY-TWO

"Is he there?" Fiona asked, crouching down in the bracken beside Diarmid.

"See for yourself." Diarmid passed her the small spyglass.

She lifted the elegant little telescope to her eye. Immediately Allan Grant came into focus in the field across the burn.

She hadn't seen Allan since he'd pursued them out of the Thistle at gunpoint. He looked older, and dressed in black as he was, he put her in mind of a funeral. Her empty stomach clenched in trepidation, and her gloved hands trembled. Even when he was a quarter of a mile away, she couldn't shake the habit of fear.

"I can't see Christina," she said, ashamed of her unsteady voice.

"There's a coach over under the trees. She'll be in there, I suspect."

"If he's brought her." Fiona swung the telescope around, until she saw the shabby closed carriage in the shade of a grove of beeches.

"He wants his money." He paused. "I'll wager he's brought his henchmen with him."

"You said to come alone."

"I did. But then I havenae come alone either." At Diarmid's shoulder was the reassuring bulk of his cousin Hamish, Laird of Glen Lyon, who owned an estate near this isolated brae. Last night, she and Diarmid had been Hamish's guests in a lovely house she'd been too nervous to appreciate.

The meeting with Allan followed a fortnight of frantic planning, with letters flying between Inverness, Invertavey, Bancavan, Edinburgh, and Glen Lyon.

"Everything will be fine," Hamish said in his subterranean rumble of a voice. He spoke with a crisp English accent, legacy of a London childhood.

As far as she was capable of devoting an ounce of attention to anything but the plan to retrieve Christina, she approved of Hamish. He wore his heart on his sleeve more than her husband did, but she liked that she knew where she stood with him. She also liked that he'd placed himself and his considerable resources at their disposal the moment Diarmid asked for help. It was clear that a deep bond of affection and respect united the cousins.

After three weeks of marriage, she commended anyone who valued her wonderful husband as he deserved.

This approval didn't stop her from wanting to slap Hamish for his easy assurance that right must prevail. Neither of the cousins knew what Allan was capable of. They underestimated their foe's animal cunning and his obsession with winning.

She'd tried to make Diarmid and Hamish understand that for Allan, the game had changed from merely keeping Christina and retrieving Fiona.

It had now become a compulsion to best Diarmid Mactavish.

More than best him. Destroy him utterly.

Since she and Diarmid had settled on final arrangements, she'd been sick with dread for the man she'd married. Barely able to sleep, picking at her food, finding surcease only in the passion that blazed like an inferno between them.

"Courage, Fiona," Diarmid murmured, putting his arm around her shoulders and kissing her cheek. He must guess that she was tense to the point of shattering and so afraid that she felt like vomiting.

"I can't bear to think, even now, that something might go wrong." She returned the telescope to him. "Don't trust Allan for a second. Even if it seems as if you've beaten him, he's always got another plan."

"Aye, he's dangerous, which is why I wish ye hadnae come," Diarmid said.

"Allan insisted." This argument had raged since the last correspondence from Bancavan. "Anyway, Christina needs me. She doesn't know you or Hamish, and she's been frightened enough already. I have to be here."

All good reasons, but she didn't speak the most powerful reason: that she intended to step in if Allan played some last trick. For her sake, Diarmid put his life at risk. She wouldn't let him lose it, whatever it cost her.

"I'd still feel better if ye were safe back at Glen Lyon."

"And I'd feel better if I'd never met Allan Grant, and my life was nothing but sugar plums and honey crumpets," she said with asperity.

"For heaven's sake, we've got other fish to fry." The laughter in Hamish's voice made her blush with mortification. "You two need to stop squabbling like an old married couple."

"And only wed three weeks," Diarmid said drily.

Hamish rose to his full six foot five. "From what you say, an eventful three weeks."

Diarmid was right to describe his cousin as a Viking. He was large and vigorous and golden fair. It wasn't difficult to imagine him leaping off a long ship in a berserker fury. Fiona still struggled to accept that this brawny Highlander was a highly respected astronomer.

"We should go, Diarmid," Hamish said. "No point extending everyone's misery."

The morning was cold and rainy, typical of the end of a wet Highland summer. The woolen shawl covering Fiona's head was uncomfortably clammy. Her husband had insisted that she hide her distinctive hair. Like her, he expected trickery.

Diarmid rose, slipping slightly on the muddy grass. When she moved, he placed one hand on her shoulder.

"No, Fiona, wait here. We agreed you'd let me make sure all is safe before ye get close to Allan."

"You told me. I didn't agree," she retorted as she subsided. Behind them, twenty armed men from Glen Lyon waited. Nobody knew what lay ahead of them today.

"Let's go, Hamish." Diarmid strode forward from under the shelter of the trees. Hamish followed him down the slope to the small stone bridge where the exchange was to take place.

"Dear God, keep him safe," Fiona whispered, and was surprised that her prayer was first for Diarmid and not for Christina.

She rose onto her knees to see better. Her heart fluttered in her throat, and coiling snakes of terror writhed in her belly. At her waist, her hands twisted together so tightly that they hurt. Had she and Diarmid come so far, only to fail now?

Diarmid knew a crowd of people watched from the wood behind him, including Sir Quentin Avery, the Englishman who owned the land he currently walked across. He was the local magistrate, and Diarmid had invited him as a witness, in case there was any treachery.

But as Diarmid walked away, he could only feel one set of eyes, Fiona's. Her gaze burned into his back like a brand. Since the day he'd found her, every moment had led to this confrontation. Diarmid couldn't let her down.

To secure Christina's future, she'd faced danger, she'd committed crimes, she'd traveled across half the Highlands, she'd submitted to an unwanted second marriage.

Except in their time together at Inverness, she hadn't seemed a reluctant bride. He'd started to feel a cautious optimism about his future with his lovely wife.

Och, well, they would sort out everything else, once Allan was no longer a threat and Christina was back in her mother's care.

Allan strode forward to meet him. With no particular surprise, Diarmid saw Thomas sidle around from behind the coach.

"Mactavish," Allan said flatly, stopping at the end of the short bridge.

"Grant," Diarmid responded, waiting at the other side. "This is my cousin Hamish Douglas, Laird of Glen Lyon. He's here to see our transaction takes place as agreed."

"Aye," Allan said sourly. "I brought my brother, too, as ye see. I ken no' to trust a Mactavish. Have ye got my money?"

"Aye. Have ye got the girl?"

"She's in the coach."

"Let me see her."

"Show me the payment first."

Diarmid reached into his coat pocket and produced the pile of notes. At the sight, Allan's eyes brightened, and he rushed forward, reaching out a greedy hand.

Diarmid retreated. "Show me Christina. We want her whole and unharmed, along with a signed paper relinquishing any claim to her or my wife."

"Aye, I hear ye married the slut."

"I'm no' above punching ye in the face, you bastard," Diarmid said sharply. "Fiona's told me how you treated her. It was enough to turn my stomach."

"She was always a foul wee liar, Mactavish. You're welcome to the besom."

Neither of them believed Allan meant that.

"I wouldnae be too quick to accuse someone else of lying, Grant. You told me Fiona and Thomas were married."

"Laddie, ye must ken that in the Highlands, a vow made before witnesses is as binding as a vow before a minister," Allan said with insufferable condescension.

"Aye, maybe so, but both parties need to agree to the match. What ye intended for Fiona was little better than rape."

"An ugly word from the devil who kidnapped the lassie away from her family."

"I wouldnae leave a mongrel dog in your custody, ye swine."

"Gentlemen, this achieves nothing," Hamish said from Diarmid's side.

Diarmid was surprised to recognize that for once, his volatile cousin was the voice of reason, while he had difficulty controlling his temper. The sight of this man who had made Fiona's life so wretched stirred a rage to kill that had grown since Diarmid first heard her history. "Hand over the bairn, sign the paper, we'll pay the agreed amount, and our dealings are at an end."

Allan's already narrow lips turned so thin, they almost disappeared, but he nodded at Thomas who crossed to open the door of the coach. For a long moment, nothing happened.

Diarmid's gut clenched with dismay. If Allan hadn't brought Christina to this meeting, the whole scheme would fall to ruin.

He only took a breath when the carriage shifted and a skinny child stepped down onto the muddy ground. She wore plain but good quality clothes, and a plaid shawl was wrapped around her head, obscuring her face.

"Take off the shawl, Christina," he called.

At the sound of his voice, the girl stopped and turned in Allan's direction. Allan gestured to her. "Obey the man."

Visibly trembling, the girl unwound the length of wool. Pale blond hair appeared. Hair the color of warm moonlight.

Relief flooded Diarmid, and he took an instinctive step forward. "Christina."

The girl's large eyes fixed on him, and she retreated. Her face was as white as marble. "Aye, sir."

"I'm here to take ye to your mother."

The girl didn't show any immediate pleasure at the announcement.

"Ye see she's here," Allan snarled. "Give me my money, and let's finish this. There's a stench in the air that makes me ill."

Now Christina was finally within reach—the lassie was the image of her mother, so there was no doubting her identity—Diarmid could ignore the puerile insult. He stepped forward, the wad of notes extended. "Here. My cousin will stay to see ye sign the paper, while I take the bairn back to Fiona."

Allan snatched at the money and counted it quickly. "Aye, all seems above board."

Diarmid's lips tightened. He wanted this over. "I'm a man of my word. That's the full amount I promised for the girl. Now ye just have to fulfill your half of the bargain, and we're square."

A lie, when Fergus already made progress on the legal issues of Fiona's dowry, but true enough at the moment.

"Aye, I see that. Ye were gey desperate to pay over the odds for this useless scrap of a lassie."

Diarmid didn't respond to the jibe. "Come with me, Christina. Your mother is waiting up in the trees on the hill."

The girl made faltering progress across the field, but her eyes remained fixed on Allan. The thought of Fiona living in such fear made Diarmid want to smash something. Preferably something bearing the name of Grant. But so close to achieving what he wanted, he wasn't going to shatter the fragile truce.

Allan jammed the notes into his coat pocket. "We can go on as planned."

Then everything seemed to happen at once. Fiona shouted her daughter's name as she broke clear of the trees and darted down the brae. Christina gave a broken cry and dashed forward past

Diarmid. A loud sound from nearby set Diarmid's ears ringing.

The pain took a few more seconds to hit him. When it did, he staggered and collapsed back against the edge of the bridge.

CHAPTER THIRTY-THREE

The crack of a gunshot made Fiona stumble on her headlong race down the steep hillside toward the bridge. With sick horror, she saw Diarmid reel and collapse. Her vision narrowed to a long dark tunnel, with her husband lying quiet and still at the other end.

"Diarmid!" she screamed in despair, finding her balance and forcing her legs to move faster.

The shock of seeing him fall was so powerful that it took her a few seconds to realize that a small figure had pushed past him and now darted up the slope toward her.

As another shot rang out from the bridge below, she came face to face with the daughter she hadn't seen in so long. "Christina..."

For a year, she'd spent every minute hungering to see her child again. Now, as the world turned to nightmare, she did.

The moment was so overwhelming that she hardly noticed Sir Quentin and the Douglas men thunder past her on their way to the bridge. From the other side of the burn, about a dozen men wearing the black and yellow Grant tartan streamed out of the trees behind the carriage that had brought Christina to this isolated brae.

"Mamma!" Christina flung herself at her mother with a force that left Fiona winded.

Fiona's arms closed hard about the too-thin body. For the space of a second, she shut her eyes and breathed in the scent of her little girl who rested in her embrace at last. As she clutched her baby to her, her heart felt too big to fit inside her chest. The surge of love that flooded her made her shake. Love and relief and overmastering gratitude that she saw her child again, when there had been so many days when she'd been sure she never would.

But the reunion was bittersweet and at least for now, by necessity curtailed. Fiona drew back, wiping at her eyes. Christina needed her. She knew it. But Diarmid needed her more. She had to go to her husband, who lay shot at the base of the hill.

Pray God he was still alive. The thought of the rest of her days without Diarmid Mactavish was too cruel to endure.

"Sweetheart, I'm sorry. I'm so happy to see you, but I have to find out what's happening down at the bridge," she said urgently. "Quick. Go up to the trees at the top of the hill and wait there. Don't come down again until I come and get you."

Distress and bewilderment darkened the large blue eyes that peered up at her from a pale, drawn face. "But, Mamma..."

It was unfair to expect a child to understand that Fiona had obligations that outweighed her immediate duties as a mother. Yet she had no time for long explanations.

"Go, Christina. Don't be afraid. I'll come and find you, and I'll make it up to you, I promise." She didn't wait for the inevitable protest, although pulling free from her daughter's clinging arms felt like cutting off part of herself. "I'll fetch you as soon as I can."

Biting back a sob, she picked up her skirts and sprinted down the hill. Halfway down, she turned back to check that Christina obeyed her. The slumped shoulders spoke of defeat in a way that tore at Fiona's heart, but at least the girl was heading toward the trees and safety.

With dogged determination, Fiona faced downhill again and headed toward Diarmid. When she skidded on the muddy track leading up to the bridge, she saw Hamish on his knees, supporting his terrifyingly still cousin and pressing a sodden red handkerchief to his shoulder. In the distance, bands of fighting men clashed near the carriage, but she had no attention to spare for anyone other than her husband.

"Oh, Diarmid, what have you done?" she cried, as she dropped onto the cold, wet stones at his side.

Her frantic gaze struggled to work out the extent of his injuries. Under the dark coat, it was hard to see exactly where the bullet had hit him.

At the sound of her voice, Diarmid's dark eyelashes fluttered on his ashen cheeks. He slowly opened his eyes to focus with difficulty on her face.

"Fiona?" he asked groggily, reaching out for her with his uninjured arm. "What the devil are ye doing here?"

"Rescuing you, you gallant fool." Catching his hand in a crushing grip, she tried to use her touch to instill every ounce of strength into him that she could.

She wouldn't let him die. She wouldn't. Everything he'd done since he'd found her on Canmara Beach had led to this appalling moment, and she wished she'd never been born. Her voice lowered to a cracked whisper. "Please, please stay alive. Please. I can't bear it if I lose you..."

"I'm pretty sure the bullet missed any vital organs," Hamish said. The misty rain plastered his blond hair to his head, and he looked serious but not frantic. "If we can stop the bleeding, he should be fine."

For what felt like the first time since she'd seen Diarmid in his cousin's arms, Fiona gulped in a full breath of cold, damp air. Uncaring of her audience, she bent to cover his face with kisses. She felt almost unhinged with relief that he wasn't dead. "Thank God, you're alive."

"It seems so." Diarmid moved his bad arm and groaned. "I certainly hurt enough. What in God's name happened?"

"Allan pulled a gun out of his pocket and shot you," Hamish said. "Don't you remember?"

"Aye, that's right." Diarmid's eyes sharpened on Fiona's face as she leaned over him. "What in hell are ye doing here, lassie? I left ye safe in the trees. I remember turning when ye called out..."

"That saved your life," Hamish said. "Otherwise, at that distance Grant could never have missed your heart."

Awareness of lingering danger pierced Fiona's panic over Diarmid's welfare, and she glanced around her. "Where on earth is Allan?"

"He's dead. I shot him," Hamish said in a voice that conveyed deep satisfaction. "Bugger deserved it."

That must have been the second gunshot she'd heard. She'd dreaded that Allan might have shot Diarmid twice to ensure his enemy really was dead.

"Good for ye, cuz," Diarmid said in an unsteady whisper.

"He's over there." Hamish jerked his chin in the direction of an unmoving figure spread-eagled on the grass a few feet away. In death, the man who had tormented her for so long looked strangely small, almost insignificant. Thomas was on his knees beside his brother, his shoulders heaving as he cried in ugly, gasping sobs.

"What about Thomas?" Fiona asked. "Is he armed?"

"Not anymore." This time, Hamish's chin indicated an old-fashioned pistol lying on the bridge beside him. "Don't worry, I emptied it."

There was renewed shouting and scuffling over near the trees where the Grants offered what looked to be half-hearted resistance to the Douglases under Sir Quentin's command. Even in her distraction, she noticed that without Allan to spur them on, his kin weren't putting up much of a fight.

With a shiver, she whipped her plaid shawl from her shoulders. The bridge was cold and wet under her knees, and the wind had a bite to it. They needed to get Diarmid to somewhere dry and warm. "This might work better to stanch the blood."

"Good idea." Hamish lifted his red-stained hand away from the wound.

Fiona pushed the coat to the side to reveal the blood blooming over Diarmid's shirt, turning the white linen a vivid scarlet. She sucked in a shuddering, horrified breath and fought dizziness.

It took her a few seconds to gather enough composure to notice that Hamish was right about the location of the wound. The blood seemed to be oozing from Diarmid's shoulder, not his chest.

Steeling herself, she forced clumsy hands to bunch up the thick woolen shawl and press it hard to the wound. "Don't you dare die, Diarmid. I'll never forgive you if you die."

"Willnae...die," he whispered, his eyelids flickering as he struggled to stay conscious.

She'd known there would be treachery. Curse Diarmid and his honorable heart that he hadn't taken her warnings seriously. She shifted against the paralyzing cold seeping up through her skirts from the bridge.

"Is yon bastard dead, then?"

Startled Fiona looked up from Diarmid's dear, haggard features to see Thomas standing over her. He looked like he'd aged twenty years since they last met.

"No, he's not," she snapped. "And he won't be, if I have anything to say about it."

"For God's sake, if you try anything now..." With impressive speed, Hamish disentangled himself from Diarmid and stood to counter any threat from Thomas. Even that small amount of jiggling had Fiona flinching on her husband's behalf. She heard Diarmid bite back a long groan of agony.

Gently she took his head onto her lap, cradling his cheeks in her shaking hands. He was as pale as paper, and the heavy black lashes lay still on his cheeks. Despite Hamish's reassurances, she was sick with anxiety. There was so much blood, and nothing she did seemed to stop the flow. Her gown was sticky with it.

"This is all your fault, ye troublesome bitch," Thomas said bitterly. "Why the hell couldn't ye stay at Bancavan and do your duty by your kin?"

Hamish saved her from answering. "What in blazes were you and Allan thinking of, shooting Diarmid? You couldn't hope to get away with murder when I was here to report what happened."

"Och, we had a dozen clansmen to swear that Mactavish produced his gun first. You're the mongrel's cousin. Nobody would believe you're an unbiased witness."

"You should have just taken your thousand pounds and left," Fiona said in a broken voice, looking up at the man whose weakness had encouraged his brother's evil to thrive. "That's more money than any Grant has seen in twenty years."

"A thousand?" Thomas's voice was snide. "A Mactavish cannae buy a Grant so cheap, ye wee besom. Allan got ten thousand out of the devil, and he'd started to wish he'd asked for more."

Ten thousand pounds? It was a mad amount of money. She wanted to give Diarmid a good shake. Or she would, if she wasn't worried sick about him.

"You great, wonderful idiot, Diarmid," she muttered, stroking the damp black hair back from his brow. He felt so cold beneath her touch. The weather became as large a threat as his blood loss.

She wondered if he'd drifted into unconsciousness again, but a ghost of a smile stretched his lips. "Had to. Worth it." His voice faded. "To see ye happy."

Oh, Diarmid...

She lifted her head to watch through tears as Sir Quentin approached them. Behind him near the trees, the Grant clansmen now stood in a disconsolate bunch under Douglas guard. "Lady Invertavey, how fares Mr. Mactavish?"

Fiona stared misty-eyed down at the man she'd married so unwillingly and now couldn't imagine living without. "He's lost a lot of blood, but I pray he'll survive."

"Let's hope so." After all the violence, his polite bow to Thomas struck Fiona as incongruous. "Mr. Grant, I'm Sir Quentin Avery. I own this land we're standing on, and I'm also the local magistrate."

"You'll want to take me into custody for shooting that bastard, I suppose," Hamish said in a grim tone. "I'd like it on record that Allan Grant had a second pistol. I knew if I didn't do something, he'd finish the job of killing Diarmid after he failed with the first attempt."

"It was cold-blooded murder, what ye did to my brother," Thomas said. "You'll hang for this, Douglas."

Sir Quentin shook his head. "Not if I have anything to say about it. I already saw there was a second gun. Mr. Douglas shot Allan Grant in self-defense and to save his cousin. When we get back to Glen Lyon, I'll take statements from you all, but I can't see that this matter needs to proceed to any sort of charge."

"Bloody corruption and collusion. I'll carry this further," Thomas snarled, his hands closing into fists at his sides. "Ye see if I don't."

"Your prerogative, Mr. Grant," Sir Quentin said in a cool voice. "But any publicity about this incident is only going to tarnish what little reputation your brother has left."

Fiona hardly cared that Thomas blustered about setting the law on them all. At last, Diarmid's blood loss seemed to be slowing. A faint trace of color seeped into his ashen face. Perhaps there was a chance he might come through this after all.

"We expected trouble. Hamish and I were both armed," Diarmid said in a failing voice. "Fiona warned me."

"You're going to have a dashed uncomfortable trip back to Lyon House, and the sooner, the better," Sir Quentin said. "I've got one of our men bringing the Grants' carriage over for you."

A timorous voice spoke from the end of the bridge. "Mamma?"

"Christina?" Fiona said, turning her head in her daughter's direction.

Her grip on Diarmid tightened, as she struggled to contain the turbulent oceans of emotion swelling inside her. Fear for her husband. Fear for her child. Relief at Allan's death. A mother's powerful yearning to clutch her daughter close and reassure her that the danger had passed.

"Go to Christina." Hamish smiled at her with compassion and understanding in his blue eyes. "She's frightened and bewildered, and we've left her alone too long."

"But Diarmid…"

"Don't worry about my cousin. I'll look after him." With competent hands, Hamish kneeled down and transferred Diarmid into his hold with a minimum of painful fuss. "Can you stand, old man?"

"Aye, I think so," Diarmid said unsteadily. "But ye might need to lend me your brawny shoulder."

Fiona's arms felt empty without him. But she trusted Hamish's opinion about Diarmid's chances. Right now, she had to look after Christina.

She stumbled to her feet on the damp, slippery stones. "Darling…"

The first time she saw Christina, she'd been too frantic about Diarmid to take in many details. Now the sight of her daughter made her heart cramp with an agonizing mixture of regret and love and longing.

In the last year, Christina had grown so much. When her daughter left Bancavan for Trahair House, she'd been a child. Now her thin, serious face hinted at the beautiful woman she'd become.

Christina looked aghast at the mud and red gore staining Fiona's clothes and hands. "You're covered in blood."

"It will wash out, sweetheart."

"Aye, that it will." To her surprise, Christina managed a nervous smile. "Can I come away with you now?"

Fiona swallowed to shift the painful lump of emotion blocking her throat. Her hands itched to grab her daughter and hug the life out of her. But the child had been isolated and afraid for the last year, and today had been crammed with confusion and danger that must scare her even more. Fiona didn't want to do anything likely to worsen her fear.

Did Christina know her loathsome uncle was dead? Fiona hadn't seen her cast a single glance toward Allan's unmoving body on the other side of the bridge.

"Indeed you can come with me." Tears thickened her voice, but she refused to give in to them. Christina needed her to be strong now. She couldn't let her daughter down.

It gradually sank in that she and Diarmid had won against the Grants. Allan couldn't hurt them anymore. Nobody had any reason to keep Christina away from her.

She should be happy. She was. Or she would be if Diarmid hadn't been hurt.

"I'm glad." The wariness in Christina's eyes threatened to break Fiona's heart. "Who is that man you were hugging?"

"He helped me find you. His name is Diarmid."

"Is he going to die?"

Not if I can damn well help it.

"I hope not."

Fiona swallowed again. So many times, she'd imagined this reunion. In her mind, it had been bright and joyous, unmarred by the shadows of the past. Laughter and smiles. Not this awkward encounter where she dreaded that every word she spoke widened the distance yawning between them.

She reminded herself that for a nine-year-old, a year was an eternity. To Christina, she must seem like a stranger. Finding one another again would take time and patience. Now, thanks to Diarmid, they had an opportunity to rebuild their closeness and give Christina the childhood she'd never had.

"What about Uncle Allan?" Christina asked, still without looking at Allan's body. "Is he dead?"

"Yes, sweetheart."

"That's good. I didn't like him."

"I didn't either." Fiona ventured a step closer. "I know I'm all mucky, but is it all right if I give you another hug?"

This time there was no mistaking the misgivings in Christina's expression. "Do you want to?"

Fiona frowned. What on earth was this? "Very much."

"Then why did you send me away to Cousin William? Was I naughty? Don't you love me anymore?"

For the first time, Christina's unnatural composure showed signs of cracking. Her face was drawn, and her mouth trembled. Shock kept Fiona silent a moment too long, and Christina retreated a pace.

"Your mother loves you more than ye ken, Christina," a deep, wonderfully familiar voice said from behind Fiona. "She risked her life over and over to save ye and bring you back to her, where ye belong. You're verra lucky to have such a brave, clever mamma, who wanted to find you so much, that she's been running all over Scotland facing untold dangers while she looked for ye."

Startled, Fiona turned to see Diarmid upright and leaning against Hamish. Hamish had rigged her bloodstained shawl into a makeshift sling. Her husband looked pale and in pain, but steady on his feet.

"Diarmid..."

Diarmid kept looking at Christina. "Your mamma is a real heroine."

"Uncle Allan said—"

"Uncle Allan was a liar."

"So you still love me, Mamma?"

"Of course I do," Fiona said in a husky voice. Longing and desperate love made her voice shake. She wanted to kill Allan all over again when she saw the mistrust in her daughter's wan face. "You're my girl, don't you know that? I've missed you every day since they took you away, and I'll never let anyone take you away again."

"You promise?"

"I promise." Fiona held her hands out, wishing they weren't bloodstained, wishing she'd been strong enough to protect her daughter from the wrongs the Grants had done her. "Christina?"

After a pause that cut like a razor, Christina stumbled forward and flung herself at her mother. Fiona's arms closed hard around her daughter's shaking body.

Tears poured down her face, as at last Christina's nearness filled the agonizing absence that had tormented her for a year. Every difficult moment, every terror, every sacrifice was worth it in return for the chance to hold her child close.

"I've missed you so much, Mamma," Christina said, her voice muffled with tears.

"And I've missed you so much. There wasn't a second I didn't think about you. I love you, Christina."

"I love you, too." Christina pulled away and sniffed loudly. Fiona noted that her daughter already looked less frozen and more like the little girl she remembered. "Do we have to go back to Bancavan?"

"Never," Fiona said fervently. "Never, never, never."

"So where are we going?"

Fiona hesitated, as she wondered how much she should tell Christina right now. But when her delay in replying brought the fear back into her daughter's eyes, she rushed on. "I've got so much to say to you. But first let's go somewhere safe and warm and let me change out of this frock."

A flash of the earlier vulnerability. "You won't go away again?"

"Never, my darling." She reached out to cup Christina's face. Such a simple action. Such a privilege to touch her child after all these months apart. "Believe me."

"I do."

"Then give me another hug."

As her daughter stepped back into her embrace, Fiona turned her head to say thank you to Diarmid. But he was already several yards away, climbing into the shabby carriage with Hamish's help.

"Diarmid?" she called after him, and he turned to give her a brief wave with his good arm.

"Lady Invertavey, Mr. Mactavish asked me to return you and your daughter to Lyon House in my carriage." Sir Quentin was at her elbow, his spare, undistinguished face full of concern. "I'll ride with the driver and give you both some privacy on the way back."

"I wanted to..." Her voice trailed off, and she noted the sympathy in his gray eyes.

"We've sent for a doctor to see Mr. Mactavish. It's best we get him to the house as soon as possible."

"Thank you." It was the right decision, but still she felt bereft. Some deep instinct told her she should be with Diarmid. "What about Allan?"

"I've sent one of my men for a cart to collect the body. His kinsmen will want to take him back to his estates for burial, I assume, but first we'll need an inquest."

"I see." She shivered. The rain had retreated, but the wind still cut like a knife.

"If you'll come this way?"

"Mamma, why did that man call you Lady Invertavey?" Christina asked, her gaze darting with fearful curiosity between her mother and Sir Quentin.

Fiona bit back a sigh. She'd hoped to put off making some of the more difficult explanations. "That's part of the long story I have to tell you about my adventures since Allan took you away. Let's go back to the house, and I'll give you the whole tale."

CHAPTER THIRTY-FOUR

*D*iarmid stirred from a restless, dream-muddled sleep and opened his eyes on a lamplit room and a lovely woman sitting beside his bed. He shifted to reach out to her, and the shaft of pain through his shoulder proved a sharp reminder of the day's dramatic events.

"Diarmid, how are you feeling?" Fiona asked softly.

"Like my head is full of cushion stuffing."

"That's the laudanum." She smiled. "Once he'd dug Allan's bullet out of you, the doctor said he wanted you to sleep."

Mercifully he'd fainted during the worst of the extraction, although he remembered gripping Fiona's hand so tightly he suspected he must have hurt her. Now his shoulder felt like it was on fire.

"Ye didn't have to stay to watch that."

"Yes, I did," she said steadily. "Can I help you to sit up?"

The tight bandaging restricted movement. "Aye, please."

"It might be painful."

It was.

By the time he was propped against the pillows, he was grinding his teeth and fighting to clear his vision. Still he felt better sitting upright. He hated lying flat and helpless. While he sipped the glass of water Fiona gave him, he waited for the throbbing agony to subside.

"Where's Christina?" he asked, as the drugged fog receded from his mind. "Should ye no' be with her?"

"She's asleep down the corridor. There's a maid with her, so if she asks for me, I'll know straightaway."

"Dinna ye want to be there?"

"Of course I do."

"Then?"

"But I also want to be with you, and I can't be in two places at once. I sat with her until she dozed off. Unless she has a bad dream, she'll sleep now. The poor wee poppet is tired out." He heard such tenderness in her voice when she spoke of her daughter. "I'm just so happy to have her under the same roof. I can hardly believe it."

"Aye. You're reunited at last. Your quest has succeeded."

"Thanks to you."

He didn't want to deal with that right now. "Did ye tell her about me?"

"Yes, I did. I tried to keep things simple, but even then, I'm not sure she took it in. She's still trying to grapple with Allan being gone. She's never known a minute without his evil influence."

Poor wee poppet indeed. "She'll need time to come to terms with her new life."

"She's young. God willing, she'll heal with kindness, patience, and love."

"Aye, with kindness, patience, and love." The last word in that prescription echoed through his mind. He was achingly conscious that his wife hadn't kissed him, hadn't even tried to hold his hand.

"Does your arm hurt?"

Like the devil. "No."

"Liar."

He didn't argue.

"You don't have to be heroic all the time, you know. You've already been quite heroic enough for one day. Dr. Gillies left a sleeping draft, if you're in pain."

"Nae more potions, by heaven." With an unsteady hand, Diarmid set the empty glass of water on the nightstand. He felt ridiculously tired. And downhearted, which was mad when they'd succeeded. He'd returned the child to her mother, he'd beaten Allan Grant, he'd even emerged unscathed. Mostly.

What did Fergus call him? The white knight? If so, he'd done his duty most satisfactorily.

But the stories never said what the wandering knight did after he won through. Did he ride off with the damsel and set up a home and family, or did he go away lonely and return to his endless questing?

"Do you remember talking to Dr. Gillies about your injury?"

"Aye." Diarmid paused. "But I was in nae state to take in what he said."

"He believes that as long as there's no infection, you should recover full use of your arm."

At last, Fiona reached across to take his hand. Och, that was better. The roiling discontent in his heart settled. Her touch had such power over him.

"You're lucky," she said.

He laced his fingers through hers. "A mere flesh wound?"

"A little more than that, but it could have been worse." She leaned in closer, and her eyes darkened as she stared at him. "I warned you to expect trouble when you met Allan. How on earth did you let him shoot you?"

"An oversupply of confidence, damn it. I thought the danger was past. Allan had got his money, and Hamish was there to see everything stayed honest. It was madness to try and kill me at that stage. A sane man would have gathered up the cash and headed for the hills."

"Allan wasn't sane." Her free hand made a dismissive gesture. "Oh, I don't mean he was a raving lunatic, but he couldn't bear for anyone to best him. He never could."

Diarmid forced his mind back to those chaotic seconds before the bullet hit him. Everything had a strangely unreal edge, as though he'd heard about the events, instead of lived through them. "I heard ye cry out."

She'd called Christina's name in a tone that would ring in his mind forever. Love and fear and longing. The sound had startled him, and he'd looked up to see his wife darting down the brae like an arrow shot from a bow.

"I couldn't bear waiting any longer." Her voice roughened with emotion, and he realized she wasn't nearly as calm as she seemed on the surface.

"I ken that. When I saw you running away from the trees, I remember cursing the way ye put yourself in danger."

"Hamish says that turning to look at me must have saved your life. That's why the bullet entered your shoulder and not your heart."

He found it in him to smile. "Och, lassie, and now I suppose ye want credit for the fact that the treacherous bastard didnae kill me."

Characteristic dry humor flattened her mouth. "Well, you should give praise where it's due."

"When I should be furious with ye for disobeying me. I *was* furious with ye for disobeying me."

The amusement faded from her eyes. "Speaking of furious, how dare you give Allan ten thousand pounds for Christina?"

This was one argument he knew he'd win. "Was she no' worth it?"

It was Fiona's turn to look embattled. "How can I say she wasn't? You can't imagine how it felt to take her in my arms after a year apart and know we were free of Allan at last."

"I can guess."

She studied him with a serious expression, before her rare, unfettered smile lightened her features. He hoped to see that smile more often, now that she'd escaped her vile kinsman's power.

"Yes, you probably can. But that doesn't mean you had a right to keep secrets from me."

He shrugged. Very briefly. He kept forgetting that he'd just had a bullet cut out of his shoulder. A flash of agony radiated through him and had him seeing stars. As he fought the encroaching darkness, he inhaled on an audible hiss.

"Diarmid, I hope you haven't opened your wound again." Fiona sounded cross. He didn't mind, because at last she perched on the edge of the bed and slid her arms around his waist. "For heaven's sake, be careful."

As the pain slowly ebbed, he opened his eyes. "Och, lassie, I'd go through it all again if it means lying in your arms."

Keeping a loose hold on him, she shifted to fix wide blue eyes the color of heaven on his face. Unhappy blue eyes. "You shouldn't even want me anywhere near you. After all, it was because of me that Allan shot you."

Diarmid caught her fingers and brought them to his lips for a quick kiss. "Don't be a silly widgeon, Fiona. I always want ye to touch me."

With a gentleness that eased his pain better than any laudanum ever could, she drew him down to rest against her. For a sweet interlude, he lay silent and unmoving in her embrace. Her warmth surrounded him, and the world took on Fiona's soft, floral scent. The horrors of the day retreated to the edge of his mind.

"That's good," she said, without moving and as if there had been no break in the conversation. "Because I like you to touch me. I like it very much indeed. I'm hoping you have plans to touch me soon and often."

That sounded promising. Perhaps the knight was about to cease his wanderings after all. His dejection faded with every moment. "How do you feel about more children, lassie?"

To his surprise, her answer came swiftly. "I'd love to have a family with you. More than I can say."

"That's grand."

Diarmid wasn't sure whether he was up to settling the details of his future this very instant, but it seemed the time had come to make confessions and commitments. The most difficult confession of all loomed ahead, but he could no longer bear to hide the truth in his heart, however Fiona received the news.

This was the greatest risk he'd ever taken, greater by far than meeting Allan Grant today on that bare brae. "The ten thousand pounds I offered Allan isn't the only secret I've kept from ye, sweetheart."

"Oh?" To his regret, she sat back and regarded him with familiar uncertainty. "You're making me nervous, Diarmid."

His lips turned down in self-mockery. "You'll be bloody terrified before I've finished."

"You were already married when you married me? You have a mistress and ten children stashed somewhere at Invertavey?"

He didn't smile, although he knew she was trying to lighten the atmosphere. "Much worse," he said gravely.

"What is it? Stop playing with me and tell me. Whatever it is, I can bear it."

He swallowed. Now the moment was here, his courage threatened to desert him. "I've done a rash and dangerous thing."

"By helping me?"

"By falling in love with ye, lassie."

She went white and scrambled off the bed. Disappointment heavy as an anvil smashed down on his heart. Not unexpected, but wretched all the same. He'd never seen a woman look less ready to respond to a declaration of love with a declaration of her own.

"You can't," she whispered, one pale hand rising to where her pulse hammered in her throat.

"Aye, I can. I have."

Perhaps he'd have been wiser to keep quiet. But if they were to stay together at Invertavey as husband and wife, she had to know how he felt. He couldn't spend the rest of his life with that lie between them. A lie of omission perhaps, but still a lie.

"I know ye, Fiona. I know ye, and I love ye, and nothing will change that until the day I die." He felt like he dredged the words up from the depths of his soul. "I'm no' a fickle man. I've never been in love before. I willnae fall in love again. It seems I'm just like my father, after all."

"Because you, too, fell in love with the wrong woman?" Her voice was bitter.

"You're no' the wrong woman."

"I am if I can't make you happy." She stared down at the floor. She looked less shocked, but no more gratified. "I'm not sure I know what love is, Diarmid."

"Ye love Christina."

"Yes, but that's not what you're asking for."

"No."

The gaze she raised to him was flat and desolate. "It would be easy to lie to you."

His good hand made a sweeping gesture. "A lie dishonors everything between us."

"Yes, it does. But I hate that I'm hurting you. Are you sure that you love me?"

His lips tightened. "That's an insulting question."

She didn't flinch. "Fergus says you suffer from an excess of chivalry. Is there any chance that you're confusing your urge to rescue a damsel in distress with something more profound?"

"You're nae damsel in distress." He snorted with scornful amusement. "You're a force of nature. Nothing can stop ye. Just ask Allan Grant. Or at least, you could ask him, if ye hadn't comprehensively trounced him. He came to grief today because he underestimated how strong and dangerous ye are. How can I help loving you? You're powerful and brave and loyal. And sweet and warm and passionate. And bonny. You're so bonny, it nigh breaks my heart every time I look at ye."

Fiona stared at this remarkable man who laid his heart at her feet and felt utterly sick with herself. She swallowed the bile that soured her mouth and made herself speak the harsh, unwelcome truth.

"Diarmid, I honor you. I admire you. I like you. I like being with you. I like what we do in bed."

"Like, like, like," he said grimly.

How she wished she could get away with a comforting falsehood, but he knew her too well. And something within her flinched from telling him a lie when he'd been so honest with her.

"Yes. I wish it was more." She forced herself to proceed to the difficult truth. "But we've only had a few weeks together, a handful of days for me to learn what it is to live in the sunlight, to trust a man, to be friends with a man."

"Before that, ye had ten years of Bancavan."

His tone hinted at hard-won acceptance. He understood. Of course he did. But understanding didn't stop her rejection from wounding him. She flinched to think of the pain she inflicted.

"Yes. Ten long years. I let a vicious old man use my body. I had my child stolen away from me. I was beaten and confined and treated with contempt. Something inside me was broken then. Despite your kindness and care and...love..." Even saying the word was difficult. "...I'm still broken."

"I cannae believe you'll be broken forever."

"But it's possible that I will be." Possible? So probable it was certain. "I can't hold out any hope that I'll ever be capable of loving you the way you deserve to be loved."

The telltale muscle flickered in his cheek. He maintained an outward calm for her sake, but she knew that every word she spoke wounded him. "Once you thought ye were incapable of passion."

"Love is more complicated than passion—and passion is complicated enough."

"Aye, it is."

She stared at him, seeing him clearly for what felt like the first time. One thing was apparent—he'd loved her for a long time. Now that he'd put a name to the glow in his eyes when he looked at her, she realized that light had been there at least since he'd married her. Maybe even before that.

"I'm sorry, Diarmid," she said with aching regret. "If I was to love any man, it would be you."

"No' much consolation."

"No," she said bleakly. Not much consolation at all.

For a long time, she stared into his face, willing what she saw there to be an illusion. But he was as steadfast as she was. She couldn't doubt that he loved her. Nor could she doubt that he suffered because she couldn't love him in return.

Eventually Diarmid shifted, wincing as he jolted his sore shoulder. When he reached out to take her hand once more, she didn't pull away. "Och, lassie, it's no' the end of the world."

He was so gallant. She crushed his hopes to nothing, yet he found the generosity to offer her comfort.

Fiona started to cry. Because she wanted to love him and couldn't. Because when she'd seen him fall to Allan's bullet, she'd feared that she lost him forever and that prospect had turned the world into a blighted desert. Because the day had been full of too many overwhelming emotions, and she reeled with the rapid changes from fear to fury to joy, all ending with this excruciating conversation that threatened to tear her apart.

"It feels like the end of the world," she sobbed, trying to dash the tears away with shaking hands.

"I'll survive."

"But I hurt you."

His smile conveyed the piercing tenderness that should have warned her long ago that he felt more for her than mere physical attraction. "This time, I dinna have a handkerchief on me. But dry your eyes. We'll work something out."

Fiona fumbled in her pocket and found a useless scrap of lace. Masculine handkerchiefs were much more practical. With shaking hands, she wiped her eyes. "Do you want me to leave you?"

"Now?"

"No. Forever."

"Do ye want to go?"

"You might come to hate me because I can't love you."

"Never." Diarmid sounded so sure, she couldn't doubt he meant it.

"I'd like to stay with you," she said in a hoarse voice. "I'd like Christina to grow up at Invertavey. I'd like her to have the example of a good man in her life."

"In that case, stay." He squeezed her fingers. "I promise I willnae annoy ye with endless pleas for your love. In fact, ye have my word, I'll never mention the word again."

She studied him, knowing yet again he was acting with a pure-hearted benevolence that put her to shame. "Won't that be difficult?"

"Not as difficult as going on without ye. But you need to know the truth before ye commit to your new life. I love ye, Fiona, and that will never change."

"I wish things could be different," she said, hating that she started to cry again.

"We've got Christina back. The Grants are no longer a threat." He looked strained and defeated, although she saw he did his best to pretend he was at peace with a lifetime of unrequited love. "We've come through our travails."

"Except Allan shot you."

"I'll heal. We'll stay together, and we'll build a good life. Dinna cry anymore. We still have plenty to celebrate."

"It doesn't feel like it," she said thickly.

"It will in time. You're just tired and overwrought right now."

"You're the one who was shot. You're meant to be resting, and all I've done is upset you."

"I'd rest better, if you lay down beside me," he said softly. "Never fear, we'll find a way forward. After all, we mightnae have love, but we have so much else. And I miss sleeping with my bonny lassie beside me."

She summoned a shaky smile and slid into the bed to curl up at his side. Despite everything, when she twined her arm around his waist, a fugitive peace filled her heart.

Diarmid was right. They'd already achieved so much together, more than she'd ever imagined they would. Who knew what else the coming years would bring them?

CHAPTER THIRTY-FIVE

Invertavey House, August 1820

 "I won! I won!" Crowing over her convincing victory, Christina flung her cards down on the baize table.

Diarmid laughed at her childish delight and folded his hand. "Aye, you did, ye canny brat. I'm beginning to be sorry I taught you piquet."

"So that means I can have a kitten from the litter that Mags's cat had last week? I know just the one I want. The wee black and white girl."

"It does. Serves me right for making such a reckless bet against a card sharp like ye. Ye should run and tell her now, before she gives your kitten away to someone else."

The prospect of losing out on her choice had Christina scampering out the library door. Diarmid found himself smiling as he watched her go. What a difference a year had made in the lassie.

The Christina who first came to live at Invertavey had been quiet and subdued, and inclined to start at her own shadow. She'd accepted her mother's second marriage as she accepted everything—too placidly for a nine-year-old girl. Diarmid read a lifetime of fear into the way she shied from his presence. She'd suffered months of bad dreams, too, filled with the dramatic events of that day near Glen Lyon, but also featuring other, older miseries.

Only gradually had the playful, happy child emerged. Now the house echoed to her chatter. Diarmid hadn't put much thought into what it would be like to have a lively young girl in his home. To his surprise, he took to his role of stepfather as if born to play the part.

"You spoil her," Fiona said from the window seat, where she was sewing some pink ribbons onto one of Christina's dresses.

"Och, she's overdue a bit of spoiling," Diarmid said, smiling at his wife and unable to deny the charge. "When I think of what that swine Allan Grant put ye both through..."

As he looked at his wife sitting in a pool of sunshine on this lovely summer's day, he knew he was a deuced lucky man to have both his gorgeous lassies in his life. Christina wasn't the only one who had blossomed with kindness and contentment.

Fiona was more beautiful than ever, now that strain no longer tightened her features. It had taken a long time, but the haunted look had at last left her azure eyes. She smiled more often, and her silvery laugh had become the music of his life. His wife was a lover who turned his nights to fire, but just as precious were quiet, sweet moments like this one, where they shared a closeness he'd never felt with anyone else.

How grateful he was that he'd discovered his mermaid on Canmara Beach that stormy morning. He'd even face another bullet in his shoulder in return for a life with Fiona. The wound had healed, although cold weather brought twinges that he suspected would remain a permanent reminder of Allan Grant's spite.

A small price to pay for the fulfillment he'd since found.

This last year with Fiona had flown. Once Diarmid had recovered from his wound and settled Christina and Fiona into their new home, he'd pursued the legal case to restore Fiona's property. That matter, too, had found a satisfying ending. Without Allan, the Grants had lacked the will for a long, bitter fight through the courts in Edinburgh. Correspondence last week indicated that the wrangling would be resolved in Fiona's favor next month. At her urging, he'd demanded his ten thousand pounds back, and to his surprise, even that would now return to his coffers as part of the settlement.

Nor had he and his wife neglected family and friends. Visits to and from Fergus and Marina, and to Hamish's house at Glen Lyon had punctuated the months. Everyone had celebrated Christmas at Achnasheen, where Elspeth and Brody's baby son Percival had been the center of attention.

Life was good and promised to get even better. Fiona made him happy and banished a loneliness that before his marriage he hadn't recognized he felt.

The fact that he loved his wife more with each minute and she didn't love him back should be no more than a minor niggle.

To his regret, it was worse than that, but with every day that he woke up beside this glorious woman, he lectured himself about not baying for the moon. He should be content to settle for what he had.

Because what he had was marvelous.

Fiona bit into the thread and set her sewing on the seat beside her. "I happen to know that you told Mags on Tuesday to keep that particular kitten for Christina."

"Och, you're getting a little too clever for your own good, lassie. I'll soon have nae secrets from ye at all."

"Neither you should." She glanced out the window behind her. "It's a bonny afternoon. Would you like to take a walk?"

Without a qualm, Diarmid put aside his plans to check the estate accounts. When a comely lassie invited a man for a stroll, only a clodpoll said no. He might coax his wife into sharing a few kisses, once they were out of sight of the house.

Perhaps more than kisses.

"That's a braw idea. The gardens?"

"I have a fancy to see Canmara Beach."

"Then Canmara Beach it is." He rose from his chair and held out his hand. "Lady Invertavey?"

The day was warm, with just enough of a breeze to set the pines whispering as they entered the woods leading to the dunes. In the shadowy, mysterious light, Diarmid felt that he and Fiona ventured into an enchanted kingdom. Which suited his plans very well.

"Come with me, lassie," he murmured, drawing her off the path and into the trees. At this time of day, the estate workers should be busy, but he didn't want to take the chance of anyone interrupting him.

"Diarmid, I have a feeling that you're about to shock me," Fiona said, although he noticed she followed him readily enough.

"Och, I hope so," he said with a low laugh, gently pushing her back against a moss-covered trunk.

"We're outside." She landed with enough of a bump to gasp. Or perhaps she gasped because she was excited. She linked her hands around his neck, and the eyes she raised to his were bright with sensual interest.

"We are indeed."

He'd often fantasized about taking her in the open air. Today provided the perfect opportunity.

"And it's daytime."

"Och, we've made love in the daytime plenty of times before."

"In our rooms." Fiona had got into the habit of afternoon "naps," although precious little sleeping ever took place.

"Time for a change of scene, surely. If you're missing the night, I'll do my best to make ye see stars."

"That's a rash promise, my cocky laddie." The carnal promise in her smile sent heat rippling through him. She dragged his head down toward hers. "Just make sure you keep it," she murmured against his mouth.

The eagerness in her lips made his head swim, and he kissed her back with unabashed appreciation. She fumbled at the front fall of his breeches until he sprang free, full and ready.

When her fingers curled tight around the hot column of flesh, he groaned.

"Aye, that's it, my darling," he bit out as that clever hand squeezed the head of his cock. He reached forward to gather up her skirts, but she brushed his hands away.

"No."

"No?"

"Not yet. Let me service you first."

His heart crashed against his ribs. "Fiona?"

"Take a step back."

Dizzy with anticipation, he retreated far enough to allow her to sink to her knees in front of him. She'd taken him in her mouth before and even seemed to enjoy it, once she'd recovered from her astonishment at the whole concept. But the prospect of her doing this to him here, with nothing above them but God's bonny blue sky, made him shake with sinful excitement.

When the wet heat of her mouth enclosed him, he released a long, shuddering groan. His hands framed her head, tangling in silky blond hair as she drew hard on him. The sensations rocketing through him flared to a wildfire.

As she fondled his tight balls, she adjusted the angle and took him deeper. Struggling against losing himself, he ground his teeth together. Her tongue swirled around him, and as she began to move her head up and down, he was the one who saw stars.

He sucked in a breath that tasted of pine needles and arousal. The pressure built higher and higher. He was so close...

Clumsily, he staggered back. He'd come in her mouth during prior encounters, but today he wanted to share the pleasure in the most intimate way he knew. "Wait, sweetheart."

She tilted her head to regard him with a puzzled expression. "I want this."

Her lips glistened where she'd taken him. He closed his eyes briefly and wondered if he was mad to stop her at this point, but he burned to be between her legs when he spilled his seed.

"And I want ye." He caught her under her arms and hoisted her to her feet. "Turn around and put your hands against the tree."

Once she might have hesitated to obey him, but the trust between them now was so strong, it was invincible. Panting, she shifted to place her palms flat on the rough tree trunk.

"Push your hips out toward me," he said in a voice that rasped like a file on metal.

"You're going to use me like a stallion covers a mare," she said in wonder.

"Aye."

She lowered her head, lifting her hips toward him in silent invitation. With shaking hands, he flung up her skirts and petticoats to reveal luscious buttocks draped in sheer lawn drawers.

Diarmid ripped the strings of her drawers and shoved the filmy material down to her ankles. The sight of her bare arse had him bending to scrape his teeth over the firm flesh. She moaned and edged back in wordless encouragement.

"Step out of them," he growled.

Once she did, he reached between her thighs to stroke her cleft. She shivered under his touch. She was close to ready, even before his fingers explored the delicate folds. When he teased the center of her pleasure, she rewarded him with a broken cry and a gush of feminine heat.

He didn't linger. They were both hungry for what was about to happen. With urgent hands, he caught her hips and slid into her, basking in her body's avid welcome. Miraculously he felt her clench around him in swift ecstasy. On a groan, he thrust hard.

The world transformed into hot, scarlet lightning. As the mighty climax thundered through him, he let go of her hips and cupped her breasts in his hands. She pressed her back up toward him, urging him on as he shuddered over her.

When at last he withdrew, she was trembling beneath him. She clung to him as he slipped free, as if she never wanted him to leave her. He bent to kiss her nape, inhaling the delicious fragrance of floral soap and musky perspiration.

Half-falling, Diarmid dragged her down until they were sitting on the thick layer of pine needles. He leaned back against the tree and hauled her into his arms.

With a choked sound, Fiona plastered herself against him, and buried her face in his shirt. It took him far too long to realize that she was crying.

"Tears, Fiona?" he asked in dismay. For the love of heaven, had he been too rough with her? "Dinna tell me that I hurt ye?"

She shook her disheveled head without answering. On a broken sob, she pressed into him and her hands made frantic fists in his shirt.

"Please, talk to me, *mo chridhe*." Seriously worried now, Diarmid tightened his embrace. "Tell me I havenae done anything too bad."

"Nothing...nothing bad at all," she forced out. She struggled to sit up, and shaking hands dashed the tears from her eyes. "Good. Wonderful. Glorious."

All of that would have sounded fine, if she wasn't bawling her heart out when she said it. As Diarmid struggled to make sense of what was going on, he fastened his breeches. "Then why on earth are ye crying, lassie?"

"I feel..."

He caught her chin in his hand, so she couldn't hide the truth from him. If he'd hurt her in his desperate passion, he wanted to know. "What do ye feel? Tell me."

"What can I say? I feel overcome, transformed, swept away from myself. Sometimes it's just too much. The beauty of it all makes me want to cry." She twisted out of his hold and surveyed him with eyes glittering with tears. "It happens whenever we're...together."

He gradually came to realize that whatever had brought on this emotional storm, his headlong seduction hadn't caused her any injury, at least. But he was still at a loss to explain her powerful reaction. "Pleasure?"

"That." She kneeled at his side, her green dress crushed and drooping at the neck where he'd tugged on it, touching her breasts. Her once-tidy chignon was half-undone, and strands of hair hung about her intent face. He'd never seen her look more beautiful. "But much, much more than just pleasure."

"Good more?"

"Oh, yes." She bit her lip as she seemed to struggle to find the words to explain. Instinct told him not to interrupt her with more questions. "When you're inside me, Diarmid, I feel like we become one person."

The unexpected answer slammed through him like a killer punch from a champion bare-knuckle fighter. He swallowed to loosen his tight throat and made himself respond with a calmness he didn't feel. "I feel like that, too."

"Do you?"

"Aye. Always."

"With other women?"

He frowned. Where the devil was Fiona going with this? "Since I met you, there havenae been any other women. I promised ye my fidelity."

"But before we married, you had lovers."

Diarmid shifted in discomfort. "Aye."

"Did it feel the same?"

"No." Now it was his turn to struggle for an answer. "It was nice. But what I feel when I'm with ye shakes the whole world."

It was no mystery why. When their bodies united, she felt like the only woman in the world, because to him, she *was* the only woman in the world. He loved his wife beyond all reason. A year of marriage had only worsened his affliction.

"That's what it's like for me." She went on in an urgent rush. "But I don't just feel like that when we're in bed together. I feel like that all the time. Every morning, my heart overflows with joy when I see you. I miss you when you're not with me. I hardly have a thought that doesn't relate to you in some way. It's like you've become a part of me. Every day my sense of the two of us joined heart and soul grows stronger and stronger."

Heart and soul? His own yearning heart slammed to a halt, then set off on a wild gallop.

"Have I made ye happy, Fiona?" he asked unsteadily, as fragile hope stirred inside him that against all his expectations, the impossible might have come to pass.

"So happy. I never thought I could be so happy." A stray tear trickled down her cheek, as she seized his hand. "You saved me, Diarmid."

Damn it all to hell.

Like that, his optimistic expectations shriveled to nothing, and he snatched his hand back from hers. What a fool he was. Would he never learn?

"Have we no' passed beyond gratitude yet, Fiona?"

She frowned. "But I am grateful."

"I ken that," he said with grim finality. He heaved to his feet and wondered at how quickly a perfect afternoon could turn sour. "Do ye still want to go on to the beach?"

She didn't take the hand he held out to her. "I've made you angry."

He sighed. "I'm no' angry."

She accepted his hand and rose. "You always hate it when I try to thank you."

"I do."

"But gratitude can be part of...love."

He went as still as the tree trunks ranged around him, and his hand tightened on hers. "What did ye say?"

He didn't mean to bark out the question, but hearing her speak that one word "love" left him floundering.

She stared at him with a trace of her old uncertainty. "I said love." Before he could respond, she rushed on. "I feel like we share one soul. What else can that mean but that I love you?"

"Fiona..."

She still wouldn't let him interrupt her. "You said you loved me once. Perhaps you don't anymore. I can hardly blame you. I've been so unforgivably slow to understand my heart. I've felt like this for months. I loved you when I married you, but I didn't know enough of love to recognize that. Even then, you'd become the center of my thoughts. When Allan shot you and I feared you were dead, God forgive me, I wanted to die, too. Despite knowing Christina needed me."

He reached out and caught her arms in shaking hands. "Fiona, sweetheart, for pity's sake...stop."

"I shouldn't be saying all this, should I? Now I know how you felt when I told you I didn't love you." The tears came faster. So did the words. "How could I have done that to you?"

Diarmid silenced her in the only way he knew. He swept her into his arms and kissed her.

On her lips, he tasted the salt of her tears. She moaned into his mouth, before she kissed him back with a desperation that heated his blood and fed his hungry soul.

When at last he drew away, they were both breathing in great gusts. Her expression was dazed as she stared up at him.

"You do still love me." It wasn't a question.

He laughed with sheer elation and kissed her quickly, because he couldn't resist. And because it seemed that all was well in his world after all.

He loved Fiona, and Fiona loved him. That truth, so profound yet so simple, sank deeper into him with each second.

"Of course I do, ye daft lassie. I told ye long ago that I'll love ye to the day I die."

With wondering tenderness, she reached up to caress his jaw. Her eyes sparkled like the stars he'd promised to show her. "And I'll love you all my life, Diarmid. Our child will be born of love."

Diarmid had imagined he was immune to shocks, now that his wife had done the unbelievable and fallen in love with him. He was wrong. "Our...child?"

In an age-old gesture of maternal protection, Fiona placed one hand over her midriff. "Yes. Sometime in February, Mags says." She sent him a searching look. "Are you pleased?"

A bairn? The woman he loved was telling him that she carried his baby?

Shaking he caught her up against him, while he struggled to come to terms with an announcement as overwhelming in its way as her declaration of love. "Och, I'm reeling."

"That's why I asked you to come for a walk, so I could tell you." She smiled with a smugness he admitted she had every right to feel. "But you distracted me from my purpose, you wicked man."

A bairn. In February. He would soon become a father.

And his wife loved him. That astonishing fact still had the power to knock him flat. Could life offer him any greater happiness?

"Is it all right that we…"

"Mags says marital relations are no danger to the baby."

He caught her around the waist, already looking forward to seeing her grow round with his child as the months went on. "Just in case, I'll restrict myself to a bed from now on."

"Must you?" The look she shot him was pure temptation. "What we did today was so very thrilling."

"Aye, it was thrilling. But so is this news." He shook his head in dazed confusion. In the space of half an hour, his whole life had changed. "A bairn…"

"Yes."

"And ye love me."

"More than I can say."

"Well, devil take me for an Englishman." A slow smile curved his lips as giddy joy took possession of his heart. "That's what I call a bonny outcome for this tale of a mermaid and a laird."

"I agree." Still smiling, she stepped closer and slowly slid her hands up his chest. "Not to mention a damsel in distress and a knight in shining armor, my beloved."

Feeling as though his wife had invited him to step through the gates of heaven, Diarmid curled his arms around her and stared into her unforgettable face. "Kiss me, my darling."

"With the utmost pleasure, laird of my heart." Rising on her toes, Fiona pressed her lips to his in a kiss that promised a lifetime together of dreams come true.

ABOUT THE AUTHOR

Australian Anna Campbell has written 11 multi award-winning historical romances for Avon HarperCollins and Grand Central Publishing. As an independently published author, she's released more than 30 bestselling stories. Right now, she is working on a new series called A Scandal in Mayfair, set amidst the glamour and sensuality of Regency London. Anna has won numerous awards for her stories, including RT Book Reviews Reviewers Choice, the Booksellers Best, the Golden Quill (three times), the Heart of Excellence (twice), the Write Touch, the Aspen Gold (twice), and the Australian Romance Readers' favorite historical romance (five times).

Anna loves to hear from her readers. You can find her at:

Website: www.annacampbell.com

facebook.com/AnnaCampbellFans

twitter.comAnnaCampbellOz

bookbub.com/authors/anna-campbell

The Laird's Willful Lass:
The Lairds Most Likely Book 1

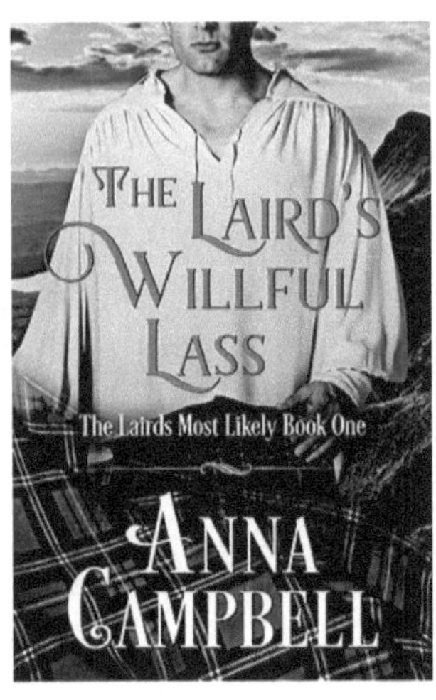

***An untamed man as immovable as a
Highland mountain...***

Fergus Mackinnon, autocratic Laird of Achnasheen,
likes to be in charge. When he was little more than
a lad, he became master of his Scottish estate, and
he's learned to rely on his unfailing judgment. So
has everyone else in his corner of the world. He sees
no reason for his bride—when he finds her—to be
any different.

***A headstrong woman from the warm and
passionate south...***

Marina Lucchetti knows all about fighting her way
through a wall of masculine arrogance. In her
native Florence, she's become a successful artist, no
easy feat for a woman. Now a commission to paint a

series of Highland scenes promises to spread her fame far and wide. When a carriage accident strands her at Achnasheen for a few weeks, it's a mixed blessing. The magnificent landscape offers everything her artistic soul could desire. If only she can resist the impulse to smash her easel across the laird's obstinate head.

When two fiery souls come together, a conflagration flares.

Marina is Fergus's worst nightmare—a woman who defies a man's guidance. Fergus challenges everything Marina believes about a woman's right to choose her path. No two people could be less suited. But when irresistible passion enters the equation, good sense soon jumps into the loch.

Will the desire between Fergus and Marina blaze hot, then fade to ashes? Or will the imperious laird and his willful lass discover that their differences aren't insurmountable after all, but the spice that will flavor a lifetime of happiness?

The Laird's Christmas Kiss:
The Lairds Most Likely Book 2

Down with love!

Ever since she was fifteen, shy wallflower Elspeth Douglas has pined in vain for the attentions of dashing Brody Girvan, Laird of Invermackie. But the rakish Highlander doesn't even know she's alive. Now she's twenty, she realizes that she'll never be happy until she stops loving her brother's handsome friend. When family and friends gather at Achnasheen Castle for Christmas, she intends to show the world that she's all grown up, and grown out of silly crushes on gorgeous Scotsmen. So take that, my gallant laddie!

Girls just want to have fun...

Except it turns out that Brody isn't singing from the same Christmas carol sheet. Elspeth decides she's

not interested in him anymore, just as he decides
he's very interested indeed. In fact, now he looks
more closely, his friend Hamish's sister is pretty
and funny and forthright – and just the lassie to
share his Highland estate. Convincing his little
wren of his romantic intentions is difficult enough,
even before she undergoes a makeover and
becomes the belle of Achnasheen. For once in his
life, dissolute Brody is burdened with honorable
intentions, while the lady he pursues is set on
flirtation with no strings attached.

Deck the halls with mistletoe!

With interfering friends and a crate of imported
mistletoe thrown into the mix, the stage is set for a
house party rife with secrets, clandestine kisses,
misunderstandings, heartache, scandal, and love
triumphant.

The Highlander's Lost Lady:
The Lairds Most Likely Book 3

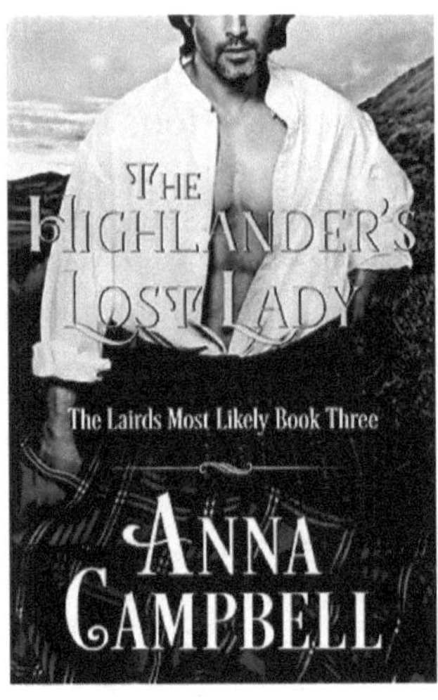

A Highlander as brave and strong as a knight of old...

When Diarmid Mactavish, Laird of Invertavey, discovers a mysterious woman washed up on his land after a wild storm, he takes her in and tries to find her family. But even as forbidden dreams of sensual fulfillment torment him, he's convinced that this beautiful lassie isn't what she seems. And if there's one thing Diarmid despises, it's a liar.

A mother willing to do anything to save her daughter...

Widow Fiona Grant has risked everything to break free of her clan and rescue her adolescent daughter from a forced marriage. But before her quest has barely begun, disaster strikes. She escapes her brutish kinsmen, only to be shipwrecked on Mactavish territory where she falls into her enemies' hands. For centuries, a murderous feud has raged between the Mactavishes and the Grants, so how can she trust her darkly handsome host?

Now a twisted Highland road leads to danger and passion…and irresistible love. But is love strong enough to banish the past's long shadows and offer these wary allies all that their hearts desire?

The Highlander's Defiant Captive: The Lairds Most Likely Book 4

Peace in the glens means war in the bedchamber!

Scotland. 1699. In a time of heroes, the greatest hero of all is Callum Mackinnon, Laird of Achnasheen. Brave, reckless, canny, and handsome enough to turn any lassie weak at the knees, Callum is a legend in the wild corner of the Highlands where he rules. Now the young laird is determined to choose a new path for his clan and end the violent feud with the Drummonds, a conflict that has painted the glens red with blood for centuries. This means taking Bonny Mhairi Drummond, the Rose of Bruard, as his wife. When negotiations with her pig-headed father break down, Callum seizes matters into his own hands and kidnaps the fairest maiden in Scotland, swearing to make her his own.

Bonny Mhairi is the adored only child of Clan

Drummond's doughty chieftain and she's inherited all her father's courage and stubbornness. Not to mention his undying hatred for anyone called Mackinnon. When the Mackinnon chieftain steals her away from her home and vows to woo her into accepting him as her husband, she swears that she'll never consent to be his bride. But trapped inside her foe's castle, Mhairi finds it hard to cling to old certainties. She detests her arrogant jailer, even as he sparks a fierce, forbidden hunger in her soul.

Loving the enemy...

As Callum and Mhairi wage their passionate war of hearts, danger, treachery and desire circle closer and closer. When her father's army masses at the gates of Achnasheen, will Mhairi prove herself a Drummond now and forever? Or will new allegiances trump ancient hatred, as the desperate laird battles to win the lass he loves more than his life?

The Highlander's Christmas Quest:
The Lairds Most Likely Book 5

She's found the man for her, but he has no plans to stay on her island. Perhaps it's time to try a little sabotage!

Scotland. 1725. The moment she sees handsome Dougal Drummond, Kirsty Macbain tumbles headlong into love. A chance storm a few days before Christmas has blown the gallant Highlander off-course to her father's isle of Askaval, but once he's repaired his boat, Dougal is determined to continue on his way. His bright blue eyes are firmly fixed on valiant deeds and a distant horizon. What does he care for a smart-mouthed, independent lassie who forms no part of his plans for his future?

Kirsty is convinced that if only she can keep Dougal on Askaval, he'll see how perfect they are together. With his boat out of action, he's trapped in her company. Some surreptitious midnight destruction with a drill and a hammer might help true love to win out. On the other hand, if Dougal discovers what she's been up to, there will be the devil to pay.

Will this madcap Christmas deliver Kirsty's heart's desire – or will her scheming see Dougal sailing away to a life without her?

The Highlander's English Bride:
The Lairds Most Likely Book 6

An impossible pairing...

Hamish Douglas, the mercurial Laird of Glen Lyon, has never got along with independent, smart-mouthed Emily Baylor. Which wouldn't matter if this brilliant Scottish astronomer didn't move in the same scientific circles as Emily and if her famous father wasn't his mentor. But when Emily looks likely to derail the event which will make Hamish's career, he loses his temper with the pretty miss and his recklessness leaves her reputation in ruins.

A marriage made in scandal...

Emily has always thought her father's spectacular protégé was far too arrogant for his own good. But what is she to do when the only way she can save her good name in society is to wed the unruly laird? Reluctantly she accepts Hamish's proposal, but only on the condition that their union remains chaste. That shouldn't be a problem; they've never been friends, let alone potential lovers – except that after they marry, Hamish reveals unexpected depths and a host of admirable qualities, and he's so awfully handsome, and now the swaggering rogue admits that he desires her...

From the ballrooms of London to the grandeur of the western Highlands, a battle royal rages between these two strong-willed combatants. Neither plans to yield an inch – but are these smart people smart enough to see that sometimes the greatest victory lies in mutual surrender?

The Highlander's Forbidden Mistress: The Lairds Most Likely Book 7

A week to be wicked...

Widowed Selina Martin faces another marriage founded on duty, not love. When notorious libertine Lord Bruard invites her to his isolated hunting lodge, he promises discretion – and seven days of hedonistic pleasure before she weds her boorish fiancé. All her life, Selina has done the right thing, but this no-strings-attached chance to discover the handsome rake's sensual secrets is irresistible. She'll surrender to her wicked fantasies, seize some brief happiness, then knuckle down to a loveless union. What could possibly go wrong?

In a lifetime of seduction, Brock Drummond, the dashing Earl of Bruard, has never wanted a woman the way he wants demure widow Selina Martin. When Selina agrees to become his temporary lover, he soon falls captive to an enchantment unlike any other. He sets out to slake his white hot desire until only ashes remain, but as each day of forbidden delight passes, the idea of saying goodbye to his ardent mistress becomes more and more unbearable.

When scandal explodes around them and threatens to destroy Selina, Brock is the only person she can turn to. After so short a time, can she trust a man whose name is a byword for depravity?

Will this sizzling liaison prove a mere affair to remember? Or will their week of passion spark a lifetime of happiness for the widow and her dissolute Scottish earl?

The Highlander's Christmas Countess: The Lairds Most Likely Book 8

The new stableboy has a secret!

Kit Laing is a genius with Glen Lyon's horses and a favorite with his employer's family, but he isn't all he seems. In fact, the shy stablehand isn't a he at all. Kit is actually Christabel Urquhart, Countess of Appin, on the run from a greedy, violent stepbrother with designs on her fortune.

And the laird's handsome nephew has worked out just what it is.

Quentin MacNab, the dashing heir to Cannich, has had his suspicions about the new stable lad from the first. Kit is far too pretty to be a boy – and far too well spoken to be a servant.

Now passion and danger combine to create a Yuletide like no other.

When a snowstorm traps Kit and Quentin overnight in an isolated hut, the discovery of her true identity sparks a rushed marriage to stave off a scandal. But can the Christmas Countess learn to trust her charming new husband's promises of protection? Or will their fragile alliance fall victim to the evil forces assailing her?

The Highlander's Rescued Maiden:
The Lairds Most Likely Book 9

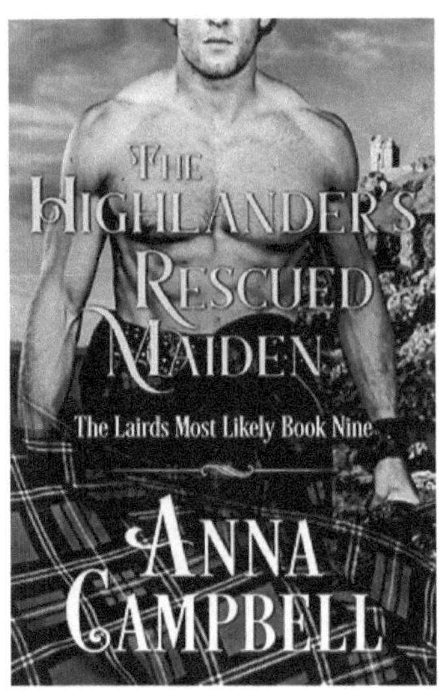

The myth of Fair Ellen of the Isles.

Across the Highlands, people recount the legend of a beautiful lassie in a tower, locked away from her clamorous suitors by a tyrannical father. Any person of sense dismisses the story as a fairy tale, no more substantial than a wisp of Scottish mist.

Rogue or hero? Or a little bit of both?

Dashing Highlander Will Mackinnon is a devil with the ladies, disinclined to fall for such romantic nonsense. But one day, his storm-tossed boat washes ashore at a rocky island dominated by a stone tower. Inside the tower, he discovers lovely, gallant Ellen Cameron and a passion that eclipses anything he's experienced before in his reckless life.

Danger and desire...

This brave adventurer vows to rescue the captive
maiden and make her his own forever. But dark
shadows gather about the lovers and threaten to
destroy all their hopes for happiness. Will has
found the love of a lifetime – but will it end up
costing him his life?

The Highlander's Christmas Lassie: The Lairds Most Likely Book 10

Young love torn apart.

As teenagers, Malcolm Innes and Rhona Macleod fell passionately in love. But Malcom's parents were horrified to think of the aristocratic heir to Dun Carron marrying a humble crofter's daughter. Desperate to crush the affair, they locked Malcolm up and exiled Rhona to London where she disappears. But Malcolm is faithful and stubborn and devotes his life to searching for his beloved and the child she was carrying when they were cruelly separated.

A chance to mend two shattered lives.

On a snowy Christmas Eve, Rhona opens the door of her isolated farmhouse to find the man she never

thought to see again, the man who betrayed her.
When she was pregnant with his son, Malcolm
abandoned her to find her way alone in a cold,
heartless world. Now she discovers that her long-
held hatred is based on lies and that he's been true
to her. Yet surely after all these years, it's too late to
awaken the love that once united them.

*As Christmas Eve turns into Christmas
Day, Malcolm and Rhona discover that
their mutual desire has never died. Will this
Yuletide reunion lead to a lifetime
together? Or has old tragedy ruptured their
bond forever?*